For Cara and Sam, whose strength and friendship helped me through my own personal fire.

DUST TO DUST

C. E. MCCLELLAND

Acknowledgments

I never realized that writing a novel, like raising a child, takes a village. My village began with my mom, Bonna Hill, who left Stephen King books lying around when I was only ten and turned a blind eye when I snuck them into my room. My dad, Charles Hill, is the real-life inspiration for William McConnelly's father. Many members of my family have battled cancer. Right now, cancer is winning 3-1, but in the case of my father, he put up a hell of a fight.

I read the first half of *Dust to Dust* to my wife Amanda when we were dating. She said I should probably finish it, then gave me the personal space to do so. Thanks, sweetheart. A former student and good friend, Rachel Meeks, read the entire manuscript and offered a lot of great advice. Can't wait to see her work out there someday! Thanks also to *I Love You A Latte* for such an inviting atmosphere for writing. You're just a little place, but you have a lot of heart!

My drama lit professor in college, Dr. Thomas Porter, gave me a love for the Irish dialect, and Dr. Dennis Maher encouraged my fascination with writing of every kind. Thanks to both of you. Of course, all this encouragement would have been for nothing if Sharona Wilhelm and Scarsdale Publishing hadn't taken an interest in my book at #Pitmad, December 2019. Then Kimberly K. Comeau took me under her editorial wing, and I've never been the same. For forty years, I have read things like "to my editor, without whom this novel could not have happened." I never really understood until now. Casey (Kimberly Comeau? K.C.? Get it?) obliterated my manuscript with notes and showed me how to rebuild it bigger and better. The absolute truth is that *Dust to Dust* is half the book it became thanks to Casey's stern yet loving guidance. I also learned to never hit the "accept changes" button in the editing layout. I came away from that email conversation slightly in fear for my life.

Strangely enough, I'd like to thank another Stephen, Steven Spielberg. When I first began working on this story, it was a film script. I wanted to move people like Spielberg does, with tears and "oohs" and "ahs." I wanted to create an *E.T.* or an *Always* or a *Hook.* Something magical but not distant. Magical and personal, like it could have happened next door to you and you would have never known. At some point, the story was getting too large for a screenplay, so I changed course and wrote the novel.

I'd like to thank my personal hero, Jim Henson. His magic and craft and sense of humor inspired me from my youngest days. I was twenty when he passed, and I cried for a full day. Thank you, sir, on behalf of the billions of children who learned love, humor, and the letter A from you.

I'd like to thank God for the inability to move through a week without writing. It's not a choice, really. I think most writers will tell you that.

Finally, I'd like to thank you, whoever you are. You picked up this book or downloaded it onto your Kindle. You gave it a shot. Reading a new author is kind of like going on Tinder. The cover might look good, but a novel is no one-night stand. So thanks, you sexy reader you, for swiping right. Now I think it's time we get to know each other a little better. I'll get the fireplace going. Why don't you open the wine? Nice. I've put together a little cheese tray for us. There are the tissues, just in case. All set? Okay, big breath…and exhale. Here we go.

Cliff McClelland
  February, 2021

Chapter One

FIRE

DAMN, Will thinks. He steers his Prius between rows of poorly parked cars, barely squeezing past a silver Expedition.

Can't he use the driveway?

Incandescent lights brighten the streets and sidewalks in the housing community, aptly named Sherwood Park. Will passes Robin Hood Drive and Nottingam Lane, then a series of cul-de-sacs. Marion Way. Locksley Lane. Mostly Tudor homes with gabled roofs and timber framing. He enjoys this particular part of the drive from the small college where he teaches drama. After all, Robin Hood originated on the medieval stage. In the 1500s, the Catholic Church loosened restrictions on theatre, which allowed playwrights to feature the famous bandit in ballads and plays. Will can see himself moving to this community someday. For now, though, he's happy living in the less expensive, two-bedroom, arts-and-crafts-style edifice he calls home.

Home.

He smiles through exhaustion, and a line from *As You Like It* pops into his head.

When I was at home I was in a better place.

"True," he murmurs. Home is where his beautiful wife, Cara, waits, and Samuel. Sam, the three-year-old bundle of energy who doesn't understand work or exhaustion. He does know that there is nothing better in the world than to launch himself at Daddy as he arrives home from work every evening. Sam's first attack took Will by surprise. They fell into the well-tended bed of cyclamen and pink skullcap Cara had planted along the walkway. The child's eyes welled with tears until he realized Will wasn't crying but laughing. Then Samuel laughed, too, and hopped up and down on Will's stomach.

"What the hell are you two doing in my flowers?" Cara had yelled.

Will and Samuel simultaneously looked up at her, wide-eyed and guilty. Then Will hooked his feet around her leg and knee and twisted her on top of them. They rolled around in the pink and purple flowers, tickling and giggling and creating a huge replanting project for Cara the following week.

Samuel.

Will smiles at what started as an overly exuberant greeting and has become ritual. What will Sam do when he has a little sister following him around every day? Or brother. It will be another seven or eight weeks before the ultrasound reveals the sex of the baby. Then they will tell Samuel about "the baby in Mommy's tummy."

Cara's difficulties in getting pregnant with Sam sparked her doctor's suggestion that she and Will consider adoption. Her Irish stubbornness wouldn't allow that, though, and the next pregnancy yielded the wonderful little terror who even now lay in wait near the front door.

Will glances at the dashboard clock. 11:08.

"Double damn," he says, an expletive acquired from his mother when he was a kid.

Sam will be in bed by now, so no tackling tonight. A twinge of disappointment sticks in Will's throat like a piece of food, but he swallows it down. Where did the night go? Oh, yeah. *A Midsummer Night's Dream* had morphed from a two-and-a-half-hour dress rehearsal to a four-hour disaster. Before Puck could finish her final monologue, Will had hurled his script onto the floor and shot to his feet.

"Go home and memorize your goddamned lines and be here at ten tomorrow morning for a real dress rehearsal!" Probably not his finest moment as a college professor, but hey, what was theatre without a few dramatics?

As he makes the final turn onto his street, a wail of sirens rises. Will cranes his neck, searching for flashing lights, as the shrill screams crescendo. A red beam slashes through his window and slices across his face.

"What the hell?"

He turns down the radio and slows to fifteen miles an hour, then ten. A fire engine brakes at the house next to his.

Mr. Owens? He's older, but—

Black-and-white Suburbans with red and blue strobes turn the night into a strange club. Police and firefighters pour onto the street and yards, while neighbors in sweats and bathrobes cluster at the curb and weave through some sort of danse macabre.

The Owens place looks fine, though. The police vehicles slow to a stop in front of Will's house, blocking all traffic on the small, suburban street. Police officers spring from their cars and wave onlookers back across the street, away from Will's house. One team of yellow-jacketed firefighters plow through Cara's flowerbeds carrying a high-pressure hose. Two more firefighters muscle the plug off a fire hydrant. Will swerves to the side of the road and throws the car into park, leaving the motor running. Smoke billows through a partially open living room window on the first floor. Will's hands twitch against the steering wheel. His stomach flips and he almost vomits.

A firefighter clutching an axe tromps through the ruined cyclamen and over the fire hose. He smashes the blade into the front door jamb. The wood splinters but the deadbolt holds. He wrestles the axe loose and swings again.

Will opens his car door and almost falls out, but rights himself and bolts. He pushes through his neighbors. A hand grabs his sleeve but he slaps it away.

"Please," he says to the house, to the nightmare before him.

A familiar voice shouts his name.

A tsunami of fear crashes inside Will's head. Faces rush past him like rocks in an avalanche. He emerges from the crowd as upstairs windows explode.

Sam's room!

"NO!"

Flames leap skyward as slivers of glass pelt his forehead and cheeks and even the inside of his mouth, still open and screaming. The coppery taste of blood trickles down his throat. He wipes away anxious tears, embedding slivers of glass deeper into his face. Cara must be scared to death, and Sam?

Gotta get in there.

A huge gust of wind blows ashes and smoke into his face. Will lunges into the wind. The world turns red. He rubs a palm across his forehead. Blood. From the glass.

He trips over a firefighter's hose and sprawls across the grass. The impact causes him to vomit.

"You need to move back, sir!" yells a police officer.

Will stumbles to his feet.

"Cara!" he yells.

Two sets of hands drag Will away from the house.

"My wife is in there!"

He struggles against the police officers. An arm encircles his chest.

"Leave it to the firemen," says one of the officers.

"They don't know where they are," Will screams. "I can find them." He twists and makes eye contact with one of the police officers, an older man.

"Please!"

"Let him go, Murphy." The older man grabs Will by both shoulders. "Son, we're doing everything we can to save your family. You gotta give us a chance and stay outa the way."

The words slice through Will's panic. He stops struggling. Exhaustion hits him and he collapses into the grass, his screams devolving into sobs.

A drop of water hits his head, and then another. The rain the weatherman predicted all week has arrived. In a matter of seconds, the drops swell into driving sheets.

A trembling hand pushes its way into Will's; Mrs. Williams from across the street, the kind, older widow who would sometimes join Will and Cara and Sam for grilled chicken or fish. She kneels beside him.

"I thought you were home, Will," her tremulous voice vibrates through the noise in his head. "You always park in the garage, and it was late. Are Cara and Sam...?" She glances at the house.

Will latches onto hope. Maybe they got out. Maybe they went to visit Cara's father. Maybe....

Will's mouth tastes of vomit and blood. He stares at the wet grass, which reflects the glow of the fire. *Please God. Please.*

Will folds his shaking hands in an effort to strengthen the prayer. He squeezes his eyes shut.

Please God, please. Please please please, God, don't take them. I'll do anything.

Behind his eyelids, Cara smiles, her face freckled with dots of paint. Samuel throws his arms around Will's legs.

The firefighters *will* reach them in time. They have to.

Right, Lord? They'll be okay?

Will slides to the ground and falls onto his back. A guttural scream escapes him. He uproots fistfuls of grass and rubs the scratchy blades over his face. His stomach contracts again, pulling him into a fetal position.

"Please," a whisper. One last prayer.

Amid the cacophony of fire and rain and sirens, the only voice Will hears is his own.

Will enjoys the warmth of the setting sun on his closed eyelids. A breeze teases his forehead like a feather. Cara's nose tickles his cheek as she snuggles closer on the red-and-white picnic blanket she'd bought because it was so stereotypically a picnic blanket. She sighs, and her breath smells of the strawberries they ate for dessert. Leftovers packed, they lie together in the park enjoying the April sun. Will expects a couple more weeks of what Texans call "spring" before the relentless Texas summer descends like ants on a discarded candy bar.

"Penny for your thoughts," Cara whispers.

Will doesn't want to spoil the moment with words.

"Will?"

He pulls her closer. "I don't sell my thoughts for anything less than a quarter."

She smiles against his cheek. "That's kind of expensive."

"They're good thoughts."

"Okay. Give me one."

He turns his face toward her, his eyes opening the tiniest bit. "On credit?"

Cara grins and nuzzles her nose into the crook of Will's neck. "I'm good for it."

"Mmmm." He turns his face back toward the sun. He's so close to sleep that he might be dreaming, and so close to dreaming that he never wants to wake. A perfect day.

"Well?" Cara asks.

Will sighs and mentally pushes aside the cobwebs. He inches away from her.

"No no no." She pulls him back.

"I want to look at you," he says.

She releases him, and he rolls onto his side. He crooks his arm and rests his head on his hand. "God, you're beautiful."

Cara laughs and gently slaps his arm. "Shut up." She rolls against him, spooning.

"I think God made you just for me," he says.

"Why is that?" She grabs his arm and pulls it around her waist.

"Because we fit. Like yin and yang. You're my missing puzzle piece."

"You're a dork." She giggles. "A big, romantic dork."

"You made me this way."

"Really?"

"Before you, I was totally different."

"Sure, you were."

"I was. Got into fights at the bar. Rolled packs of cigarettes up in my shirt sleeve."

"I bet."

"I slapped a puppy once for being too cute."

"Sounds like you were pretty badass."

"I was. And then I met you, and now I'm all...touchy-feely." Will fake-shivers, and Cara laughs again.

"I like the touchy-feely part," she says.

"You do, huh?"

"Especially if you touchy-feely me the right way."

Will pauses, then a real shiver runs through him. He grins. "Maybe we should pack up and head home for some real touchy-feely, then."

Cara rolls over and faces him. "You can...touchy-feely me here."

Will frowns. "We're in the middle of a park."

"Yeah?" Her eyes twinkle like a fairy's.

"And there's a lady and her two kids about thirty feet behind you."

"Really?"

"Yep."

Cara takes his hand. "I bet they won't mind."

Surely, she's joking.

She places his hand on her stomach. "See? Just touchy-feely right there."

"Oh," Will says. This is not what he had in mind. Then a thought pops into his head. His eyebrows rise. "Are you...?"

Cara nods, her smile unwavering. "Ten weeks. I didn't want to tell you in case...you know."

"And you're...there's nothing...?"

Cara laughs, her bell-voice ringing.

The woman looks their way. One of her kids runs past her toward the parking lot. She turns and yells for him, grabs the other child, and chases him.

"The doctor says everything is fine." Her hand leaves his and caresses his stubbled chin. "We're gonna have a baby."

Will pulls her close, then abruptly releases her in a panic. "Did I squeeze too hard? I don't want to—"

"Stop," she laughs. "I'm pregnant, not brittle. Squeeze all you want."

Will puts his arm around her and squeezes, not too tightly, but not gently, either. Two bodies become one for several minutes. That night, when they get home, two bodies become one for several minutes more.

"Then said Martha unto Jesus, Lord, if thou hadst been here, my brother had not died. But I know, that even now, whatsoever thou wilt ask of God, God will give it thee."

The priest, garbed in a traditional black chasuble, continued the funeral rite, but his words passed over Will's ears rather than into them.

Will knew the story, had heard it at other Catholic burial masses, but Lazarus had no place here today. Good Catholics were supposed to be buried whole, not cremated. The fire had given Will no choice in the matter.

A simple urn sat on the altar, scant feet away. Mourners filled the pews behind him. So many people had loved her. Will had never suffered the delusion that she was air and light and water and earth to only him. The crowded church bore witness to Cara's charity, grace, and good nature.

Aidan Brady, Cara's father, sat next to Will. Though Will was numb, Aidan's grief radiated like a fever. The older man's eyes were dry, but he trembled slightly, as if he might explode. He'd lost his wife to cancer almost five years ago, and he'd buried his sorrow in the warmth and love of his only child and his grandson Samuel. Now, there was no comforting hand to hold, no strong voice to insist that the world was a good place.

Will descended into his wifeless, sonless abyss. Finally, the mass ended. Incorporeal hands led him to a mausoleum, where the bronze urn was laid to rest. More hands guided him to Aidan's house, where people traded tears and casseroles. Common practice would have been to go to the home of the deceased, but that house was a blackened shell.

After a few hours, the mourners filled the refrigerator with leftovers and promised to bring more during the coming week. Will and Aidan bid them goodbye, thanked each for their kindness, and closed the door.

Will turned to Aidan, who stared at him. Then the older man locked the door and, wordless, shuffled the million lonely miles to his bedroom. Will didn't say good night. If Aidan slept, if either of them slept, it would be due to exhaustion and grief. There was no good about the night. There would be no comfort in the morning.

Will sat on the couch and stared at his hands. Tears eventually came again, as they did every night. The world dissolved into blobs of light behind a wall of water that flooded Will's eyes and cheeks. Eventually, he slept.

Thomas Putnam slid a preprinted leave of absence request across the desk. Will sat quietly, holding his hands to keep them from trembling.

"Are you sure about this, Will?"

"Yes."

Tom, a gaunt skeleton of a man who reminded Will of Mr. Sowerberry, the undertaker in Charles Dickens' *Oliver Twist*, was the Dean of the School of Drama at Tarrant County College. The leave of absence form indicated a start date of October 7th, today, and no end date. Will signed the document and passed it back.

Tom accepted the paper and placed it in the wooden outbox at the corner of his desk. "I'll hold the position for you as long as I can," he said. "I've already got Frieda Martin from the community college coming in to cover your classes for the semester, and your A.D. is finishing up *Midsummer*."

"Thanks." Will tried to smile, but his lips just wouldn't stretch that way. The best he could offer was a sort of pursed grimace that he hoped didn't look too sad. Will didn't think he could handle any more condolences.

"I know it's hard," Tom said, "but you're a damned fine educator. The students need you."

Tom picked up a coffee cup filled with about seventy percent coffee and thirty percent brandy. He sipped. Fumes of the strong alcohol wafted over to Will. He thought about asking for a cup, but he was afraid that if he climbed into a bottle he might never emerge. Then again, what did it matter?

Tom was still speaking. Will realized that he didn't know what was being said.

"Come again?" he asked.

"I said, are you sure you want to do this?"

"Very."

"We could just have Martin take your classes for a couple weeks, long enough for you to get your mind a little more wrapped around what it needs...to wrap around."

Will shook his head. "I can't."

"But—"

"Not right now."

Putnam set his cup down and leaned back in his leather desk chair. "The kids here love you, Will. Love and respect the hell out of you. Don't you think it'd be good to be surrounded by that rather than off on your own?"

Will shook his head again. "I need some time, Tom. To process. To mourn."

Tom nodded, his demeanor empathetic.

Will stood and extended his hand.

The dean took it in both of his and gave it two quick shakes. "God bless you, Will, you and your father-in-law both. I never met your son, but Cara was a dear. Everyone in this department loved her."

"Thanks."

Tom led Will from his office and patted his shoulder, then disappeared behind a closing door.

Will trudged to his Prius, hoping against hope that he wouldn't encounter any of his students or fellow professors. For the first time in days, God was kind. Will saw no one.

Chapter Two

GLITTER

"FIRST ROW, three seats down from the center aisle," Richie whispers.

Will peeks around the curtain into the audience, trying to locate the girl his friend is talking about. "There's too many, dude," he breathes. "All of 'em are hot."

"I'm not just talkin' hot. I'm talkin' give-you-instantaneous-wood hot."

"Okay, okay. First row, right or left?"

The audience sits about forty feet away from offstage. Will peers through already dying prop foliage for some unknown goddess, or more than likely, a nice pair of boobs. Richie is a breast man. The thing is, they're both post-grad students in Austin, Texas, and there are tons of beautiful girls on campus. Then he sees her, a blonde girl, and yes, she's in the first row and— "Damn, Richie. She looks like a Victoria's Secret model."

Richie leans away from the curtain, sighing. "What I wouldn't give for a shot at that."

Will laughs. "Go for it, man."

"Yeah, right. Tammy'd kill my ass."

"Tammy's rock solid. You're lucky she puts up with your shit on the regular."

A loud "Shhh!" hisses from the corner. The guys turn to see their bespectacled stage manager, Taylor, glaring at them over her promptbook.

"Sorry, Taylor," says Will, and Richie follows with "Yeah, sorry."

"We're at places," Taylor whispers.

"We said we're sorry," Richie says. "And we're ready."

"That woman's not a piece of meat, by the way," she adds. "Have some respect."

Richie's mouth snaps shut.

"Truth," Will says, nudging his friend. "Have some respect."

"I'm talking to you, too, Will McConnelly," Taylor says.

"Oh, milady," he replies, his improvisation skills kicking in, "let apologies be rain, and mine will shower around thee like a spring storm."

Taylor rolls her eyes. "You're like a ten year old with a good vocabulary."

Richie and Will stare at each other, fighting serious giggles. Over their heads, music rises. It's almost time for the show. Richie glances back out at the audience.

"You should invite her to the cast party," Richie whispers.

"Taylor?" says Will. "She's cute, but I'm not sure she's into dudes."

"No, dumbass! The blonde. At the meet-and-greet after the show, you should invite her to the cast party."

Will smiles. "I don't think so. I've got finals coming up and every-thing. I need to focus."

Richie grabs Will's shoulders.

"Come on, man. You can't tell me you wouldn't hit that."

Will peeks around the curtain again, watching the house lights dim. The blonde is chatting with her seatmate, a woman, and there's another woman on the other side of her. No boyfriend. At least, not here.

"Maybe," he says.

"Sweet!" breathes Richie.

Will straightens his tunic and prepares for his entrance. "If she'll talk to a guy in tights."

"Are you kidding?" Richie asks, pointing at Will's crotch. "With that codpiece?"

Will looks down at the large, rounded costume piece covering his crotch. When he'd been cast as Mercutio in the production of *Romeo and Juliet*, he'd jokingly asked the costumer for an oversized codpiece, the traditional covering for male genitalia in the 16th century. In return, she'd obliged in spades. The director had gotten such a laugh out of it that she'd decided to keep it in the show.

Will heard Gregory and Sampson's verbal conflict on stage. He grabbed his saber from the props table. "We'll see," he says, his brow arched and mischievous. "But right now, it's time we kicked some Capulet ass."

"Hells to the yeah," says Richie. "Let's do this."

A clash of arms draws them past the curtain and onto the set. The evening disappears into tragedy.

"So...what's your major?" asks Will.

The blonde, whose name is Summer, says, "Marketing. I'm a Libra and I like long walks on the beach. Oh, and I'm in *Playboy's Girls of the Big 12*. Any other small talk you wanna get out of the way?"

Will stares at her, stunned. As an actor, he thinks he's grown adept at reading people. Summer doesn't seem upset or bored, so why the diatribe?

"Look," she says. "I liked you on stage. Your...." She looks down at his crotch, and Will feels instantaneously awkward. "Your...whatever that thing you were wearing over your tights—"

"It's called a codpiece," Will says.

"Your codpiece...you've gotta have a lotta confidence to walk around in that thing. I like that."

Summer slides her hand from Will's knee to his inner thigh. -"My dad owns a million-dollar software firm and my mom's a former pro tennis player. I'm kinda used to people who walk the walk, you know?"

Flustered, Will manages a quick, "Uh...sure."

Summer laughs, and then she snorts, and with that, she becomes human.

Will smiles, finally, an honest smile rather than an affectation.

"Okay," Summer says, giving Will's thigh a squeeze, "I'm gonna go freshen up. To finish my perfect upfrontness, I'm kinda horny tonight. I want somebody to pull my hair in bed, and fairly soon, 'cause I have to be up early in the morning. If you want that to be you, and your codpiece wasn't lying too much, we can head to my place." With that, she launches herself toward the bathroom.

Out of nowhere, Richie takes her place next to Will. "So?" he asks.

"So what?" Will says.

"Are you serious?" Richie nods toward the hallway where Summer exited, then back at Will. "Are y'all hookin' up or what?"

"I don't know, man." Will shakes his head. "I've never said this in my life, but that woman might be a little too much for me."

"Dude!" says Richie, crumpling to his knees in fake/real consternation. "You've gotta be kiddin' me! That is the hottest chick in this town."

"Now *you're* exaggerating."

"No, I'm not."

"She is in *Playboy*, though."

"What?" says Richie. He grabs his head with both hands as if to stop it from exploding. "I'm gonna kill myself right now!"

"Why are you gonna kill yourself?" says a new voice, a girly voice.

Will glances up, over Richie's shoulder, at a cute brunette with long hair and a strained smile. "Hey, Tammy!" Will says. "Having fun?"

"If by 'having fun' you mean watching my boyfriend ogle your date for the last ten minutes, then yeah. I'm having a shitload a' fun."

"Come on, baby," says Richie. He shoots to his feet and throws his arms around his girlfriend's waist.

Tammy pushes him away. "Screw you," she says, her voice light but her eyes angry. "Why did you invite me to the party if you weren't gonna talk to me?"

"Look," says Richie. "I was the one who talked Will into inviting the blonde."

"Summer," adds Will.

"Summer, yeah. I'm just checking on his progress. Gotta have my brother's back, right?"

Tammy crosses her arms and cocks her head. "So, this isn't about her?"

Richie shakes his head. "No."

"Not about the fact that her boobs are so big that they maintain their own zip codes?"

"There are only two boobs in the world that I care about," Richie says, gently taking her arms and putting them around his neck. "And those are these." He wraps his arms around Tammy's back, plunges his nose into the center of her cleavage, and motorboats her with a loud "Pbbbbbttt."

Tammy screams and laughs and the whole room turns to stare.

"Stop it! Stop it!" she yells as Richie picks her up to get even more depth. She starts slapping his shoulders as she laughs. Richie sets Tammy back on the floor and kisses her.

"You believe me now?" he asks.

"You are such an asshole," Tammy says, smiling. She kisses him again.

"Wanna dance?"

"Sure."

Richie leads Tammy onto the dance floor.

Summer ambles over to the couch. "That guy walks the walk," Summer says, staring at the couple.

Will turns to her.

"So, what do you think, Romeo?" she adds. "Thirty minutes of heaven and some awkward snuggling afterwards?"

"Actually, I played Mercutio," Will says.

"Whoever." She grabs his hand and leads him to the door. Fifteen minutes later, they're fumbling around her bed like drunkards. Twenty minutes after that, she's asleep, her back turned and her body half a mile away across a king-sized bed. Will puts his pants and shirt back on, grabs socks and shoes, and heads for the living room.

It's a nice apartment, Will notices. Open design. Earlier, there'd been too much kissing and groping on the way to Summer's bedroom to appreciate the aesthetics of the place. He sits on the couch to put on his socks and takes a moment to look around. The décor is tasteful, very modern. Lots of mirrors and candles and artwork. Mostly Pottery Barn, from the looks of it. He pulls on his left shoe and reaches for his right. The painting above the fireplace catches his eye. It's a mess of a thing, really, blobs of paint thrown around haphazardly on a canvas. He stares at it for a moment, unsatisfied but curious. He leaves his shoe and ambles to the center of the room, trying another angle.

"Diddle diddle dumpling," a voice says behind him.

Will jerks around and sucks in his breath. He almost chokes on a stray bit of spittle.

The woman laughs. "Sorry," she says. "I wasn't trying to sneak."

"That's okay," Will says. He coughs again. "Ummm, are you—"

"Summer's roommate, yeah."

"Have you been here all night?" Heat rises to Will's face.

She laughs again. "Don't worry, I keep my door closed and my headphones on when I go to bed. Summer's quite...well, she isn't shy about bringing guys home."

"Yeah, not shy, for sure. Hope we didn't wake you."

"Nope. I've been studying and now I can't sleep. I was gonna grab a glass of milk. It helps sometimes."

"The sugars," Will says. He sits on the couch and grabs his other shoe.

"What?"

"The sugars in the milk. They give you a little sugar high, and then a bit of a crash. Sometimes that's enough to help you sleep. I read it in some health magazine."

"Didn't know that." She sits on the couch, a couple feet away. Her scent—something like vanilla and lavender—tickles Will's nose. He smiles, then gets a whiff of his own smell—sweat and sex. The smile disappears.

"I should prob'ly get out of your hair," he says, rising. He looks at the shoe in his hand, unsure of why it still isn't on his foot.

"Sure," she says. "I just saw you looking at my painting, so I was gonna ask you what you thought of it."

Will nodded toward the fireplace. "That...you painted that?"

"Yeah."

"Cool. It's...ummm, yeah. Cool."

"Thanks."

A big pause as Will stares at the painting.

"Of course," adds the woman, "cool isn't necessarily a compliment."

"Uh, yeah."

"The critics never said that about *Starry Night*. 'It's ummm, yeah. Cool.'"

Will nods. "You're prob'ly right. Sorry."

The woman shakes her head and laughs. She grabs Will by the crook of his arm and pulls him far away from the painting, almost to the apartment's kitchen. Then she walks to the fireplace and flips a switch. A small light illuminates the painting.

Colors leap at Will, as if he's put on 3D glasses.

The woman saunters back to his side. She takes the shoe from him and sets it on the coffee table. "Now," she says. "Try not to think about anything, at all. Just look."

Will looks.

"Wait," she says.

"What?" He swivels his head toward her. Her brow is knitted in concentration.

"Not me," she says. "Face the painting. Now close your eyes."

"Why?"

"Just do it."

Will closes his eyes.

"Stare at the back of your eyelids. At the darkness there. Empty your mind."

"This is a little weird."

"No. Weird would be me dressed in a tutu with an eyepatch and a parrot on my right shoulder riding a unicycle through the kitchen."

Will chokes back laughter. Then he can't choke it back and it tumbles out. "What?" he asks.

"Never mind," she says. "And shush. You'll wake up Summer."

Will breathes through his mouth to control the giggles and, after a moment, they dissipate.

"Okay," she says, and then Will starts snickering again. "Hey!" She slaps his arm.

"Sorry, sorry," he says, trying to catch his breath. The image of her in a tutu and the...the parrot and eyepatch and the unicycle....

I'm gonna die trying to hold it in.

His eyes are still closed, so he jumps when she places a hand on each side of his head. She pulls his face to hers and kisses him. The need to laugh falls away like a dropped penny as the vanilla scent of her skin and the mint on her breath envelope him. As she pulls away, Will's eyes pop open.

Green eyes, he thinks. *Pretty green eyes.*

She releases his face. "Now that I have your attention...." She pulls his eyelids shut with the sweep of one sideways palm. "Empty your mind."

Will opens his eyes in protest. "You just kissed me!"

"So?"

"So, how am I supposed to empty my mind after that?"

"I don't know. You're an actor. Don't you work on things like that in class?"

Will shakes his head. *What the—* "How do you know I'm an actor?"

"I saw you in *Romeo and Juliet* a couple nights ago." She smiles. "Who could forget that codpiece? Now focus!"

She passes her palm over Will's eyes once more. Her hand warms his eyelids, then disappears. Her kiss still vibrates on his lips like a downed electric line.

Will takes a deep breath and focuses. He expels a breath and then pulls in more, this time imagining the air as a bright, golden light. He holds that breath for a moment, then releases it again, the image in his mind that of expelling a black, poisonous gas. In with the light, out with the dark. His breathing slows a little, and he relaxes his shoulders, empties his mind. Actor training one point oh. Will giggles.

"Better," she says, a thousand miles away.

He's in a zone now.

"Open your eyes."

He does so, and he sees the painting as if for the first time. The blob is now an older man walking down the street, his hand extended to that of someone very small. Perhaps his grandson? The pictures aren't exact, but they're what Will feels must be right. The town in the distance. The dark blue windows with dots of light inside

Faces.

They stare at the day with no expression because they're no more important than a piece of grass in a field. The two in the center and their relationship is where the painting finds its truth. The whole thing looks as if it's underwater, but that only adds to the beauty of it.

"What do you call it?" he breathes.

"*Apocalypse,*" she says, and he turns to stare at her, confused. She laughs. "Just kidding. I call it *Shan.*"

"*Shan?*"

"It's short for Seanathair. It's Gaelic for 'grandfather.'"

"Shan-aw-her?" Will asks, trying to get the pronunciation right. "How's it spelled?"

The woman laughs. "Don't even bother. You'd never get the pronunciation if I spelled it out. Just stick with the phonetics."

"'Kay."

"So, do you like it?"

"The name?" Will asks.

"The painting," she says, her brow creased.

"Oh. Yeah, definitely. I don't really go for Impressionism that much.... It is Impressionism, right?"

"More or less," she says.

"I like the way the colors blend into each other," Will says. He glances back and forth between the painting and her green eyes. "It's like everything is connected. There aren't any hard lines between objects. Just one color leading to the next leading to the next."

"Thanks."

"Be nice if the world was like that."

"It can be," she says, smiling.

Her teeth are straight on top and a little crooked on bottom. Absolutely beautiful against her full lips. Will feels himself staring and looks away. "I uh, guess I shouldn't keep you any longer."

"I can't sleep anyway," she says. "Summer won't wake up until eight or so. Are you tired?"

"Ummm, no," Will says, surprised. "Not really."

"Want to watch a movie or something? I have a pizza we could cook, and there's beer in the fridge."

"Uh, I guess?" Will laughs a little. "Do you always hang out with guys your roommate brings home?" He instantly regrets how insulting that sounds, but the woman doesn't take offense.

"Never," she says. "Have a seat."

Will settles on the couch as she grabs a couple Coronas. She hands one to him.

"Thanks. I'd take something cheaper if you've got it."

"Summer doesn't keep anything cheap. Her dad's rich, so it's only the best for his little girl. I get the benefits." She slides a pizza out of the freezer and turns on the oven. "If I was living on my own, you'd be getting Keystone Light."

"I've got PBR in my fridge," says Will, sipping the cold, Mexican beer. "But I won't complain about Corona, either."

"Good," she says. She slides the pizza in the oven and sets the timer, then plops down beside him. She grabs the remote. "'Cause I might have to kick your ass if you complain about good beer."

"God help me," Will says.

"I'm a black belt in Tae Kwon Do."

"Really?"

"I can kill you five different ways right now and not even spill my beer."

"That would be impressive."

"Not to you. You'd be dead."

"True."

"Yeah." She turns on the television and satellite box. "So, what do you like?"

"I'm not too picky. Comedies are good."

The woman flips through channels. "Ooh, what about that?"

Onscreen, a woman and a man kiss in the rain.

Will laughs. "Seriously?"

"What? Ryan Gosling is a god."

"A wimpy god."

"Wimpy, hell! Have you seen him with his shirt off?"

"Yeah. No big deal."

"So, you have seen *The Notebook*. Or do you just go through issues of *Teen Beat* checking out the dudes?"

Will stops in mid-sip. "Uh...this girl I was dating, she—"

"Yeah yeah. That's the excuse every guy uses. You can't tell me that Rachel McAdams doesn't do it for you."

"She's cute," Will admits.

"Cute." The woman glowers at him. "Hot girl. Wet shirt. All over you. That's how you define...cute."

Will sighs. "Promise not to rip up my man card?"

She smiles. "It's safe."

"Okay, I like *The Notebook*."

She pats his leg. "See, that wasn't so hard, was it?"

"No."

"I mean, learning to admit that you're a wuss is the first step to inner peace."

Will turns to her, shocked.

She grabs a pillow and buries her laughter in it.

He grabs a pillow, too, and having nothing better to do with it, bops her on the side of the head.

The woman stops laughing and her eyes grow wide. She launches herself at him with a gleeful shriek, raining pillow attacks on his head so fast that he can barely block them. "You killed my father!" she yells. "Prepare to die!"

Will ducks under her blows and jumps onto the couch. "But I know something you don't know!"

The woman stares up at him, smiling, panting. "What?" she asks.

"I am not left-handed!" he says.

Will looks at his pillow and realizes that it's in his right hand, so he grabs it with his left and, with a sword-like flourish, tosses it to his right. The silky pillow slips through his hand and lands on the floor.

"You are defeated, sir." The woman points her pillow at Will. "Concede."

"Never!" he shouts.

Will leaps from the couch, lunges for his pillow, but trips over a small conversation chair at the head of the coffee table. He falls and smashes his head on the edge of the table.

"Ooh," he says. A sharp pain erupts just above his ear. "Ow!"

The woman rushes to him. "Are you okay?"

Will touches his scalp, and his hand comes back bloody. "Shit."

The woman grabs Will's wrist and pulls him to his feet. "Come on." She leads him to the kitchen sink. "Bend over."

He does.

She grabs some paper towels and wets them, then dabs at the wound.

"Ouch," he says.

"Don't be a wuss," she returns.

"You really like that word," Will says.

"I really do."

"What's going on?" a voice mumbles from across the room. They both turn to see Summer, wearing a Victoria's Secret "Pink" nightshirt. She stands at her bedroom door staring at them through barely open eyes.

"Your guy just injured himself," the woman says. "Go back to bed."

Without a word, Summer closes the door and, presumably, returns to bed.

The woman giggles.

"What?" asks Will.

"Oh, I love her bunches, but she's kind of a goof. Tries to be a big party girl, but if she's out past midnight...."

"Carriage turns into a pumpkin?" asks Will.

"Her Beamer, yeah. All right. It's stopped bleeding."

"That's good," Will says. "I don't feel like going to the emergency room."

"You'll survive." She tosses the paper towel into the trash can. "It's just a flesh wound."

"Thanks." Will leans back against the island stove. *Princess Bride and Monty Python references? Who is this person?* She'd made another reference earlier, one he hadn't recognized. What was it?

"Hey, what'd you mean earlier when you said 'Little little dumpling.' Or whatever you said."

"Diddle diddle dumpling," she corrects. "From *Mother Goose.*"

"Sounds familiar."

She turns to rinse off her hands, then dries them on a dish towel. "Diddle, diddle, dumpling, my son John, Went to bed with his trousers on; One shoe off, and the other shoe on, Diddle, diddle, dumpling, my son John." She points at his feet, and he remembers that he's still only wearing one shoe.

"Oh," he says.

"Just popped into my head when I saw you."

"Random."

"That's me. And speaking of me, or us...maybe we should introduce ourselves?"

"Oh," Will says. "Yeah, I'm sorry." He extends his hand. "Will McConnelly."

"McConnelly?" she says. "That's a nice Irish name." She shakes his hand, her grip firm and warm.

"Maybe. My mom used to say we were. My dad died of cancer when I was seventeen and Mom followed him in a car crash not too long after."

"That's horrible. I'm sorry."

"It happens."

"Well, my name is Caralin."

"Car-a-leen?" he says. "How do you spell it?"

"C-A-R-A-L-I-N," she says.

"It's pretty."

"Kind of formal. My friends just call me Cara."

"What should I call you, then?"

"I don't know. Are we gonna be friends?"

He smiles and she smiles. Hours later, Will hears a door creak open. He twists his head around to see Summer standing in the kitchen, a surprised look on her face. Cara's head rests on Will's shoulder.

"Morning," he whispers. He holds his finger up to his mouth signaling Summer to be quiet.

Behind him, a short loop of *The Notebook* trailer plays on the television screen. Will closes his eyes again and drops back into a perfectly peaceful slumber.

WILL PULLED A SHOPPING CART FROM THE ALCOVE JUST inside the Walmart entrance. He tested it to make sure none of the wheels squeaked or pulled to one side, then pushed it through the second set of automatic doors and into the store. Even this close to midnight, the place was busy. Customers navigated their carts around pallets of boxes set out by the night stockers. A small, blue-vested Asian man pushed a floor waxer up and down the aisles. Invariably, customers stopped right in front of him to look at one item or another. A little Hispanic boy, probably three or four *Samuel's age* giggled and ran from his mother, who appeared to be about six months pregnant. She grabbed him by the hand and pulled him back toward her cart as he laughed and laughed.

Will took a shortcut down the school supplies aisle, then rerouted when he saw a man on a tall ladder trying to hang a sign above the shelves. The employee, balanced precariously at the top of the ladder, leaned on several unopened boxes stored on the top shelf. Will also steered past the next aisle, where an industrial fan pointed at a wet spot on the floor. The third aisle was the charm. Empty. Will turned right and made his way through the school and business aisles to housewares.

Dishes, he thought. *Silverware. Pots and pans.*

He stared at the various designs and collections on display. Cara had spent hours picking out the dishes they'd listed in their bridal registry. So many hours, that most of the people at Macy's knew her by name. After the wedding, she'd taken Will to pick up a few odds and ends they hadn't been gifted. Every single person they passed in the department stopped her and asked for details about the ceremony. They wanted to see her ring and, of course, meet Mr. Cara McConnelly. Will went along with this good-naturedly, having gotten used to the fact that Cara never went anywhere without making friends. How she remembered every-one's name was beyond comprehension, though. It was one of her gifts.

Something else lost to the world.

Tears swelled. He fought to blink them away, to not let them carve pathways down his cheeks in the middle of Walmart. The guy with the floor waxer whooshed by him. A few aisles over, the Hispanic boy giggled again. Will figured the little guy was off on another escapade, followed by his frantic mother. For Will, though, there were dishes to be bought. Dishes to fill the empty cabinets at the townhome he'd just leased. There hadn't been much salvageable from the fire, so Will needed dishes and pots and pans and furniture. He needed everything and didn't want any of it. Except his wife and son back.

He took a deep breath and grabbed the box of dishes closest to him. What did it matter? They were just dishes. He needed something to eat on and eat with and drink with. Especially drink with. He was going through a liter of Jack every other day now. He'd resisted alcohol at first, but what else did he have to do besides stare at the television for hours at a time? Everybody needed a hobby, right?

Will headed for the flatware, but something bugged him. What was wrong?

Just go to the flatware.

He started again, then stopped. What the hell was wrong? Then it came to him. Cara would want him to have nice dishes at the new place. Not nice necessarily, but right. The dishes had to be right. They had to work with the kitchen and the paint and the counters. They had to reflect something about the person using them, because Cara was an artist. Aesthetics were important to her. But how was Will supposed to pick out dishes that made sense without her, because without her, nothing made sense anymore. He was stuck here in this goddamned store in this goddamned life without the person who made everything work. How could he do this without her?

Another giggle, this time closer. The little Hispanic boy ran down the main aisle, swerving back and forth. This time, he wasn't being chased by his mother but by the floor guy and his waxer. The smile on the

Asian man's face showed that he also knew games that little boys played. Perhaps he'd even played a few when he was three or four.

The boy whirled around a corner, and the cleaning man followed, both of them giggling.

"Hey!" someone yelled.

Above the shelves, the man on the ladder tipped to one side.

Oh, shit, Will thought. *The little kid or the waxing guy must've hit the ladder.*

The man swayed toward the top shelf and grabbed boxes to save himself from falling. He found his balance, then pushed himself back up onto the ladder. That final shove sent one precariously balanced box hurtling to the second aisle floor. Will didn't see it hit, but instantaneously, a billion little silver sparkles filled the air. They floated toward him like a fog and covered him.

Glitter, he thought. *It was glitter, and it hit the floor fan.*

Will stepped to the edge of the dishes aisle. Everyone in the area stopped and looked up. Time seemed to slow as the silver rain fell around them—on them. For a moment, Will had a crazy notion that they would all start to float, to rise up and fly through some magic portal to Neverland. Except him, he realized. He would never be able to fly, no matter how much fairy dust landed on him. The most basic premise of flying was that you had to have a happy thought, and all of his had been stolen, burned away by fire.

Still, he needed dishes. Will brushed the silver glitter off his shirt and shook it from his hair. He drifted back to the aisle to find the perfect designs and colors to fit his new kitchen.

For Cara.

Will struggled up the stairs of his townhome three times with various boxes and bags. The counter was now covered in new stuff—dishes and pans and glasses and everything he needed not only for him but for three other people. Four cups, four plates, four spoons. Why did things come in fours? Was that the prerequisite whenever people started packing dishes into boxes? Was it that nuclear family concept from the 1950s of husband, wife, two kids?

Will just needed one of everything. He didn't plan on entertaining, and the option of not having to wash dishes but every third or fourth day was probably not good for his state of mind. He needed to keep things neat and clean, or as neat and clean as he could. He'd already scheduled maid service every month on a Saturday, and the little bit of lawn outside would be maintained through his Homeowner's Association dues.

Neat and clean was the order of the day. That meant Will needed to get all of his purchases into the dishwasher so they could go into the cabinets clean. He grabbed a can of Coke from the refrigerator and filled a plastic 7-11 Super Big Gulp soda cup with ice. He poured in half the can and topped off the cup with Jack Daniels, then sipped the drink while he pulled items from boxes and filled the dishwasher. By the time he'd started the first load, the cup was half empty. When he'd taken the first load out and replaced it, the cup had been emptied, filled again, and was now down to a few ice chips. He dumped the ice into the sink and shoved the cup into the dishwasher alongside his new pots and pans.

He hit the dishwasher start button and stumbled into the living room. The Jack was hitting him hard because he hadn't had anything to eat since lunch.

He grabbed a large manila envelope from the coffee table and fell on the couch. Inside was his copy of the fire report. He'd already talked to the police and the insurance adjustor, so he knew that the fire had been caused by old wiring in the wall of his study. The flames had spread quickly because of the number of books and papers he kept on his shelves and in drawers. The fire chief noted that Cara and Samuel had probably died in their sleep. They were found in their beds after the fire was extinguished.

The report was something the insurance adjuster wanted, along with a list of all the items lost in the fire. Will was able to provide that list because Cara had taken pictures everywhere they went, in every room they lived in. The pictures were all online "in the cloud," where she also kept the digital portfolio of her artwork, both sold and unsold. Will had copies of all their sales receipts, and since they'd been organized in a metal filing cabinet, most of them were still intact.

Will looked down at a couple silver specks on the report. More glitter.

"Jesus," he breathed. He used a fingernail to scrape the sparkles onto the coffee table. He'd tried to brush himself off before he'd gotten into his car, but he guessed he'd missed some.

"Be finding glitter forever," he muttered. He stumbled out onto his small balcony, took off his shirt and pants, and shook them into the night air. Then, he ran his fingers through his hair, trying to remove the remaining sparkles.

Back inside, Will tossed his clothes into the washer and grabbed a quick shower, using lavender soap. Then he lay down on the new queen-sized bed, grabbed a pillow, and held it to his face. He breathed in the Vanilla Lace Body Spray scent Cara had worn. He'd picked up a bottle of it and sprayed the pillow, hoping the scent would help him sleep. All it did was make him long for the warm silk of her skin, the way her hips pressed his when they lay together, spooning after making love. Tears welled, and because he was no longer in Walmart, and there was no one there to judge him, he let them flow. They mingled with the vanilla and lavender ghost of his lost wife. Eventually, he slept.

Chapter Three

ASHES

IT WAS AMAZING how easily a person could fall off the face of the earth. The first week after Cara's and Sam's deaths, Will's cell phone rang nonstop. Dozens of well-wishers left message after message of concern and love. After a week, only ten percent called back. Will discovered that if he didn't return phone calls, people eventually gave up calling. Dean Putnam still left the occasional "We miss you," as did the technical director at the college, but as fall drifted into winter, and winter thawed to spring, even their voicemails became few and far between. Will figured that if they hadn't started a job search for a permanent drama professor already, they soon would.

Only one other person called Will, and when that call came, Will never let it go to voicemail. That person was Aidan Brady, Cara's father, Samuel's grandfather.

April third—Cara's birthday—dawned cold. Will's cell phone rang. "Hello?"

"Mornin' Will. Yeh outa bed yet?"

Will looked at the time on his phone. 7:30. He hadn't slept nearly long enough to touch his hangover. "Just barely, Aidan." Will sat up against the headboard of his no-longer-new bed. "What's up?"

"Are yeh goin' to the cemetery today? It's Caralin's birthday, 'a course."

Will struggled through his mental fog. "Yes, of...right. I ordered an arrangement from McShan Florist a couple days ago. Something for Samuel, too."

"Good lad. Well, then. I'll be meetin' yeh there when? Ten thirty?"

Oh god...no way.

"Why don't we make it noon, and we can get some lunch after?"

"Actually, I was hoping yeh could come with me to Trinity Hall after."

Will thought what he'd heard must be a mistake. "Trinity Hall?"

"Tá," Aidan said, which Will knew meant "yes." Sometimes, Aidan slipped into the Gaelic-Irish he'd grown up on, and at other times, it was just a soft lilt in the way he spoke. Both were beautiful in Will's ears, and because they reminded him of his family, sent daggers through his heart.

"Isn't Trinity Hall in Dallas?"

"Tá. I've saved us two rooms at a hotel across the street, reserved them in both our names. I ken we might have a pint or two, and maybe a Jameson. It's the house whiskey there, yeh know."

"We have a couple Irish pubs here in Fort Worth. Why don't we just stay on our side of town for free?"

"Because an Irish pub ain't an Irish pub unless it's owned by an Irishman." Something slammed on Aidan's end of the line.

Will imagined Aidan with a beer bottle in his hand, striking a table to punctuate his declaration.

"I tell yeh bye, Trinity Hall is as Irish as me, or as you might be if yer parents were still around to talk about it. So, we go to Trinity Hall to celebrate me poor baby's birth, and if they have to haul us to the hotel in a cart, why that is what they'll do."

Aidan's statements were wet with emotion. Even over the phone, Will heard the tears and snot coating the older man's words.

"Ay," breathed Will. "Whatever you'd like, Aidan. We'll drink 'til the cows come home."

"Noon, then," said Aidan. "And by the way, 'ay' is fer the feckin' Scots."

The phone went dead. Will stared at it, dumbfounded. He'd never heard his father-in-law say the f-word before. Will had gotten out of the habit of saying it when Samuel began to repeat everything he heard. Will almost laughed, but the sound felt so wrong in his throat that it stuck halfway out. He struggled to choke it down.

Will hadn't bothered to check the weather before leaving. Standing in a chilly April rain in front of a mausoleum made him wish he had. The wind was strong, twenty or thirty miles an hour maybe. The rain hitting his face and arms felt like ice pellets. He set the vase of flowers down in front of the mausoleum door and leaned a small wreath against the vase. One for Cara and one for Samuel, as he had promised. He looked to Aidan.

"Good," the older man said. "Good and right."

Will backpedaled two steps, preparing to leave, but Aidan bent to the ground and knelt in front of the mausoleum door. Will stopped and closed his eyes.

"Hail Mary, full of grace," said Aidan. "The Lord is with thee. Blessed art thou among women and blessed is the fruit of thy womb, Jesus. Holy Mary, mother a' God, pray for us sinners now and at the hour of our death. We're here today to remember the life a' me beautiful girl, Caralin Deirdre Brady McConnelly, and me grandson, Samuel Aidan McConnelly. They are waitin' for Jesus with open arms and hearts, and we left here must be glad for them, tá. But it's hard, Lord, when we were given so little time together with Caralin and even less with Samuel."

The wind rose. The rain hitting his face now felt like daggers, but still didn't pierce him like Aidan's words. Will wanted to fade more with every sentence. Gravity pulled him to his knees beside his father-in-law.

"If you can but intercede on behalf a' these poor hearts left here on Earth, dear Virgin Mother, and somehow steal a little a' the pain away, then we will be even further in debt ta yeh than we already are."

Will's world spun. He fumbled for something to hang on to. The sureness of his father-in-law's prayer, perhaps. What he found was a small seed of anger.

Anger?

Yes. Why should he pray? Why should anyone pray to the same God who'd allowed Cara and Samuel to burn to death on a night when Will should have been home? He imagined himself sitting at his desk. A hint of hot wood and wire tickles his nostrils. He rises and sees smoke behind a wall of books. 9-1-1. A small blaze dowsed by the fire department. Will and Cara and Samuel standing in front of the house, Samuel crying but alive. All of them, alive. Will picks up Samuel, and his son buries his face in his daddy's shoulder. Will pulls Cara in close. "Thank you, Lord," he whispers to a loving God. "Thank you for protecting my family."

Will rose and stared at the sky. Dark clouds raced above, and a sudden fork of lightning traced a spiky path through the dark gray. Trees bent in the deserted cemetery as the wind's strength grew. In the distance, the burgeoning screech of an air siren rose.

"God damn you," Will whispered. The tempest ripped the words from his lips. "God damn you," he repeated.

In the distance, Aidan's words stopped. The old man regarded him, watched as Will approached the mausoleum, stepped onto the outcropping of stones that bordered the door, and began to climb.

"Jesus, bye!" yelled Aidan, barely intelligible in the roar of the mushrooming wind.

Sticks and leaves whipped past Will as he climbed the side of the mausoleum. A hand pressed his shoe just as he stepped out of Aidan's reach, and then a stabbing pain as the fingernail on his right index finger caught on stone and ripped off. A trail of blood followed him up, up to the roof of the tomb.

Will stood tall, rain and blood dripping off the end of his fingers. The wind receded, then blew in a gust that threatened to toss him back down the ten feet to the cemetery lawn. He braced himself and held up his hands as if challenging God and nature. He screamed, "Why?" but the question became a guttural roar of hatred that no longer held a word. His temples throbbed as the roar threatened to shred his vocal cords. He didn't care. Pain and anger poured from his very being.

The howling blast dissipated and the torrential downpour slowed to a drizzle, as if Will's anger had rebuffed the tempest.

Will's scream died with the wind. The world hung on silence, as if waiting for God's response. Nothing. More nothing.

Then the distant roar of an oncoming train emerged from the silence. Air horns blasted nearby. Heaven opened, and a tornado descended blocks from the cemetery. Will blinked twice, and below him, Aidan said, "Jesus, Mary, and Joseph."

Will gawked at the tornado, a huge, twisting monster of destruction. It staggered toward him like a drunken giant: his answer, at last.

"Get down here, Will!" Aidan shouted.

The tornado touched down at the opposite end of the cemetery. It uprooted trees and tossed cars as if they were Hot Wheels. A section of metal fence sprang from the ground and whirled up and out of sight. Will stood before the fury of God and whispered, "Lord, forgive me for my blasphemy. Take me. Take me to my wife and son."

The roar of the train was deafening, so Will spoke louder, his words a litany. "Forgive me for my blasphemy. Take me. Take me to my wife and my son!"

Tears poured down his cheeks, and Will smiled in the face of the tornado. "C'mon, you sonuvabitch! Take me! Take me to my wife and son!"

"Will!" Aidan screamed. "Get down here now!"

Will growled, "Come on, you piece a' shit! Come get me!"

The tornado tore through the cemetery, ripping through headstones and statuary as if they were Styrofoam. A stone cross hurled past Will's face and crashed somewhere behind him. Will didn't blink. He waited for the tornado to make up its mind, for God to decide to be cruel or kind.

The tornado lunged forward, screaming, then leapt into the sky. It flew over Will's head and landed briefly in a field before disappearing altogether.

Will's surge of anger vanished just as quickly. He fell to his knees, exhausted.

Aidan stared up at him, eyes wide and bushy eyebrows creased. "Ya know somethin', bye?" Aidan said.

Will could barely ask, "What?"

"You're a feckin' dope."

Will's sight glazed over. Aidan and the rest of the world blurred out of focus.

"Now getcher arse down here. We're due to check in to the hotel, and after a nap, I'll need that pint."

The air raid sirens faded, replaced with police and fire sirens. They were headed this way.

Will looked at his finger. "I'm bleeding."

"Yer lucky yer not buried headfirst into a sidewalk," Aidan said.

Will nodded. He didn't feel lucky.

"An' the tornado was right there," said Aidan, pointing to an imaginary whirlwind. A group of old codgers stood around the table, listening intently. "It almost seemed to stop and listen to 'im."

"What was he sayin'?" one of the old men asked.

"Who could tell," said Aidan, "what with the roarin' of a tornado right in yer ears?"

One of the other men slapped the first on the shoulder, as if to say, "What were you thinking?"

"But he was yellin' jus' the same," Aidan continued. "Wavin' his fists as if he were challengin' the very wind to a scrap."

"This is a' bunch a' bullshit," said one of the men. He grabbed his beer and strode to another table.

"Believe what yeh want," said Aidan. "I was there. I'd swear on a Bible if I could, but that's a sure way ta hell no matter if it be truth or lie an' yeh damn well know it!"

The man shrugged and returned to the table. "So, what happened then?" he asked.

"Look at the news, ya git!" yelled Aidan.

A couple of the old men backed away, as if Aidan and the other man might have a go.

"The tornado lifted off the ground and jumped over the rest of the cemetery, as if William had told it ta hie away."

"Bullshit," the other man repeated.

The bartender, a pleasant man in his sixties named Marius, held up his hands. "He's tellin' the truth, lads. I saw it on YouTube. Someone was filmin' the whole damned thing on their phone. Two hunnerd an' fifty thousand views so far."

He held up his cell phone, and Will saw himself from someone's window across the street from the cemetery. It was a long, blurry shot, but Will was standing on the mausoleum with his hands reaching toward the heavens. Aidan stood on the ground behind him as the stone cross flew past Will's face.

I look insane, he thought. *Thank God, my back was to the camera.*

"So how did it end, Aidan?" asked Marius.

"Well, the bye just sat down on the mausoleum like a gargoyle on top a' Notre Dame Cathedral. And then, me friends, we came to the best Irish pub in the state a' Texas to drink with yeh!"

Everyone at the table cheered the end of Aidan's story and Will's ebullience. Marius grabbed a bottle from behind the bar and brought it to the table.

"What've we got there, Marius?" asked another of the old codgers. His name escaped Will, but by this time, between Guinness and Jameson, everything was escaping him.

"*We* got nothin', Brody," replied Marius. "But Will here...." He patted Will on the shoulder. "Bye, yellin' down a tornado prob'ly takes more bollix than even *you* know yeh have. Here." He poured a generous shot of whiskey.

"What is it?" asked Aidan.

"And how do I get a shot of it?" added another.

"You two cough up thirty dollars," said Marius. He turned to Will. "This is my favorite, Will. Twenty-one-year-old Bushmills single malt. It's a shame you're already all in, but still. I ain't seen no one do nothin' like that in my lifetime."

Aidan reached into his wallet and pulled out a wad of money. "Pour me one, too, Marius. Me bye ain't gonna drink alone."

There were "yeahs" and "tás" in agreement. Several men pulled out wallets, though a couple of them offered something like, "Make mine a regular Jameson" or "What about Connemara, do you have any a' that?" Soon, there were filled shot glasses all around the table.

Marius raised his glass. "To bollix," he said, and the rest of the men chorused, "To bollix." They all turned to Will, who had not yet raised his glass. He did so. "To love," he said. The older men lowered their glasses a moment and looked at each other. The cheer hung in the air, and then Marius nodded. "To love." Everyone echoed the new cheer and drank.

The Bushmill's single malt was warm and smooth in Will's mouth, with none of the schizophrenic notes of some whiskeys. This was simple and fruity and delicious. Will pulled out his wallet and handed Marius a credit card. "Six more, for all of us."

The old men stared at him as if he were nuts, and then they cheered. Cries of "love" and "bollix" echoed around the pub, mixed with laughter and loud pats on the back. Blush rose to Will's cheeks—his first moment of pleasure since the fire. Marius poured, everyone drank, and then he poured again.

After about three hundred dollars of this, Aidan put his hand on Will's shoulder. "We should switch back to Guinness, Will, or yeh'll be rememberin' this night crouched over the bog."

Will tried to focus on Aidan's face. "The what?"

"The toilet," Aidan said.

"Oh," Will said. "I do that all the time."

"Perhaps tonight we'll make a change, eh?" Aidan strode to the bar. "Two more Guinness for me and mine."

"Two more it is," said Marius.

"So, no more of the good whiskey?" asked one of the old men.

"Yeh got more than yeh deserved, Casey," said another. "Unless yer buyin' the next round now?"

Casey changed the subject to Shamrock Rovers Football so quickly that even Will, in his inebriation, found it funny. In fact, he found it a riot. He started laughing. Though it seemed foreign to him, once he'd started, he couldn't stop. The old men looked at him as if he might be contagious. They stepped away to give him room to lean on the table. Will realized at some point that Aidan had placed another pint in front of him, and for some reason, that seemed funny, too. He laughed harder.

"He's bewitched," someone said.

The laughter was starting to ease off, and he looked up at the concerned faces surrounding him. Will knew his stomach was going to be sore tomorrow, whether he hurled in the bog later or not.

"Oh, geez," he said when he'd finished.

"What was that about?" asked Casey. The amazement on the man's face was like the expression of an old cartoon character. Will imagined Elmer Fudd or Daffy Duck with his literal jaw on the floor. Bubbles of laughter started to float up into his nose again.

What the hell? he thought.

Will burst into laughter once more.

CARA SNORES BESIDE HIM, A LIGHT SHEEN ON HER SKIN glowing orange from the bathroom light down the hall. The hotel room is in shambles, a tornadic collision of clothes and bedsheets. The aftermath of the first time they'd made love. Will's heart taps against his chest, a beat that he puts silent words to.

I can't / believe / I'm here / with her / tonight, he thinks, the iambic pentameter coming easily after the seventeen-performance run of *Romeo and Juliet* he's just finished.

Will supposes he should feel like a douchebag. He's never been the "stud" that sleeps with a lot of women. Yet here he is, lying next to the second in less than a week.

And they live together.

Will smiles. He's too happy to feel like a douchebag. Since the night at Summer's, he and Cara have seen each other almost every day—coffee, dinner, running into each other on campus—and now? A spontaneous decision—Cara's—the Courtyard by Marriot a mile-and-a-half away from her apartment. After all, having sex with your roommate's recent conquest just one bedroom away seems "a bit gauche," according to her.

Will rolls over to stare at the side of Cara's face in the dim light of the hotel lamp. Her forehead slides down into a perfectly formed nose. That tiny bit of perfection drops onto her philtrum—thank you, theatre makeup class—and up into swollen lips and a strong chin. Will longs to trace her profile with his finger, but her mouth opens and the daintiest little snore pops out.

God, she's perfect, he thinks. *Even her snores are—*

A gigantic inhalation interrupts Will's thoughts, followed by the loudest snore he's ever heard outside of television sitcoms.

Cara opens her eyes in the midst of the snore.

"Huh? What?" she says. "Where are the rainbows?"

"What rainbows?" Will asks.

She smiles, and her eyes close again.

"You know," she whispers. "The penguin ones."

She's still asleep, thinks Will.

Another snore pours out of Cara's slightly open mouth. This one's somewhere between the first and the second. Not tiny, and not giant. For a snore, it's *Just right, just like you.*

Will pulls the cover up to Cara's chin and watches her sleep until his eyes begrudgingly close.

AIDAN SET TWO COFFEE CUPS ON THE TABLE AND SHOVED one in front of Will.

Will accepted it gratefully. They were seated at a Café Brazil five minutes from The Highland Dallas, the hotel Aidan had booked for them. Will didn't want to know how much Aidan had paid for the rooms. The standard rate on the inside of the door was listed at $325 a night. Will knew that you could get a better deal than the standard rate, but still....

Will took a sip of coffee. Bitter and hot and fresh. It soothed his dry throat with its heat.

"Did we get copies of our tab from the bar last night?" he asked.

"Pub," Aidan corrected.

"What's the difference?" Will tore into a pink packet of Sweet'N Low and poured it into his cup, then stirred.

"A bar is where yeh go to listen to loud music and get drunk. A pub is where yeh meet friends and have good conversations."

"We got drunk."

Aidan paused. "Yeh can get drunk almost anywhere. I'll still take a pub over a bar any day."

"Cheers to that," Will said, raising his cup.

Aidan didn't toast him back.

A reserved but friendly waitress, probably a college girl from Southern Methodist University just across the highway, stopped and asked for their order. Aidan glanced at Will.

"Huevos Rancheros, please, with the turkey."

"Sure," she smiled, then turned to Aidan. "And for you?"

"Just two eggs over medium and some toast."

"Okay. Be out in a few."

She shuffled to the kitchen and stuck the order on a turnaround in the window.

"I thought the cure to a hangover was a big breakfast," said Will, playing in his coffee with his spoon.

"I'm not hungover," replied Aidan, "but I had a bit of a bloody Mary this morning through room service while yeh were still snorin' next door."

Will stopped playing and looked up. "You could hear me through the wall?"

"Everyone who walked by could hear yeh, lad," Aidan smiled. "Through the walls. Over the vacuum."

"Hmph," Will said. "Not sure I snore that loudly."

"Well, I could hear yeh anyway, as I live and breathe."

The two men sipped their coffees in silence. For Will, it was just another day without Cara and Samuel.

What about last night then?

Right. Last night he'd laughed for the first time in months. From what he could remember, he'd had a decent time. How was that possible? Sam and Cara were still gone, weren't they? Had he forgotten that? Will glanced up from his coffee.

"So why did we do it?" he asked.

"Do what?" replied Aidan.

"Last night. The bar."

Aidan shot him a disapproving glance.

"The pub, I mean."

"Wasn't it time? Time to get back to the order a' livin'?"

Will sipped.

"Look, bye. I know yer still hurtin'. I am, too. Every mornin' I wake to no daughter and no grandson and no wife, and it's hell. I tell yeh this, though. I'm damned proud to have a son-in-law like yeh. That's enough to give me strength to start plannin' fer the future."

"What future?" Will asked. *No tears*, he told himself. *No goddamned tears*. "I can't see a future right now."

"Course yeh can't, an' it's hard for me to see, too. But I know it's there. We just have to start lettin' go a' some of the past."

"Let go? Of what?" Will's voice started to rise. "Let go of Cara? Of Sam? How the hell am I supposed to do that?"

"William...."

"Why would I even try?" Tears struck his cheeks before he could stop them. He shoved his napkin against his eyes, hard.

Back, he thought.

Will took a deep breath and sighed it out. Returned the napkin to his lap. He grabbed his cup and took a long sip of the now bittersweet coffee; drank for so long that it burned his tongue. He put the cup down. "Sorry."

Aidan's wrinkled hand covered Will's.

He looked up, and the older man smiled.

"We'll never stop missin' 'em." Aidan's voice was a deep whisper. "But this is no way to remember. We've buried 'em in sorrow, in the dark. That was not the way they lived."

"You're speaking metaphorically, right?"

"Yes. And no."

"Everyone's buried in the dark, Aidan. You're talking about their spirits, right?"

Aidan finished his coffee. "I need a refill. How about yeh?"

"Sure." Will handed his cup to Aidan. The older man ambled over to the large coffee bar and began to refill both cups.

What the hell is he talking about?

Aidan was no poet—at least, not the Aidan Will knew. Cara's mother, Betha, had relayed stories of how Aidan had courted her in Ireland, but that was past. Betha died shortly before Samuel was born. It seemed as if she had taken Aidan's poetry with her.

"Here we go," said Aidan, setting the cups on the table. Will added Sweet'N Low, and the two men sipped. The waitress approached from between two other tables with Will's plate full of food and Aidan's spare eggs and toast. Eating offered an excuse for the silence, so they ate.

"Yeh know Caralin and Samuel ain't buried in that mausoleum, right?" asked Aidan, breaking his second egg yolk with a corner of his bread. He dipped the golden crust in the rich yolk.

"Sure," said Will, looking up from the sizeable dent he'd made in the eggs, turkey, jalapenos, and feta cheese on his plate. "They're in heaven. Or waiting for Jesus. Why do you keep bringing this up?"

Aidan paused, then put the rest of his toast down beside the little bit of egg left on his plate. "Yer not understandin' me, Will. They ain't in that mausoleum. At all."

"What?" Will couldn't wrap his mind around what the old man was saying. Had his father-in-law gone off the edge?

Aidan reached down beside him and grabbed a handled paper bag. In the midst of his hangover, Will hadn't noticed the bag. Aidan reached into the bag and extracted an ornate, lidded vase, emerald green with a golden latch and lock. He set it on the table.

"What's that?" asked Will.

The old man said nothing. He stared into Will's eyes, unblinking. Then it hit Will, not like a load of bricks, but like a truckload. A semi-trailer truckload.

"You...you've gotta be shitting me!"

Will felt the entire restaurant turn to stare as he stood and grabbed the side of the table. Fury pounded up his throat like vomit. He leaned across the table, inches from Aidan's calm face.

"Are you fucking insane?" he yelled.

A lady at an adjoining table said, "Hey! There's kids here!"

"Well, God bless you!" said Will, whirling on her like a viper. "Maybe you'll be lucky and not lose them in a fire like I did mine."

"Will!" said Aidan, standing.

"Don't even—"

"Sit your bloody arse down right now, laddie."

Sound caught in Will's throat. Aidan's voice was soft, but the tone struck like a hammer. Will rocked back and forth for a moment, dizzy, almost sick. Then he fell back into his seat, shaking.

"Sorry, Ma'am," Aidan offered to the lady, and then turned to the rest of the mid-morning crowd. "To the rest of yeh, our apologies, as well. In Ireland, we say "Ta bron orm.""

People awkwardly offered "that's okays" and nods and half-smiles. Aidan returned to his seat.

"Now see here—"

"You see here," Will interrupted. "And yes, I'm sorry. Of course. But you...." He placed his hand on the cool side of the vase. "This is...?"

"Ay," said Aidan.

Will's mind whirled.

"You've got.... Why did...? Wait a minute." Will paused, then half-smiled. "The Scottish are the ones who say 'ay.'"

Aidan looked up with a bit of a grin. "Tá. A' course they do, ignorant dopes."

"So, these are...these are the ashes?"

Aidan nodded.

"How did.... Why?"

"Yer not finishin' many sentences this mornin'," said Aidan.

"I don't.... Do you blame me?"

"There's a lad. I'm outa coffee again. You?"

"No, I'm.... Wait a minute."

"It'll hold." Aidan grabbed his cup, leaving Will with the emerald vase. He thought of Cara and Sam inside the thing, ashes. How could that be? How could his beautiful, vibrant family fit in such a small container? He was short-breathing, almost hyperventilating, when his father-in-law returned to his seat.

"Okay," said Aidan, his hands encircling his cup as if it were a goblet in the Middle Ages. "Jus' let me chat for a minute like I was talkin' to meself. Whatever yeh might say after...well, at least I had me moment."

Will took a deep breath and slowly let it out, allowing his shoulders to relax. He rolled his head a couple times, then took another breath and released it. He looked back at Aidan. "Okay."

A huge, expectant pause hung between them like a bubble. Aidan popped it with three tiny words, "I said no."

Will started to ask him what he said no to, but the old man held up his hand. "The night it happened, I said no. No to God, who I know is All and good, but no to Him, just the same. I said no to electricity and fire and homes where smoke alarms don't work. I said no to studies where books burn too fast. I said no to everything, and I said it over and over to meself and to every single thing in my home. My three-bedroom home that only came to life when you brought my daughter and my beautiful, beautiful grandson to see me. I cursed almost everything that night, including you, Will."

"I deserved it," said Will.

"No, bye. Yeh didn't."

"I should've smelled something. I should've—"

"Yeh couldn'ta smelled nothing, Will. Yeh gave my babbies a good home and all the love in the world. It weren't nothin' neither of us could rail at except for God and nature. God listens and doesn't answer, at least not out loud, and nature? Well, she answers all the time. Sometimes her answer is a light wind across the trees brushin' a tree limb against a window, and sometimes it's a tornado rushin' through the middle of a cemetery that decides to change direction and leave yeh be."

Will redirected his gaze at the table, at a beveled saltshaker that had absolutely nothing to say and was an excellent companion because of it.

"The thing is, I couldn't stop sayin' no, not when they gave us that urn they were expecting us to put in a cold piece a' stone to wait on Jesus. I said no, Will. I bought another urn, and when I had a few minutes to meself, I put their ashes into this one."

"Why?" asked Will. "Why would you do that?"

"Gettin' there, bye, in me own time." Aidan took a sip of coffee and laughed. "Yeh'll never find chocolate-cinnamon flavored coffee in Drumkeeran. Tá, that's sure enough." He turned the coffee cup in circles between his hands and smiled.

"I said no to the mausoleum, Will, because I don't want my family in the ground. When I go, I'll go to ground because it's my time, and perhaps you, as well, when you go, because if God is just, neither of us will be ripped outa life the way our loved ones were."

In his head, Will disagreed. If God had truly been good and just, he would've ripped Will out of his life yesterday when he'd faced down the tornado. He would have reunited Will with his family in some world beyond this one. He knew in his heart that Cara and Samuel were somewhere else, somewhere happy, because the universe could not be so unjust that it would allow them to be in a cold and barren afterlife. Maybe Aidan was right. They did deserve more than the ground.

Will looked up to see Aidan waiting. "Did I.... What?" he asked.

"You were woolgatherin'," said Aidan. "I was just waitin' for yeh."

"Sorry. I'm back."

"Not for long, me bye. Yer goin' to Ireland."

Will did a double take. "Say again?"

The old man smiled all the way this time, a huge grin. He placed an envelope beside the vase. "Here's yer ticket. Yeh leave day after tomorrow."

"Why would I.... What?"

"Don't worry, lad. It's round trip. I'm not tryin' to get rid a' yeh."

Will picked up the envelope and looked inside. Aer Lingus. William Greyson McConnelly. He looked back to Aidan. "I don't understand."

"I'll speak slowly, then, and use small words." Aidan was teasing, but it didn't seem mean-natured. "I want yeh to take these ashes to Ireland. I want yeh to go to Drumkeeran and take them into the drumlin hills and release them into the Irish wind."

Will heard the words, but they didn't make sense.

"Why? Why would I...? Is that even legal, transporting ashes by...? Shouldn't they be here, with us? Aidan, I...I can't."

"It don't matter if it's legal or not," said Aidan. "We're not tellin' a soul. An' we don't need 'em here, not in the ground. We have 'em here"—Aidan touched his chest—"and here." He pointed to his head. He smiled and tapped the urn. "They're not really here anyway, right? Isn't that what you told Caralin at her ma's funeral?"

The older man sipped his coffee, then continued, "As for why I would want them there...yeh'll see that the first mornin' yeh wake up and look at an Irish sunrise. I want them in the wind there, Will, where there's still magic and beauty. I love America, but I want Caralin and Samuel where my Betha can look over them."

"Your wife?" asked Will.

Aidan nodded.

"But she's buried in the same mausoleum where Cara and Sam are...where the other urn is."

Aidan shook his head. "That's an empty casket. I put it there for Cara to have a place to go and mourn her ma. Betha is in a little plot a' earth outside Leitrim, where we met and had our first wee house. It's where I'll go when I leave this earth, as well."

Will shook his head. "So, all this time...you lied to your own daughter?"

"Cara loved her ma. She needed a place to go and talk to her now and again. I would have told her eventually."

"Eventually could've come sooner than later," said Will, downing the rest of his coffee.

"Tá, it coulda," Aidan spat. "A lotta things coulda, like me takin' you and yer family to Ireland for a proper trip. I'd always promised to take Cara there when she was a child, and then a teenager, and a college lass, and I never did."

He met Will's eyes again. This time, his gaze was desperate. "Help me, Will. It's the only promise I made her that can still come true."

"Why don't you go?" asked Will. "Or, at least"—he touched the envelope with the ticket inside—"go with me."

Aidan bowed his head a little, still looking at Will. "Because I'd never return, and I know that yeh could never stay there. I feel the two of us are bound up now. By grief, maybe. By love of our children, most assuredly. Maybe even a little love between us, as well."

Will had never thought about it much, but yes. He loved the older man.

"You know what yer name means, Will?"

Will smiled. "Protector. Cara told me that I would always...." He couldn't finish because the tears leapt into his eyes.

Aidan's hand covered his. "Yeh can still protect her, Son. Protect and send her into the beauty of the place I'd always promised to take her. I beg of yeh, Will. For me. For her and Samuel. Maybe even for you."

"All right," Will managed. "I'll go."

Aidan looked as if a hundred years had lifted from his face. "Thank yeh, Will. God bless you."

"Just one question."

"Tá. Anything."

"What's in the urn in the mausoleum? If this is Cara and Sam, what's in their place?"

Aidan took the last sip of his coffee, looking quite serious. "About five pounds of Kingsford Match Light briquette ash from those steaks we cooked in the backyard last September."

"You're kidding me," Will said, shocked.

"Actually," said Aidan, grabbing the emerald vase and paper bag, "I'm not kiddin', at all." He headed out the door, leaving Will to pick up the check and his airline ticket.

Chapter Four

AIR

"ATTENTION, travelers. Aer Lingus flight 237 is now boarding. If you're flying business class with us today you may now board. We will board other travelers in just a few minutes."

Will looked at his phone. 6:45 p.m. at O'Hare Airport in Chicago, where he was changing flights from American Airlines to Aer Lingus.

Cara's and Sam's ashes were safely tucked away inside the emerald green vase in Will's checked suitcase. Aidan had also packed a variety of fake flowers and greenery, so that a customs official might assume that Will was some sort of florist bringing work with him on vacation.

"That doesn't make any sense," Will had said to Aidan the night before. "Who would do that?"

"Doesn't have to make sense," Aidan replied. "That's the beauty of it. Yeh can travel with as many bags as yeh want, really, as long as yeh pay the fee. It just can't look like ashes."

"I can prob'ly get permission to take the ashes on the flight."

"Nah. I Googled it, or what have yeh. Yeh've got ta talk to everyone and his ma to get permission, and that includes the American embassy in Ireland. They'll ask what yer gonna do with the ashes and yeh can't very well say what yer gonna do, 'cause that's illegal fer sure."

"Then why don't I just put them in something else? This is ridiculous!"

"Just do it, bye," said Aidan. "Have a little faith."

Now Will was sitting at the airport waiting for some official to tap him on the shoulder and say, "Mr. McConnelly? You need to come with me. We have to discuss your checked baggage."

He caught the movement of an airport security guard out of the corner of his eye. The man was talking to a pilot, and they were both pointing toward Will.

Oh shit.

The security guard left, and the pilot made a beeline for Will, wheeling his suitcase behind him.

I knew it. Sonuvabitch.

Will's heart pounded against his chest. The pilot made eye contact, smiled, and walked right past him. Will watched as the man leaned against the check-in desk to whisper something to the very attractive gate agent making the announcements. She giggled, and the pilot laughed. His hand moved around her back for a side hug, and then he left, pulling his small, wheeled suitcase behind him.

Close call, Will thought, then realized that it wasn't really a call, at all. Totally unrelated.

The lady at the desk called for any guests in wheelchairs or parents with young children. There were no wheelchaired guests, but two families with babies boarded.

A nine-hour flight with babies. That'll be fun.

The gate agent finally called group D, and Will grabbed his laptop and carry-on bag. Aidan had assured him, rural setting aside, that there would be internet in Drumkeeran. Will thought he might try to write out some of his feelings about the last year: the fire, the funeral, and the seemingly bottomless well of heartache. He hadn't written a play in forever. Perhaps the magic of Ireland would inspire him.

Darker thoughts stirred, as well, an idea he'd been playing with for the last month or so. He pushed that aside for now. There would be plenty of time for those thoughts in the Drumlin hills, where he would put the remnants of his life into the Irish wind. That reminded him of something...*what was it?*

The Aer Lingus gate agent interrupted his reverie with a perfunctory "Good afternoon," to which Will replied, "Thanks." He grabbed his ticket and trudged down the air bridge to the plane. It wasn't a crowded flight. Aidan had planned that out well. Though people vacationed in Ireland up to mid-November, the best time to go was in the summer. It wasn't necessarily because of temperature differences.

Aidan had said, "The only way yeh can tell the difference between summer and winter is by how cold the rain is." Will had found much the same in his internet research. The temperature year-round stayed between thirty-two and sixty-eight Fahrenheit.

Will waited patiently for others in the half-full plane to store their luggage. Then he grabbed a script from his carry-on before shoving the carry-on and laptop bag into the overhead compartment.

"Excuse me," he said to an older, white-whiskered man sitting on the aisle side of his row.

The man glanced up and said, "Yes?" in an accent that didn't seem quite Irish but close.

"Sorry. I'm in the window seat," said Will.

"Oh, ay," said the man. "There ya go then." This time, Will caught the rolled "r" and the brogue. Scottish. "Let's get in there."

The man stood and moved into the aisle just long enough for Will to move past. They both plopped down in their seats. Will stuck *A Midsummer Night's Dream* in the magazine holder in front of him. He raised his butt off the seat long enough to find the lapbelt, which he fastened.

"This yer first time to Ireland?" asked the Scotsman beside him.

"Yes," said Will. "You?"

The man raised his eyebrows.

Will noticed that they were amazingly bushy, like gray and white monkey grass. "Stupid question, right?"

The man laughed, a nice guffaw. "Ay, since I'm right across the pond. Well, not *the* pond. But close enough."

"Visiting relatives?" asked Will, trying to be polite. He used to enjoy talking to strangers. Now, words felt like poorly written lines delivered by the worst of actors.

The man laughed again. "No, lad. But it's a hop across to Edinburgh, a lot easier than flying into London. And Ireland's a beauty, indeed. Almost as pretty as our Highlands. Are ye on business or holiday?"

Between the two designations, Will was probably on business, but he couldn't really talk about that. "Just getting away for a while."

"Ah. Well, when ye're done on the Island, drop by Scotland for a touch. Then ye'll have seen the two most beautiful places on this earth, and I tell ye that's the truth. I've traveled a lot."

"I'll see," said Will, smiling a little.

"Ah, here." The man pulled out his wallet, and then a business card. He handed it to Will. "I live in Musselburgh with me wife and daughter. She's still at Queens College. Studying philosophy...this week." He laughed. "You give me a ring when ye get into town, and I'll get ye set up in a nice little cottage we own, free a' charge."

"That's.... Thank you."

"Ain't nothin'. We rent it out, but we've got another month before the new tenants come. It's just sittin' there across the street lookin' sad. We'll have ye over for some of me wife's steak pie. Good home cookin'.

"That's very kind of you. I'll try to make time for it."

The man put his hand out. "I hope so. Name's McCulloch. Alistair."

Will took his hand and shook it. "Will McConnelly."

Alistair's eyebrows shot up in amusement. "McCulloch and McConnelly. It's like we're related!" He put his other hand on top of Will's, shaking with both as if they had been friends their entire lives. He released Will's hand and eased back into the seat, smiling. "I do hope ye'll come. I see it in yer face that ye won't, but maybe ye'll change yer mind."

Am I that easy to read? Will thought.

"It's been a difficult year. I'm trying to get away from...from myself, I guess."

Alistair stared into Will's eyes, and his face melted from friendly to sad. All the laugh wrinkles pulled downward into age. "I'm sorry, lad.

You must miss them very much." He reached over and grabbed Will's hand again.

His grip was like iron, and so personal that it made Will want to jerk his hand back, move out of his seat, and deplane.

He knows. How the hell does he know?

Alistair released his hand. "I'll leave ye be now," he said. "But if ye do make it to Scotland—if ye don't do what ye're plannin' on doin' in Ireland—we'll have a nice room and some good conversation waitin' on ye." He turned away.

Will wanted to ask how he knew, but the flight attendant began her diatribe about seatbelts and oxygen masks. Will turned to the window, trying to clear his mind. Fifteen minutes later, they were in the air, flying over Chicago, and a couple hours after that, the Atlantic. Will saw a hint of ocean beneath misty white clouds, and then he was asleep and dreaming.

Ahead of him, Cara springs up the gangway with laughter bubbling like water from a mountain spring. Will can't help but laugh, as well, and neither can others on the cruise ship. The pure joy she exudes sprouts smiles on the faces around her.

She rockets back down the gangway

Oh shit.

and launches herself into Will's arms, knocking the suitcases out of his hands.

She kisses him, first on the lips and then all over his face. Little dry smacks that almost tickle. "I'm so excited!" she says. "Raaaah!"

Will really starts laughing then. How can life be this good? Cara halts her flurry of kisses, but her arms and legs still encircle him.

"Are you happy, William McConnelly? Are you one hundred percent truly happy?"

He nuzzles her nose with his. "One hundred percent happy, Mrs. Cara McConnelly."

Her face turns semi-serious. "You know what's weird?"

"What?"

"I'm already used to that name, even though I've only had it a day now."

"You'd better be used to it. You're gonna have it a long, long time."

"My whole life," she says. She kisses him again, almost embarrassingly hard and deep.

Will feels more eyes on him, and he breaks away long enough to murmur, "Maybe we should find our room."

Cara lowers her gaze until she's looking at him underneath her eyebrows. She sticks her index finger in her mouth sideways, mischievously.

"Oh, yeah. We should definitely find our room. Come on." She grabs his hand and starts up the gangway again.

"Wait, wait!" he says, gesturing to their luggage with his free hand.

"Oh, oops!" She turns, grabs one of their giant suitcases and dashes up the gangway, wheeling it behind her like an out-of-control rickshaw.

"Be careful," Will yells.

Cara makes a beeline for one of the cruise ship personnel, a deck crewman. By the time Will gets there, she's off again, waving for him to follow.

"First cruise?" asks the deck crewman.

"Yep," says Will. He turns as he passes the man. "First time for both of us."

"Welcome aboard. Don't forget the safety drill. Directions are in your room. It's required before we set sail."

"Okay," says Will.

Up ahead, Cara has stopped, waiting with one impatient hand on her hip. Will hurries to catch up with her, narrowly avoiding an elderly lady with a walker.

"Come on!" Cara groans. "You're taking forever!" She kisses Will again and shoves her way through the crowds like a Dallas Cowboys lineman. She stops at a bank of elevators, and Will almost runs over her.

"In here."

Will stares at the overcrowded cab. His hands start to sweat. "Let's wait for the next one," he says, but Cara is already through the doors, pushing people gently aside with her beautiful smile.

"Sorry, sorry," she says to the disgruntled riders. "It's our honeymoon."

Her declaration is like adding sugar to bitter coffee. A chorus of "congratulations" and "awwwwws" provide the accompaniment as everyone scooches together to make room for Will. He shakes his head and wheels his suitcase into the cab. The doors close.

Will finds himself nose-to-nose with his wife. He can't even move enough to turn around and face the doors. Cara cranes her neck forward and brings her lips within centimeters of his. She opens her mouth slightly and runs her tongue along her lower lip. Not only does Will have almost no room in the elevator; he now has very little room in his jeans.

A little old man, back bent with age, taps Cara on the shoulder. She twists her neck around just enough to see him.

"You were just married?" he asks. His voice is a soft, gravelly bass barely louder than the mechanics of the elevator.

"Yesterday." Cara smiles.

"Excuse me," says someone else. A woman in a big sun hat. "This is our floor."

Of course, she's in the back, Will thinks and steps out of the elevator to allow two women to exit. Now there's enough room, but he still faces the back of the elevator.

Cara turns sideways to more easily talk.

The elderly man, Will can now see, holds the hand of an older woman. He pats it gently as both of them smile at Cara.

"Jenny and I have been married for sixty-five years," he says, and the old woman nods. "We've had our ups and downs, but if you remember to say that you love each other every night before you go to sleep and every day when you wake up, you'll remind yourselves of the only thing that's important." The man turns to his wife and they share a brief kiss before turning back to Cara and Will.

Cara beams down on them, then turns to her husband. "Every morning and every night. Can you handle that?"

Will smiles. "Every morning and every night and a hundred times in between," he says.

The little old lady pipes up, "Oooh, I like him. He's a bullshitter."

Several exclamations of surprise follow the dainty cursing.

The lady winks at Cara, then leans in conspiratorially, "This one's a bullshitter, too, and I'm gonna tell you this little tidbit. The bullshitters are the best in bed."

Cara covers her mouth to stifle giggles, and the old woman looks over at her husband affectionately.

"Eighty-three, and he still can't keep his hands off me."

"She loves it," the old man says.

The elevator dings. It's Cara's and Will's floor, so they roll their bags out into the hall.

"Every morning and every night," the old man reminds them.

"For sure," says Will, and the elevator doors close.

Cara presses herself into him. "She had your number, didn't she, Mr. Bullshitter?"

Will laughs. "Except you know I'm not bullshitting."

A couple passes by, a little boy in tow between them.

"So, you'll love me even when we're a little old couple like that?" she asks.

"I'll love you 'til the stars turn to dust," Will says. His brain suddenly fills with a little poetry. "My love is not an option. It's a must."

Cara smiles so widely, Will thinks it might split her face in two.

He takes her hands and kisses her softly on the side of her mouth. "Each morning and each night, I'll promise now. To speak the words 'I love you,' as my solemn vow."

"Mmm," says Cara. "She was right."

"Who? What?"

"That lady. Bullshitters *are* the best lovers."

"Come on," says Will, grabbing his suitcase. "Let's find our room."

"Amen to that."

They powerwalk down the hall, trying not to run, until they find room 875. Will fumbles with the key card, and then they're inside. The door closes behind them. They set their suitcases by the bed.

"Look!" says Cara, pointing. In the center of the bed sits a towel folded into the shape of a swan.

"Cool!" Will replies, already on his way to the balcony.

"I can't believe there's so much room," Cara says.

"I know. Come here."

Cara joins Will on the balcony, an area big enough for a couple of chairs and a side table. He puts his arms around her waist as she stares out at the other ships docked in Miami Harbor.

"This is gonna be amazing," she says.

"It already is," Will says.

"I love you so much it scares me," she breathes.

"It doesn't scare me."

They step together and their lips meet, mouths open. One of Will's hands caresses Cara's face as the other slips around her waist to pull her close. For a moment, it seems if he pulls her just a little closer, they will occupy the same space and time, become one being.

Cara pulls away and looks up at him, her eyes a little wet. "What are you thinking?" she asks.

"How I haven't even begun to discover how much I love you. How important you are to me."

She pulls his head down to hers, lips together then open, tongues dancing. They stumble back through the balcony doors and fall onto the bed. Cara unbuttons Will's shirt as he slips his hands under her blouse to her soft, warm breasts. He pops the clasp of her bra as she helps him out of his pants.

Will lifts up her sundress to find her warm and ready, and he slips into her effortlessly. Cara gently bites his neck and pulls his face back into a long kiss that leads to sighs, and then to moans. She wraps her legs around his back as if she'll never let him go. For a long time, she doesn't.

WILL WAKES WITH A START, NOT SURE WHERE HE IS. HE twists in bed to see his beautiful wife, and behind her, the setting sun dripping gold through the balcony window. He relaxes back into his pillow.

Cara blinks and opens sleepy eyes. "Is it morning already?" She yawns.

"I don't think so. Sunset."

"Oh. Good."

"We must've missed the safety drill."

"What safety drill?" She snuggles her face closer into his chest.

"Something we're supposed to do before the ship launches."

"Ummm."

"That's it? Ummm? What happens if the ship goes down?"

"Ain't nothin' goin' down on this cruise but me," she says, giggling.

Will laughs. "Naughty."

"Just wait 'til I wake up. I'll show you naughty."

Will kisses her forehead. "I bet you will."

"You'd better believe it." She relaxes into him, her breath slowing. Then she pushes up into a sitting position, looking around like a groundhog.

"What?" Will asks, startled.

"I'm starving," she says. She hops out of bed and grabs her dress from the floor.

Will sits up. "How the hell do you do that?"

"Do what?"

"Instantaneously wake up like that, in one second."

Cara bounces back onto the bed and kisses Will. She shoves him down and climbs on top of him.

"It's a gift," she says. "I've always been this way."

"It's kinda weird."

"Mmmm," she hums through a kiss. She hops back onto the floor. "Do you think we missed dinner?"

Will rolls over and grabs his pants. "They said there's not a seated dinner today, but there are twenty-four-hour buffets on the fourth and fifth floors.

"Look at this, Will."

He hops toward the balcony, his pants around his knees. Cara stands there, still holding her sundress, bathed in the setting sun.

Golden hour. That's what they call it in the movie industry. That one hour at sunset and again at dawn when light makes gods out of mortals.

Will steps out of his pants and joins her on the balcony. The wind blows soft and cool against his skin, and the waves crest white atop the blue-black water of dusk. Cara leans on the rail, and the wind blows her hair gently.

"I know other people are beside us and below and above," she says, "but right now, it's like we're the only two people in the world."

She closes her eyes and continues to lean on the rail. To Will, she looks like a goddess there. Venus born on sea foam. Artemis sprung, fully formed, from Zeus's head. Cara's face shines gold.

Will bends his head to her shoulder, and Cara tilts her head so that he can kiss her neck.

"I don't ever want to leave this moment," she whispers.

"Should I take a picture?" Will asks.

"No. Let's just put it somewhere in our memories where we'll never forget it. This one perfect moment."

Will gazes out at the ocean, at the sun framed by Cara's beautiful face. He never will forget that image, not if he lives to be a hundred.

She turns away from the ocean and looks at him, then down at his nakedness. She points. "That, sir, is gonna have to wait until after dinner."

"Aw, c'mon!" he says in mock consternation.

She slides past him, and he gets one nice slap on her ass as she dons her sundress.

"Nope," she says.

"Oh, yes." Will pulls the balcony doors closed behind him.

Cara rushes to the stateroom door and flings it open.

Two large women in swimsuits walk past. The movement attracts their attention, and they see Will in all his naked, enthusiastic glory. A moment later, he hears laughter erupt down the hallway.

"Close the door!" says Will, covering himself.

"Get dressed," Cara says. "I'll meet you in the hall." She leaves the room, closing the door behind her.

Will looks down. "You're just gonna have to wait 'til later, man," he says.

Cara throws the door open. "Boo!"

Will turns in surprise, trips over the end of the bed, and hits the floor. "Goddamnit!" he yells.

Cara giggles and shuts the door again.

Will struggles into his clothes. "Just wait!" he shouts. "Revenge is a dish best eaten on a cruise!"

"I love you!" she yells back.

"That's not fair!" he returns.

"I'm your wife! I don't have to play fair!"

She's right. I'd let her get away with almost anything.

He finishes dressing, throws on his socks and shoes, and stumbles to the door. Cara stands across the hall looking totally innocent.

"A lady just told me they're serving a seafood buffet on the aft side of deck four," she says, "on the port end. Now, I don't know what any of that means, but once we figure it out, I'm gonna gorge like a tick."

"Just a snack," Will says.

"Are you kidding? This is all-inclusive!"

"A full belly," says Will with a slight Asian accent, "does not a honeymoon bed make."

"We have maids for that," Cara says. "And they make birds out of towels."

"I wasn't really talking about making the bed," Will says.

"I know." Cara's hand wanders down from Will's waist and into his back jeans pocket.

"I love you," he says.

"Mmm. Say that to me tonight before we go to sleep."

"And again tomorrow when we wake up. Every day for the rest of our lives."

Cara slides her hand out of Will's back pocket and around his waist. He slides his arm up to her shoulders.

"I think I'm gonna like my first marriage," she says.

Will stops. "First?"

Cara bends double laughing. "Just kidding."

Chapter Five

GREEN

WILL POPPED the latch on the overhead bin and grabbed his carry-on. He was glad there weren't more passengers, because he had a mild case of Enochlophobia and hated crowds. Tight spaces themselves were no big deal, but when people packed in around him, Will felt like screaming.

Up ahead, Alistair McCulloch swam through the crowd like Michael Phelps in the 200-meter medley. He was lithe and swift, and out the door before many of the other passengers had managed to retrieve their carry-ons.

Prob'ly for the best.

Something about the man gave Will the—he chuckled at the word choice—willies. He was a little surprised Alistair hadn't said something before he left, though. More than a little surprised, actually.

Will grabbed his travel bag and laptop and jumped into the aisle traffic, now flowing steadily toward the air bridge. The flight attendant, the one with the lilt, said, "Thank you for flying Aer Lingus." Her smile seemed almost real, if not a little tired. Will didn't blame her. Theirs was a long flight, and *he* hadn't served two meals and drinks.

That's what I need.

He wondered how soon he could get a shot of Irish whiskey. Surely, the airport had a duty-free shop. Will needed something he could take with him on the bus to Drumkeeran. He stepped from the air bridge into the terminal.

He followed some of the same backs he'd seen deplaning. They were all moving with determination, motivated walkers trying to find their ways to their luggage and beyond. It was as if they all had a path.

Two roads diverged in a wood, he thought. *And I took the one that led to a fire.*

Lost in thought, Will ran into the back of someone.

"What're yeh doin'?" a middle-aged lady asked, turning. "Are yeh daft?"

"So sorry," Will replied. "Wool gathering."

The woman stopped, and her demeanor changed. "American?"

"Yes."

"I went there last year. Saw *Wicked* on Broadway."

"I teach drama in Texas," he said. "We do a musical every year."

"Oh, yer a lucky lad! What're yeh doin' next?"

The question hung in the air a moment. "I'm not sure. I've taken a, uh...small hiatus from teaching."

She stared at him for a moment, then harumphed. "Well, get back to it," she said. "Then it'll be safer here in Ireland!" She dismissed him with a wave and took off for the baggage claim.

"Get back to it," whispered Will. *God, I wish it were that easy.*

He followed the lady to the baggage claim and waited for his luggage to drop onto the carousel. Finally, a black, rolling suitcase with gray trim appeared. Will found bare floor space next to the conveyor belt and grabbed his suitcase. He strapped his carry-on travel bag to the rolling suitcase's telescoping handle, then slipped his laptop's backpack over his shoulders.

He headed to the customs line, where he waited for a tall, gap-toothed agent to stamp his passport.

"Hi," said Will. "I was wondering if you have a duty-free shop for travelers entering Dublin." He noted the agent's name on a small silver badge on the man's lapel. "Is it Shawn? Shee-han?"

The agent gawked at Will, then his passport.

"Is it Will-I-aim?" the agent asked. "Wyle-ee-am?" He aggressively stamped Will's passport.

Will finally understood the true meaning of the word "stamped." "Sorry."

"It's Key-An. Emphasis on the 'key.' An' yes, I know it's not spelled that way. It's not me fault, and it's not me ma's, neither. Are yeh here fer holiday or business?"

"Holi—"

"Never mind. Don't care, to be honest." He shoved the passport across the table to Will.

"Thank you. About the duty-free—"

"No duty-free fer incoming flights unless yer connectin' to somewheres outside the EU. Next, please."

I thought Americans were sensitive.

Will ambled toward the sliding glass doors. He glanced back at a digital clock above the ticketing counter. *Ten a.m.*

A bus was scheduled to leave the Dublin Airport Atrium Road en route to, eventually, Drumkeeran. Bus Éireann was the name of the company. Aidan had written out a list of times just in case Will's flight arrived early or late or even, God forbid, on time, which it was. He simply had to find which way the Atrium Road station was.

Will stepped through the sliding glass doors into the Dublin morning. The air reeked of cigarettes and gasoline exhaust. He glanced at the dozens of smokers clustered in the designated areas, feeding their habit. Dublin, like many cities, must have banned the cancer sticks.

Vaping should be next.

Will set out for the taxi stand to ask directions. A horn honked, and Will twisted around to see a red Volkswagen Golf pull between two taxis. As if in reply, the taxi drivers laid on their horns.

The driver of the Golf stuck his head out of the driver's window, which was right next to Will. It was Alistair.

"Get in, lad," he cried.

Will strode over to the window and bent down. "I thought you were on a connecting flight to Edinburgh."

"I am," said the Scotsman. "Well, that's to say, I was. Just throw yer bags in the back and hop in."

Will shook his head. "I'm fine. I have a route all planned out by my father-in-law."

"Ah, fer Chrissake," said Alistair. He opened his door and hopped out of the car.

"Get outa the transportation lane, yeh eejit!" yelled one of the taxi drivers.

Alistair ignored him. Instead, he pulled the rolling suitcase from Will's hand and lifted it into the trunk, carry-on still attached. He opened the left, back door of the Golf and pointed to Will's laptop bag. "Toss it in there, that's a good lad. Now, get in before one a' these maniacs decides to run us down."

Will climbed in the left side of the car, and Alistair tore out of the space. Will grabbed the seatbelt and attempted to fasten it as Alistair almost crashed into another blue-and-white taxi trying to park. He zoomed out of the airport and headed for, according to traffic signs, the M4.

"Can I—?" started Will.

Alistair interrupted. "No, you canna."

Will stared back at the road, waited a minute, then, "But I got in here with—"

"Jesus, would ya just gimme a chance to get the bloody hell outa this godforsaken airport first?"

Frustration bubbled up and exploded into, "Just pull over and let me out, okay?"

The Scotsman looked over at him then, his monkey-grass eyebrows bristling over narrowed eyes. "Really?" he asked.

"Just...pull over, right here."

"Sure."

Another long stare, alternating between Will and the road. Alistair laughed. "Yer daft, yeh know that, William McConnelly?"

Will's frustration turned to anger. "I'm not daft, but you're definitely starting to piss me off."

"Oh, I *am* now?"

"Yeah. So, you'd better pull over right now."

Alistair's face broke into a wide grin. "Or what, bye?"

"Well...." Will stopped. What the hell was he gonna do? "I'll...I'll call the police."

"Really? What's their number?"

"I assume it's 911. Isn't it?"

"You think I'm gonna tell ye?"

Will jerked his head as Alistair swerved around a sluggish Fiat. "Jesus!" said Will. He grabbed the overhead handle on his side like a mountain climber's rope. "Slow down!"

"Oh, you'd like that now, wouldn't ya? I supposed you'd try to grab the wheel then?"

"No. NO! I'm not the crazy one here."

"I'm thinkin' yer just that," Alistair said. He abruptly wheeled the car over to the right side of the road and threw it into park. Will was so shocked he forgot his whole plan of grabbing his luggage and calling a cab.

The two men stared at each other for about five seconds. Then, Alistair put his hand on Will's shoulder.

"Look," he said. "My family, at least some of 'em, have this gift. Sometimes we get glimpses of things that might happen to people. They're not carved in stone, and sometimes they're so common that I don't even mention 'em. Like the other day, I accidentally brushed the hand of someone at a 7-11 in Chicago and saw that she was gonna win one dollar from a lottery card. Why tell her, right? She'd think I'm some sorta bugger and it's all for a dollar."

Will looked down at his hands. Was this guy for real?

"But you," Alistair continued, "yer goin' through somethin' fierce and important, and maybe somethin' that could affect someone else. A couple someones. We're all on paths, bye."

"Predetermination," Will scoffed. "We're on a path and there's nothing we can do about it. I heard all that growing up Baptist."

"Oh, aye. I've heard that shite, as well. Me parents were Presbyterian, if'n ye can believe it." Alistair laughed. "Oh, it were a scandal around our little town."

When Alistair said town, it sounded like "toon." Will stifled a laugh.

"There are paths out there, though," the older man continued. "Dozens of 'em, if ye ken it. God leads us, if ya believe in such a thing as God, but I think He leaves us alone a lot, too. What good would free will be without the free part?"

"What does that have to do with me?" Will asked.

Alistair looked into his rearview mirror. "Uh oh."

Will turned in his seat to see flashing lights pull up behind them. A moment later, a police officer stepped out of his car and approached them on the right.

Alistair lowered the window. "G'day, Officer," he said. "Can we help ya?"

"Jus' wonderin' why yer pulled over. Any problems here?"

Will noticed the patch on the officer's right arm. It said, "Police Service, Northern Ireland."

"Not at all," Alistair laughed. "Me friend here, Will, he was...er, checking his pockets. Thought he mighta left his wallet at the airport."

The police officer removed his glasses, revealing kind eyes housed in a round, pudgy face. "That true, son?"

"Yes, sir," said Will, removing his wallet from his pocket. "I was kinda sitting on it, and I couldn't feel it on top of my jeans. I panicked. Sorry."

"Yer from America, are yeh?" the officer asked.

"Yes, sir."

"In fer business or holiday?"

Again, the question. Will said, "Holiday. Visiting a cousin of my father's up in Drumkeeran."

"Ah," the officer smiled. "I have an aunt who lives up there. It's a small village, only a couple hundred folks. If yeh see Fiona Coneely, tell her Emmet says hello. She'll know who it is tellin' yeh."

"I will, sir."

"All right, then. Carry on. Have a good holiday, son."

"Thank you."

Alistair raised the window and turned to Will. "Now, can we finish this conversation on the road, or are ya gonna be gettin' out with all yer luggage in front of the constable?"

Will sighed. "The road's fine," he said.

"That's me bye." Alistair smiled. He pushed his turn signal up, glanced behind him, and jammed his foot down on the accelerator. The little Golf swerved into traffic like a dervish.

Three minutes later, they were on the N3 speeding toward, Will assumed, Drumkeeran.

"So...." said Will.

"Aye?" returned Alistair.

"Were you...gonna finish your story?"

"Oh, we've got plenty a' time fer that now. It's a two-and-a-half-hour drive to Drumkeeran, dependin' on traffic, which shouldn't be too bad this time a' day. No need to rush. Why don't yeh tell me about your family?"

Will turned to look out the window. They were still passing a lot of buildings, albeit a different style of architecture than what he was used to. Everything here felt...older.

"Bye?" said Alistair, but Will ignored him.

There was an age about the country that made the oldest city in Texas feel like it'd been founded yesterday. Then they passed an Enter-prise Rent-A-Car, which destroyed the illusion.

Will mused that it didn't matter how magical a land might once have been. The twentieth century saw fairy rings ploughed under and paved over. Fairy tales were fed into the Disney machine and turned into movie franchises rather than stories for bedtime. Then, the twenty-first century digitized the stories and quantified them into digital streaming services.

The feeling was different here. Buildings melted into green trees and fields. Vines gradually overgrew and concealed modernity under millions of leaves. Will had discovered his own time machine. The farther from the city Alistair drove, the older everything seemed. The cool green flora persuaded Will's eyelids to droop and then close. He slept.

A voice climbed inside Will's ear. Not loud, but insistent. "Will," it whispered. "Laddie."

"What?" said Will. "Just a few more minutes, Aidan."

"It's Alistair, Will. We're here."

Will's eyes opened. He and Alistair were passing a series of white, gray, and brown buildings made of brick and stone, perhaps concrete, too, or some other smooth building material. Some had a kind of town-home look. Others were lofts perhaps, with small stores underneath and living areas above.

Will rubbed his eyes and tried to make sense of his surroundings. Where was he, and why the hell was some guy driving on the wrong side of the car? Small droplets of rain hit the window, a soft tattoo in the near silence. He remembered where he was.

"We're here?"

"Ay, son. We're here, even though yeh need to tell me where exactly in Drumkeeran yeh need to go."

"Uh..." was as far as Will got before a huge yawn climbed into his nose and forced his mouth wide open. He wiped his eyes. "There's a bed and breakfast called the...the Drumkeeran Bed and Breakfast."

"Leave it to the Irish to be that bleedin' obvious," said Alistair, shaking his head. "We passed it right before I woke ye. Hang on."

Alistair made a U-turn in the middle of the road, sending two pedestrians scurrying to the sidewalks and earning a series of honks from several cars he almost sideswiped.

All of this shook Will wide awake. "Jesus! How the hell do you stay out of the hospital the way you drive?"

Alistair smiled at him. "Well, where I live, everyone knows me car."

That got Will to smile, albeit weakly.

"All right, bye. We ain't got much time now. I've got to be on the road right after I drop ye at the door, so listen. Remember how I was tellin' ye that me family had the gift of sight?"

Will thought a moment. "I remember you saying something right before we got pulled over. A one-dollar lottery ticket, was that it?"

"Part of it, ay. The point is, I tetched ye while ye were sleeping, and I saw something."

"Touched me?"

"Hand ta hand, bye. Nothin' inappropriate."

"Just sounded weird. I'm still half asleep." Will yawned again.

"Then listen with yer wakin' half."

"Okay."

Alistair took a deep breath. "Tail, blindfold, shadow."

Will waited. Nothing. "And?" he asked.

"That's it. Tail, blindfold, shadow."

"What does that mean?"

"Dinna know," Alistair confessed. "I just saw a lotta confusin' images, and some beautiful ones, too, but at the end, those three words were there, in me head."

"What were the images?"

"That, me bye, is fer ye to find out." He shoved the car into park in front of a large white building adorned with many windows. He hopped out of the Golf and started retrieving Will's luggage from the trunk.

Will grabbed his laptop from the back seat and met Alistair at the front of the B&B.

"You rented a car for a two-and-a-half-hour drive—"

"Actually," Alistair interrupted, "we made it in two hours ten minutes." He smiled proudly. "A new personal record."

"You drove me out here for three words?" said Will, exasperated. "Three words."

Alistair shrugged. "That's what they gave me, so that's what I give to ye. At least, ye got a free ride, an' a quick one, at that."

Will pulled out his wallet and started counting out bills. "At least, let me give you something for the trip."

Alistair closed his large fist over the wallet. "I'd hate ta wallop you right now, when we're so close ta bein' friends."

Will took a step back. "I'm sorry."

Another kind, Scottish smile. "As the Aussies say, 'No worries.'" He extended his hand, and Will shook it. "Just give me a call when yer on yer way home, if it pleases ye to do so. This may be a story I'll want to hear."

Alistair opened his car door, jumped in, and, without another word, sped back toward Dublin. Will shook his head. "What the hell?" he whispered.

. . .

"AND HERE'S YER ROOM, DEARIE," SAID THE MATRONLY proprietress of the Drumkeeran Bed and Breakfast. She opened the door to reveal a simple yet nice room with a desk, queen-sized bed, and a couple paintings featuring the Irish countryside. Will thought that, without the window to the Irish afternoon and a rectangular door, he might well be in a hobbit hole in the midst of a Tolkien novel.

"Dinner's at six, straight on the clock up and down, so's everyone remembers. We have some singin' in the main room most nights, though yer certainly welcome to walk down the road to the Forde Ian and grab a pint there. Won't find a stranger in the bunch, I suppose. Do yeh have any questions, luff?"

Will set his bags beside the bed. "No, Ma'am," he said.

The owner laughed. "I'll not be called 'ma'am' until me ma's six feet underground. I'm Meg, tá?"

"Okay. Thanks, Meg. I'm fine right now."

"All right, then. I'll leave yeh to be unpackin' and what not. Feel free to come down and chat us all up at any time."

"Right."

"You here fer work or holiday?"

Third time's a charm, Will thought, and said, "Holiday."

"Have yeh been here before? To Ireland? Drumkeeran?"

The questions were machine gun fast—almost too fast to answer. "Ummm, no. And...no."

"We're a bit off the beaten path. How'd yeh find us, if yeh don't mind me askin'?"

Will scratched the back of his neck. "My father recommended it. He has a cousin over here."

Meg tapped her head. "That's a smart da yeh've got there. Better keep up with him."

"I'm trying." Will fought back a yawn.

"Well, I can tell yer a little outa sorts from yer trip, so's I'll letcha be. Like I said, yeh need anything, just yell fer Meg. Or Hamish, me bye. His father passed on not two year ago, so it's just us and the cottage and the field mice now. We'll see yeh at dinner." She started out.

"Oh," Will blurted. "Ummm...."

"Yes?"

"My father, he made the reservation, but...did he put down a credit card or anything?"

"No, lad."

"Ah. Well." He fumbled for his wallet, but Meg put her hand on his arm.

"We...what was yer name again?"

"Will."

"Will, we don't ask fer payment up front. Just pay after breakfast in the morning, or yeh can wait until yeh check out to go home, if yeh'd like."

Will's brow furrowed. "You don't want a deposit or anything?"

Meg shook her head. "I know it's strange to some, but we figure, yeh came all these thousands a' miles to visit us, as if we're relatives or friends. Askin' fer rent up front would be rude. Afternoon." She sauntered back into the hallway.

"Afternoon," said Will. He pushed the door closed behind her. No deposit? This was, indeed, a trip to another time. He lifted his rolling suitcase gently onto the bed and retrieved the locked vase. It was intact, and the case looked as if no one had touched it. Maybe Aidan had been right. Will placed the vase on the desk and, as an afterthought, lay plastic flowers around it.

He sat on the bed and stared at the makeshift shrine. So many things to ponder. So many things to do, and none of them easy. To tell the truth, he hadn't touched a gun since he was a kid, when he'd gone dove hunting with his dad. Finding one in a foreign country? That would probably be even more difficult. But how else would he do it?

He stared at the vase. His plan seemed sound. He would scatter Cara's and Sam's ashes, then he would follow them into oblivion. He and his family would be together again, unless God was so unkind as to send him to hell. But wasn't he there already? Hadn't he lived there for the last eight months? So, yes. He'd find a gun. Somehow.

~

"Stop!" Will commands, and the actors freeze, almost fearfully. Will pops out of his seat and strides up the four steps to the small, proscenium-style stage. He stares at them, hands on hips, then motions with both hands, palms down, for them to sit. He joins them. "What's the problem?"

"What do you mean, Professor?" asks Tracy, a cute, extremely tall sophomore in the college theatre program. She and the rest of her cast are working on *Children of a Lesser God*, Mark Medoff's award-winning play and Oscar-nominated movie. Much of it is in sign language, and Will has brought in an ASL interpreter to help them with the text, but....

"There's no link between the sign language and the emotion," Will says. "It's like you're doing two different plays up here."

"We barely have the sign language down," says Andrew, the lead. "We just need more time."

"That would be great, Andrew," Will replies, "if we didn't open in two weeks." He pauses, sorting through random theatre exercises and games. "Okay," he decides. He holds his hands out and together, palms up. "I have a gift for all of you."

"I like gifts," says Amber, batting her eyes. She's sitting directly across the circle, so none of the other actors see. Will does. He knows she has a crush on him, or whatever they call it in college. He also knows that she keeps wanting to come to his office after hours for tutoring, but that's never gonna happen. Not that she isn't gorgeous, but he has Cara. Why would he want anyone else?

"Take it, then," he says, holding his palms out to each of them in the group. One after the other, they pantomime taking something, until the last person in the circle holds an invisible object. "Tracy, you're first."

Across from him, Amber immediately pouts.

"What did I give you?"

Tracy opens her hands and watches an imaginary something fly away. "A beautiful, pink butterfly," she says, still watching it.

"Okay," says Will. "Jenny?"

"A good grade," says a petite senior with nice dimples, and everyone laughs, including Will.

"Fine. Amber?"

Amber bites her upper lip. "It's a gold heart on a necklace."

"Not on a professor's salary," Will says, and they all laugh again, except for Amber. He continues around the circle, having given one girl a puppy, another guy a Texas Rangers cap, and then a final student, Caleb, a Matchbox car.

"Why the car?" he asks.

Caleb smiles and shrugs. "I liked Matchbox cars when I was a kid."

"You're close there," Will says, smiling. "Very close."

"What did you mean to give us, Professor?" asks Tracy.

"Let me tell you a story first. So, I don't know who my real dad is. My mom never told me, except to say that he was kind of a shady character who disappeared after she got pregnant. So, she raised me on her own until she met my dad."

"Your adopted dad," said Caleb.

"He never adopted me," Will replied. "Didn't need to. He loved me more than a name could ever mean. He was a truck driver and crass and would throw a hammer every once in a while when he was pissed off, but he was my dad. He loved me and my mom something fierce. Well, when I was thirteen, he got prostate cancer."

He looks around at his students, his actors. Most of them glance back with pity. Nicole, a sweet young woman with a lot of baggage, looks away.

"Nicole?"

She looks back. "Yes?"

"It's in your family, isn't it?"

She nods. "My uncle."

"Right. Hang in there." She tries to smile and fails, but after three years in his classes, he's seen her strength.

She'll be okay.

"So, they do the radiation, and the chemo, and his hair falls out, and he gets the sores in his throat that hurt so badly he can't eat. He drops weight like a"—a somewhat bitter laugh escapes Will—"like a cancer patient. But he makes it through, and we think everything's fine. For five years."

No one speaks.

"It's ironic, really," says Will. "They said if we reached the five-year mark, we should be fine. Well, that turned out to be bullshit. It was five years and two months when they said the cancer had metastasized to his lungs, and that he would need more chemo. But he'd been through that already, and he wasn't doing it again. He was sixty-five, and he made peace with his disease."

Will pauses and swallows, finds his throat dry. "Makenna, can you bring me my water, please?"

His stage manager grabs his bottle of Dasani and brings it to the stage.

"Thanks."

"No problem," she says. She wanders over to the edge of the stage and continues working on her notes.

"So, that's only part of the story. The other part is about my dad's ring."

One of his actors begins to nod off.

"Not boring you, am I, Mitch?"

"No, no," says Mitch. "Sorry, dude. Up all night doin' freakin' biology homework, and then I worked all afternoon."

"Sounds like you need a break."

"Hey, I'm a senior. It's gotta get easier after college, right?"

Will laughs. "As soon as you win the lottery...or an Oscar."

The students laugh.

"Okay, so my dad had this ring. It was one of the first things he and my mom bought together. It had an irradiated diamond on top—yellow. I don't think they do that anymore. Anyway, it had four diamonds around it and, his favorite part and mine, two horseshoes on the sides filled with little diamonds. My dad loved the old cowboys. John Wayne, Clint Eastwood. The badasses. So, the ring meant a lot to him.

Well, I grew up teasing him about it. I would say, 'I can't wait to get that ring someday,' and he'd say, 'You're never getting this ring.' I'd say, 'You're gonna die someday,' and he'd say, 'I'm gonna be buried in this ring.' I'd follow that with, 'I'll dig you up and rip it off your dead hand,' and so on.

"It was our thing. A litany, if you will, part of our religion and our relationship." He stuck his hands in his pockets. "One day, after we'd found out about the metastasized cancer, I came home. It was near my birthday, and there was a wrapped gift on the kitchen bar. My mom and dad were sipping coffee, almost like they were waiting on me.

"'Got sumpin' for you,' my dad said.

"I said it was too early for my birthday.

'Go ahead and open it,' he said."

Tracy starts to tear up, and a couple of the other students do, as well. Amber looks away.

"I opened it, and of course, it's the ring. The irradiated diamond and the four diamonds and the horseshoes, and all of a sudden, I don't want it, at all. I shove it back so hard that I feel the bottom of the box give way a little.

"'I don't want this,' I say. I push the box back across the bar, controlling an urge to throw it at the wall.

"My dad grabs my hand and he says, 'It's always been yours. I just wanna see ya wear it before I go.' I can barely even see, because my eyes are windshields in the midst of a blowing rainstorm, and the wipers just...they don't work."

Will opens the Dasani and takes a sip, then recaps it.

"I put on the ring, which they'd had sized for me, and I threw myself into my dad's arms. This truck driver, who never hugged anyone except my mom, pulled me in and held me like a drowning man would hold a life preserver. 'I love ya, Son. And I'm damned proud a' who you are.'"

By now, several students are out and out weeping, and Makenna, unasked, pushes a box of tissues into the midst of the group.

Will grabs a tissue himself. "Every gift has to have that much meaning. It doesn't have to be sad, but it can't just be a butterfly, or a baseball hat, no matter how much we like butterflies and baseball. It has to connect to us in a visceral way. It has to stir something in our guts. That's why we can't wait on these movements to mean something, because hearing-impaired people can't wait. Every sign means something for them instantaneously, and they should to us, too. Let's take ten."

The group breaks up, heading off to bathrooms or outside to smoke. Amber slowly approaches, eyes full of tears, and gives Will a huge hug, pushing her ample chest into his.

Damn this girl.

Aloud he says, "You too, Amber. Get away from the room for a minute and come back fresh."

She looks up at him, and for once, there's nothing in her eyes but innocent empathy.

He smiles. "And thanks for the hug." She releases him and saunters to the door. Will looks over at Makenna, who just stares back.

"That didn't get to you at all, did it?" he asks.

"Stage manager rule number one: never cry in front of the actors," she says.

Will laughs.

"But it was nice," she finishes. "My dad's my hero, too." She closes her book and heads for the door, leaving Will alone with his stage. What he hasn't told them is that his mom died two months after his dad in a car crash. She'd left a note for him, though no one knew it except Will. He'd hidden it deep inside a memory box he kept with yearbooks and medals and other little mementos of a life lived.

"My dearest boy," it read. "I just want you to know how much I love you, and how proud your dad and I are of you. You're so much more than a truck driver and an English teacher could've ever hoped to raise, so much smarter. You're really important to me, but...every day without Jim is like a dagger in my heart. I don't know how much longer I can stand it. If something happens to me, just know that there wasn't anything you could've done. It's just that, sometimes, two people aren't meant to be without each other, even when it means moving heaven and Earth to make it happen."

She'd put that letter in her safety deposit box. Will found it as he'd sorted through her things after the funeral. He remembers it, now that he has someone in his life who means the world to him. Finally, he understands exactly what his mom meant.

WILL SAT DOWN TO DINNER IN THE LARGE COMMON ROOM with about twelve other guests. Irish, Scottish, and British accents provided an almost musical underscore to the meal. He sat away from everyone else, near the fireplace, and tried to enjoy a bowl of Irish stew. Thick chunks of mutton, cabbage, and various other vegetables steamed in the thick gravy, with a large slice of soda bread on the side to mop up the juice. It was okay, he guessed, although the seasonings weren't familiar to his palate. Will didn't care much about food anymore. It was just something to keep him alive, which was almost a moot point now, as well.

"'Lo, Dearie," said a voice. He glanced up to a very heavy-set woman, probably in her sixties, who held a plate of half-finished pie. A dab of whipped cream dotted the corner of her mouth like a white beauty mark.

"Hi," said Will. His smile felt more like a line than an arc.

"And what would yer name be?" she asked.

"Will," he replied.

"Top a' the evenin' to yeh, Will! I'm Emma Barry."

"Good to meet you."

"Yeh're from America, right?"

"Yes."

"Yeh've come a long way to be sitting by yourself. Would yeh like to join me and me husband Robert at our table?"

She gestured toward the tables, where a gaunt-looking man smiled and waved.

Will raised his hand in response, then cocked his head toward the woman again. "I'm pretty tired from my trip. I don't think I'd be very good company."

"Oh, come now. Yeh don't have ta talk around me, dear. I can talk fer the both of us. Fer the three of us, including Robert. I just don't like seein' such a nice-looking young man alone." She reached down and grabbed Will's arm.

Given no choice, he grabbed his food and followed her to the table where her husband sat.

"Robert, this is Will."

Robert stood and shook Will's hand. "Pleasure, Will," the man said, his voice quiet and quick.

"He's not much of a talker, me husband," said Emma, "but he's got a good heart. We've been together thirty-six years, and I don't think I've heard him say over a dozen words." She laughed and sat.

Will followed suit.

"So, what is it you do back in America, in...what state?" she asked.

"I'm a college teacher," Will replied. "Texas."

"Oh, and ain't that interestin', Robert?"

"Tá, it is," replied Robert. He stuffed a large spoonful of stew into his mouth.

"What is it you teach?" asked Emma.

"Drama. Theatre."

"Oh, that's wonderful," she said, clapping her hands together once. "We have a lovely little playhouse where we're from near Belfast. They perform in Gaelic. We don't understand it all, but it's lovely to hear. And they dance. Oh, the dancin' is simply perfect. Surely, yeh've heard of the *Lord of the Dance?*"

"I have." Will dipped his bread into the gravy and took tiny bites.

"Well, they're all lords of the dance there, and it's just a little place. No fancy lights or sound. A fiddle and concertina and drums, but the dancing is just...ah." Her sentence trailed off into a sigh.

"So, why are you two here?" asked Will. "In Drumkeeran, I mean."

"Oh, it's our anniversary, isn't it, Robert?" She turned again to her husband, and the affection in her gaze hurt Will's heart.

"Tá, it is," said Robert.

"We can't afford ta travel off the island, but every year, we try ta go someplace different. We've been ta castles and villages all over, really, and fishin' in the ocean and some of the loughs. Robert's been a fisherman fer forty-five years, and he says fishin' is nothin' like a holiday, so we try stay inland. Are yeh plannin' on doin' any fishin', Will? Lough Allen has a goodly amount of brown trout in it."

Will shook his head. "I'm not really a fisherman. I've done a little hunting though. Deer and dove and quail." Will paused for a drink of tea, then continued the lie, "Is it hunting season here?"

"Thinkin' about bringing some rabbit home fer the stew, are yeh?" Emma laughed.

"Something like that."

"Well, I tell ya this, Will. Out here in the Irish country, everybody's happy to help. Yeh go down the street ta the pub and buy a couple pints, and I bet yeh can find an old gaffer who'll take yeh on a hunt. Prob'ly a couple more who'll offer just ta keep the Guinness pouring. Ain't that right, Robert?"

"Tá, it is," he said, scraping the last of the stew from the bottom of his bowl.

"Would yeh like a bit more, dear?" she asked, and he nodded. Emma grabbed his bowl and started toward the kitchen.

When she was eight or ten steps away, Robert turned to Will with a conspiratorial smile. "That's my lass," he whispered, giving Will a bit of a shock.

"You talk," he said, and Robert nodded.

"I used ta toss me share a' blarney about, but Emma? She could talk a post into a panic, so I just keep me thoughts ta meself unless I'm around the lads. I love her, though. I do. And she's right, ya know. Ain't no strangers out here in the country. Folks in Dublin or Belfast, they're a little different. City drives 'em crazy. But out here where the sun glows gold over the green fields? They're a kind folk. A queer folk a'times, but kind just the same. Yeh make yer way to the pub an' yeh'll see." He glanced over at Emma, chatting at the door to the kitchen. "An' I tell yeh, if yeh wanna be doin' that tonight, yeh'd better leave before Emma gets back with me stew. She'll not let yeh go until her throat's sore, and that'll be judgment day." He patted Will on the shoulder. "Go ahead, lad. I'll make yer apologies."

"Thanks," said Will. He glanced over to see that Emma's back was still turned.

"We'll talk again sometime, mebbe." The old man smiled. "Have a pint fer me."

"I will."

Will shot out the door and upstairs to his room. He grabbed his jacket and plunged back downstairs and into the Drumkeeran evening. The street was well-lit, though the night air was a little cold. Will was glad he'd grabbed his jacket. He glanced left and right, wishing he'd asked directions to the pub. What was its name? Forde Ian?

Down the street to his right, a couple men ploughed out of a building, arms around each other and singing. That was as good a place to start as any. He pushed his hands into his coat pockets and started walking. A light drizzle began to fall. The smell of rain mingled with the scent of burning peat, and the combination made Will feel like he'd left his century. This could easily be the early twentieth century, or the nineteenth. This village probably wasn't that different back then, except for the streetlights and electricity and the cars.

Will strode closer to the two men. They weaved across the sidewalk, laughing and singing in a foreign language.

Gaelic?

The men passed him, and one tipped his hat. Will nodded.

He strode past a small, lamp-lit shop with the name "Clarke" painted on the window. Will could see a glass counter with several beef and chicken cuts laid out, along with various other meats. He slowed but didn't stop. He remembered a time when there were a couple old butcher shops still around the small Texas town where he'd grown up, but they'd eventually failed against the Walmarts and Krogers and Targets.

After the butcher, there was a small shop named "Kenny's Grocers." It seemed almost smaller than a 7-11. Will stopped for a moment to peer inside, but there was no inside light, and the streetlight cast scant beams on the aisles near the window.

Will continued down the street. The music grew louder the closer he got to what he hoped was the pub. He stopped in front of a door with a hanging wooden sign on the building's eave that read "Forde Ian." Muted laughter and music pounded against the door, as if wanting to be let out into the night.

Will reached for the door handle, then put his hands back in his pockets. Was he sure this is what he wanted? Go in, buy some drinks, find someone who'd take him out hunting, or maybe just borrow a gun. That'd be easier. Then wander into the hills and—

The music stopped on the other side of the door, and a sharp Irish voice, a woman's voice, yelled, "Yeh'll be gettin' the hell outa here right now! Talkin' like that, yeh feckin' knacker!"

Before Will could react, the wooden door slammed open, catching him hard in the face. Something went flying past him and fell onto the sidewalk. A bright pain burst across his nose and white lights flashed in front of his eyes. "Aaaow!" he howled. He fell to one knee. Red droplets splattered the sidewalk in front of him.

"Oh, Jaysus!" someone cried. An arm snaked around his shoulder and a rough cloth pressed his face. "Come in, come with me."

He pushed to his feet, eyes blurry, as the person—*woman?*—led him into the pub and through a crowd of people to the back.

"What'd yeh do, Savan," Will heard, "throw one out an' try to kill another?"

Laughter pounded around him, sending spikes shooting through his ears and into his aching head. The laughter faded as a door closed and the arm around his shoulder guided him into a chair.

"Sit," she commanded, whoever she was. *Savan?* That's what he'd heard. Maybe. "Hold this yerself. I'll get a cold cloth." Will took the rag and held it gently against his nose. He closed his eyes, fighting a sudden onslaught of nausea.

"Sam?" another voice asked, a male voice, an older voice, and Will's breath caught in his throat. *Sam?* he thought. *Sam?*

"Sammie!" the voice repeated.

"Right here, Fergus," the woman said.

"Ah. Want me ta have a look at this one?" Fergus asked.

"Please," Sam said.

A calloused but gentle hand slowly removed the rag from Will's face.

"Careful now, bye," Fergus said. "We're gonna clean this off and have a look-see."

"Fergus here's a doctor," Sam said.

"Thanks," Will replied.

"Just keep yer eyes closed fer me," said Fergus. "There's a lad."

A cold cloth glided around Will's eyes, and then across his nose. "Mmmaaa," Will moaned in pain.

Fergus said, "Almost there, bye. Hold strong fer me."

Will sighed as the cold cloth left his face.

"What's yer name, lad?"

"Will," he replied, having a little difficulty with the "ll" sound at the end of his name because of his nose.

"All right, Will. Yeh can keep yer eyes closed, but yeh need to follow my instructions. The next few minutes are gonna be very painful, but yer nose is broken, and I need to set it. Do yeh understand?"

"Yes."

"Okay. First things first. We need to get the blood outa yer nose, so I'm gonna ask yeh to blow into this towel." Will felt a towel being shoved into his hands. "It'll be better fer yeh ta hold it, since yeh can feel where it hurts the most and avoid the area. But I need a good blow ta clear the blood, so don't hold back."

Will lowered his head and used both hands to cover his nose with the towel. He blew gently, the pressure against his nose almost unbearable.

"C'mon, lad," said Fergus. "Blow like that'n we'll be here 'til mornin'."

Shit, Will thought. *This is gonna suck.* He took a big breath and blew hard, feeling a thick spray of blood and snot hit the towel. Stars popped in front of his closed eyes, and he screamed.

"There we go," said Fergus. "That was a massive blow right there." He took the towel from Will and folded it a couple times, sealing the blood and snot inside the folds. He handed it back to Will. "Hold this right up against yer nose fer a tetch, bye. Ta staunch any new flow, yeh understand.

"Now, let me tell yeh what's about ta happen," said Fergus.

Will struggled to hear him through his pounding head.

"I'm gonna pull yer nose back into line, an' it's gonna hurt like hell. Yeh might feel like passin' out, and I'd prefer it if yeh didn't. Tá?"

Will slowly nodded, wondering how a person can decide whether or not to black out. He felt Fergus's fingers against the top of his nose, barely touching the skin.

So far, so good.

The man laid his hands to rest against the sides of Will's nose, which hurt some, but Will thought he could handle it. No passing out so far.

"Here we go, lad." Fergus pushed his fingers together and began dragging them down Will's nose, sending instant, hot pain shooting into Will's skull.

A scream started in the bottom of Will's throat and, unrequested, sprang from his mouth like a thousand locusts from a field, bursting in all directions. Will pushed to his feet and stomped once, twice. His gibberish scream found words. "Aaaaaaaah son of a mother fucking oowwwwwww!" He shook his hands and then clenched them into fists. He opened his eyes to hazily see Fergus staring at him. The bald, kind-looking man was actually smiling, for godsakes!

"God damn," said Will. "Seriously?"

"I warned yeh, lad."

"Yeah, but...Jesus!"

"We're not finished yet."

Will stopped moving. "You're kiddin' me."

The man shook his head. "Sit down again, please."

"But it feels better now," said Will. "I'm sure it's fine."

"I'm a doctor, Will, and seein' as we play real sports in this country, compared to yer girly boys and all their pads, I'm kind of an expert in settin' broken noses. So, sit yer arse down and let's finish. I have a pint ta get to out there."

Will blinked a couple times, then sat.

"Thank yeh kindly. Now, we're gonna do that one more time. This time, yer gonna blow yer nose, too, ta clear out a little more a' the blood and snot. This'll straighten it up a little better. So, hold this towel under yer nose and we'll go again."

Will felt involuntary tears start in his eyes in anticipation of the pain, but he held the towel underneath his nose and said, "Ready."

The doctor put his hands on either side of Will's nose again and said, "Go."

Will took a breath and started blowing his nose as Fergus pulled his fingers down the sides of it, pulling it back into alignment. It hurt, but this time Will was expecting it. He didn't scream.

"There's a lad. Good work, good work."

"T'anks," said Will. He felt pretty good about not screaming. "Are we done?"

"Not at all. We still have to set the inside."

"Damn," said Will. "Really?"

"Really really," said the doctor, reverting for a moment into a Scottish brogue.

Will almost laughed in spite of the pain. He guessed even the Irish appreciated a good Shrek impression.

"Ah, we gotta smile out of yeh, did we? That's good anyhow. Let's keep up that positive attitude. What's gonna happen here is I'm gonna stick my fingers up yer nose and—"

"What?" said Will. "You're gonna what?"

"Yeh need to watch a few more doctor shows. It's all they have on cable."

"That and the Kardashians," said another voice.

Will had almost forgotten about the girl. *Sam*, he remembered.

"Oh, right, Sammie," the doctor replied. "All those fake celebrities yeh make over there. The young 'uns in Dublin eat that shite up. Nevertheless, I'm gonna stick my fingers up yer nose ta reform the cartilage, and when I pull my fingers out, yeh'll start blowin' again. Got it, Will?"

"Tá," Will replied. "I've got it."

The doctor laughed. "Listen to that, Sammie. We've got a feckin' Irish-American right here, as I live an' breathe."

Sam and Fergus both laughed.

"My father," said Will. "He's Irish."

"Well, yer blessed then," said Fergus. "Now hold that towel under yer nose and let's get this finished up."

Will did as he was told, and in ten minutes, his nose was reshaped and filled with cotton from the pub's first aid kit. It felt twice its normal size, but at least it was fixed.

"How're yeh feelin'?" Fergus asked.

"Better," said Will. "I guess."

"Brilliant. Well, yeh've got ta keep ice on it fer the next fifteen minutes or so. Sammie?"

The girl moved from behind Will and handed him ice wrapped in a towel. Will could see her now, a pretty girl with long, reddish-brown hair pulled into a braid. She was closer to six feet tall than five, with high cheekbones and a nose that, while not small, fit her face about as perfectly as a nose could.

"Now to the important thing," said Fergus. "I figure yeh were comin' ta the pub ta drink, that bein' the most common reason people come ta the pub. Normally, I would tell yeh ta take a couple ibuprofen or Tylenol and rest, but being a good Irish doctor, I can't recommend both drinkin' and drugs. And while I can't officially recommend whiskey as a good palliative measure fer a broken nose, it's a might tastier than an ibuprofen tablet. So, if yer stayin', yeh might get a bit a' whiskey in yeh fer the pain. If yer goin', Sam prob'ly has a couple pain relievers behind the bar she uses ta deal with the headache Conor McPherson gives her. He's the drunk arsehole she was tossin' outa here when yeh decided to visit this kind establishment."

"Either way," the girl said, "the pills or the whiskey's on the house." She turned to Fergus and added, "As well as yer tab fer helpin'."

"Yer a good lass," said Fergus. "I'll be switchin' to the good whiskey then, and another Guinness."

Sam turned back to Will. "Find yerself a table if yeh'd like to stay, and I'll bring yeh a glass, or a pint if yeh'd rather."

"Okay." Will stood.

"Yeh said yer name is Will, right?" she asked, her tone almost expectant, or...excited?

"Yes."

She smiled, a full smile that brightened her face instantly. He noticed her hazel eyes and realized that he hadn't made eye contact with anyone for a long time. "That was me da's name, and it's a good one." She held out her hand. "I'm Samthann."

"Spelled like id sounds?" Will was having trouble pronouncing words because of the cotton in his nose.

"Not at all," she laughed. "S-a-m-t-h-a-n-n, after the saint, but it's said 'Savan.' People 'round here are lazy and just call me Sam or Sammie, since it means the same. Yeh can call me whichever. But let's get back out there. Quinn'll be stealin' all me tips."

She turned Will around and lightly pushed him toward the door. "I'll let yeh open this one," she said, and laughed again.

WILL SAT IN A CORNER, THE ICE-FILLED TOWEL OVER HIS nose, feeling like an idiot. He silently corrected himself, *Eejit. Might as well think like an Irishman.*

Samthann, pronounced Savan but okay with Sam or Sammie, brought him a large Irish whiskey.

"Whud is it?" he asked.

"Oh, we like our Bushmills 'round here, but fer meself, I prefer a Jameson neat. Guess I should've asked yeh. Is it fine or wouldja like somethin' else?"

"Oh, it's fide. Thags."

"Samthann!" a voice shouted across the bar. "Give us a hand, would yeh?"

She patted Will on the shoulder. "I'll be back." She turned and yelled, "Jaysus Christ, Quinn, can't yeh handle things fer two bleedin' minutes?" She marched through the pub in mock anger, leaving Will alone with his whiskey and towel.

Will stared cross-eyed at the large, cold cloth pressed against his face.

How the hell am I supposed to drink like this?

He removed the towel and stared into the faces of two oldish men with almost identical beards, sitting across from him.

Will jumped and uttered a "Shit!"

The old men smiled, and the one on the left said, "Now that'd be 'shite' here in Ireland and more properly in County Leitrim and even more properly in Drumkeeran and most properly in the Forde Ian, and superlatively proper as to say sittin' on the bench in the southwest corner."

"Now Conor," said the other one, turning to the first and making a strange popping noise with his tongue, "the bye's already been hit in the head. Don't confuse him more with yer rattlin' off specifics."

"Ain't nothin' worth anythin' less it's right," said the first. "And bye, yeh'd better get that ice back on yer nose, or it'll be turnin' all black and blue by mornin', though it's gonna turn black and blue anyway, which is to say purple and blue. It won't really turn black. In a coupla days, it'll start yellowin' on the edge. Should be gone in a coupla weeks, unless...." He looked around the room, as if to make sure no one listened. Then he craned his head forward to whisper, "Unless yeh might be interested in somethin' that'll make that blue and purple disappear overnight, as if by magic."

"Conor," the other replied, hitting the first lightly on the shoulder with the back of his old, gnarled hand, "yeh wouldn't! That's not yers to give."

"Leave it, Seamus. It's mine fair and square, since I won it in cards from the Deamhan last Saturday night."

"No good'll come of it," replied Seamus, crossing his arms.

"Ah, yer a bleedin' culchie and yeh know it," Conor said, turning away from Seamus.

Will decided they must be brothers, or cousins. They looked far too much alike to not be related.

"I have a salve right here in me coat, and it heals a hurt overnight."

"If'n yeh believe in that sort of thing," added Seamus, "which yeh don't, so tell Conor to get sauced."

"Get sauced yerself, yeh bleedin' sack a' nothin'!"

"Guys, guys," said Will, shutting his eyes and trying to avoid another wave of nausea their back-and-forth caused. "By head feels like a pudcheeg bag. If a pudcheeg bag felt adytheeg, I guess. Dow I'b dot bakeeg ady setse, Christ."

The two old men crossed themselves.

For the first time, Will noticed just how short they were. Not midgets exactly, but short. Wizened, maybe.

"Sorry, lad," said Seamus. "Get that ice back up there."

Will started to return the ice to his face, but Conor put his hand on the towel. "Wait, lad." He dug in his pocket and pulled out a small, unmarked bottle containing a thick, white salve. He pushed it across the table to Will. "Put this around yer eyes tonight 'fore yeh go ta bed. In the morning, yer face'll be right as green."

"Right as green, tá," added Seamus. "If'n yeh believe in magic."

"Thags." Will pressed the towel back to the bridge of his nose.

"A' course," said Conor, "all I was gonna ask fer in exchange was a wee shot a' whiskey."

Will turned his head so he could see the old man, who was looking almost sad. Not sad sad. Puppy dog sad. Will pushed his large Jameson to the other side of the table. "Be by guest," he said.

Conor's eyes lit up. "Why, thankee lad. It's mighty kind a' yeh." He picked up the glass and swirled the clear brown liquid, staring at it as if it were gold. "Beautiful," he breathed almost reverentially.

Will peeked out of his other eye. Seamus seemed filled with the same strange wonder as Conor. "Id's just whiskey," Will said. "What's the big deal?"

Seamus turned a serious eye to Will. "It's not the whiskey, Will. It's the givin'."

Will closed his right eye and opened his left to see Conor staring at an empty glass, a few trails of whiskey clinging to the glass wall.

"Did you ever taste it?" asked Will, incredulous and laughing.

"Yeh arsehole!" said Seamus. "Yeh drank the whole thing an' didn't leave me a drop?"

"I couldn't help it," said Conor. "It tasted like gold would, if gold could taste."

"Well, yeh could've saved a little fer me."

"Next time."

"Very likely."

"Well, that didn't take long," said Samthann, seeming to materialize at the table.

Will pointed at Conor and Seamus. "Cad I have three bore? Two for theb add one for be."

Samthann stared at the two old men. "Two fer theb...them?" She glanced back at Will with furrowed brows. "If'n yeh say so." She retreated back into the crowd.

"She doesn't like us very well," said Seamus. "What'd she call us once, Conor?"

"A coupla knackers, weren't we?"

"Tá, that's what she said. Knackers, indeed. We've lived here a mite longer than she."

"Fer sure and certain."

Will was getting a little dizzy trying to look at one after the other around the ice towel, so he finally gave up and laid the towel on the table. He pushed it and the bottle of salve aside.

"Oh, yer gonna be a sight tomorrow, bye," said Conor. "Jus' don't forget that salve." He pointed at the bottle beside the wet towel.

"I wod't," said Will.

Samthann returned with the drinks, setting all three of them in front of Will. "Tell yer *friends* they'll be carryin' yeh home if yeh keep drinking yer whiskey like shots."

She sauntered away again, leaving Conor and Seamus scowling for about three seconds before the whiskey in front of them returned smiles to their faces.

"Give us a toast, lad," said Conor, raising his glass.

Will tried to remember something from his college days, when there were a thousand shots and a thousand toasts, but nothing was forthcoming. He shook his head.

Conor turned to his friend. "Seamus?"

Seamus raised his glass. "To Samthann, not that she deserves it. Yeh know, Will, Irish men are famous fer understanding women."

"Indeed, they are," Conor said. "In fact, there are only three kinds of women an Irishman can't figure out. Young ones, old ones..."

Seamus chimed in, and together they finished with, "and middle-aged ones!" They laughed uproariously, and Seamus slapped Conor on the back. They turned to Will, and Seamus said, "Sláinte." Conor tapped Seamus's glass with his own. "Sláinte," he said. Will said "Slaw-chuh," and the three of them upended their glasses, draining them.

"Yeh know, lad," said Conor, stacking the three glasses together, "they say there's gold hidden in the hills of Ireland, guarded by all sorts a' faerie creatures, but I tell yeh this. There's gold, all right, but it's hidden right in plain sight, in every bottle a' Jameson and Bushmill."

"True," said Seamus, "though I'm more of a Guinness man meself. Yeh ever heard about the bye who drowned at the brewery, Will?"

Will shook his head.

"T'was a sad tale indeed. Let me see if I can remember it." The old man leaned back in his seat and looked at the ceiling. He began,

"A young brewery worker named Drew

Sadly drowned in a vat filled with brew.

All the stories say he

Didn't drown too quickly

He climbed out twice ta go ta the loo!"

Conor and Seamus burst into laughter again, patting each other on the back and cackling until tears poured down their cheeks. Will smiled in spite of his dark mood. He thought that these might just be the strangest people he'd ever met.

"Aw, c'mon bye," said Conor, trying to catch his breath. "Not even a giggle? Or a chortle or chuckle? Perhaps a guffaw, or a howl or a roar or...no?"

Will attempted a small laugh. It came out more like a groan.

"How'd yeh define that one, Conor?" asked Seamus.

"A grunt, fer sure and certain. Sure and certain."

"Sorry," said Will. "I'b dot very good cupady todight."

"There's someone who could change that fer yeh," said Seamus.

"Who?"

The old man smiled. "You."

"I doad theeg so," Will said, shaking his head.

"Every face tells a story, Will," said Seamus. "Yers is full of beauty and tragedy. But the story's not finished yet. Yeh still have time fer a happy ending."

"Is everybody id this part of the world psychic?" Will asked. The whiskey burned in his chest. It was hitting him fast, for some reason, even though he'd only had one drink.

Should've eaten the pie.

"Not psychic," said Conor. "Wiser, mebbe. We've been around a wee bit longer."

At the front of the pub, a group of musicians struck up a lively tune with a concertina, violin, and a bongo-like drum. Some of the patrons clapped, and a few hopped to their feet. Arm-in-arm, they danced a kind of shuffle step. Will wondered if this was the Irish version of the Cupid Shuffle, and that made him giggle.

"See, he can laugh," Conor said to Seamus. "Yer just not very funny."

"Step off," said Seamus.

Samthann appeared at their table. "Okay, Will. How's yer nose feelin'? Those whiskeys helpin' with the pain?"

"Sure. Thag you."

"Good," she said. Her full, pink lips pulled into a smile. "Then come dance with me." She grabbed his hand and pulled Will to his feet.

"Whud?" The air left his lungs, and his stomach turned.

"Dance," she repeated. "Yeh know, when two people hold hands and throw each other around to music? I love this song, and I certainly don't want to dance with this lot."

"I...cad't," Will said.

"Oh, don't worry about the steps. I can show yeh."

"Doh, I just..." Bile rose in his throat, and the whiskey heated his cheeks. But it wasn't just the whiskey. He saw the living room windows explode and fire burst out into the night. Cara's and Sam's sleeping forms burning inside their blankets like wood.

"I'b sorry," Will blurted.

He rushed across the room and out the door, trying to get to fresh air before the tears started. When he hit the street, he ran as if pursued, ran toward nothing and away from everything. He passed streetlights and houses and then veered onto an old, dirt road. The cold air bit into his lungs, and his tears felt like icicles. He saw a fence ahead and tried to leap it, tripped, and fell, jarring his nose, the pain muted by the memory of his dead family.

Will rolled onto his back and stared at the stars. A stitch throbbed in his side from the exertion of running. The night was dark except for the stars, which were brighter than he could ever remember them.

As a young boy, Will had talked to the stars. An only child's behavior perhaps, but eight-year-old Will had considered the constellations his friends. Especially Orion. He'd read *Bulfinch's Mythology* from cover-to-cover in the third grade, so he knew the story. The giant Orion was such a good hunter that he attracted the attention of Artemis, the goddess of the hunt. He swore that he could hunt and kill any animal on Earth. This angered Artemis's mother, Gaia, who sent a giant scorpion to kill Orion. The two battled and both were slain. Artemis asked Zeus, king of the gods, to place their bodies in the sky. There, they would chase each other through eternity.

"Hey, Oriod," said Will, staring up at the sky. "Log tibe, huh?" He closed his eyes. The soft, wet grass smelled wonderfully green. There was another scent, though. Musky and thick and—

"Baaaa," something muttered. A wet nose snuffled the side of his head. He opened his eyes and stared into the shadowy face of a curious, fluffy sheep.

Seriously?

The thing sniffed around his ear and tried to take a little nibble of Will's hair.

"This does't happid every day," he said aloud. He turned and tried to pat the sheep, but it trotted away toward the far fence. Will spotted a couple dozen more lying on the ground. Of course, if there were sheep, there would be a shepherd around somewhere, or at least a herding dog. Will decided he'd better pick himself up and get off the person's property before he got shot.

Maybe that would be easier, he thought. *A little accident.*

No. He wouldn't want that on someone else's conscience. He climbed over the fence, saw a lighted street in the distance, and headed for it.

Chapter Six

MAGIC

WILL WOKE the next day to blood on his pillowcase. "Shit," he muttered, then reached up to touch his nose. It still hurt and felt the size of a cantaloupe.

Can't wait to explain this.

He threw on some shorts and an old shirt and crossed the hall to the community bathroom, where he took a quick shower. He started to shave but figured, *Why bother?*

Gritting his teeth, he managed to get the cotton out of his nostrils without screaming. His nose was orangish-pink, with bruises across the bridge and underneath his eyes.

"Jesus," he said. He dressed and stashed his bag back in his room, then looked at his watch. Eleven o'clock. "Damn." He'd missed breakfast, and the B&B didn't serve lunch. Oh well, there were a couple diners down the street. He'd pick up a sandwich and...then what? He hadn't really planned this part of the trip. He supposed he needed to walk around—what did Aidan call them? The drumlin hills?—and see if he could find a nice spot to spread the ashes. He'd already decided that he would do it at dawn, let them go in the beauty of the morning. He needed to power up his laptop and type a note for Aidan, but he could do that later. Right now, he was hungry. Very.

He stepped downstairs and peeked into the community room. No one there, which was good and bad. Good, because he didn't have to feign interest in someone's conversation. Bad because he wanted some suggestions on where to eat. He wandered over to the check-in desk and rang the bell. Meg appeared, talking on her cell phone.

"The twenty-first. Fer how many days?" She held up a hand for Will to wait, then punched some buttons on her old desktop computer. "Okay, dearie. No, we don't need yer credit card until yeh check out. Just call us if yer plans change. Thank yeh kindly." She closed her phone and looked up from her computer. "What can I.... Oh, dear!" She stared at Will's nose. "What happened, Will? Yeh be fightin' yer first day in town?"

"Absolutely," he replied. "I had a knock-down-drag-out with a door last night at the pub."

"Ah!" she said with a smile. "Now that's an Irishman fer yeh. First night in town an' passin' out in the pub."

"Actually"—Will smiled—"a guy was getting thrown out of the pub as I was about to go in." He made his hand into a door and pantomimed it smashing into his nose. "Boom," he said. "Bad timing."

"Oh," Meg said, sounding almost disappointed. She leaned in and whispered, "When yeh tell the story next time, say it my way. More entertainin'." She stood erect again. "Now, what can I do fer yeh, love?"

"I was wondering where the best place for lunch is, and then how far the drumlin hills were. I was going to...have a picnic."

"Picnic? With who, dear?" Meg smiled. "Yeh meet someone last night? A cute lass perhaps? Tell me all about it."

"No," said Will, shaking his head emphatically. "It's just me."

"A picnic fer just you, hey? Seems a bit lonely. I could prob'ly introduce yeh to some a' the guests here." Her face brightened. "There's a little old couple from Belfast. Emma and Robert. Now, she can talk a day away like no other, but they like ta wander around the town an' look at things. A picnic would be a right fit fer them, like as not."

"I think I'd prefer to go by myself," said Will. "This time, at least," he added.

Meg sighed. "Well, if that's the case, then have a stop at the Rowan Tree Restaurant, an' they can pack yeh a lunch. An' there's a market right beside, so's yeh can pick up some beers or drinks. The hills ain't far, but if yeh don't want to walk the six or seven kilometers out there, yeh can borrow me bicycle. It's out back, behind the shed."

"Thank you," said Will. "Which way to the restaurant?"

"Just out the door and take a right. Yeh'll be there in five minutes. An' when yeh leave fer yer...picnic, then go up Main Street past Dowra Road an' take yer first left. Follow that an' yeh'll be in the hills before yeh know it."

"Great. Have a good day, Meg." Will started for the door.

"Will?"

He turned.

"Don't forget yer jacket. It'll rain today. Yeh know how I know?"

"How?"

Meg smiled. "Coz it didn't rain yesterday." She disappeared into her office.

Will picked up a steak and grilled onion on potato bread (the lady at the bar called it a "sammy") and a bag of crisps (chips). He bought a couple bottled waters and cans of Guinness at the market next door. The bike, an older model with large, curved handlebars and a banana seat, stood behind the shed as Meg had indicated. Will set off for the hills.

It was a beautiful day, with not a cloud in the sky. In spite of that, Will brought his jacket as Meg had suggested. He hadn't ridden a bike since junior high, but his feet found the pedals and he was instantly good at it again.

That's why it's called "Just like riding a bike."

The air was cool on his face, and the town, except for the exhaust from passing cars and the occasional drifting scent of a lit cigarette, smelled...what was it? He'd thought green last night, but it was different out here in the street. Old? Maybe. Not in a bad way, though. Well-seasoned, with rich flavors of farmlands and rain and stonework.

Will took a left off Main and began the journey out of town and into the country. He passed fenced farms and fields, cows and sheep, and several dogs frolicking in the sun. It reminded him a little of the hill country just north of Austin, green and peaceful.

He could imagine Samuel running through the green fields, chased by a dog, maybe an Irish Wolf Hound. Will and Cara had gone to the Irish Festival at Fair Park in Dallas several times, and one of their favorite places to stop was the Irish Wolfhound adoption center. The first time they had gone, Will had come face-to-face, almost literally, with one of the huge creatures. The thing's head was bigger than his, and when the wolfhound stood, its nose almost reached Will's chest.

"Is this a dog or a horse?" he asked one of the volunteers.

"Isn't he gorgeous?" she said.

"What's his name?"

"Tiny."

"What?" said Cara. "Tiny?"

"Well, he was the runt of the litter, so they named him Tiny. He made up for it eventually, but the name stuck."

"What's up, Tiny?" asked Cara, running her hand through the thick, tousled hair on the back of the dog's head. Tiny closed his eyes and cocked his head a little, trying to show her where to scratch.

They'd returned to the booth every year, vowing that, as soon as they had a bigger yard, they were gonna get an Irish Wolfhound. Then Samuel was born, and they'd decided to wait until he was five or six and then get him the dog for a birthday present.

Another unfulfilled wish, Will thought. *A whole lifetime of them—birthdays, Christmases, baseball games, choir and acting classes, and football and homecomings and prom and college....*

His mind tried to go on, but he focused on the road instead. He was entering an area with more trees, and the road was getting a little steeper. He pushed for more speed and less internal monologue, rushing past what looked to be alternating groves of oak and ash. A dirt road appeared up ahead as the one Will was on curved left. He decided that it might be time to get off the beaten path.

He went straight on the dirt road, and the path almost immediately got much steeper. He wasn't riding by the trees anymore, but through them. Where they blocked the sun, the air grew a little cooler. Not quite cold, but definitely crisp. The path leveled off a little, and Will raced through the trees and into the sun again. Despite the cool wind, he started to sweat. His lack of exercise the last few months definitely showed in his shortness of breath and muscle fatigue. He rode into another copse of trees. The path turned steep again, swerving first left and then right around a huge, ancient oak tree. After that, it straightened out once more.

Will was about to get off the bike and walk it for a while when he burst through the trees and found himself near the top of a small clearing. He cycled another fifty yards or so and coasted to a stop. Soft, green grass filled the clearing, with a tree near the center completing the scene. To his right, a brook gurgled down the other side of the hill, cutting its way to a bigger stream below.

The clearing was high enough that it overlooked several small hills and, in the distance, Drumkeeran. He could make out another, even larger clearing near the stream, probably a few hundred feet down the north side of the hill. The path climbed another, slightly taller hill, but Will felt that he had found what he needed. He climbed off the bike and walked around for a moment, then stretched his legs a little so he didn't get a cramp when he sat. He grabbed his lunch and found a nice spot in the center of the clearing to eat.

He took a bite of the steak sandwich. The meat was tender, and the taste rich. The steak was drowned in a thick, hearty gravy and covered in grilled onions, just a little crisp. The potato bread was cut so that one side was still attached, making a pocket to hold the filling. He opened the bag of sour cream-flavored crisps and crunched a few, staring into the distance and letting the sun warm his face.

"Yer a ways from home," said a voice.

Will gasped in surprise and sucked a small piece of potato chip into the back of his throat. He choked and started coughing.

"Good job, Seamus," said another voice. "Jes' kill the poor bye."

Will coughed again and struggled to his feet, grabbing his water bottle and managing a couple short swallows before coughing some more. The chip rocketed into his nose.

"Here, bye. Here," said the first voice, and a handkerchief was pressed into Will's hand. He looked up at the sun, felt a sneeze build in the front of his face, and covered his nose and mouth with the handkerchief before it let fly. Instantly, the pressure disappeared, and he looked in the white cloth to see not one but three small chip pieces. He looked at Conor and Seamus, leaning on walking sticks.

"Thanks," he managed, then coughed again.

"Sorry, bye," said Seamus, looking contrite. "We didn't mean to surprise yeh."

"Don't be lyin' now," growled Conor. "Yeh were over there an' said, 'We should give Will a big surprise. Let's creep up.'"

"Well, maybe I did say that, but it were all in fun. Sorry, Will."

"That's okay," said Will. "What're y'all doin' up here?"

Seamus turned to Conor with a big smile. "He said 'y'all,' Conor, just like them folks on *Dallas*." He turned back to Will. "We watch *Dallas* every time it's on cable, and now they have those new ones, too."

"Seamus does love that show," added Conor, "fer sure and certain. But ta answer yer question, our house is nearby, so this is part of our daily walk."

Seamus nodded. "At our age, you either exercise a' bit or it all goes 'round yer middle. The ale, that is."

Looking at the two men's pudgy bellies, Will believed that the ale had *already* gone 'round their middles.

"So, yer havin' a day out by yerself, are yeh?" asked Conor.

"Yeah. Grabbed a sandwich—a sammy—at the Rowan Tree, and a couple Guinness at the market. What?"

Conor and Seamus were no longer just looking at him anymore. They were staring at him now, eyebrows raised.

"Didja...say Guinness?" asked Seamus.

"'Cause Guinness makes other things, yeh know," added Conor. "Chocolate and stews and rugby shirts. But yeh say yeh brought Guinness, an' yeh were talkin' about yer sammy, so it'd be common sense ta think yeh were talkin' about somethin' ta drink."

"Yer smarter than yeh look, Conor," said Seamus, and then to Will, "So it's ale then, is it?"

Will nodded and laughed a little. He reached into the bag sitting beside his sammy and grabbed the two cans of beer. He held them out to the old men.

"Fer us?" said Conor, blinking at the cans as if he were staring at the sun.

"For you," said Will.

"We couldn't take both of 'em," said Seamus, "unless yeh have more fer yerself."

"I have water," said Will. "That's prob'ly better for me anyway, after that uphill ride."

"So, we're really helping yeh out," said Conor, "drinkin' these fer yeh."

Will smiled. "Yes. You're absolutely helping me out."

Conor slapped Seamus on the arm. "Well let's help the poor bye out, then!"

"All right," said Seamus. They grabbed the beers and opened them, downing the thick brown liquid as if it were water.

How the hell do they drink so fast?

Whiskey was one thing. At least, its consistency approached that of water. Guinness, on the other hand, was a thick brew with a lot of foam. Will belched suddenly, tasting the steak and onions and bread mixing with...something. Probably a spice in the sauce, or maybe they used Guinness. Aidan did that for his stews, or he used to when he cooked.

"Excuse me," he said.

"Not at all!" said Conor. "Thank yeh kindly fer the beer!"

"Indeed!" said Seamus. "Glad yeh decided to interrupt our walk with yer lunch."

"Ummm, speaking of walks," Will said, "I was wondering what the hunting laws are around here. I saw a lot of game when I was coming up through the hills."

That was a lie; Will had barely seen anything except the road on his way up here, and maybe some songbirds. Still, it was an acceptable lie, at least to him. A harmless one perhaps, to everyone but himself.

"A hunter, eh?" said Conor. "A fisherman, too? We've got some nice brown trout over in Lough—"

"Allen," said Will, interrupting. "Meg at the bed and breakfast told me."

"She's right. Nothin' like a little trout fishin' fer a calm afternoon."

"I'm not much of a fisherman. Not too much of a hunter, either, but I know my way around a gun." That much *was* true. Will had gone dove hunting at the opening of the season every year when he was young. It had scared him initially, especially the first time he'd shot a dove and hadn't quite killed it. His father had popped the bird's head off with his thumbs. Yech. He'd gotten used to it after a while, though, and they'd always eaten the doves they'd shot.

"Okay, then," said Seamus. "Yeh follow that road on up about another half a mile, an' there's pheasant and pigeons, maybe even a deer or two. Not that yeh'd want to shoot one a' them by yerself. Are yeh bringin' someone with yeh?"

"I wasn't planning on it."

"Have yeh got yer license?" asked Conor.

"License?"

"Yeh need a license to hunt, or else it's illegal."

Will's head began to swim a little in the sun. He hoped the sandwich he'd eaten wasn't bad. "I don't have a license. I was...I was hoping just to borrow a gun and...you know."

Seamus and Conor glanced at each other, then back at Will.

"Yeh know," said Conor, quite serious, "a lad could get into a bit a' trouble fer loaning out a gun, especially if somethin' bad happened. Like an accident." He paused, then laughed and slapped Will on the back. "But seein' as yer our new friend and a trustworthy soul, if'n I can read a heart like any good Irishman, I'll lend yeh me shotgun. A box a' shells, too."

Will began to breathe a little harder, and his stomach turned. Was this really happening? "Thank you," he said. "I'll be careful."

"Whaddyeh think, Seamus? Can we trust the bye?"

"I think we can, Conor. Indeed, I do."

"Meet us at the pub tonight then, Will," said Conor. "This might, uh...cost yeh another shot a' whiskey."

Will tried to laugh, but the sound was fake and deep and more of a bark. The brothers didn't seem to notice. "It'd be my pleasure," he said.

"Well then, we'll let yeh finish yer meal in peace." Conor looked around. "This place is my favorite part of our walk. Yeh see that patch down there, near the stream?" He pointed at the clearing Will had noticed earlier.

"Uh huh."

"Yeh'll prob'ly think I'm daft—"

"Yeh are daft," said Seamus.

"Shut it, yeh old bag a' wind. Anyway, when I were a lad, I was doin' a little huntin' of me own in these hills, fer a lass named Moth. Well, that were her nickname, a' course. She was a tiny, pale, snip of a thing, an' she might have left an article or two a' clothin' to help me find her. So, I was full on runnin' through that field, an' all of a sudden, there were a man with a full red beard and a green suit jus' sittin' on a rock a-starin' at me."

Will's eyes squinted in disbelief. "You saw a leprechaun?"

"I never said it was a leprechaun."

"Daft," Seamus repeated.

"Never said it weren't, either. But he was a full foot shorter than me, and I'd say I'm the shortest in Drumkeeran, on a bet."

"Shorter than me," said Seamus.

"We're the same size, yeh eejit." Conor turned back to Will. "So, I stopped, like I was restin', an' I said, 'Pardon me, sir, but have yeh seen a lass run by?' The little fellah reached down and pulled a handful a' clover out a' the ground, threw it in the air, and caught just one, just one little clover between his thumb and forefinger. He put it in me hand. 'Go back to town and put this on her windowsill, and she'll come to yeh. Or yeh can keep chasin' her past those trees and up the hill.' The lad pointed up towards the largest hill, and I got to thinkin', 'Conor, me bye, would yeh rather be chasin' this lass to kingdom come or conjure her to yer own front door?' Then I turned to ask the little guy what he'd do, but—and I swear on the names of all the saints this is true—he'd disappeared."

"Seriously?" asked Will.

"Swear on me dear mam's memory, Will!"

Seamus laughed, and Conor kicked him in the shin.

"Aw, shite!" screamed the old man. "Why'd yeh have ta go and do that?"

"'Cause yer bein' a right gimp!" said Conor.

"So, what'd you do?" asked Will. "Did you follow her or take the clover to her house?"

"Well," smiled Conor, "I was about to turn around and head back to town, and then I saw it, in all its glory, hanging from a tree at the bottom of the next hill."

"What?"

Conor continued to smile.

"What was hanging?" Will asked again.

Conor laughed. "Why, it was her bra, bye! A beautiful thing, too, wavin' in the breeze like a ship's flag. So no, I didn't make it back to town 'til later, and by then I had grass stains all over me clothes. C'mon, Seamus!" Conor turned and clapped his brother on the back.

"I should just stay up here with Will," said Seamus. "It'd be safer."

"Aw, let's go find some lunch of our own, why don't we?" He waved. "See yeh later, Will. At the pub. After dinner."

"'G'bye, guys."

"Oh," said Conor, "I almost forgot." He reached into his pocket and brought out the bottle of white salve from the night before. "Yeh left so quickly last night that yeh forgot this." He tossed it to Will, who caught it. "Under yer eyes and across yer nose tonight, can yeh remember?"

"Sure," Will replied.

"Have a good day," said Conor, and Seamus added, "Tonight, then." He limped behind his brother until he finally got his feet back under him, and they entered the trees.

Will sighed, then sat back down to the rest of his sammy. Maybe it was the sun and the food, but he was sleepy all of a sudden. He reached up and felt his nose. "Ouch."

He thought about applying the salve. He knew it wasn't magic, but home remedies sometimes worked just as well as over-the-counter medicines. Conor had said to do it right before bed. Of course, Will didn't think he'd be going to bed tonight. Or ever again, for that matter. He decided that he didn't want to finish his sandwich, after all. He lay back in the clover and looked up at the sky just in time to see clouds cover the sun. One drop, then two. The rain came. Will slipped his jacket over his shirt.

I'll be damned, he thought. *Meg was right.*

CARA MOANS AND SQUEEZES WILL'S HAND HARD, LIKE A lemon she's trying to drain for a batch of guacamole.

"Hang in there, honey," he says, wincing.

Cara's hair entwines her face in sweaty strands. She's been in labor since Tuesday night, and now it's Thursday morning. Will thinks he's been awake for…for….

Eight thousand hours. Shit, I'm too tired to do the math.

"Will, we're at ten centimeters," says Dr. Callahan. Will had thought it funny at first, the doctor's name, because Callahan's was also the name of a big plant nursery in Texas. A doctor named Callahan who delivered children to nurseries was almost too apropos.

"Is that good?" asks Will, and then realizes it's a stupid question. Of course, that is good. That means—

"The baby's crowning. Everything's very normal right now. All I need Cara to do is push."

The nurse, a pudgy, sweet woman named Elan, moves to the head of the bed and begins talking softly, "Okay, Cara. We're gonna wait until the next contraction hits, and then I'm gonna ask you to push, okay? We've talked about this already, right?"

Cara nods, her face filled with tears. She looks over at Will. "I'm supposed to cuss you out now, right?"

He smiles. "Whatever you need."

She releases his hand and gently caresses his face. "You know I'd never do that," she says.

"I know."

"I love you so much."

"You're my world."

"I'd better be. Forever."

"Forever and ever."

Her face begins to contort. "Oh. Oh no!"

The nurse squeezes Cara's other hand. "Okay, honey. Here we go."

Cara looks at the nurse, shakes her head. "No. No. Let's wait."

"Now's the time, baby," says Will.

"No no no no no no," Cara moans. "I'm not ready."

Will turns to the doctor. "Can we wait a little longer?"

"No," says Callahan. "The baby's coming. We've just gotta help him along."

Will pulls Cara's hand to his chest. "It's time, sweetheart."

"Okay," she groans, her body tensing. "Tell me you love me."

"I love you."

"Tell me again, Will."

"I love—"

"Ohhhh, god fucking damnit, sonuvabitch!" She clenches Will's hand and pulls him to her with almost inhuman strength. They're face to face now, tears pouring from her eyes. "Hurts. God. Will." She starts crying for real, tears pouring down her cheeks.

"Push, Cara," says the nurse, and she pats Will on the shoulder.

He looks up. "Help her." He looks back at his wife—her stringy hair and red, puffy eyes. He's never seen anyone so ragged and beautiful in his life. "We're gonna push now, honey, and we're gonna meet our baby."

She shakes her head. "I can't I can't I can't."

Will puts his free hand on her forehead, wipes away the hair and sweat, and says, "We'll do it together. Now push, you gorgeous, strong...bitch."

Cara's eyes grow wide, and Will smiles. "Fuck you," she breathes. The contraction hits. "Ohhhh, shit!"

"Take a breath," says Will, and she inhales. "Now push, baby! Push it out!"

She pushes and screams and crushes his hand with her grip.

"He's coming," says the doctor. "One more contraction and he'll be out."

"You hear that?" says Will, near tears with relief. "He's almost here."

"He needs to...fucking...hurry up," grunts Cara. "Oh, shit!"

"Big breaths," says Will. "Just like in class."

Cara breaths with him.

"Here we go," says the nurse.

"Okay," adds the doctor. "Let's bring this baby home!"

Will stares at the doctor.

What is this, the Stanley Freaking Cup?"

"Ohhhh!" moans Cara, gripping Will's hand again.

"This is it, sweetheart," Will says.

"If it's not," says Cara, "I might rip your...ahhhh, shit!"

The doctor and nurse both yell, "Push!"

Cara screams and pushes.

"Focus on me, Cara!" Will says. He stares into her eyes and tells her over and over how much he loves her. The room dissolves like a watercolor painting in the rain. The whole thing is just a huge blur, the entire world out of focus. Then....

A shrill little voice, a baby's voice, slices through the confusion. Will jerks his head from Cara to the foot of the bed. This thing...this little, red and purple, slime-covered thing with dark hair plastered against its head, screams with all its might.

"Samuel?" he whispers. He glances back at Cara, but her eyes are closed. Her chest heaves with the exertion of forty-four hours of labor—yeah, that's it, forty-four hours. The math was there the whole time.

"We're going to clean him up here on your wife," says Nurse Elan. "The doctor likes to leave the baby attached to the mother for about ten minutes so he can absorb her body warmth and get extra blood from the placenta. That helps prevent anemia. He went over that with you, right?"

Will nods. To be honest, he doesn't remember much of anything the doctor went over in the months that led up to the last forty-four hours of brainwashing labor. Cara's hand rests in his, limp. Her eyelids flutter a little, then stop. She's asleep. Will's legs are so exhausted that he wants to sit down in the chair that's two feet away, but he can't make it there. Not because it's too far away, but because it's too far away from *her*. He looks down at Samuel, his weird, tiny, alien child. The nurse slowly cleans him, and he cries a little. She puts a little blue cap on his head, propagating a gender stereotype. If Cara weren't asleep, she'd probably be pissed. Will's vision doubles, then quadruples, and....

Someone taps him on the shoulder. "Mr. McConnelly?" Will's eyes blink open and closed, open and closed, and open and....

"Will?"

He jerks awake and realizes that he's kneeling beside the hospital bed, his hand still holding Cara's. A huge drool stream courses down the side of his face. Will stands and tries to get his bearings. He faintly remembers that he's in a hospital, and that he has a baby. He gawks at Cara like an idiot, unable to shake the fog from his brain. He hears someone crying in the background. *Samuel.* Will wipes the drool from his cheek with a sleeve.

"Mr. McConnelly?"

He finally homes in on the nurse. "Yes," he says. "Hey."

She smiles, her eyes warm with understanding. Maybe she's not as inexperienced as he'd thought. "Would you like to meet your son?"

"He...." Will begins. "Where?" Monosyllabic conversation appears to be the order of the day. The nurse puts her hand on his shoulder and leads him to a small, squarish pen.

Incubator, idiot.

A tiny boy lies there, crying his eyes out. Will knows it's a boy because of the knobby little penis between his legs. Otherwise, he's just this beautiful little lizardy thing...

You'd better never tell Cara you thought that.

...whose eyes are closed. His tiny arms beat the air as he proclaims his existence to the world. Will remembers a song he had sung to Cara's belly a hundred times when she was pregnant. He begins to sing, "Why are there so many Songs about rainbows...?"

Will knows that his son can't really see him. He and Cara have spent a lot of time researching birth over the last few months. Samuel, like all newborns, sees in black-and-white and focuses at about eight inches away. Still, the little guy *seems* to look up at Will, and his crying stops.

The banjo continues to play in Will's head as he sings to his beautiful son.

The Muppets had been something Will and his father had shared. When he wanted to sing to Cara's belly as her pregnancy progressed, Kermit the Frog seemed a natural choice. Now, he reaches down and touches Samuel's tiny hand, so small that it can't even wrap around Will's little finger. It seems like a beautiful light shines from behind his baby boy. Even if the light is a figment of Will's exhausted imagination, the image is something he will never forget, the corona that gilds his new baby in his temporary home.

"Will?" he hears. He turns to see Cara stirring from sleep.

"Hey," he says. He steps away from Samuel, the Muppet movie fading from his ears like a radio volume being turned down.

Cara looks up at him, totally spent.

Will takes her hand.

"Where's our baby?" she croaks, her voice as tired as her body.

As if on cue, Elan appears on the other side of the bed, Samuel wrapped in a blanket, like a burrito. She loosens the blanket so that Samuel can lay skin-on-skin and sets him gently in Cara's arms.

"He has your nose," Cara says.

Will doesn't see it, but he smiles anyway. "He definitely has your eyes."

"We're a family now, aren't we?"

"We've always been a family." A little laugh plays through his words like a song. "We're just a bigger one now." He kisses her forehead, then leans way over and kisses Samuel's forehead.

"Does he need anything?" Cara asks.

"Just the same thing you do," says the nurse. "Sleep. Here we go." The nurse gently takes the baby from Cara's arms and returns him to the incubator.

"Mr. McConnelly?" the nurse says. "Can I see you for a moment?"

Will follows her into the next room.

"Okay, Will. This next part is kind of hard. There was just a little bit of internal bleeding, and—"

"What?" Will says, her words squeezing the exhaustion from his body like a sponge and resoaking it with fear. "Is she okay?"

"It's nothing," says the nurse, smiling. "Totally natural, especially with a first birth. There was just a little tearing on the inside of her vaginal wall."

"Shit!" says Will, panicking. "I need to get back in there."

"Wait!" says the nurse, her voice and face suddenly sharp.

Will stops.

"Just let me finish, okay? Now, take a deep breath and say these words: I'm listening."

Will feels a little like a child, but he takes a deep breath, exhales, takes another, and says, "I'm listening."

"Good," says the nurse, relaxing a bit. "The doctor has already stitched your wife up, and it was only a couple stitches. That's nothing, trust me. I've had worse playing softball."

Will wonders if a person could get vaginal tearing playing softball.

That's prob'ly not what she means.

"The thing is," the nurse continues, "she has a few little blood clots inside of her, and they need to come out. So, I have to palpitate her stomach once, maybe twice, to expel them."

"What does that mean?"

"That means I have to shove on her stomach pretty hard. It won't really hurt unless she tightens up, and she won't if she doesn't know what's coming. So, I need you to distract her while I do it. Then we'll lay the baby back with her so he can feed. Do you understand?"

"You want me to distract my wife. So you can shove blood clots out of her vagina."

"Yes."

Will sighs. "She's gonna be pissed."

Nurse Elan smiles. "It's the best thing for her right now. You can do the best thing, right? Even if she gets a little mad?"

Will realizes that he's never lied to Cara, except when it was a surprise like a Valentine's Day gift.

"Come on, Will. It'll be over in two minutes."

"Okay." Will nods.

"Good. Let's go."

He follows the nurse back into the birthing room, where Cara is once again sleeping.

"Never mind," says the nurse. "Just be ready to grab her hand." Nurse Elan pulls the sheet down, revealing Cara's naked body and slightly spread legs. "We just have to wait for her to exhale."

Will looks at Cara's chest as she breathes in, and then exhales. Like a piston, the nurse's hands shoot down into Cara's stomach. Cara screams and bolts upright just as Will sees two large bubble-like clots, like giant alien marbles, shoot from her vagina. He faints.

WILL ATE DINNER IN HIS ROOM, DETERMINED TO AVOID THE community room and the inquisitiveness of the bed and breakfasters. The beef pie tonight was better than any meat pie he'd ever had. On the other hand, he'd only eaten about five in his life.

As he ate, he powered on his laptop. He'd made sure that he had all the cords and transformers plugged in correctly. He'd heard horror stories of people traveling overseas and blowing up their electronics because they weren't prepared. The computer booted up fine, or as fine as Microsoft Windows 10 ever did. He missed Vista, or to be more honest, he missed his MacBook, but he used his Dell computer more than anything else because he was comfortable with its size, especially the keyboard. Sometimes, he felt that his largish hands didn't really fit on the Mac keyboard, and he felt silly buying an auxiliary keyboard for a laptop that already had one.

He double-clicked Microsoft Word and took a couple more bites of pie while it loaded. "Jesus," he breathed. He stared at an image of the *Midsummer Night's Dream* program he'd been working on the day of the fire. Had he really not opened this laptop for nine months? He read through the names of actors and their characters. Puck...DEVON WORSHAM, Oberon...MICHAEL WESLAKE, Titania...SARA STILES,

Hermia...ELIZABETH MCCALLA, etcetera, down the page. Students he hadn't seen in months. They'd sent all sorts of e-mails for a while and then, receiving nothing back, had finally stopped. He saved and closed, then opened a blank document. He typed, "Dear Meg. This is the number for my father-in-law, Aidan Brady. You probably already have it since he made the reservation, but...please call him immediately and have someone read him the letter that continues on the next page. I have enough money lying here beside the computer for the call, my room for the last three days, and a generous tip for having to deal with all of this. Thanks for your kindness and the beauty of your home. This was an amazing place to be for me to—"

Will needed to finish the sentence. It was incredibly easy to think *"end my life,"* and nearly impossible to type. Yet, he managed it, changing the word "life" for "pain." He hit Ctrl+enter, making a hard return to a blank page.

"Dear Aidan," he began. His fingers lingered over the keys, impotent. How could he do this to Aidan, the last person in the world he wanted to hurt? The only person he could still hurt.

Will removed his hands from the keys, lifted the plate of pie, and swallowed a couple bites, barely chewing. He grabbed a bottle of water and took a drink.

He set the pie and bottle down on the desk and stared at the computer screen. He could scatter the ashes and head back to America. Try a fresh start.

"No," Will breathed. He shook his head at the thought and saw a reflection of himself in the computer screen. The reflection was shaking its head, too.

How could he live with the nothing that was his life? Wake up every day for nothing. Get another job to make money for nothing. Eat dinner and drink and exercise, all for nothing. Will stared into the abyss of his thoughts, and unlike Nietzsche, found that nothing stared back at him. Or was that Nietzsche's point after all? His hands, unbidden, returned to the keyboard. He typed, "I know this is hard for you. I can only say that I am so so sorry I am doing this, and even as I'm typing, I still can't believe I will go through with it. But maybe I will, and I don't want to take a chance of not getting to say goodbye to you. You have been an amazing father to Cara and me, and a wonderful grandfather. I wish there were a better word than amazing. I love you, Aidan. I wish that were enough for me to stay here in this world, to comfort you and have you comfort me, but it's not. Every day, I wake up in heartache that Cara and Samuel are gone. It's not like I just miss them. It's more physical than that. It's like a stabbing pain in my chest every single day. Nothing tastes right, and the wind is too harsh and the sun is too hot, even in winter. The world is askew because of all the pain, and I can't handle it anymore."

Will pulled his hands away, then said, "Don't reread. Finish it." He closed his eyes and continued typing. "So please forgive me, and know that I love you as much as I loved my own father. If there is any justice in the universe, I'll be in Cara's and Samuel's arms by morning. If not, then God will have to deal with the shame of keeping us apart. Much Love, Will."

He clicked the "save as" button, typed in the file name, "Final Letter to Aidan," and hit save again. Then, as an afterthought, he added, "I am leaving the vase here for you. If possible, can you cremate me as well and spread us together? I know that's not a fair request, but it's my last wish. You're my beneficiary on my life insurance, and on the savings account at Regions Bank. That should cover all your expenses and leave you with a little bit at the end. My will is in a safe deposit box at Regions. The key is in the kitchen drawer with the plastic utensils. Everything I have left in this world is yours. It's not much. It's not enough."

Will hit save again and moved back to the first page of the document. He went into the menu, removed the screen saver, power saver, and password protection options. Now the computer would stay booted up until someone physically shut it down.

He looked at the time. Ten o'clock. Time to head to the pub.

This time, Will opened the pub door immediately. Several of the customers saw him and elbowed each other, nodding to him as he headed toward the back of the bar. A couple of them pointed at their noses and laughed, and Will put on a fake, good-natured smile and tipped an imaginary hat in their direction. No one was seated at his table yet, but he figured Conor and Seamus wouldn't be far behind. He sat.

"So there yeh are," said a very disapproving voice.

Will turned to see Samthann staring down at him, hands on her hips.

"Hi," he said.

"Yeh run outa here last night like a ghost at dawn an' then meander back in without a word? Not even payin' yer tab last night?"

Will blinked, confused. "You said you would get my tab."

"And why would I do that?"

"Because you broke my nose."

Samthann bent down and inspected Will's face, her breath a nice mixture of something sweet and alcoholic, like an Irish cream. "Yer a sight, that's fer sure, and I was buying yer drinks. But yeh didn't need to run off."

"You were...you were dragging me to the dance floor, and I didn't want to go."

"That's not my fault!" she said, standing upright.

Will laughed, incredulous. "How is that not your fault?"

"Because I'm a pretty girl and I'm askin' yeh ta dance an' if yer fool enough not ta, then that's yer own fault. Now whaddya be drinkin' tonight, and no more free drinks unless I break yer nose again, which I've half a mind ta do right now."

"Three Jamesons, just like last night."

"Oh, are yer"—she made air quotes—"'friends' joinin' yeh?"

"Yes, they are."

"Well, good. I hope yeh all have a merry time."

"I'm sure we will."

"Good!" She marched from Will's table like a soldier.

"What a shrew," Will whispered before he saw customers near the bar staring in his direction.

I wonder if there's another pub around here.

Samthann returned with the drinks and slammed them on the table. "There's yer drinks," she said. "That'll be fifteen."

Will handed her a hundred pound note. "Keep thirty for yourself, and let me know when the other…fifty-five's gone."

"Yeh drinkin' that much, are yeh?" Samthann asked, and then she snorted. "I'll put the doctor on alert."

At least she's smiling this time, Will thought, and when she walked away, it wasn't with a march but a saunter. A very hip-swaying saunter.

"Amazing, idn't it?" said Conor over Will's shoulder. He and Seamus moved from behind the table and slid in across from Will.

"Don't seem natural," said Seamus, taking off a gray golfer's cap and tossing it on the table. "Do they learn that in secondary?"

"Ah, it's natural, fer sure and certain. Swingin' back and forth like a clock? It's a gift ta all mankind, I say. So, how're yeh feelin', Will?"

"Pretty good, Conor. How are y'all?"

"Good, good, and gettin' better. Jus' waitin' fer the storm."

"Storm?"

"There's one comin'. It'll be a coupla days, but then yeh won't see yer hands in fronta yer face."

Will turned to Seamus. "Is he right?"

"Conor ain't right about much, lad," Seamus said, "but the weather? He ain't never wrong."

"When is it coming?" Will asked Conor.

"Like I said, a coupla days. Now uh, not to get off subject, but these wonderful cups a' gold right here, they wouldn't happen ta be fer us, would they?"

Will smiled. "They are, indeed." He picked up his glass.

"Well then, here's ta yer, what? Yer huntin' expedition tomorrow?"

Will set down his glass, his smile gone. He nodded. "Here's to the hunting."

The three clinked glasses and drained them without a breath.

"Amazin'," said Conor.

Will felt the familiar burn in his throat and chest, and the abyss in his head closed just a little. Not much, but for some reason, the combination of the whiskey and the two old men comforted him a little.

And why not be comforted a little on my last night on Earth?

Aloud he said, "To-morrow, and to-morrow, and to-morrow, creeps in this petty pace from day to day to the last syllable of recorded time, and all our yesterdays have lighted fools the way to dusty death. Out, out, brief candle! Life's but a walking shadow, a poor player that struts and frets his hour upon the stage and then is heard no more. It is a tale told by an idiot, full of sound and fury signifying nothing."

Will looked across at the two old men, who were sitting there, staring at him.

"*Macbeth*," he said. "Act five, scene five."

The old men burst out laughing, and Conor came out of his chair and clapped Will on the back. "Yer a dramatic after all, Will, fer sure and certain. Good work, bye!"

That got Will to laughing, too. They were all laughing until Conor stopped suddenly and backed away from the table. Samthann approached them, three more drinks in her hands.

"Findin' a bit a' merriment, are we?" she asked, staring down at the three empty glasses.

Will was breathing heavily. "Aye, we are. At the expense of the Scottish play." He felt a little woozy.

Maybe I should've finished that pie.

"Yeh know the only thing worse than a drunk Irishman, Will?"

"No."

"A drunk Yank. And save the 'aye' fer the Scots!" She put the drinks down on the table and strode off with the empty glasses.

Will glanced across the table at Conor and Seamus, who were trying their best to look contrite. Then the three of them burst into laughter again.

Two hours later, Will, Conor, and Seamus staggered out of the pub laughing at one thing or another Conor had just said. Will had never been so drunk on three Irish whiskeys in his life, but that was okay. It was three o'clock in the morning. Dawn came at five-thirty, and he thought that would be a beautiful time to rejoin his wife.

"Oh, me bye, me bye," said Seamus, slurring his words and inverting vowel sounds so much that it came out, "my bee, my bee."

Will put his arms around their shoulders and said, "Yer a pair, yeh are," his drunk Irish accent sending the two older men into hysterics. The three collapsed against the side of the pub, well away from the door. Their laughter disappeared into chuckles and giggles and finally, silence.

"It's really quiet out here," said Will. "What happened to the band?"

"Why, they all left, they did," said Conor. "An hour ago. Didja ferget already, Will?"

"That's right. They left, and then Samthann threatened to throw us all out if we didn't finish our drinks so she could clean up."

"She did, at that," said Seamus. "That lass, she has a thing fer yeh, I can tell."

"Bullshit. She hates me."

"No, bye. She hates us. You, she likes."

"She just met me!"

"Doesn't matter, lad," said Conor, putting his hand on Will's shoulder. "Yeh like who yeh like, an' if it's after ten years, it's ten years, and if it's a minute, well...then it's a minute. She likes yeh."

Will smiled, just a brief moment of wonderment. "Conor?"

"That'd be me," Conor said, giggling a little.

"You said you were going to loan me your shotgun. Did you remember it?"

Conor glanced at Will with an expression so serious and sad and—*sober?*—that Will wondered, for just a moment, if the old man knew what he intended to do.

"Just a stitch," said Conor. He staggered over to the corner of the pub and disappeared down an alley. After a moment, he returned with a shotgun and a box of shells.

"You hid it outside?" said Will. "Isn't that kinda dangerous?"

"I hide things well, lad. So well, someone passin' by might mistake it fer an old stick."

Will and Seamus straightened from the wall. Conor passed the shotgun, stock first, to Will. The wood was smooth in Will's hand, polished and fine, and the barrel glistened in the light of the pub. He stared at the reflection of the light, and in his drunkenness, almost imagined seeing himself in the barrel. Perhaps this was fate, too, like Conor *or was it Seamus?*

said about a person liking a person. Within a minute? Was that it? Or ten years? This gun fit his hand perfectly. Felt warm and...right. Conor held out the box of shells.

"Just be careful out there, Will. Like I said, up in the hills, so pryin' ears can't hear."

"I will."

"After a night's rest, a' course," added Seamus.

"Of course," said Will. He started to say more, make some comment about "it's too late to go hunting now," or some other pretensical—*is that even a word?*—nonsense to shift attention from the fact that he was about to take his new friend's shotgun and blow his head off. It didn't matter though, did it? The gun was in his hand, and the path chosen. He threw his arms around Conor and picked up the old man.

"Will!" Conor sputtered. "Wouldja be putting me down?"

Seamus cackled until Will grabbed him, too, squeezing both of them hard.

Seamus said, "Jaysus, bye! Yer breakin' me ribs!"

Will put them down and wiped the tears from his cheeks. He hadn't realized he was crying.

"What's wrong, Will?" said Seamus, taking Will's hand, like a father might a son's.

"Nothing," said Will, pulling his hand away and staggering back a step. "Just...."

"What is it?" asked Conor.

"Thank you. Thanks for being here."

Tears started again, and Conor slapped Will hard on the shoulder, surprising him and stopping the tears. "Yeh've a mighty heart, Will. Big and mighty and colossal, like a mountain. It's a gift just as much as anything in the world. Let it beat again."

Will teetered where he stood, feeling too much. He turned and staggered up the street, back toward the B&B. He grabbed the bike from behind the shed and pedaled up Main Street, weaving across the road like a slalom skier. The shotgun lay across the curved handlebars, and the box of shells were compressed into his pocket.

Will took the left turn and struggled up into the hills. Lights were staggered here and there, but when he eventually passed the small houses, he had only starlight and a soft, crescent moon to keep him on the road. Somehow, he managed, his weak, sloshed legs pushing him up the pathway. He rode through the trees, where the overhanging branches blocked the moon and stars. He only stayed on the path by how the bike wheels felt on the dirt road versus the thicker grass. Finally, he broke through the trees and into the clearing. He braked but overcompensated, flying end-over-end into the clover.

"The gun," he muttered. There it was, a couple feet away. He stood and managed to stay upright for about five seconds before he fell again, his exhausted legs failing him. He rolled onto his back and stared at the sky. There he was, Orion, staring down at him a few million light years beyond the moon.

"'Sup," he said. The stars seesawed. Will closed his eyes to keep the spinning from going to his stomach. He was starting to feel nauseous. The world began to spin in earnest. He turned over and crawled as far as he could away from the bike and vomited into the grass, a projectile of snot and liquor and pain. He rolled onto his back, praying for the nausea to pass, but it returned with a vengeance. He reeled back onto his hands and knees and retched again.

Finally, there was nothing left. Will fell onto his back once more, away from the vomit, and wiped his mouth on his sleeve.

"Jesus," he sputtered. "Jesus."

He sat up and put his head in his hands, pushing his hair away from his face. He took a huge, malodorous breath and expelled it. Sound came with it, building from a cry into a loud, angry scream. Will fell back into the clover and the tears fell again. He felt so...messy. Like Cara's paintings, where nothing was clear, but those were beautiful. He was just splatters of paint on an empty canvas—more empty than paint. He staggered back to his feet and struggled toward the bike and the shotgun.

He stumbled to one knee and grabbed the shotgun, sprang to his feet, and rushed toward the edge of the clearing. He fell, rolled, and sat up, stood up, and found himself staring at the moon.

"Four days will quickly steep themselves in nights," Hippolyta had said. "Four nights will quickly dream away the time, and then the moon, like to a silver bow new bent in heaven, shall behold the night of our solemnities."

Will wondered if his production of *Midsummer* had gone okay. He knew they hadn't canceled the show, but it definitely had to have been a blow, your director losing his family and his mind all in the same day. He hoped it had gone well, for his students' sakes. He loved teaching....

Had loved teaching.

Yeah, that. Had loved teaching, especially at the moment when a student "got it"—understood what it meant to put on the mask of someone else, to walk in his shoes. In that moment, eyes would fill with knowledge that hadn't been there seconds before. Even one revelation was worth every minute he spent banging his head against the wall over kids who would never get it.

An image of Cara lying on the beach in Cancun swam before Will's eyes. He remembered that teaching was *almost* the best thing in the world. The actual best thing, though, Cara and Samuel, were dead and ash and sitting in a vase on his desk at the bed and breakfast. At their side, humming the soft note of a computer fan, sat his Microsoft Word suicide note. He pulled his eyes away from the moon and to the shotgun. His gaze lost focus as he mechanically flipped the latch and broke the double barrel. He pulled the box of shells from his pocket and shoved two into the empty slots, letting the rest spill onto the clover. He reset the latch.

"Two triggers, no mistakes," he said, and he turned the end of the barrel toward his neck, realizing that he really should have had longer arms to kill himself with a shotgun. He stretched and managed to get the barrel underneath his chin. His fingers barely reached the trigger guard, but they were there.

"God forgive me," Will said. He closed his eyes and pushed the trigger. A loud POP erupted in his brain, followed by a flash of bright light that pulsed through his eyelids. The gun fell away. Its stock struck the springy clover, then fell onto its side. He waited, eyes still closed, for eternity. Nothing. Just the bright light that continued to pulse through his eyelids.

Will opened his eyes to a brilliant, glowing mass of gold and silver shooting like fireworks around him.

Is this it? Am I dead?

He tore his eyes away from the light to find the gun lying in the grass.

Did it misfire? Both shells?

He blinked twice and looked again at the light. He realized the radiance lit the lower clearing on the hill, the larger one he'd seen earlier in the day.

Where Conor said he saw a leprechaun.

The light began to swirl, the gold and silver interweaving in some pattern Will couldn't identify. The beams danced, snake-like in their movements. The light spread over the field like fire, then shot into the air. It continued to weave in and out, threading the air into a huge woven ball. Colors swirled through the silver and gold, bright blues and greens and reds, like molten thread. The ball was huge now. It illuminated the entire hill, from tree line to tree line. The weaving and swirling slowed, and the colors melted back into silver and gold. The entire ball grew translucent, transparent, then disappeared altogether. Behind it—

"No effing way," he whispered.

—stood a castle, an ancient gray palace with smooth stone walls and grayish-blue roofs covering the chapel and the parapet walks. The central tower, the keep, shot up in the air seventy or eighty feet, like a stone giant guarding the rest of the structure. At the four corners stood towers linked by battlements, turrets, and, in the center, a guardhouse and a large, open bailey. A footbridge provided passage through two barbicans to a drawbridge, which spanned a moat filled with the remnant of the ball of light. Gold and silver swirled in the moat bed like molten ore.

Will's feet moved of their own volition. He staggered toward the edge of his clearing and down, down through the trees. He tried to keep the castle in sight, but that became impossible with the thick foliage.

His only choice was to hurry as fast as his tired legs would carry him and hope that the castle hadn't disappeared when he reached the lower clearing.

This is crazy, Will thought, and then, *I'm drunk and passed out and dreaming*. He didn't feel drunk anymore, as if the ball of light had sucked the alcohol out of his system. He certainly could be dreaming about not being drunk and finding a castle in the middle of the woods. That seemed much more plausible than actually being awake and finding one.

He ran into a low-hanging branch that slapped him hard across the chest. Welts rose underneath his shirt.

Do you feel pain in a dream?

Leaves crunched beneath his feet as he ran. A smell hit his nostrils, fresh yet perfumed, like a floral refrigerator. If this were a dream, it was the most vivid one he'd ever experienced.

Maybe I'm passed out face down in the clover. That was a possibility. Or...*is this heaven? Could it be?*

The trees thinned, and the walls of the castle rose up behind them. He sprinted now, pressing his unfit body through the woods like a man pursued. He broke through the tree line, thirty or forty yards from the castle. The keep's pinnacles shot up as if to pierce the pre-dawn sky. A drum sounded somewhere inside the battlements, and then—

Exhaustion and amazement toppled Will into the clover. He pushed into a sitting position, ninety-nine percent sure he'd gone mad.

"Fairies," he breathed, and laughed. *I'm out of my fucking mind.*

Thousands of the small creatures poured over the drawbridge, dove from the battlements and towers. Will couldn't see their wings, yet they flew toward the field from all directions. Each fairy glowed silver or gold and pulled wide, colored ribbons of fabric behind them. They glided past the footbridge and began weaving through and about each other, creating a giant, living loom. The woven ribbons became a rainbow-colored walkway that arched into the field angled toward Will, who crab-walked backward into the safety of the trees.

The fairies completed the walkway and flew back to the castle, landing on the walls. Will could finally see their wings, soft and opalescent, shimmering in a light that seemed to emanate from the castle itself. Someone *or something* began to beat the drum again. A company of huge, armored creatures marched from the castle and over the draw-bridge in military formation, their captain leading like a drum major. They split into two lines, tramping along the outside of the rainbow-ribboned pathway until they reached its end. The captain yelled some-thing that, in fairy language, must have meant turn and halt, for that's what the creatures did.

Will pushed himself farther into the woods, heart in his throat.

The captain raised his helmet visor, revealing deep, olive green skin and huge incisors shooting up from his jaw and over his upper lip. Red hair burst from underneath the helmet. Huge, bushy eyebrows grew above reptilian eyes. He raised a giant, spiked mace and tapped it against the vambrace protecting his forearm. Then he tilted his huge, sunken nose into the air and sniffed. He must have caught a scent on the wind because he started toward Will.

Jesus Christ, Will thought. *That thing'll murder me*, forgetting that ten minutes before, his intentions had been to murder himself. The creature had almost reached the tree line now, and Will prepared to turn and run.

Yeah, right. Like I can outrun him.

Music began.

A tiny, soft soprano lilt arose, as if the very air around them spoke. The creature cocked his head, then returned to his place at the head of the line. He strode almost gracefully now, as if in a dream.

The note grew louder, and a beautiful, powder blue light glided across the drawbridge. As the light approached the ribbons, a beautiful woman—not human, but beautiful and feminine—took form. Her hair, like that of an Andalusian's mane, as white and opalescent as fairy wings, flowed thick and smooth down her back. Her face, the color of the sky on a perfect spring day, held elongated eyes that curved diago-nally toward her temples. Tiny purple areolae, like flowers, adorned her small breasts. Will didn't look lower, suddenly embarrassed that he might see her sex. He glanced back at her face. Her nose was thin and tiny, as were her lips, although it seemed they would curve into an elon-gated heart when closed.

She sang a melody so beautiful that Will felt tears well, divined by the song. She had almost reached the end of the path now, and he could discern her eyes better—a violet that glowed with the same light as the castle.

Behind her came a myriad of creatures, things that flew and crept and walked and slithered. They all glowed with that same light—a train of servants for a queen.

Titania.

The woman knelt at the edge of the ribboned walkway and sang to the clover. The tiny leaves danced softly in time to the gentle movement of the lyrics. A yellow light blossomed before her. From that light a plant appeared, grew, and budded as she sang. The bud swelled, grew pregnant, then opened. The Fairy Queen reached into the flower and removed a body three inches long. She stopped singing and brought the little creature to her face. The world seemed to stand silent as she bent her head to the tiny thing and kissed its face. Nothing happened for a moment, then the creature stirred in her hand, stood up on tentative legs, and unfurled miniature wings. It flitted its wings like a baby bird about to leap from its nest.

The fairy folk laughed and applauded, except for the queen's guard, which stood taciturn and ready to protect her.

The little fairy took to wing and flew about its queen's head. She laughed, her voice a hundred crystal bells ringing in harmony. The tiny fairy landed on the queen's shoulder and nuzzled her cheek.

The first beam of daylight shot over the hills, and the queen's laughter disappeared. She dissolved into blue mist again, and the guards executed an about face and marched double-time over the drawbridge. The fairy folk raced for the castle walls, shooting across the footbridge and disappearing even as the castle began to shimmer and grow translucent in the light of dawn. As the last fairy darted inside its gates, the castle disappeared, leaving the ribboned walkway in the grass.

Will stepped out of the woods and knelt beside the walkway. He tried to pick up the strange fabric, but it dissolved into dew and seeped into the grass. In a few short hours, even that would evaporate in the morning sun.

"Conor and Seamus are never gonna believe this," Will said, then added, "I don't even believe this." He slogged back up the hill to the smaller clearing to retrieve the gun and bike. He paused halfway up and turned back to the clearing.

"Am I dead?" he yelled.

He waited, but if the field had an opinion on the matter, it kept its secret. "Sonuvabitch," Will muttered. "I'm outa my friggin' mind."

Chapter Seven

HOPE

WILL AWOKE WITH A START. The moon, still a thin crescent, shone through his bedroom window.

Night. How long have I been asleep?

He grabbed a towel and his toiletries bag, then quietly left his bedroom and headed down the hall to the bathroom. He'd barely touched the knob of the bathroom door when a familiar voice called, "Ah, there yeh are, Dearie!"

Will turned to see Emma Barry plowing down the hall, her husband in tow.

"Hi, Emma. Robert."

"Evenin', Will," said Robert.

"We thought yeh'd left, what with not seein' yeh the last day-and-a-half."

"Yeah. I've been kinda busy." Will shuttled his bag between hands, impatient to enter the shower.

"Busy with what, Dear?" Emma asked. Her nose wrinkled a little, and she looked down at Will's shirt. "Oh, Will. What have yeh done to yerself now?"

Will glanced down to see the remnants of last night's alcoholic debauch covering his shirt in the form of dried vomit.

"Oh, uhhh. Yeah, I really need to...excuse me."

Will turned the knob and almost leapt into the bathroom, slamming the door behind him and locking it. Outside, he heard, "Well, I.... Are yeh okay, Will?"

"I'm fine, Emma. Really. I just need a shower."

"I should say so. Well, good night then. C'mon, dear, let's to bed. We should get an early start in the mornin' if we're gettin' to the lough by eleven."

Go to bed? thought Will. *It must be later than I thought.*

He sized himself up in the mirror. Circles under his eyes enhanced the still dark bruises there and over his nose. He hadn't shaved in three days, and dried bits of vomit clung to his neck.

I look like dogshit. Then he caught a whiff of his smell. "Ugh!" He stripped and tossed his filthy clothes in the corner.

He grabbed his body wash/shampoo and jumped into the shower. The soft, hot water opened his pores, and he felt last night run off and down the drain. How'd he gotten home, anyway? He vaguely remembered running in the burgeoning light and finding the bike but not the shotgun. A gnarled walking stick lay on the ground nearby, so he'd grabbed it.

Why the hell did I do that?

He hoped that he'd returned the bike to the shed behind the B&B, because the next thing he remembered was waking up to darkness just minutes ago. The crazy thing was, he didn't feel hung over, at all. No headache or jitters, no dry throat or fatigue. Well, his muscles were tired, but he'd had more exercise riding that bike than he'd had in almost a year. Even for that, he felt pretty good. Pretty damned good.

He cut off the water and towel dried. As he stepped out of the shower, he realized that he'd brought no fresh clothes with him. He wrapped the towel around his waist and opened the bathroom door just in time to see Meg poking her head into his bedroom. She held a tray of food.

"Will?" she said. "Are yeh here, love?"

"Meg?" he said.

"Oh!" she said, jumping a little and tipping the tray. Will's hands shot out to grab it before the plate and cup of tea slid off the edge. His towel dropped. The only thing between his manhood and Meg's curious eyes was a tray of pork and cabbage.

"Uh...'lo, Will. Thought you might like some supper."

"Thanks, Meg," he said. "You got it?"

She bent forward a little, trying to surreptitiously peek over the tray. "Oh yes, yes. Of course, I do."

He released the tray, grabbed the towel, and encircled it around his waist. This time, he tucked one end into the top of the wrap. He looked back to see Meg still staring, her eyes wide.

"Oh, well then. Ummm, where can I set this fer yeh?" She headed for the desk, where Will saw his lit computer. She was almost there before he remembered what was on the screen.

"Meg!" he shouted. She started again, but this time, didn't tip the tray.

"Yeh've got ta stop givin' me the frights, Will" she said, "or yeh'll have ta eat this off the floor."

"Sorry," he said. "I just thought I'd like to...eat here." Will hopped into his bed, sitting against the headboard, and patted his lap. "Nothing like dinner in bed, right?"

Meg stared at him as if he were crazy. "Well, I suppose not, if'n yeh like that sort a' thing." She set the tray across his legs. "I've heard a' breakfast in bed, but not supper."

"Americans do it all the time." He smiled. "A custom, I guess. Netflix, chill, and eat dinner in bed."

"Really?" she said.

"Oh, yeah! It's really popular."

"Hmmm. All right, then."

"Thanks so much for bringing this to me," Will said, meaning it. "I know this isn't part of the regular service."

Meg smiled, the strangeness of "dinner in bed" apparently diminished by the compliment. "We have customs here, too," she said. "One of 'em is makin' sure everyone gets their fill. Yeh slept the entire day away."

"I did."

"Course, ya didn't come home 'til seven in the morning." Meg's eyes squinted and her eyebrows lifted, accusatory.

"I know."

"Off on a little adventure?" she asked.

She does love to gossip, doesn't she?

Will could imagine her tomorrow at breakfast. "That Yank, Will. Yeh know him?" she'd say. "Well, he was out all night, and do yeh know why?" The guests would all lean in, hanging on her every word. "Somethin' from somewhere, blah blah blah, doin' somethin' he's not s'posed to be doin', that's what." Everyone would gasp and pretend to be shocked, eating it up like pastry.

"Oh, yeh shoulda seen him before his shower," Emma would add. The breakfast crowd would turn to her. "He looked like he'd drunk half the pub and afterwards took to spreadin' it all over himself like finger paints."

Meg would steal back the conversation with, "And after the shower, he dropped his towel right in front of me and was as naked as Jaysus was before Mary swaddled him and put him in the manger."

"A little adventure," he agreed. "Nothing to talk about."

"Oh, it's aaaalways somethin' to talk about, love," she said. She stood there like a Baptist in church, staring down at him. Will picked up his fork and knife. He carved off a nice bite of roast pork.

"Mmmmm," he said, his mouth full. "This is amazing. Thanks so much for bringing it."

Meg stared a moment more, until Will took a large bite of cabbage so soft that it almost dissolved in his mouth without chewing. He swallowed and grabbed more pork.

Meg sighed. "Well, I'll leave yeh to it, then. Just bring the tray down with yeh in the morning."

"I will. Thanks."

Meg grabbed Will's doorknob and turned. "That is, if yeh get home by breakfast." She closed the door. Will heard her laughing as she wandered back down the hall.

"Oh, I had an adventure all right," Will said, jamming another bite of pork in his mouth. The seasonings were pretty good, though still a little strange. He was hungry enough to eat two or three platefuls worth.

You wouldn't believe it, Meg. I saw a giant ball of light appear in the middle of the woods, and it turned into a castle with fairies.

Meg would've had something to talk about then. The insane American. Will wondered if she would call somebody. Aidan, maybe. She had his number. Or the local doctor. Hey, maybe it'd be the same one who fixed his nose. Will touched it, gingerly. Still a little sore, but not bad for just two days.

He finished his meal, set the tray aside, and threw on his clothes. He paused at his computer and looked at the document.

Did I write this just yesterday?

He sat and read the note, his mind wandering away from his depressed, suicidal thoughts and back to the drumlin hills. His heart beat faster. Why was he so excited?

A dream? He was sure that's what it had been. He'd been staggering toward the edge of the first clearing, drunk and off-balance. He'd probably fallen down the path, grown disoriented, and passed out in the lower clearing. Everything else was a dream.

If we shadows have offended, he thought, *think of this and all is mended. That you have but slumbered here, while these visions did appear.* Puck's monologue at the end of *A Midsummer Night's Dream*. Probably the most famous words from the bard besides, "To be or not to be. That is the question." Hamlet, prince of Denmark, another suicidal person. Except, he wasn't real, or, at least, not the one in Shakespeare's play. There *had* been a prince in Denmark's history named Amleth, and some scholars believed that Shakespeare had married that story with historical facts about King James I of England to create Hamlet.

"O, that this too too solid flesh would melt," Will whispered, "thaw and resolve itself into a dew. Or that the Everlasting had not fix'd his canon 'gainst self-slaughter!"

He pushed himself up from the computer and trudged to the window. Tears again. Would they never stop? Will turned from the window and leaned back against the cool glass. He slid down to a sitting position. His mind was still in Hamlet's text, and he recalled for a moment, just how much he had enjoyed playing the role in college. The black clothes...so goth. That was after he'd met Cara, and he couldn't even think depression, much less act it. Performing the role was a fight the entire time. One day—*God, why am I remembering this now?*—the director, Professor Proctor, had kept him after rehearsal and asked him what the problem was.

"I dunno," said Will, frustrated. He knew he was letting the entire company down.

"You're not connecting with the character at all out there," said Proctor.

"I know," said Will, clenching his fists. "I'm trying. I've got all the lines, it's just...I don't know."

"Have you experienced this kind of loss?"

"That's what's pissing me off! Both my parents are dead. I miss them so much, but—" Will stopped, then laughed.

"What is it?"

"It's stupid, but I'm dating this amazing girl right now. She and I get along like.... It's hard to be sad with her in my life."

Proctor's eyes glazed over for a moment, then grew alert again. "What if *she* were gone?"

Will's eyes narrowed. "Gone?"

"What if something happened to her? Like your parents. Just gone. What if you got a call tonight from the hospital? There was a car accident and—"

"No!" said Will, instantly panicked and angry. "Don't even put that out there!"

"It's acting, Will," Proctor said, his voice soft. "You're getting in touch with that...'magical what if.' What if you never got to see her again?"

Will paused. They'd only been dating a couple of months, but those months were damn near perfect. The way Cara's hand fit in his as they walked across campus to the university kitchen. The way they didn't laugh at the exact same jokes and how that ended up being even funnier than if they had laughed. How their bodies moved together as Will put his fingers through Cara's hair and pulled her lips to his when they made love.

"Do I have to go there?" Will asked.

"You have to go somewhere," said Proctor. "You can't stay here."

The metaphor was not lost on Will, and he ended up giving one of his strongest performances. Now, the dark words he'd used alongside his "magical what if," the one that had turned out not so magical, grew on his lips like a bubble. They burst into sound.

"How weary, stale, flat and unprofitable, seem to me all the uses of this world!" he said, rising. "Fie on't! Ah fie! 'Tis an unweeded garden that grows to seed; things rank and gross in nature possess it merely. That it should come to this!" Will struck the desk hard, barely resisting the urge to slide his hands across it and send his computer crashing into the wall.

"But two months dead. Nay, not so much, not two. Nine months," Will added. "Nine." Then the Shakespeare began to blend with the McConnelly, giving life to a new play fabricated from the lives of a long dead prince of Denmark, a long dead king of England, and a practically dead drama teacher. "So excellent a wife, so wonderful a child that was, to this, Hyperion to a satyr; so loving to his mother and me that he might not beteem the winds of heaven visit her face too roughly."

Will grabbed his pillow and clenched it to his chest. "Heaven and earth! Must I remember? Why, they would hang on me as if increase of appetite had grown by what it fed on: and yet, within a year. Let me not think on't."

Will collapsed on his bed, suddenly too tired to stand. "Frailty," he said, and he clenched his eyes to dam them against the tears. "Frailty, thy name...is William." He clenched the pillow tightly to his chest as if it were Samuel and began to rock back and forth, back and forth.

I'm going crazy. No wonder I'm seeing fairies in a field.

That led to the image of the fairy queen, the beautiful, not-quite human being crouched in the grass, creating a brand-new life that fluttered around her like a bee to honey.

"Get outa there," he said, shaking his head as if to clear the memory, but the image wouldn't leave. The song she'd sung crept into his ears.

Will closed his eyes, remembering every single note as if it were happening here and now. He tried to shut out the song by thinking of every one-hit wonder, every bad jingle that had ever stuck in his head. As if in revenge, the song grew in volume. Will shoved his hands over his ears, not to keep the notes out but to keep them from spilling into the night, waking the temporary residents of the B&B.

I've got to get the hell out of here.

Will shot to his feet, and the fairy tune stopped like an unplugged radio. He waited, holding his breath. Silence.

Thank God for small favors.

Yet, the vision of the fairy queen remained. Will suddenly realized that there was no countdown timer for his suicide. Right now, though, he *needed* to find out what he'd seen. How could he join Cara and Sam with that massive question hanging over him? And if anyone would know about fairies, it'd be someone who'd once met a leprechaun. Will grabbed his coat and hit the stairs running.

Will sat at his booth, two full drinks across from him and one half-empty in front. Head in hands, he perked up every time the front door opened, but each time, it happened to not be Conor and Seamus. Not that it needed to be both of them, but after two nights, he'd begun to think of them as a pair. He closed his eyes and sighed. He wasn't tired; in fact, he hadn't felt so awake in a while.

"Where're yer friends?" said a voice, and Will jumped, his eyes popping open. Samthann had slipped in across from him, her arrival masked by the violin music across the bar.

"Uh. I dunno. Have *you* seen 'em?"

She shook her head and laughed. "I can't tell if yer pullin' me leg or not. Yer a strange one, Will McConnelly."

"I feel strange today," he admitted.

"Why?"

"It's just...a strange day." He motioned to one of the whiskeys. "Can I buy you a drink?"

Samthann picked up one of the glasses and sipped.

"You like whiskey?"

"Like any decent Irish girl, though we'll dip into the beer, as well. We leave the fruity drinks to yeh Americans."

Will smiled a little. The only thing Cara would ever drink in college was a Midori sour, which, to Will, tasted like a lollipop. She got into wine eventually, thank God. Those fruity drinks gave her the worst hangovers in the history of their history.

"A smile," said Samthann. "That's original."

"What?" asked Will.

"Yeh've come in the last coupla days lookin' like yeh'd lost yer best friend."

Will looked at the liquid gold in his glass. "I guess that's a fair statement."

He watched as her hand slipped over his, and he caught his breath. The touch was almost electric. He fought to not jerk his hand away as though she were a live wire.

"Would yeh talk about it then?" she asked, her voice soft.

He looked into her hazel eyes, beautiful and concerned. Real concern. He slowly pulled his hand back to his glass and sipped.

"I can't right now," he said.

"Good!" said Samthann, slapping her hand on the table and smiling.

Will jumped again.

"Then we can discuss it tomorrow when I show yeh 'round the village."

"What?"

"Have yeh got another date lined up?"

"Uh, date? Nuh, no. Not at all. But—"

"No buts. I'll be pickin' ya up at the B&B at noon. Don't make me get mean." She upended her glass and downed the rest of her drink, leaned over to kiss him on the cheek, and ran off toward the bar.

"What the hell?" asked Will. He noticed that half the patrons were staring at him, grinning. He swallowed the rest of his drink, slid twenty-five pounds underneath the empty glass, and grabbed the still full whiskey across from him. He stopped on his way to the door and set the drink down in front of an old, semi-toothless man in a newsboy cap. "Enjoy."

"Go raibh maith agat," the old man said.

Will stopped, having no clue how to respond, and said, "Bless you." He pushed his way through the front door and into the chilly, Irish night. As he took a left back toward the B&B, he mentally began a list of excuses as to why he couldn't meet up with Samthann the next day. He was so lost in this imaginary list that he almost bowled over Conor and Seamus.

"Jaysus, bye!" exclaimed Seamus. "Are yeh tryin' to kill us or just give us a nose like yers?"

"Sorry, sorry," said Will. "I didn't know.... Where were you guys? I've been waiting all night."

"Oh, we've been all over town," said Conor, "listening to stories about you!"

"Me?"

"Indeed. Why, when we got up fer our early morning walk today—"

"We walk twice a day," said Seamus. "Once at sunup and once around noon."

"Keeps the blood runnin'," added Conor, "but as I was sayin', we came across my shotgun, and there was hide nor hair a' yeh anywhere."

"What time was that?" asked Will. He shivered.

Shouldn't have forgotten my jacket.

"Oh, yer gonna freeze, bye," said Seamus. "Let's get ya inside the Forde and have a shot a' whiskey to warm yeh up."

"Oh, ummm...I've kinda worn out my welcome in there tonight."

"Nonsense, Will. Yeh could send an Irish bartender ta the hospital one day and he'd welcome ya back the next with open arms."

"Uh, yeah. Is there any place else, though? Other than...here?"

The brothers regarded each other, their faces reflecting puzzlement.

"Well," said Conor, "there's another pub down the street, I s'pose, but it ain't like this one."

"Samthann doesn't work there," said Seamus with a wink.

Will sighed. "Let's go there then. Which way?"

Conor shook his head and pointed. "All right, Will. It's thisaway."

"Awesome."

The three set off down the hill. "So, what are people sayin' about me?" asked Will.

"Oh, it's a book, bye," said Seamus. "Heard yeh didn't come in until jus' before breakfast, fallin' up to yer room like a goat in a glass factory—"

"Didn't get up 'til after supper," said Conor. "And what I heard about yer appearance, yeh wouldn't want ta know."

Will shook his head slowly. "I was kind of a mess last night. Uh, this morning, I mean." He smiled. "And that's why I was looking for you two."

"Why?" said Conor.

"What is it, bye?" said Seamus.

Will opened his mouth, then shut it.

"Will?" said Seamus. "Yeh okay?"

"I'm fine. Well, the truth is, I don't know if I'm fine." He hurried a couple steps in front of the old men, turned, and stopped them. "The real truth is—I haven't been fine in a long time."

"Here we are, Will," said Conor, pointing over Will's shoulder. Will turned to see another wooden door, much the same as the other up the hill, with a sign over it reading, "Siog Public House."

"Okay," said Will. He pushed the door open into the pub, followed by Conor and Seamus.

"Yeh've got ta order at the bar here," said Seamus. "No beautiful bartender and waitress like the Forde Ian. This isn't even really a pub, Will. Yeh sure yeh don't want to go back up the hill ta the Forde?"

"No, let's stay here." Will looked around. The place was deserted except for a couple older women sitting across from each other knitting and gossiping. Every once in a while, they'd take a sip of whatever they were drinking, something clear. Did people drink vodka in Drumkeeran? Will thought Samthann would definitely look down on the practice.

Will ordered three Jamesons from a short, surly bartender who scowled at him from behind a reddish-white beard.

"Twen'ee pounds," the man demanded. Will tossed him twenty-five.

"Keep it," he said, and the bartender, without a word of thanks, pocketed the money and turned to watch television again. Will handed the drinks out and headed to a little table near the rear of the pub.

"That guy was rude," said Will. "I should tell the owner."

"That was the owner," said Conor.

Will snorted. "No wonder this place is empty." He sat down at the table and had the strangest feeling that something was staring at his back. He turned, but there was only more empty bar. "Man, I am freaking myself out."

"About what, bye?" said Conor. "What's happened to yeh?"

Will raised his glass. "Let's drink first."

The brothers raised their glasses. "May yeh be poor in misfortune," said Seamus, "rich in blessings, slow to make enemies, and quick to make friends. And may you know nothing but happiness from this day forward."

"Sláinte," said Conor.

"Sláinte," said Will and Seamus together. They drank. Three glasses hit the table almost simultaneously.

"Now," said Conor, wiping his mouth on his coat sleeve, "what happened to yeh last night when we left the Forde?"

Will began the tale, leaving out the part about trying to kill himself. He told them that he had decided to get an early start on the pheasants by going up the hill before dawn. He paused before he described the ball of light and the appearance of the castle, but by the time he got to the Fairy Queen singing to the clover, the words were flowing from his mouth like a river. Not until he stopped did he realize that Conor and Seamus were staring at him like he was a madman.

"Oh, Will," Conor started.

"I know, I know," said Will, interrupting. "You think I'm crazy." Will's gaze fell to his empty glass, and he wished that he had the magical ability to fill it with whiskey.

Conor said, "We don't think yer crazy, Will. On the contrary, we think—"

"We think yer blessed," said Seamus, "if I'm readin' me brother's mind right."

"You are, fer sure and certain, Seamus. Fer sure and certain."

Will didn't know if he should breathe a sigh of relief or get up and run. Conor and Seamus had to be just as crazy as he was.

"But how?" he asked. "How did I see what I saw?"

"Now that's a story that's ripe fer the tellin'," said Seamus.

Will stood. "Let me buy you another whiskey then, and let's hear it."

Conor shook his head. "Ah, no thank yeh, Will. No more fer me."

Seamus said, "Thank yeh kindly, though."

Will did a double take. "You two don't want any more whiskey? This day *is* crazy."

"This whiskey doesn't taste the same as the Forde's," said Conor. "Plus, yeh've already got a couple nights tied up in yeh. Better hear this sober."

Will inched back into his chair. He heard a sound and involuntarily glanced over at the two old women who were talking. For a moment, they didn't look old at all, but almost like children. Then he blinked and there they were, normal and talking about how loudly one's husband farted in bed.

"Okay, Seamus," said Conor. "Be this yer story er mine?"

"Yeh tell it better," said Seamus. "An' I have ta piss or I'll leave a trail like a snail when we leave." Seamus stood. "But go ahead and start. Yeh can catch me up when I'm back."

"I'm not gonna 'catch yeh up,'" said Conor. "Yeh'll have to jump in wherever I am."

"Fine, fine," said Seamus. He disappeared into the back of the pub.

"So," said Will, leaning back against the chair and crossing his arms. "What are we dealing with here?"

"Oh, *we're* not dealin' with anything, lad. That's all you. Me and Seamus are too old to go wanderin' about the countryside chasin' fairies."

"It's just an expression," said Will.

"Ah," said Conor, and laughed. "Then *we* are dealing with somethin' right special, Will." Conor glanced around suspiciously, then leaned in. "Fairies are real, bye. Real as yeh or me." Will started to interrupt, but Conor held up a hand. "If I'm gonna tell the story, I'll need yeh to listen more than talk."

Will let his hands fall into his lap. "We've gotta be crazy, Conor. You and me both. Fairies? At least I was drunk last night. If I believe anything now, well...I believe I've lost my grasp on what's real and what's not."

"Leave the doubtin' to Thomas, lad. Yeh know, people believe in prophets and gods they've never seen, jus' because a' some writin' in a book or two. If they can do that, maybe yeh can believe in what yeh saw with yer own two eyes, because I've seen it, too. An' I weren't drunk, at all. But let me tell yeh about fairies first, if'n yeh don't mind. What think yeh?"

Well...what the hell? If I'm insane, listening to another insane person won't kill me. We'll just be insane together. Or start a club. In a nice little home with padded walls.

"Will?" said Conor. "Yeh there, bye?"

Will nodded. "Yes. Go ahead."

"All right. Yeh ever hear the name J.M. Barrie?"

Will thought about it. There was something on the tip of his tongue, but it wouldn't come out. "Not sure."

"He was Scottish, but we won't fault him fer that. Not everyone can be born in Ireland. No, Barrie wrote a book called *Peter Pan*—

"That's it!" said Will. "Damn."

"Indeed. Anyway, he wrote 'When the first baby laughed fer the first time, its laugh broke into a thousand pieces, and they all went skipping about, and that was the beginning of fairies.' Nice thought, that, but not anywhere close to the truth. Fairies have been here far longer than we have.

"Will, there are hundreds of kinds of fairies, all over the world. There's alvens and banshees and bogles and brownies. Changelings and dwarves, dryads, elves, fauns, gnomes and goblins, leprechauns, and I told yeh already I met one of those, pùcas and pixies, selkies and trows, and the list goes on and on. We don't know where they came from, though some believe them to be angels, or fallen angels, or daemons. Others believe they're spirits of the trees and woods around us. A few believe they're creatures from another dimension who travel here only on a special day, or a special time, and otherwise live in a place that can't be seen or heard by humans. Where they stay is a place of eternal beauty and play, with sweet streams and evergreen fields. There ain't a morsel a' regret or sadness there, and that's what I want ta talk to yeh about."

At that moment, Seamus returned. He sat down and drummed his hands lightly on the table. "What did I miss?"

Conor stared a hole through him. "If yeh don't have the fergettin' disease, then I'm a potato farmer." He returned his gaze to Will. "When I was a bye growin' up just down the road a spell from here, there was this sad young man in the village. Everyone knew he drank too much, and one day his mam, she said, 'Nothin' more I'll have with yeh, whether yeh be sober or not. Get yeh from me place. Yer me bye no longer!' "

"Well, that killed the bye on the inside, 'cause it don't matter none how yer mam treats yeh growin' up, she'll always be yer mam until yeh pass on or the world takes it in its head to end itself. Well, this man— his name was Liam—went to an old apothecary woman who lived in the very hills you were in yesterday, Will. He asked her fer poison, 'cause he'd decided that livin' was just not his cup a' tea. But this old woman, she'd lived a long time, an' she knew stories told by her mam and her mam's mam. She saw the bye's sadness and recognized it fer despair. So, she said, 'Bye, yeh need no poison to escape the misery of this world.' She told him of the kingdom of the fairies and an old ritual to call up the Queen, so that one could ask permission fer entrance to her kingdom. Liam took her advice, bade this world a not-so-fond farewell, and disappeared into the hills."

Conor stopped and swallowed. He wiped his dry lips.

"Are you sure you don't want a drink?" asked Will, and then shuddered at the sound of his own voice. The fairy tale had drawn him in like a self-hypnosis CD.

"Not much left of the story," said Conor, "but a wee bit that happened years later, when I was in the middle a' me life, with a sick wife and no children. A' course, the whole town knew the story a' Liam Flynn, just like the whole town knows the story a' crazy Will McConnelly. No offense, Will, but we're a village a' two hunnerd an' forty-three. If people don't talk about each other, there's a wee bit a' nothin' to talk about."

"Sure," said Will. His cheeks grew hot with embarrassment.

Will became aware of a soft rumble. He looked to the window, expecting rain, but the sound was almost too close. Then he noticed Seamus's face, which was slowly inching its way toward the tabletop. The rumbling was the snores pouring out of Seamus's nose.

"Funny, ain't it?" said Conor. "He can stay awake fer two days a' hard drinkin', but put a tale in his ears and watch him shake the rafters." He grabbed a pepper shaker from the table and shook a handful of black pepper in front of Seamus's nose. On the next inhale, Seamus began to wheeze, rub his nose with his hand, and then he sneezed so hard that he blew the rest of the pepper off the table and into Will's face.

"Argh!" screamed Seamus, and "Oh, man!" yelled Will, wiping pepper from his face just before his own, "Aaaachew!" Will opened his eyes to see both of Conor's hands pressed against his nose and mouth. A moment later, Conor's loud cackles filled the resonant pub. The two older women stared at him as if he were a giant mole with hair growing out of it. Will giggled at the mental image of a giant, laughing mole, and Conor laugh harder. His face turned a bright pink, while Seamus stared at them, trying to figure out what the hell had happened.

"Ohhhh," breathed Conor. "Oh, dear." His laughter slowly tapered into a giggle, and the giggle into a wheeze. He finally collapsed against his chair, winded as if he'd run a marathon.

"What are yeh about then?" asked Seamus.

Will shook his head. "It's...you...never mind."

"Just stay the bloody hell awake fer five more minutes," said Conor, still wheezing a little, "and then we'll head to the meadow."

"The meadow?" asked Will.

"That's where we live, a little cottage in a meadow up in the hills. It was our da's, and when me wife passed, we thought to move in and spend our aging years together rather than alone. But there's still the end o' the story."

"Oh, right," said Will. "Hold on just a sec, okay?" He rose and sauntered to the bar. "Hello?" He peered behind the counter and saw nothing but a reddish-white field mouse picking at an old piece of grain on the floor. It saw Will, grasped the grain in its mouth, and scurried for a hole in the wall.

"This service really stinks," muttered Will. He returned to the table.

"What is it?" asked Seamus.

"Oh, I was getting thirsty, but the bartender's nowhere in sight."

"The Forde Ian," said Conor. "Didn't we tell yeh?"

"You did," said Will. "And you were right. Much better service, for sure and certain." Will plopped back down in his seat. "So, how about the rest of the story?"

"Like I was sayin' before the thunder started," Conor began. He winked at Will, who smiled.

"Thunder?" asked Seamus. "Bloody hell. I didn't bring me coat."

"Yeh'll survive," said Conor. "So...." His eyes narrowed in concentration. "Where was I again?"

Will said, "Everyone in town knew the story of—"

"Oh, yes yes yes. Everyone in town knew the story a' Liam Flynn an' how he disappeared. Well, one day, I was out wanderin' through the woods, feelin' the weight a' the world on me shoulders, an' I heard someone laughin' in a nearby field. I said to meself, 'Mayhap some soul might share a little happiness with me,' fer I was ridin' so low that me beard was constantly in me soup. I crept quietly in the direction of the laughter."

"Well, I come to the field, and there's this lad chasin' a spry, little fox. Not huntin' it, mind yeh. Just chasin' it. The fox weren't runnin' away neither. It were runnin' here and there, dodgin'...playin' with the bye. Smiled at him almost, as if it were all in good fun. Then the fox made fer the part of the wood where I was hidin'. The lad followed. Now, I hadn't seen Liam Flynn since I was a boy, an' when I saw him then, it was on the side of the street passed out by a rubbish bin, likely as not. This lad, though, the one chasin' the fox? It were Liam Flynn or his twin. I swear it on the sweet mother a' Jaysus.

"I was shocked, and I stepped outa the woods and said, 'Liam?' The lad looked up, startled, as did the fox, and then both of 'em cut and ran toward the opposite end of the field. I ran after 'em, yellin', 'Liam, is it yeh, bye?' The fox cut back into the woods and was lost there, but the lad?" Conor took a dramatic pause. He stared at Will.

"Go on," said Will, impatient. "What happened?

"Well, like I said, the fox cut into the woods, but the bye? He just kept on running, me right on his heels. Now, this is the daft part, so when yeh say yer crazy, Will, I understand what yeh mean. I've been there. One second, this lad is runnin' breakneck speed toward the other side of the field. I'm keepin' up though. Truth be known, I think I'm gonna catch him. Then the world shimmers a little in front of him, as if it's meltin' in the afternoon sun. I don't know if that makes any sense. Anyways, the bye runs into that shimmer and..." Conor pauses, waits for Will to crane forward until they're almost nose to nose, "he disappears."

"Bullshit!" Will laughed. He fell back into his seat.

"It's every bit as true as the day is long, Will. One second he was there, and then the shimmer. Poof. He was gone. Yeh know what I felt at that moment? 'Cause sometimes yeh can feel strange things inside yer chest, an' yeh know they're true even if they don't make sense. I knew if I'd been closer, an' if I'd been as spry a lad as once I were—well, sir, I believe that I woulda leapt through there with 'im. Where I'd be sittin' today, God knows, but it wouldn'ta been in this world."

Will shook his head. "It's impossible."

Conor smiled. "Nah. What's impossible is not believin' that *anythin'* in this world is possible. Anythin', Will. There are doors just waitin' to be opened all the time. Yeh just have to find the knob."

Will sat up straight. "This Liam Flynn, he went on some sort of quest to find the fairy kingdom?"

Conor nodded. "An' I believe he found it, an' happiness besides. There are a lotta ways out of this life, Will, some worse than others." Conor stared at Will intently.

"So, what if someone else was tired of being here, Conor?" Will asked. "Really tired and wanted to leave. How would a normal person find the fairy kingdom?" He suddenly laughed. "Jesus Christ, it's almost like I'm believing this bullshit." He dared another look at Conor. "How would someone find that place?"

Conor smiled. "Oh, there's ways. Sometimes one just stumbles upon it in the wee hours before dawn, when he's out huntin' with a borrowed shotgun that he never returns."

Will felt himself blush. "That wasn't my fault. Well, I guess it was, since I lost it, but I did try to find it and I just found the walking stick."

"That's okay, bye. I found the gun later that mornin', like I told yeh. An' yeh might hold on to that walking stick. Somethin' good to have, 'specially if yer gonna take on a quest."

"So, there is a way to find the Queen again?" Will's heart beat faster. As impossible as everything was to believe, he...he wanted to try. Needed to.

Conor nodded. "Yeh have to complete three tasks. It's a tradition fer heroes or seekers, the number three bein' magical in and of itself."

"What three tasks?"

Conor started to speak, but the pub began to rumble again. They looked over to see Seamus's face resting on the table, a thin rivulet of drool dribbling down the side of his mouth.

"We'll palaver on it tomorrow," said Conor. "I need ta get Seamus home before he brings the ceiling down. Meet us in the field at noon. The field where yeh dropped the shotgun. Bring yer walkin' stick and a lunch. Yeh never can tell what might happen." Conor rose and patted Seamus on the back.

"Huh...hmmm?" said Seamus, suddenly awake and looking lost again.

"Let's go home, lad," said Conor.

"Ah. Good idea." Seamus yawned. He stood up and almost fell over, but Conor caught him around the waist.

"C'mon, yeh right wee babby," said Conor, shaking Seamus.

"A'right, a'right," said Seamus. "I'm awake." The two started for the door, followed by Will.

"*Oh, crap,*" thought Will, and then he said, "Conor, I'm supposed to meet Samthann tomorrow at noon."

Conor turned, his eyebrows reaching for his hairline. Seamus was suddenly awake.

"Are yeh now?" said Conor. "And why would yeh be doin' that?"

"She's supposed to take me on a tour of the town?"

Both Irishmen laughed.

"A tour?" said Seamus. "Why, Will, if yeh've been down Main Street, yeh've had the tour."

"Aw, shut up, yeh ninny," said Conor. "Will, meet the lass at noon and then us at two-thirty, but no later. In the clearin', all right?"

"Sure," said Will. "Or I could just cancel with Samthann, leave her a message."

Conor's face grew dark. "I told yeh yesterday that yeh've got a big heart, Will. Don't prove me wrong."

Will nodded. "Right. That would be kind of an asshole thing to do."

"Good then. Two-thirty?"

"Two-thirty."

WILL SITS IN HIS SATURN AND STARES UP AT THE SMALL, one-bedroom apartment he and Cara share in Austin. He's angry and, at the same time, ashamed of his anger. His feet twitch, longing to climb out of the car and leap back up the stairs.

What the hell happened?

They'd been having dinner. Cara made a very good lasagna with ground turkey and wheat pasta—she was *that* person. She cared about what she put into her body and liked to recycle and wanted people to bike more and drive less.

The lasagna was delicious and the conversation lighthearted, more or less. Cara had changed her program of studies from art to nursing after her mom passed; she and Will were discussing the last few classes she would need to finish her degree. Then they moved on to the color of their living room wall. Cara had repainted before they'd moved in, and now she wanted to do it again. She was going through her "blue" period, and the paintings she wanted to hang wouldn't complement the walls.

"Are we going to have to get new furniture again?" Will asked.

Cara laughed. When they'd moved in together, one of the first things she'd insisted on was replacing Will's furniture.

"Gotta go," she'd said.

"What?"

"Your furniture, Will. It's old."

"I'm in college. I'm supposed to have old furniture."

"It doesn't go with my new walls or my paintings."

Will had surveyed the room. His furniture had been a combination of garage sales and friends who were getting rid of their stuff. It *was* old. And ugly.

"How are we gonna pay for new furniture?" he'd asked.

"Let *me* figure that out."

She was biting the side of her little finger, which, for some unknown reason, instantly turned Will on. She'd grabbed him and pulled him in for a long kiss.

"Fine," he'd said. "As long as we get to use the couch one more time." Forty minutes later, sweaty and content, they'd hauled the furniture down to the giant dumpster at the back of their building.

Will smiles at the memory, and the ire drains from him. The resulting void leaves an open seat, though, and melancholia takes anger's place. What did he do? He'd said something, and then she'd said something. Her words were a little sharp, so he'd known he'd said something wrong, but he didn't know why, and.... Why are relationships so hard sometimes? Will loves Cara more than anything in the world. Most of the time, he's walking on clouds just thinking about her. So, what happened tonight?

A light blinks in the apartment window. On, then off. Again, on and off. Then it stays off.

What's going on?

Will steps out of the car, clicks the lock button on the door arm rest, and shoves the door closed. He glances back up at the apartment. The lights don't come on again. He takes a step toward the stairs and stops. Is he giving up some sort of battle here? Should he just stay in the car and wait for her to come down? What if she doesn't?

No.

One of the best things about their relationship so far is that there is no power struggle. The two of them are in this life together, not fifty-fifty, but one hundred-one hundred. Why should he let some macho caveman bullshit inside of him dictate how he reacts to what he's sure was just a stupid misunderstanding?

Once Will comes to that decision, he races up the steps. He reaches the front door. He was wrong about the apartment being dark. This close to the window, he can see a soft yellow flicker through the curtains. He opens the door and smiles.

Cara reclines on the couch against the far wall. She's dressed in a see-through robe that she's pulled to the side, making Will wonder why she's wearing it at all. Yet, she looks perfect. Candlelight casts a soft glow across her body. He tears his eyes away from her smiling naked-ness to the wall above her. Normally, a watercolor of a little girl playing in a grassy field hangs there. Now, the painting is nowhere to be seen. Instead, rows of computer paper cover the wall, one letter painted on each like the Hollywood sign. They read, "This is stupid. Can we never do it again?"

Cara picks up a glass of wine and offers it to Will. He accepts it, sips, then sits beside her.

"I hope—" he starts, but she presses a hand to his lips.

She runs her fingers across his lips and face. She grabs the back of his head and pulls him into a deep, sensual kiss that starts with his mouth and moves across his neck to his ear. "Promise," she breathes.

He pulls away enough to make eye contact. "I promise," he whispers. "What am I promising?"

"To never fight again," she says.

Will nods.

Cara takes the wine glass from him and sets it beside hers on the small end table. She unbuttons his shirt, kissing her way down his chest as she wraps her arms around him. Then she reaches back around his neck and draws his face to hers, her lips so close that they share breath. She whispers, "Bedroom."

Will lifts her from the couch and carries her to bed. It isn't until later, as Cara rests her head against his chest, sleeping, that he realizes he's locked his keys in the damned car.

Will woke the next morning without a hangover and realized it felt pretty good. No headache. No tremors or vomit breath. Nice. After breakfast downstairs, he returned to his room and found he'd missed a call from Aidan.

"Shit." Will had called the first day, and when Aidan hadn't picked up, felt relieved that he didn't have to talk. Since then, he'd been in an alcoholic stupor most of the week. He hadn't even touched his cell phone.

He grabbed the phone and hit the message button. "Hi, Will," said Aidan. "Hope yer findin' my homeland as hospitable as I promised it'd be. There's no hurry to you comin' back. I told the manager there that you might stay a few days. I bet what you're doin' is damned difficult, so if yer not answering yer phone? Well, I figure it's coz it's hard to talk to me, as well. Just know that I'm here an' prayin' to the good Lord." There was a pause, not long or short, and then, "I love ya, Son. Take care."

The message ended, and Will sat on the bed. He replayed the last few words in his head, the catch in Aidan's voice when he said, "I love ya." What would he have done if Meg had called him yesterday morning with the news that Will's brains were sprayed over a patch of clover? He pushed the morbid thought away and focused on…. What?

Fairies?

Will laughed out loud. He couldn't even speak the word with calm, rational daylight pouring through the window. Fairies? Was he daft? And why was he even thinking in words like "daft"? He'd only been in Ireland four days.

He turned to face the wall. "O, that way madness lies;" he said. "Let me shun that." Will paused as if waiting for a response. "*King Lear*," he told the wall.

He fell back on the bed and stared at the ceiling. He wished it was night so he could talk to his old buddy Orion, but it was…. He grabbed his phone. Eleven o'clock. He still had an hour before Samthann arrived. Maybe just enough time for a nap. The heavy sausages and beans...

Pork and beans. Who ever heard of pork and beans for breakfast?

...and eggs and toast sank in his belly like an anchor.

Gravity works differently after eating, Will thought. His full belly pulled him down into the mattress. He flipped onto his left side and let the sausages and beans gently pull him all the way through the bed and into sleep.

BANG! BANG! BANG! Will woke with a start, his heart pounding against his chest as if inspired by the knocking on the door. He grabbed his phone.

12:45? Shitshitshit!

"Just a second," Will yelled. He pulled at the bottom of his shirt, trying to smooth out the wrinkles. Then he grabbed his jacket and leapt for the door. Behind it was a not-so-happy Samthann.

"Yeh still on American time, are yeh?" she asked.

"I fell asleep," Will said. "I'm really sorry."

She stared at his hair.

"Yeh look like Ronnie Wood on a bad hair day."

"What?" Will reached up and felt his hair, which was flat and plastered on one side and sticking straight up on the top. Yeah, he probably did look like the guitarist for the Rolling Stones.

"Shit. Just a second." He rushed back into his room to grab his comb and a towel.

"There's...eighteen hundred plus nine hundred...twenty-seven hundred seconds in forty-five minutes. I've given yeh plenty already."

He turned the knob on the bathroom door. It didn't move.

"Shit." He sighed.

Samthann flipped his hair around with her long, cool fingers. "Hat," she proclaimed.

"Hat?" Will asked, and then, "Oh, duh!" He returned to his room and grabbed a red Texas Rangers baseball hat from his suitcase. He pulled it onto his head. "Ready."

"Let's go, then." Samthann thrust her right hand into the crook of his left arm and pulled him toward the stairs. Her grip was awkward and pleasant at the same time. His reflexes had forgotten what it was like to have someone hold onto him.

Who could hold onto you? You've been spinning out of control for months.

They passed Meg on the way out the front door.

"Hi, Will. Got yeh a date ta the fair, do yeh?" Meg winked at Samthann.

"Fair?" he asked.

Sam didn't slow down, at all, almost as if she feared she might lose Will if she stopped. They stepped into the warm, Irish afternoon and into the midst of a crowd, at least by Drumkeeran standards. There were people everywhere up and down the block, along with street vendors and musicians.

"You didn't say you were taking me to a fair," Will said, his eyes a little wide.

"Would yeh have agreed to come out if I had?" she asked, smiling.

"I don't know. You didn't give me much of a chance to say no anyway."

"Indeed, I didn't." She laughed. "Now c'mon. I want some candy floss!" She grabbed his hand and pulled him into a run down the street. Candy floss, it turned out, was the Irish name for cotton candy, and they soon had two large paper sticks of it. Will took several, sticky bites of the pink sugar, but it soured in his stomach. Somewhere in his head, a door clicked open.

SAM—SAMUEL—SITS IN WILL'S ARMS AT THE STATE FAIR OF Texas. He feeds his cotton candy to a llama as the animal's keeper yells at him to stop. Samuel laughs and laughs. The door slams shut.

WILL TOSSED THE STICK IN THE FIRST TRASHCAN THEY passed.

"Yeh don't like it?" asked Samthann.

"I had a huge breakfast," he said.

"Hmmm. Okay."

They stopped to watch some Irish dancers tapping in time to a violin and hand drum. The girls laid a stick on the ground and danced a fast step around it. The crowd of onlookers clapped in appreciation.

The girls broke from their clogging, grabbed people from the audience, and pulled them into another dance. No tapping this time, just whirling around each other, holding hands. Maybe it was the Irish version of the Cupid Shuffle, but in a circle. A young girl, maybe ten years old or so, hopped over to Will and held out her hand.

"Go dance with the lass," said Samthann. She laughed and gave him a shove, but Will couldn't move.

"Sorry. I don't dance."

"S'okay, sir," said the little girl. She curtseyed and danced over to an older gentleman, who allowed her to pull him into the circle.

"Yeh really don't dance?" asked Samthann. "Not even slow, with someone hangin' on yer shoulder?"

Will shook his head. "No. Not at all."

"Hmmm," she said again. She stared at him through narrowed eyes.

"What?"

She shook her head slowly. "Nothin'. I just have a strange feelin' about yeh sometimes, and then yeh prove it wrong." There was a note of sadness in her voice.

Will had absolutely no idea why. "Sorry?" he said.

"Why?" she smiled. "Yer here. We've a whole afternoon to get to know each other."

Uh oh.

Will's gaze dropped to his feet.

"What?" said Samthann. "Yeh have another date lined up now?"

"Not a date. I'm supposed to meet my friends up in the hills."

Sam's eyes narrowed again, not in a puzzled way but in anger. "Yer friends again, is it?"

"Yes. I...they're helping me work on something—"

"On what? Your tale-spinnin' skills?" Her voice rose into a storm. Will felt the fairgoers begin to stare.

"Hey, I don't want to upset you—"

"Well, yer doin' a nice job a' not upsettin' me, Will. A damned fine job, indeed!" Tears filled Samthann's eyes, and her face grew beet red.

Will turned and power walked away from the crowd. He heard steps behind him, running, and then Samthann's hand snagged his elbow. She turned him around to face her. Anger and disappointment and pain covered Samthann's face like a bruise. Will didn't understand how he could possibly hurt her like this. They'd only met four days ago.

"The face is the same," she said, pushing his cheeks in with her hands. "The nose and the ears and the chin, and yer tall like him. But yer eyes, they're dull. Where's yer soul, Will? What happened ta yer soul?"

"What?" he asked.

"The light behind yer eyes, it's gone." She released him and took a step backward. "Who stole yer soul?"

What is she talking about?

"Samthann—" he began, but she pushed him.

"Don't talk with his voice." She shook her head. She stepped past him, then broke into a run, racing out of sight down the street toward the pub.

Will's mind reeled. He felt like a total ass and didn't know why. Except for being late, had he really done anything wrong? He felt eyes staring at him from all directions, then felt something tugging at his jeans. He looked down to see the little girl who'd asked him to dance.

"Mister?" she said.

"Yes?"

"Why did yeh make the pretty lady cry?"

Will shook his head and backed away.

"I du...I don't know," he stammered.

Will turned and jogged back to the B&B. He grabbed his walking stick and the bike and headed up, up into the drumlin hills.

Chapter Eight

QUEST

WILL LAY IN THE GRASS, trying to puzzle out why Samthann had gotten so upset.

"Ah, there yeh are, an' early, too!"

He sat up and watched Conor and Seamus make their ways up the hill.

"Thought we might see yeh at the fair," said Seamus. "Did yeh go?"

"I went," said Will.

"Uh oh," said Conor. "Why do I think a thing happened with a certain lovely barmaid?"

"She's a bartender," said Seamus. "It's not the 1800s anymore."

"True enough. True enough. What happened, Will?"

"I don't know," Will said, standing. He brushed a stray clover leaf off his jeans. "We were watching some girls dance, and I told her I had to leave to meet you two. She totally flipped out."

Seamus and Conor looked at each other. "She really doesn't like us," Conor said.

"Not a bit," Seamus agreed.

"I was a little late to meet up with her," said Will.

"How little?" asked Seamus.

"Forty-five minutes."

"Oh, that'd never work fer a woman," said Conor. "Now if *she's* late, be it ten minutes or an hour, well that's just what women do. 'Makin' an entrance,' they call it. But a lad being three quarters of an hour late? Why, yer lucky she didn't punch yeh!"

"An' I've seen her punch, Will," added Seamus. "She's got iron in her fist, that one. Knocked a poor bye right ta the floor."

"I'll remember that," said Will. He shook his head. "I guess she thought we were spending the whole afternoon together, but I never said that. She forced me to go with her in the first place."

"She did now," said Conor. He seemed a bit skeptical.

"At the pub last night. She said she'd pick me up and to be ready to go at noon. Then she told me not to make her mad."

"Well then," said Conor, "I guess she had it comin' to her, the poor lass." He sighed. "Still then. We've got places ta go and parlayin' ta do. Follow us, Will. Yeh can leave the bicycle here if yeh'd like. Nobody'll touch it."

"No no," said Will. "If someone steals it, Meg'll kill me. I don't need two women pissed off at me on the same day."

"Push it alongside then," said Seamus. "Let's go, Conor."

They strode toward the wood, Will awkwardly balancing the walking stick across the bicycle's handlebars. The brothers led him onto a path that was almost hidden from the field. Several bushes covered one side, where it zigged, and then several more covered its zag. From a distance, it looked like one, long patch of bushes. Brief minutes later, they arrived at another, smaller clearing at the center of which stood a modest stone house with a thatched roof.

"Watch yer head," said Connor. Will leaned the bicycle against the side of the cottage. "No one in my family's been over five foot six fer ten generations." He and Seamus ducked inside, and Will followed.

The little cottage was warm and inviting, with several ancient-looking tapestries hung on the walls and a few rugs covering the stone floor. An unlit fireplace sat near one of the other doors...a bedroom, probably. The small kitchen housed a wood-burning stove and a sink. The place stood dark and quiet, like the clearing in which it rested.

"You don't have electricity, do you?" asked Will.

Conor shook his head. "Fer sure and certain. No lines up here to spoil the beauty, and we like it that way. We can cook a meal, and there's an icebox to keep our food cold. We don't keep enough here to worry about spoilin'. That's what town is fer."

Seamus called from the other room. "Found it!"

"Good," said Conor. "Bring it on out." He gestured to a worn chair near the fireplace. "Have a seat, Will."

Will leaned down and into the chair, finding its wear to be smooth and comfortable. Conor pulled a bag from his jacket and held it out. "Seaweed? I got it at the fair."

"No thanks," said Will. "I'm not hungry."

"Hope yeh don't mind me havin' some. That's why I love a fair. The seaweed and taffy and candy floss and drinks. So much ta fill a man's belly."

"It was nice," Will agreed.

"Here we go," said Seamus, appearing from one of the other rooms.

"Ah," said Conor, setting the seaweed down on the small table beside Will's chair. "Let's have a look then, shall we?"

Seamus and Conor sat down on the thick ledge of the fireplace across from Will, and Seamus opened a leather pouch he'd brought in from the other room, revealing an old, home-bound ledger of some sort. A scent hit his nose, alongside the smell of the old leather.

What is that? he thought, and then he had it. The book smelled like autumn. Like sun-warmed fallen leaves on a forest floor. Seamus opened the book, and Will leaned in to peer at the writing, instantaneously disappointed. It wasn't in English.

"Gaelic," said Conor, looking up at Will through his bushy eyebrows. He turned to Seamus. "Will yeh?"

"Indeed," said Seamus.

"It'll be three, then," said Conor, ambling into the other room.

"Three what?" asked Will, confused.

"Three pipes," said Seamus. "That means it's gonna be a long afternoon. Nothin' gets yeh through a long story like a good pipe."

"I don't smoke," said Will. "I mean, I used to, in college. I did a lot of things before Samuel was born, but...." Will trailed off into silence.

Conor returned with three timeworn pipes and a large pouch. He sat and began filling them.

"Erinmore Balkan," he said. "The best around."

The scent of orange in the tobacco swirled into the autumn leaf smell of the book and Will closed his eyes. The combined smells were so fresh and so old at the same time, like...like a library. Time reached at him with gentle hands and pulled him back to the third grade. Rather, the summer between his second and third grade year. He'd visited the public library a lot that summer because there was a prize for the student from each grade level who read the most pages. Most of the other kids read the shortest books they could find, but Will read things like *The Lord of the Rings* trilogy and Andre Norton books. He'd won the prize, beating out Becky Norsedale, who'd read three hundred pages of Dr. Seuss. It wasn't the books that took him back, though. The librarian, a sweet, ancient lady named...*what was it?* Mrs. Garrett! That was it. She'd kept the library in wonderful repair, cleaning the piles every other month with orange oil. The citrus scent mingled with the older texts, and that fresh, rich scent was almost the same as the pipe tobacco and the old Gaelic book. Will opened his eyes, and Conor handed him a pipe. He took it gratefully, bending his nose to the bowl and inhaling.

"Yeh've got to light it first, Will," said Seamus. He held out a wooden match and a stone. "Have at it, then."

Will struck the match on the stone, and soon the room was filled with thick, aromatic smoke. Will coughed a couple times.

"We'll choke in here if you don't crack a window," he said.

"We'll not be breakin' our windows," said Seamus, "but we can open the door a bit." He did so, and Will laughed.

"What?"

"Nothing. Language barriers are funny sometimes."

"Perhaps," said Conor. "But we should be gettin' to the book. There's a grave amount a talkin' that needs ta be done before the moon."

Seamus handed the book to Conor.

"Yeh sure?" said Conor.

"Yeh've got the blarney in yeh, not me," said Seamus. "If there's tale spinnin' ta be done, it should be yeh."

"Very well, then. Yeh comfortable, Will?"

"Very."

The smoke circled Will's head in patterns that seemed to capture the light like a living thing. Or a ghost, a wraith straight out of Tolkien. He started to drift and realized that he'd nodded off.

"Better make some tea," said Conor. "Young Will's eyelids are halfway to dreamin'."

"I'm fine," said Will. "Really."

"I'll need a cup too, lad, if I'm ta be readin'. Jus' relax and Seamus'll get yeh fixed up."

"'Kay," said Will. He closed his eyes and let his head slip back against the soft curve of the old chair.

THE SWEET SMELL CURLS UP INTO WILL'S NOSE THE SECOND he walks through the door.

Orange? No, not quite.

He smiles. It's apple with cinnamon. Perfect for a stressful day, with the final matinee of *A Christmas Carol* Will has directed for a local church. Add in a quick dash to the mall for last minute gifts and a pit stop at Kroger's for the can of cranberry sauce Cara always seems to forget. Will can't complain, since he himself almost forgot their Christmas Eve tradition of apple cider and homemade gingerbread.

"Daddy, daddy!" a voice cries. Samuel toddles around the corner and stops so quickly that he almost topples over. The little boy stares at the packages and grocery bags in Will's arms. "Foh me?" he asks. His voice is like the fragile snowflakes that are melting in Will's hair. The weatherman had said a "slight chance of snow for Christmas," but when it comes to snow, Texans adopt the Missouri state motto of "Show Me" before they'll believe it. Yet here it is, Christmas Eve, and snow has started to blanket the ground in soft, gentle white.

Will holds the grocery bag out to his son. "For Mommy," he says, and Sam grabs the bag and makes a break for the kitchen.

"Mommy Mommy. Pwesent foh you."

Will laughs and quickly shoves the store-wrapped presents underneath the tree.

Will felt a warm cup being shoved into his hands. "Already?" he asked, opening his eyes to see Seamus handing a cup to Conor.

"Bye, this is our second pot," said Conor. "Yeh've been asleep fer an hour."

Will yawned and stretched his back. "Seriously? I barely closed my eyes."

"Closed yer eyes and cut some wood, fer sure," said Seamus.

Will felt a sticky sensation on the side of his face. He reached up to find a dried patch at the corner of his mouth.

"I drooled?" he asked.

"A bit," said Seamus.

"Like a horse with an apple," Conor added.

Will sat up. "Sorry, guys."

"We let yeh nap," said Conor. "But now"—he tapped the book—"it's time fer a story. I'm gonna do me best to translate the Gaelic, and if I pause, just be patient. It's not somethin' I do every day."

"Okay," said Will. "Let's go."

"The title is simple. It's called *The Hidden Kingdom*."

"Where'd you get the book?"

"Eh?" said Conor, looking up as he opened the cover.

"The book. Where did you get it?"

"Oh," said Seamus. "We've had it in the family fer generations. Our grandad passed it down to his granddad and so on."

"Your grandfather passed it down to his grandfather?" asked Will. "That doesn't make sense."

"Don't ask Seamus too many questions," said Conor. "He ain't the sharpest spade in the shed."

"What?" asked Seamus.

"What he meant to say was that it was passed down from father to son and so forth. Our great great great great a few more greats grandad —we call 'em seanathair over here, Will—heard the stories in his village and, bein' a bookbinder fer trade, printed and bound it for the book-sellers. He kept a copy, and it came down the line. Our seanathair gave it to our da, and he to us." Conor took a long pull on his pipe, blowing the smoke out in rings. "The sad thing is that we have no one to pass it on to; neither of us had children."

"I'm sorry," said Will.

"Don't be. Ours isn't the saddest lot in the world. Mebbe not even the saddest lot in this room."

Will looked away. He knew that Conor was talking about him.

"No more interrupin', now," Conor said, "or I'll have ta crown yeh with me shillelagh."

"What's a—" Will started, but Conor stopped his question with a roll of his eyes. "Sorry."

"*The Hidden Kingdom*," Conor read.

"A'times, yeh live in a village and die in that same village, yeh and yer kin, fer hundreds a' years, and nary a day see somethin' amiss. A'times one a' yer neighbors mebbe borrorin' a draught a' cow's milk and ne'er return it, but nothin' more'n that. An' it's the same with yer father an' grandfather, and again with yer son and grandson. An' yeh know there's an invisible world, fer that's where the Virgin Saint and her Son and the Father live, but yeh'll never see that kingdom. Least not 'til yer soul is weighed just and right by the Lord.

"Yet, if yer eyes are sharp, a'times yeh can peek around the edge of the world errybody else sees, blindly traipses through, and there is a hidden kingdom, sideways from the kingdom a' man. I've seen it. There's will 'o wisps that shine in the bogs and lure men to their watery graves. I've seen the fairies dance in rings upon the clovered fields, too. I had ta search fer it, fer sure and certain, fer it weren't, until that very cold, cold day, willin' ta search fer me.

"T'were winter in me seventh year, an' the frost was layin' high on the grass. Me mam was fillin' a pot with water an' tossin' in the last a' the cabbage from the fall, an' she said ta fetch her some more peat fer the fire. I ran out back behind our tiny cottage to the pile a' peat we'd cut in September. I'd just popped a coupla pieces into me bag when I heard a noise, like somethin' whisperin' through the peat. It were deep, like when thunder's startin' a storm miles away. I quietly set me bag down on the peat and crept 'round the pile like a mouse, careful a' every dry piece a' brush. I pushed me way through the bushes that bordered our field from the wood. T'were a dull mornin' with little sun, an' even that dimmed as I slid into the first dense copse of trees outside our land. The voices were stronger now, so I lowered meself even further to the ground, inching along like a serpent. It was as if St. Patty had forgot one wee snake when he laid the land free of 'em a thousand years before. I heard the cracklin' of a fire, an' the low rumble broke into two sep'rate voices.

"'Ay, Copper. Tonight's the night.'

"'Is it?' said the other. 'Fin'ly?'

"'It is. I saw him through the window today, an' he's all plump and ready to eat.'

"'Tell me, Flint. Tell me what he look like, so's I can taste him in me head. The same as he'll taste in a soup tonight when we break his bones apart and suck the sweet marrow from 'em.'

"I was close now, mayhap too close. I stopped an' pulled meself up on a tree, peeked 'round e'er so slow. There, before me eyes...." Conor stopped and laid the book in his lap.

"What's wrong?" asked Will.

"Just a small draught a' tea," replied Conor, "and a fill a' me pipe."

"Really?"

"Oh, fer sure and certain. Yeh didn't think I would read a whole book, even a tiny one like this, without a few sips a' tea, didja?"

Will realized that he was leaning forward like an attacking goose. He took a breath and settled back into his seat.

"Just seemed like a strange place to stop," he said, grabbing his teacup and taking a sip, or trying to. His cup was empty, as well.

"Here, bye," said Seamus. "I'll grab yeh another."

"Thanks," said Will, holding out the cup. The older man took it and meandered toward the kitchen.

"Another pipe, Will?" asked Conor, offering the tobacco pouch to him.

"I just need another match," he said. "The bowl's almost full."

"Here yeh go then." Conor scratched a wooden match on the side of the fireplace and handed it, lit, to Will. A few quick draws, and the smell of orange rose again, tickling his nose. A moment later, Seamus returned with the tea, and Will settled into his seat.

"Now, where was I?" asked Conor.

"And there, before my eyes," said Will.

"Really?"

"Yes."

"Yeh were payin' close attention, then. Good job, Will. Nothin' like an eye fer detail." Conor lit his pipe, took a long pull and a sip of tea, then picked up the book. "Now, then. Well, perhaps back just a bit.

"'Tell me, Flint. Tell me what he look like, so's I can taste him in me head. The same as he'll taste in a soup tonight when we break his bones apart and suck the sweet marrow from 'em.'

"I was close now, mayhap too close. I stopped an' pulled meself up on a tree, peeked 'round e'er so slow. There before me eyes were two a' the strangest, ugliest brutes to walk the earth. Their faces were brown and wrinkled, with tufts of hair sprouting out of their ears. They had so much extra skin that it hung from the sides of their faces like melted wax on a candle. Their eyes were tiny and dark, black pebbles too close together above their huge, wart-covered noses.

"They hovered o'er a small fire. One of 'em—Flint I suppose, since he spoke next—was a-stirrin' somethin' in a black pot hung over the flames on a few sticks and a chain.

"'Let me tell yeh 'bout this bye,' said Flint. 'He's a small, ripe morsel, that he is. He has thick, black hair we can use to tie the laces on our shoes when all's said an' done.'

"'I like black hair,' said Copper, poking one, long-clawed finger into his nose and pulling something purple and worm-like from within. He held it to his mouth and sucked it down. I felt me stomach turn and wanted to run, but I was frozen there. Frozen, and barely breathin'.

"'He's about this high,' said Flint, holding his hand about four feet in the air. Though the creature was no bigger than I, his arms were long, like the pictures I've seen of apes and things in the wild African jungles. 'His skin is nice and pink, like a baby pig's arse. But yeh know the best thing about him, Copper, the very best thing of all?' Flint lifted a huge ladle of some thick, reddish soup out of the pot. A large, bulbous eye bobbed up ta the center a' the liquid.

"'What's the best thing about him, Flint?'

"'The best thing, Copper,' said Flint, lowering the spoon back into the pot and slowly turnin' his face toward me, 'is that he's right there, behind that tree.'

"Copper leapt to his feet, his brown tongue darting quickly over his lips. He rushed at me, quick as a fox. My feet unfroze an' I fell backwards, then turned an' ran as fast as I could. Bushes slapped me in the face like horse whips. The thing's breath was on me neck, an' its stench smelled like rotted deer flesh clotted with maggots. I burst into the clearin' an' fell over the mound a' peat, tumblin' head over feet like a clown in a play. I thought, 'Yer dead now, lad. They'll have yeh fer sure.' I huddled up with me knees in me chest like a babby, waitin'. Loud, phlegm-clogged laughter echoed from the trees, but the creatures never appeared.

"Well, I picked meself up an' ran to the house, almost run me mam right over. Like a runaway horse, I was, and then I was in her arms an' cryin' and she was asking me what were wrong. I begged fer her ta nail me winders shut, 'cause somethin' bad was comin' fer me. After a while, with many pats and hugs and kisses, I calmed, though I still trembled inside me heart. When me da got home from town—he kept a little market there—he listened to me tale alongside his evening pipe. He ne'er smiled once.

"'Goblins,' he said, his face grim. 'I've heard of 'em, but ne'er seen one a'fore. But it were goblins yeh saw, bye.' His face relaxed a bit then. 'Yeh have nothin' to worry 'bout tonight. Goblins're all talk an' no teeth.'

"'But Da,' said I, "Copper and Flint said they was gonna eat me tonight after e'erbody were in bed.'

"Me da laughed then, a good hearty laugh. 'Bye, goblins live on fear, hot wet fear like what comes from chasin' a young bye through the forest. Those goblins? They got e'erything they wanted from yeh. Big bye like you in a pot? Not likely.' He laughed again and wandered off to bed, and me? I lay there wide awake, listenin' fer two deep voices outside me winder. I finally fell asleep, nearer to dawn than to dusk."

Will found himself at the edge of his seat once more. Conor paused to take a sip of tea. Will tried to relax back into his chair.

Goblins? Were there any of those among the creatures I saw at the castle?

Conor picked up the book again. "After that, I began to look fer the invisible kingdom, and it were like a blinder had been lifted from me eyes. O'er the years, I saw dozens a' things that'd make a wise man fall to his knees and pray fer heaven, but me? I sought 'em out as a hunter does a deer. I wanted to know more, see more. I became a fisherman and moved to the coast, but every time a day a' fishin' weren't comin', I'd find me way to the forests and bookshops, searchin' fer more and even more stories.

"Then one day, I met a little man on the side a' the road, just sittin' there as if he owned it. Short an' hairy and stout, like the trunk of a chopped down tree. He asked where I were off to, and I told him me story. He said, 'If yeh love the kingdom that much, why don'tcha ask fer admittance?'

"'Admittance?' says I.

"'Why, a' course!' he says. 'All yeh have ta do is complete three tasks, and while they're not easy, well, they're not altogether impossible.' Then he told me the three things I had ta gather ta gain an audience with the Queen of the fairies. I lay 'em down here just as he said 'em. This be the end a' this journal. I'll finish me search fer the invisible kingdom or die in the effort. Either way, these'll be the last words this world will hear from me. Blessings on yeh, whoever yeh might be."

Conor closed the book.

"That's...it?" asked Will.

"Well, there's—"

"I mean, you write a whole book about the crazy things you've seen, and then you get to the best part and just stop? I don't think your relatives were very smart, no offense. Jeez!"

Will plopped back down in the chair, barely minding the protestations of the old wooden supports that bowed under his weight. He stared at Conor for a moment, then Seamus, and back to Conor. He took a deep breath and sighed it out, then rolled his eyes at himself.

"The lad's gone barkin' mad," said Seamus.

"Totally," agreed Will, and he burst into laughter. "It's like...what did I think? A guidebook?"

An image popped into Will's head, a diagram book for a piece of IKEA furniture called "Entrance To The Kingdom Of The Fairies."

ETTKOTF? Even sounds like IKEA furniture!

Will laughed harder and let his imagination run free.

Step 1. Remove all the hardware before starting the quest. Step 2. Lay out the pieces of pressed wood marked "Shit Show."

In the midst of the laughter, his breath caught, and he was sucked into an unexpected yawn. Like that, the hysteria departed, leaving him with a few tears in the corners of his eyes and a sore stomach. He wiped his eyes. "Sorry," he said.

"What were that about?" asked Seamus.

Will shook his head. "I don't know." Another giggle bubbled up and disappeared. "I guess...I was really into the story. I almost forgot that it *was* just a story. It seemed so real." He looked back and forth between the two brothers. "I used to read all the time. In the order of things, my loves were my wife and son, being a teacher, reading.... God used to be in there somewhere, back when I believed in a benevolent Creator. That was before the fire. But reading? Cara used to say that if I was in the middle of a good book, she might as well take a cold shower, because I'd end up finishing it before I finished her." Will's cheeks heated. "That was way too personal. Sorry."

Conor smiled. "We love a good story, too, Will, fer sure and certain. What I was gonna say before yeh interrupted me, is that's not the end a' the book."

Will almost stopped breathing. "What?"

"Oh, there's stories a'plenty in the book. I skipped to the last one. It seemed the end were the place yeh needed to start. An' I was tryin' ta tell yeh, before yeh started laughin' like yeh was fluthered."

"Fluthered?" Will asked.

"Drunk," Seamus replied.

"Ahem!" said Conor. "Whoever tol' this last tale, he sets down the method fer gainin' admittance to the kingdom of the fairies, jus' like he says he was lookin' fer. It's inscribed here on the last few pages."

"You kinda buried the lead there, Conor," said Will. "You could've started out with that."

"Ah, yeh younguns," said Conor. "Always wantin' ta jump ahead. Yeh'd just skip the pipe and the tea an' be out the door if'n yeh could. Ne'er so much as a 'thank yeh kindly!'"

"Sorry," said Will, and he meant it. The old men had been nothing but kind to him. Having a pipe and cup of tea was common courtesy.

"I did enjoy the evening," he continued. "Your relatives must've had crazy lives."

"Yeh don't know the half of it, Will," said Seamus. "Some a' the stories in that book...no mythology was ever as rivetin' as the God's honest truth."

Will nodded, and the three sat there, sipping remnants of tea and smoking the last of their pipes. Finally, Conor nodded to Will.

"That's enough, bye. Yeh've been polite. Now ask."

"Thanks." Will smiled. He took a deep breath. "What are they? The things you have to do to get into the fairy kingdom."

Conor turned to Seamus. "Get us a fire then, wouldja?"

"It's time," said Seamus. "Cold's creepin' through the stones, and the sun'll be hid soon."

"I really should go," said Will. "Can't you just tell me the rest?"

Conor shook his head. "We're talkin' about things that can kill yeh with a glance or a song, Will. Yeh don't rush now, whether the sun's fillin' the sky or dozin' off, waitin' fer tomorrow."

Will sighed and bowed his head. "Sure."

"Bye?"

Will looked up, and Conor's eyes were filled with so much warmth and kindness that Will felt as if he were looking at his own father.

"There's a moment in any race," Conor began, "when the whole world is still. The crowds are silent, the runners frozen, their muscles tensed and ready to spring. It's as if God in heaven Himself is listenin' fer the crack a' the gun." The old man smiled. "That's where we are now. Slow down and get ready. Once the gun sounds, the race is on, and there'll be no respite 'til the finish line and the flag."

Will heard crackles and turned to see the fireplace blazing. Seamus thrust a poker into the pile of peat, readjusting it until the flames almost leapt into the flue. The red-gold light spilled onto Seamus's face, moving paint on a weathered canvas. Satisfied, the old man lay his poker on the hearth and returned to his seat.

"Now then," Conor said.

"Wait," said Will. The two Irishmen looked at him in surprise.

"Haven't heard *that* word from 'im yet," said Seamus.

"Fer sure and certain," Conor agreed.

"Should we have one more pipe? You know, to finish the story with."

Conor's face grew a huge, Cheshire Cat-like smile. He turned to Seamus. "This bye'll make an Irishman yet. Get us one, lad!"

"Indeed," said Seamus. He lunged forward and filled Will's pipe from the old bag.

Conor laughed and rose to his feet just to clap Will on the back. He said, "Yeh're a good bye, all right. Fer sure and certain, yeh are."

Will lit his pipe and pulled the sweet orange smoke into his mouth. It snuck back out and up, into the air. His eyes watered, but it seemed that his vision was clearer now than when his eyes were dry. Conor and Seamus breathed their smoke into the air, as well, and the three of them lay back in their chairs like dragons, making fire and letting their dreams rise with the smoke to the low ceiling of the hut.

Finally, the smoking was finished. Will tapped his ash into a small bowl Seamus pushed in front of him. Will's cheeks were warm with the smoke and the peat burning in the fireplace.

"I think we're ready now, right Will?" asked Conor.

Will nodded.

Seamus nodded. "He's ready, Conor. If I have an eye in me head, he's ready."

"Then listen, Will. This is the very last page." Conor opened his book and read.

"If yeh'll listen, then, stranger or friend, to these words as the little man told them, I will impart the way into the hidden kingdom. The three keys, if yeh will, that'll unlock the door and allow yeh to ask the Queen fer admittance. Yeh might think, why yeh'd want such a thing? Why would a man wish to dance with the magicks? I'll tell yeh this, and it's straight from the mouth of the little man. Once yeh enter the kingdom of the fairies, all pain will pass away from yer heart, fer in that land, all that exists is happiness and joy. Yeh'll sleep through the day and yeh'll dance through the night and yeh'll ne'er feel sorrow again."

Butterflies started flapping their wings in Will's stomach. Even while his mind shirked belief, his heart leapt toward the knowledge that in the realm of all possibilities, magic could exist. If magic existed, then magical people, magical things, even respite from the pain of life and loss, all those things could exist, as well. He'd seen the kingdom, after all. Filled with grief and drunk, yes, a dreamer, yes, but neurotic? Never. Psychotic? Broken from reality? No. Reality woke him up every day and stomped on his heart. Magic could be real, and if it was, then this story could be real, too.

"There are three keys to the kingdom," Conor continued, "and as the little man said, they're not easy to get, but not impossible, either. Tomorrow morning, I go to the cliffs, and if I succeed there, then to the lough, and to the sidhe, and then to the Queen. So, take heed to the path, should yeh decide ta follow me. If yeh succeed and we meet in that invisible kingdom, then we'll dance amongst the honesty and drink our liquor from the honeysuckle until the end a' days, when the sun's fire retreats from the eyes of men and the earth itself ceases to be."

"Dance amongst the honesty?" asked Will. "What does that mean?"

"It's a flower, Will," said Seamus.

"A flower?"

"Tá, a little purple one."

"Is that what he means, though?" asked Conor. "When he says honesty?"

"Exactly," said Will. "Maybe this is all a metaphor. Maybe the quest is for truth."

"Don't get ta talkin' about metaphor and the like," said Conor, "or we'll be wipin' up the spittle off Seamus's sleepin' gourd again."

"Ah, yer daft," said Seamus. "But go on, yeh old fool. A'fore we lose the day entirely."

Will looked out the window and said, "Too late."

"Here I will name the three tasks," read Conor, "that lead to the talisman you must lay at the feet of the Queen. I warn yeh, read one at a time, fer in the reading of them all, there is extreme peril indeed. All one's focus must be on the task in front, not two or three ahead. It will take all of a man's strength to complete the tasks, if it even be possible."

"Is he ever going to actually tell us the—"

"Quiet, Will!" said Seamus. "We're there."

Conor continued, "The first task must take place in Donegal Bay. If yeh wish to see the Queen, then yeh must challenge a selkie in a swimming match. Not just challenge, mind you, but defeat him. The selkie will not show himself to any mortal unless he deems him worthy. Ta prove yerself, yeh must dive off the cliffs of Slieve Liag. Listen well, friend. From the very minute yeh enter the waters of Donegal Bay, yeh'll have three days and three nights 'til the Fairy Queen appears. No more and no less. Meet her at dawn at the end of the third night or naught at all. No more can I tell yeh, except that I go to the cliffs at dawn, ta perish or succeed." Conor closed the book, his face ashen.

Seamus's gaze fell to his feet.

"What?" said Will. "What's a selkie?"

Silence.

"What's the Slieve Liag?"

Conor pushed to his feet and silently disappeared into the other room.

Will turned to the other man. "Seamus?"

"Gettin' cold in here," said Seamus. He rose and grabbed a couple more peat logs and tossed them into the fire.

Conor returned, sans book. "'Bout time to be headin' home, Will," he said. "We'll see yeh back to the main path."

"Wait a minute," Will said. "What about the cliffs?"

"Don't yeh worry about those cliffs," said Conor. "Just get some rest, then leave yer ashes to the Irish wind and go home. Find yerself there, in America, not here."

He threw his arm around Will and half led, half pushed him toward the door.

"I don't...just...come on, guys!" Will sputtered. They reached the front door, Conor trying to shove him outside, when Will pushed away from the older man and whirled around. "Wait just a goddamned minute!"

Conor took a step back, blinking in surprise. "Bye," he said.

"I'm not a bye...a boy," said Will. "I'm a man, and I'm in charge of making the decisions that affect my life. Not you." He turned to Seamus. "And not you." Back to Conor. "You can't spend all evening telling me this shit and just expect me to go back to Texas and forget about it. You can't unsee things. You can't unthink things, unfeel things. That night, last night? It happened for a reason. And whatever that reason is, I'm not gonna back down from it."

"But Will," said Seamus. "Yeh don't understand—"

"You're damned right I don't understand! I don't understand anything that's happened the last year. I don't understand how a tsunami can wipe out a hundred thousand people in India and a fire can kill two and I can be shocked for a hundred thousand and want to kill myself over two, but that's my reality, Seamus!" Will's words caught in his throat. The tears were there this time, but the heat of his anger, his indignation, kept them holed in the corners of his eyes. He struggled to breathe, and dizziness forced him to lean into the door frame.

"Steady, bye," said Conor, putting his hand on Will's shoulder.

Will felt the world spin. The room filled with smoke again, and his past projected onto the smoke as if from a spinning zoetrope lantern. Cara and Samuel and Aidan and college and his life, everything smoke. Beyond it rose a palace and a queen and, perhaps, relief from the all-consuming, soul-rending pain.

"I can't go on like this, Conor. Every day I wake up with a dark mask over my face. I can't see the sun or the rain or five steps in front of me because it's Sam's face and Cara's face right behind my eyelids, every time I blink. I know it's an illusion, that they're gone and in a vase in my room at the inn, but they're more real and present than anything that's happening now. It's killing me." Will's chest heaved as he took a huge breath.

"I have to do this," he said, his voice now quiet. "In my heart, I know it." His gaze turned to Seamus. "It's my path. Death or magic, one of the two. Death will take me to my loves all the faster, and magic, if there really is such a thing? It'll keep my heart and mind occupied until I see them again."

The two old men looked at each other, and then Conor shrugged. "Well, if it's yer path, that's a different story."

"Indeed, Will," said Seamus. "If it's yer path, then yeh'd best get on it."

"We'll meet yeh outside yer place in the morning at five," said Conor.

"Five?" asked Will. "Why five?"

"It's a bit of a drive to Donegal Bay. We'll borrow a car from our friend, Kevan, in town."

"Ah, Kevan, yes," said Seamus. "A better man yeh'll never find."

Conor turned Will around and pushed him through the door. "Just stay on the path to the village, Will. Yeh'll be back in town afore yeh know it."

"I thought you were gonna—" Will began, but the door slammed behind him. "Lead me back down. Okay." He stood a moment, halfway thinking that Conor would open the door again and say, "Just kidding," or something. No. The door stayed closed, even though Will could hear whispering on the other side, and maybe even

a laugh?

Will walked toward the open window and bent down to peer inside. The two Irishmen were nowhere to be seen. "What the hell?"

Conor's face leapt into view, startling him. "Go home, Will! Me and Seamus have plannin' to do, and the night's not gettin' any younger!"

"Get some sleep," yelled Seamus, unseen, and then Conor slammed the window shut, leaving Will alone beside the hut.

When they're done, they're done, he thought.

Will shrugged and began looking for his bicycle, for the path, and eventually, for bed.

Chapter Nine

WATER

EVEN THOUGH IT was only nine or so in the morning, Will's energy lagged like an animatronic toy on its last bit of charge. His muscles burned as he tried to keep up with Conor and Seamus. They seemed to be eternally eight steps ahead of him on the tiny span of rocky path named "One Man's Pass."

Will's nerves had gotten the best of him the night before, and he'd barely slept. Instead, he'd pored over his old *Midsummer's Night* script until four in the morning. He'd thrown it in his carry-on when he'd packed for Ireland. *On a whim*, he thought, or maybe because it was the last thing he'd directed before the fire. Now, the four-hundred-year-old story of fairies seemed all too real.

Conor and Seamus woke him scarcely an hour-and-a-half later. The drive to the Bunglass Cliffs took about two hours. Will alternated between sleeping and being tossed around in the 1974 Ford Pinto that Conor carelessly piloted down the narrow Irish roads.

The walk from Bunglass parking to the beginning of One Man's Pass took another hour-and-a-half. That was when the most strenuous leg of the hike began. Giant, tooth-like stones jutted through the grass, eventually creating an uneven trail that fell away on either side while the trail grew narrower and narrower. As they progressed up the hill, larger rocks protruded from the middle of the path. The three had to squirm past or slide over the huge formations, sometimes climbing, sometimes sitting and scooching on their backsides until the path cleared again. At one point, Will had to climb onto a rock, straddle it like a horse, then pull himself slowly over, grinding his crotch against the rough stone like a Chihuahua humping a clown shoe. By this point, Will was beyond exhausted.

Now, the two Irishmen seemed to leap forward rather than walk. The burn in Will's calves morphed into cramps. He knew he was out of shape, but how were two older gaffers—Tolkien, again—kicking his ass in this climb? He almost tripped but caught himself with the old staff he'd grabbed on his way to the car.

Better watch it. One slip and it won't be a cliff dive. It'll be a cliff...died, Will died. Whatever.

Will struggled the last few yards to join Conor and Seamus where they'd stopped. They stood framed against a perfectly blue sky, and Will realized they'd reached their goal. The edge of the Slieve Liag overlooking Donegal Bay. He eased closer to stand beside the old men.

"Should I look down?" he asked, fighting to catch his breath.

"I wouldn't," said Seamus, "were it me."

"Tá, me as well," agreed Conor. "Best ta get a runnin' start, close yer eyes and jump."

"It can't be any worse than the hike up here," Will said. He looked down.

Jesus God.

Mind-numbing fear iced Will's body, tensing every muscle as if he'd just caught the eye of Medusa. He began short breathing.

"He looked, Conor," a voice said, a million miles away.

"Fer sure and certain," replied another. "A mistake if there e'er was one."

Wide-eyed, Will glanced at the two men at his side. "It...." He shut his mouth with a snap. "Ummm...."

"Spit it out, bye," said Seamus, a soft smile warming his face. "We're nowhere near the Blarney Stone, so's yer gonna hafta do it on yer own."

Will looked down again. The waters of the bay melted against the sides of the cliff, blue softly blending into the gray rock with white, ever-changing foam.

"How far?" he asked, feeling as if his face were the color of the foam.

"Nigh to four hunnerd meters or so," said Conor. "Give or take."

"Four hunnerd, fifty," said Seamus. "Or I'll move ta Scotland an' wear a skirt."

"That's...what?" asked Will. "A quarter of a mile?"

"A few years ago, mebbe," said Seamus. "But since 2005, 'tis four hunnerd fifty meters, and that's plenty fer provin' yerself to a selkie. Course, I'd ne'er be a' tryin' anythin' that foolish meself, but like yeh said, yer on a path, lad. So...godspeed."

Seamus clapped Will on the shoulder, then he and Conor took a step away from the edge of the cliff. Will glanced back, and Conor gave him a quick nod. Will returned his gaze to the bay, to the water that seemed to disappear into the mist and sky, all blended together like one of Cara's paintings.

Cara.

For a fraction of a moment, he'd forgotten her. His skin grew cold, and his mind scrambled. How could that happen? Forget his wife? Forget Sam? Only a few seconds, but the lapse felt unforgivable.

What was the highest recorded cliff dive? A hundred feet? Two? Jesus, impact with the water would kill him for sure.

For sure and certain.

Will laughed.

Behind him, Seamus whispered, "The bye's gone daft, he 'as."

He *was* daft, Will realized. He hadn't experienced a sane moment for nine months, except when he put the shotgun against his throat and pulled the trigger two nights ago. As suicides went, that seemed fairly commonplace. Looking down "four hunnerd and fifty meters" to the blue mirror below him, Will thought that taking the two steps into that particular infinity might be the least sane thing he would ever do. He shook his head. "I can't do it," he said.

"What's that, bye?" asked Conor. "Me ears are as old as the rest of me. Speak up!"

"I don't think I can do it!" Will shouted.

"Can't do it?" said Seamus. "Or won't?"

Staring at the bay, Will wasn't sure. *It's all bullshit, isn't it?* he thought. *Magic. Heh.*

Death or magic, he'd said. In the comfort of the hut, with pipe smoke swirling around the ceiling, the choice had seemed easy. Now, he faced actual water, actual...*gravity.*

Yeah, gravity. Magic was harder to believe in the face of physics. Still, there was the bay and the horizon, a vibrant picture painted by Nature herself.

A memory surfaced.

Cara at her easel, and the way her hair smells as he comes up behind her. She applies paint to the canvas, wet-blending blue and green and just a bit of pink to bring the sun over the horizon. He looks over her shoulder with her smell in his nose and the warmth of her cheek on his. Will's breath quickens as she puts her brush down and turns to kiss him. She's more present in memory than anything he feels now, and yet she's gone. Like sunset melting into a starless, moonless night...gone.

"I want to," he said, his voice shaking. "I can't take the step. I can't seem to make my—"

Two hands hit Will in the back and he shoots over the edge of the cliff. Wind rushed past, ripping a scream from his mouth.

He couldn't breath, and his body turned and twisted head-over-heels in an insane, acrobatic display. The water rushed at him like a tsunami. His eyes tried to water but were blown dry by the air blasting into them. A bitter wail burst from him as his world turned a beautiful, dark blue, and he closed his eyes, not prepared to die but ready.

He stopped falling.

He opened his eyes. He hung a few feet above the water, his body tensed for impact but so perfectly parallel with the blue mirror below him that he might be part of a magician's trick.

"What the—"

He fell. The bay surface slapped him like an angry girlfriend. The impact stung face, body, legs, and arms. He couldn't draw breath. He scissored his legs, broke the surface, and began treading water. He gulped breath after breath like a beached fish. Finally, intellect overtook panic.

We prepared for this, remember?

He, Conor, and Seamus had concocted a plan as they drove here this morning. Just in case magic actually existed.

He ducked underwater and pulled off his jeans. When he resurfaced, he tied knots in the legs and waved the pants above water to fill them with air. He cinched the waist with his belt, and—bam!—he had a flotation device.

He wore a pair of fitted shorts he used as nightwear. The water seemed even colder at first, but without the weight of the jeans, he thought he might survive. He stripped off his shirt and the water began to warm.

Magic? he thought, and then he saw the seal. It lazily paddled around him on its side, its thin, pink penis pointed at him.

So, we begin with a pissing contest.

Will realized that, with the two cups of coffee he'd drunk in the parking lot and the long walk, he could join in. He let his own warm spray spread through the water. The seal must have smelled or tasted it, because he whirled away and broke the surface, spanking his tail and splashing Will in the face.

Will laughed. "Hey, you started it!"

The seal stopped and rolled onto its back, its mottled belly catching the light of the Irish morning. It looked kind of like an otter to Will, at least in that position. A seven-foot-long, giant otter.

"I never realized seals were this big," Will said.

The seal turned and hooked its tail into the water again, sending another small tidal wave at Will's face. This time, the wave caught Will inhaling. He sucked up a throatful of brine and began choking and coughing. The seal laughed, if the loud barking was laughter. Will figured it probably was.

After he cleared his burning nostrils, Will faced the seal again.

"I don't know how this works," he said.

The seal stared at him without moving.

With the morning light behind the creature, its eyes were dull black, as if its eyeballs had receded into the thing's head, leaving soulless holes in their places. Will shivered.

"I have to beat you in a swimming race," he said.

The seal barked a reply, then laughed again.

Will laughed a little, too. "I know it's ridiculous. But I have to try." His laughter faded. "My...wife and son died in a fire and I want to ask for admittance into the fairy queen's castle." For some reason, it seemed easier to admit that to a seal that had taken a piss on him than it had to Conor and Seamus.

The seal cocked its head sideways, almost human-like, then swam a few feet away to a rock jutting out of the bay. He turned and looked at Will as if waiting. Will kicked his feet and swam to the rock. On a small, flat surface rested two piles of stones. Rather, one pile of stones, and then two small stones in a second pile. The larger pile was comprised of various shiny sea rocks, a few pearls, and even what looked like a gold coin, centuries old. The second pile was two rocks that looked as if they'd come from the land along the cliffs. They were weather worn in a rain and wind sort of way, rather than polished over time by water.

"I guess this is the record of winners and losers?" Will asked.

The seal bobbed its head and barked.

"Looks like you're the gold medalist. Only two losses." The seal stared at him, and Will sighed. "All right. Where do we race to?"

The seal turned and bobbed its head toward another land mass in the bay, a tiny island about a hundred yards away.

"Meters, bye," he heard Seamus say in his head. Will laughed.

Sorry, guys. I don't remember my conversion tables. A hundred yards'll have to do.

Will turned back to the seal. "So...when do we start?"

The seal blinked at him twice, then disappeared into the water. Will heard a bark a few yards away. The seal had crested the surface a quarter of the way to the island.

"Hey, that's not fair!"

Will pulled himself around the rock and pushed off from the other side. He shot into the water and began the freestyle stroke he'd learned in his college swimming class a million years ago.

Breathe.

Will turned his head to the side and gulped the icy air. Then it was back into the water, hoping his head was in line with his body and all of it was in line with the smallish island ahead.

After a couple minutes, Will stole a look and realized he was within twenty yards of his goal.

Yes!

He pushed his head back into the water and kicked with renewed strength. Pain raked across his legs as he grazed his shins on the rock of the outlying base of the land mass.

SonuvaBITCH that hurts.

He climbed up and saw that he was first there. He howled a victory cry, the pain in his legs secondary to his triumph.

"Ha!" he yelled. "Betcha never saw *that* coming!"

The barking laugh echoed from the other side of a large rock.

Will circled around the small island and found the seal, lying on his back, fur almost dry in the sun. Maybe it was Will's imagination, but it seemed the thing's lips curled up in amusement.

"Fine," said Will. "You got here first, but every race I've ever seen has been to the target and back. So...see you at the rock."

Will turned and dove into the cold water. His already hike-and-swim-exhausted muscles screamed. He was angry and embarrassed, which made his stroke uneven and slow. He realized that he was beating the water rather than slicing through it. He tried to calm down and get back to regulation swimming. Out of the corner of his eye, he saw something bob up in the water. The seal swam beside him, on its back. He barked at Will, then turned over and torpedoed through the water. In seconds, he was halfway back to the rock. Then he returned to Will and began swimming circles around him while clapping his flippers together in mock applause. Will stopped swimming and felt his face harden.

"You don't have to be a dick about it," he growled.

The seal stopped longways, right beside Will. It slapped him hard in the face with a flipper.

Will shouted in surprise and pain. "That hurt, you sonuvabitch!" He balled up a fist and punched the seal in the nose.

The creature rolled over, barking in pain.

"Yeah," shouted Will. "How do you like it?"

The seal swam a few yards away, turned, and then shot at Will like an insane, flippered torpedo. Will twisted in the water, and the thing barely missed crashing straight into his chest. Quick as a whip, the seal whirled and swung its massive tail at Will's face. It caught him on the side of the head. Will's neck cracked, and there sounded a sharp pop in his ear. Pain shot through him like an electrical charge. Will could no longer hear on the right side of his head.

He barely had time to notice the hearing loss, because the seal circled around and charged him again. Will pushed his arms down by his side, then cupped his hands. He pointed his feet and shoved against the water as if trying to do a jumping jack. The move pulled him underneath the surface of the bay. The seal shot past, mere inches above Will's head. Will grabbed the thing's tail with both hands. The seal stopped moving, and Will's head broke the surface of the water. The competitors stared at each other. The seal shook its tail, but Will held on...barely. He wrapped his right arm around the tail, giving himself a better hold, and narrowed his eyes.

"What now, asshole?" he said.

He imagined the seal shrugged just before it leapt forward. Will grabbed a huge lungful of air as the creature dove and plunged downward, and farther down. Pressure mushroomed in his left ear, and then in his head. At any moment, his skull would burst open like a smashed watermelon. His right shoulder hit something hard.

Shit!

Pain spiked as the shoulder dislocated. It was all he could do to keep ahold of the tail. He reached out with his other hand, trying to right himself. Fear gripped him. He wanted to scream as the seal continued its descent. The pressure in Will's head became a drill. He imagined individual capillaries beginning to pop. He thought he saw blood draining through his eyes and out into the bay water, and then...nothing.

"Oh, he's dead, fer sure and certain."

The voice was a mile away, in a tunnel, projected through a staticky

TV speaker. He managed to open his sore, weeping eyes. Seamus and Conor, out of focus, stood over him, leaning on their staffs.

"Mmm...maybe you're right," Will struggled to say. What emerged was, "Mmm."

"What's that, bye?" said one of them.

"Am...hmmm. Am I duh-dead?"

"Well, if'n he thinks he's dead, he's prob'ly alive," said Conor.

Will closed his eyes, exhausted. He reached up to an itchy part of his right arm and felt a sticky ooze. The gash there throbbed when he poked it. Mostly, though, the arm was numb.

What happened?

He looked at his arm and saw his entire right side covered in blood. His arm lay at a weird angle against the ground.

"Jesus," he muttered. "I'm bleeding." He laughed, and then he yawned. His ear was hurting, and he reached up to scratch it. A knifing pain stabbed into his dislocated shoulder and he screamed just a second before he passed out again.

Will woke again to muddled voices. His eyelids were heavy, and sound was curiously absent from his right ear. He lay still and listened as best he could.

"...fourteen hours now, Sam. He'll wake up soon. No brain damage as we can figure. His right eardrum's punctured, that's fer certain. Tá, it may heal itself given time. Everything else's patched up an' put back in place the best I can."

The doctor. What was his name?

"We should take him to Dublin, then," said Samthann. "Or someplace with a proper hospital."

Silence.

"Fergus, I'm not sayin' yer a bad doctor."

Fergus. Will's memory started to kick in, like a lawnmower that hadn't been started all winter.

Sigh. "I know, lass."

"He's hurt beyond a country doctor's care."

"This country doctor brought yeh into the world, Samthann, an' I'd say yer no worse fer it."

Will tried to form words, to tell them to stop arguing because he was fine, for sure and certain, as Seamus would say. Or Conor. He groaned.

"Will?" asked Sam. Her hand pressed his arm.

"Are yeh there, bye?" asked Fergus.

Will opened his eyes, at least one of them, and tried to focus on the two softly lit blobs in front of him. He squinted a little more and focus improved. "S-Sam," he said.

Her hazy face seemed to tear up. "Tá, I'm here, Will." She caressed his face. "Are yeh in pain?"

"I feel strange," Will said. "Do I have a right arm?"

Sam seemed to pale before him, and he smiled.

"Just kidding."

Sam slapped him across the face, sending his neck into spasms.

"Ow!" he groaned.

"Samthann!" Fergus yelled.

Will laughed. The sound tore through his throat like glass, but it felt good to hear. At least, in his left ear.

"What do yeh remember, bye?" asked Fergus. "It's as if you were beaten by thieves, but no one in the village has seen or heard a thing."

Will tried to remember. "Donegal Bay," he managed. "The Slieve Liag."

"The Liag?" said Fergus. Will saw the doctor turn to Sam, perplexed. "Why would you go to the Liag, bye?"

"Challenge a selfie," said Will. "I mean...selkie." His eyes blurred again and his mind fragmented. Memories melded one into another, creating new images in his head. A peat fire swept through a small hut, killing his wife and son but leaving two old men with walking sticks. A beautiful fairy with inhuman eyes rode a barking seal with a pink, erect penis. The two old men laughed in the distance as they clinked pint glasses of Guinness together.

"Where are they?" Will said suddenly.

"Who?" asked Sam.

"Conor and Seamus," he said. "They brought me here, right?"

Sam and Fergus looked at each other again, then back at Will.

"Who are Conor and Seamus, Will?" said Fergus.

"The two old guys I drink with at the Inn," Will said. "Sam knows."

Will turned to her for confirmation, but even in soft focus, Sam looked pissed.

"Isn't it about time you get off about yer...friends?" said Sam.

"They said..." Will began, "you didn't...."

"What is it, bye?" asked Fergus.

Will felt something pulling him down.

"Am I on drugs?" he asked.

Fergus chuckled. "Yeh were screamin' last night, so I gave yeh a nice shot a' morphine. I sincerely hope yeh've insurance fer it. Why?"

"That's good," Will mumbled. "Shit." He passed out.

BETHA, CARA'S MOM, NEGOTIATES THREE DIFFERENT DISHES on the stove, mixing and turning and tasting like an Iron Chef. She insists that Will sit down at the table and not "worry his head" about helping.

"Mrs. Brady?"

"None a' that, now," she says. "And it'll be Beth to yeh, sir. Or Betha, like Bay and Thaw, but I've given up on you Yanks gettin' me name right, so Beth is fine." She picks up a broom and starts whacking him on the leg. "Now out." She laughs all the while she's shooing him out of the kitchen. Will thinks he's never seen a merrier person in his life. In fact, he can't remember using the word "merry" outside of an Elizabethan play, but Betha...?

Whack!

That one catches Will straight on the ass. He jumps.

"Better listen to her, bye," says Aidan Brady. He sits at the head of the dining room table—a large, wooden thing with intricate carvings on the sides. A handmade tablecloth rests on the top, and a rectangular piece of glass covers that.

Practical, Will thinks.

Tablecloths are pretty but washing them every time somebody spills a few drops of wine or food is a pain. Cleaning the glass is much easier.

"Have a sit, William," says Aidan. "Tell me about yerself."

Will pulls out a chair and sits to the older man's left, on the long side of the table. He's already shaken Aidan's hand when he arrived, but Aidan carries such a sense of nobility, of pride, that Will almost sticks out his hand to shake it again. There's something else in Aidan, too. Distrust, maybe. It's the first time Will has met Cara's mom and dad, so it's a big day.

In more ways than one.

Aidan grabs a bottle of Jameson Irish Whiskey from the table and pours generous shots for Will and himself.

"Before dinner?" Will asks.

Aidan lifts his glass, playing the dining room light through the caramel-colored liquor. "The light music of whiskey falling into a glass," he says. "An agreeable interlude."

"Churchill?" says Will.

"Joyce," says Aidan. He holds the glass toward Will. "Sleinte."

"Sleinte," says Will, touching his glass to Aidan's. The glasses clink, and they sip.

"So...." says Aidan. "Where ya from?"

"Oh." Will sits straighter, then leans back a little. Interview time. "I was born in a small town south of Dallas. Lancaster."

"Like England, say. A town in Lancanshire, right on the River Lune. They have a nice castle there, tá. I used ta travel when I was a lad, with me parents."

"No castle in my Lancaster. Mostly fields and farms, at least when I was growing up. A tornado came through when I was young and took out half the town square. It's never really been the same."

Betha set a huge turkey down on Aidan's side of the table, along with a carving knife and fork.

"Too bad Aidan wasn't there fer yeh then," she said, laughing. "He coulda told the tornado to take off." She heads back to the kitchen.

"Daft woman," Aidan whispers. "Pay her no mind."

Betha returns with some sort of potato dish.

"Not daft, an' there's nothin' wrong with me ears, neither, Aidan

Brady." She smiles at Will. "He's a half leprechaun, Will. Control the weather, they can, if'n they take a mind to it."

"Ah, woman. Take yer fairy tales to the kitchen and don't bother the bye with 'em. We're tryin' to get to know each other."

Betha steps behind Aidan and grips his shoulders, lightly massaging. "Well, that's what he told me, Will, when he was wooin' me from David O'Conor, back in high school. Said he were half leprechaun and had all sorts a' mystical powers. Told me he'd take me on a picnic, but we'd need an umbrella fer the rain, and on the Good Mother's name, we did!"

She bends down and winks at Will. "Course, if there's a day it don't rain a little in Ireland, you'd better look fer Jaysus comin' back." She laughs and pats Will on the shoulder as she saunters back into the kitchen.

Will catches Aidan smiling as he watches his wife disappear and thinks, *They're totally, madly in love.*

Aidan's serious face reappears. "You were sayin'? Lancaster, was it?"

"Yes. Ummm, graduated there and went to South East Texas State for theatre."

"Yer an actor, hmm?"

"Yes, sir. I mean, I enjoy acting. But what I really want to do is teach."

"Teach what?"

"Theatre. Acting, directing. All that stuff."

Then comes the second, "Hmm" from Aidan. Will picks up his whiskey and takes another sip. Cara had told Will that her parents would love him, that he didn't have to worry.

Funny how a couple guttural hmms can totally ruin a man's confidence.

"Any money in it?" asks Aidan.

"In what?" Will says. "Oh, theatre?"

"Bye, we all know there's no money in theatre. But teachin'. There's that poster—'Those that can't do, teach.' Those that teach, do they make a living?"

Will feels the ire rise in his throat. "Man, I hate that saying."

"No offense, bye."

"But it is offensive, Aidan. Sir. And it's not true. My college professor had two agents from Austin come to our senior showcase, and both of them were interested in signing me. But as much as I love acting, I love teaching more. My mom was an English teacher. Every day, she came home with stacks of papers to grade and stories about the kids who were going to change the world. My dad was a long-haul truck driver who wasn't home much, so I was around teachers constantly. Their sacrifices and love for education soaked into my skin like oil. And crap, I just went off on a diatribe. Sorry."

Shit.

Will downs the rest of the Jameson in one gulp.

"No, bye," says Aidan. His voice is warm and kind and his eyebrows, raised and bushy. "That was me pushin' yer buttons a little. I respect a man who stands behind his vocation." He grabs the whiskey bottle and pours another two fingers into Will's glass, then adds a little to his own.

"Sláinte," he cheers.

"Sláinte," says Will, and they clink glasses.

After a sip, Aidan says, "Yeh *can* make a living though?"

Will laughs. "Yes, sir. I've just started on my master's degree, and then I'll teach college. The pay isn't amazing, but it's not as bad as it used to be. The benefits are great."

Cara appears at the top of the stairs, sweeping into the room like a queen.

"What'd I miss," she asks. She kisses Aidan on the cheek. "Daddy, are you being nice to Will?"

"Tá, lass. As nice as I can be." Aidan grabs his whiskey and takes a sip.

"You'd better be. He's the man I'm going to marry."

Aidan almost spits out his whiskey. He manages to get it down, but he chokes and begins to cough. Through watery eyes, he glares at Will.

Will knows, of course, that he and Cara are going to get married. They've already discussed how and when and where and the honeymoon. He's even shown her the ring. They've talked about almost everything, except when Will is going to ask her dad for her hand.

Betha deposits a bowl of green beans and fingerling potatoes on the table.

"You okay, mo chuisle?" she says, smiling, but a little concerned. She's sweating a little and blots her forehead with a dishtowel.

"He just choked on his drink, Ma," says Cara.

Aidan waves her away, hacking twice loudly to clear his throat. "Lass's tryin' to kill me," he manages.

Will stands. "Well, I'd hate to waste good whiskey for no reason." He removes a small box from his pocket and opens it toward Aidan and Cara.

"Mr. Brady, I'd like to formally ask you for your daughter's hand in marriage."

Cara's hands cover her mouth. At the other end of the table, Betha starts to scream and cry and smile, all at the same time.

"Will," whispers Cara. "You didn't!"

She reaches across her father, grabs the ring from the box, and shoves it onto her finger. She holds her left hand toward the light, just as Aidan had done with his whiskey.

Betha hurries around the table. "Let me see, Caralin!" she cries.

Cara holds her hand out and Betha takes it. They both burst into tears.

"Now wait a minute!" Aidan bellows. He pushes himself away from the table with a mighty shove.

"Da," says Cara.

"Not a word, lass," says Aidan, deep and serious. "Not a damned word."

"Fine."

Aidan turns to Will.

"Bye, my daughter has talked about yeh a lot, an' now we fin'ly meet yeh an' yer gonna ask to marry her all of a sudden like?"

Will's face heats. "Ummm, yes sir. I guess that's, uh...well, that wasn't exactly the plan, but it seems...yes, sir. All of a sudden...like."

"What's yer godforsaken hurry?" says Aidan, crossing himself. Behind him, Betha does the same. "Yeh've known her what now, six months?"

"Three."

"Three!" Aidan shouts, and he turns to his wife. "Three months,

Betha, and they're already makin' weddin' plans! You two are like a blind cobbler's thumb, for certain!"

"Daddy!" says Cara. "Don't!"

"Don't 'don't' me, Caralin! Three months! Jaysus, Mary, and Joseph!" Aidan crosses himself again. "Three months, bye! What can yeh know about a lass in three months?"

Will's voice is soft, like tiny droplets of rain in the midst of a thunderstorm.

"Three months, sir? Three months can be a lifetime. It only took Van Gogh one month to paint *Starry Night*, looking through his bedroom window at the asylum in Saint-Rémy-de-Provence."

"Another madman, tá," muttered Aidan.

"Jack Kerouac inscribed an entire generation with *On the Road*, a novel he wrote in under thirty days on one piece of taped-together paper. Your own John Boyne wrote *The Boy in the Stryped Pajamas* in less than three days. Mozart wrote the overture to *Don Giovanni* in three hours the night before the opera was to be performed. Sir, it's taken me twenty-two years to meet your daughter, but every moment up to that point, everything I've done, every mistake I've made, road I've driven down, second I've lived has brought me to the point when I looked into her eyes and knew she was the one. Three months seems a short time, I agree, but I've wasted twenty-two years living without her, and that's way too much time already."

Silence. Cara and her parents stare at Will. Aidan crosses his arms.

More silence, and Will sighs. "Too much?"

Aidan shakes his head and sits. To Cara, he says, "An actor?"

Betha starts laughing. "I thought I was watchin' *Romeo and Juliet*, right here in me own dining room."

"Did you write that, Will?" asks Cara.

"I might've made some notes," says Will. "And a couple rewrites." He looks up at them, guilty. "Okay, I practiced it with Alyssa and Ray. They gave me copy notes."

"Obviously not enough!" Cara says, laughing.

"Shite," says Aidan. "Oh, yer full of it, bye. Like a pasture in Drumkeeran. Sheep shite."

"That's enough," says Betha. "Don't skewer the bye." She turns her face to Will. "Did yeh mean it, Will? The things yeh said?"

"Every word," he says. "Every overwritten word." He looks at Cara. "I had a soul once, but I lost it. My heart, my soul...you have everything that I am and everything I want or ever will want." Back to Aidan. "Sir, I would be honored to have the privilege of marrying your daughter. I promise that, if given that opportunity, I will use every moment of the rest of my life trying to make her smile."

Aidan stands and clears his throat. "Well," he says. "I guess yeh'd better learn to call me Da."

Cara and her mother scream and cry. Will grabs Aidan's hand to shake it, but the older man pulls him in for a hug. Cara's scream changes in pitch. The men turn to see Betha lying on the floor in a faint. Aidan drops to her side and grabs her hand. "Betha! C'mon, lass!"

Will grabs the dishtowel she dropped and wets it in the kitchen sink. Aidan dabs her face with it, and she slowly comes back to them.

"What...Aidan? Where am I?" she looks up at them. "Who are you?" she asks Will. After they get her up and into a chair, her memory starts returning. "Strange," she says. "I guess the excitement got to me." She smiles at Will. "So, lad. When shall we be gettin' married?"

It will be another six months before the fainting spell reoccurs, and that's when Aidan takes Betha to a doctor. By that time, the tumor is inoperable. Cara and Will move their wedding up so that she can be there, wheelchair-bound but smiling. She'll even have the privilege of touching the small bump in Cara's belly that someday will become Samuel McConnelly. Sadly, that's the closest she will ever come to meeting her grandson.

WILL FLOATED BACK INTO CONSCIOUSNESS, STILL WOOZY from the morphine. The room was darker now. As his brain began to clear, he realized that he wasn't in a doctor's office. Paintings hung on the wall, and a curtained window offered a view of a tree and the sunset behind it. A bedside table lamp dimly lit the shadowy room, and a digital clock beside the lamp flashed 12:00 at him. There must have been a power outage at some point.

"Yeh awake fin'ly?" said a voice to his left. Will turned to see Samthann enter the doorway.

"Where am I?" he asked.

She smiled. "Me cottage. T'were me parents' up until two years ago, but she's mine now. Hold on."

Sam turned and disappeared from view. Will relaxed back into the pillow and closed his eyes. Sam's house? Why would he be there? He heard steps and opened his eyes to watch her carry a bowl and a chair across the room. She set the chair down beside him and picked up a spoon that protruded from the bowl.

"It's stew, Will. Fergus said yeh need food to counter the morphine or yeh'll be a right mess. Here."

Sam filled the spoon and aimed for Will's mouth. He started to ask why he was in her cottage, but she stuck the spoon in his mouth, almost choking him. Will chewed the piece of meat and potato and barely managed to swallow before Sam refilled.

"I know yeh have questions," she said, "so why don't I try to guess a couple of 'em fer yeh. Then yeh can relax an' eat."

"When did—" Will began. Another spoonful cut him short.

"Yeh eat, I'll talk," Sam said. "If'n yeh don't remember where yeh were before yeh got here, or how yeh got hurt, then we've a mystery on our hands. An Agatha Christie book—without the murder, I hope." Her eyebrows knitted, then relaxed. She smiled. "Nah. Yer no killer, right, Will? An' I'll say the only way to answer that is with a no, 'cuz I have a .45 in me chest a' drawers. I can have it in two shakes, should yeh turn all Suffolk Strangler on me." She gave him another mouthful of stew. He liked the flavor way more than anything he'd eaten in Ireland so far.

"Okay, so it were me day off. I come back from the store an' yeh're outside on me stoop, bleedin' like the proverbial stuck pig. No one else was in sight. Will, how'd yeh even know where I live?"

He opened his mouth to say he *didn't* know where she lived, but she shoved another spoonful of stew into it. "It don't matter none. I helped yeh inside an' called Fergus. He stitched yeh up and gave yeh some antibiotics fer infection."

"And the morphine?" Will managed between bites.

"Tá. Right in the middle a' stitchin', yeh woke up screamin' to wake the dead. Oh, and yeh were down to yer knickers, too. Yeh know where yeh left yer clothes?"

"Yesterday?" asked Will. He glanced out the window. "Isn't it sunset?"

Sam shook her head. "I found yeh around two yesterday, Will. It's near ta six in the morning." She nodded to the window. "Sunrise."

Will pushed up from the bed so quickly that he almost toppled Sam and her bowl of stew off the chair.

"No time," he said. His feet hit the floor just moments before he did. Pain slammed into his forehead as he smacked the wall on his way down. He tried to catch himself with his right arm, but it gave way instantly. He yelled in agony.

"Jaysus, Will!" shouted Sam. "What the hell're yeh doin'?"

Sam knelt beside him. When she looked at Will's right arm, her face went white.

"Shite," she breathed. She helped him into a sitting position against the wall and started yelling. "What're yeh thinkin', yeh bleedin' fool?"

Will looked at his arm and saw that his stitches had split. He laughed. He was, literally, a bleeding fool.

Sam grabbed a pillow from the bed, yanked the pillow out of its off-white cover, and bound Will's arm the best she could.

"Use yer hand, Will. Try to keep pressure on the wound."

She grabbed Will's left hand and placed it on top of the pillow cover. "Press hard."

Bright red blood blossom through the cover as his wound continued to bleed. Dazed, he jammed the fabric as hard as he could onto the gash. He felt so weak that he was surprised he could apply any pressure at all, even with his uninjured hand.

Interesting.

Samthann jerked her phone out of her pocket. "C'mon, Fergus," she said, punching in numbers. "Don't be nursin' a hangover today, will yeh?"

Will's laughter settled into strange giggles. He could only hear through one ear, so sound was disconnected and distant. His eyes closed, and the world began to fade. Something jerked his head around, and daggers of pain shot through his neck. He wondered if one of his vertebrae were shattered. He opened his eyes.

"Don't go ta sleep, Will!" shouted Sam. She looked at her phone again. "Dammit, Fergus! Answer yer godforsaken mobile!" She looked back at Will.

"I'm gonna hafta get 'im, Will, or yer gonna bleed out in here. Try ta stay awake while I'm gone, do yeh understand? And keep up the pressure. Yer doin' great."

Will nodded, feeling nauseous and sleepy. Was he drunk or sick? The world spun around like a carousel.

"Ah, Will. What'll I do with yeh?" he heard as his eyes closed.

He was close to giving in to the darkness when something warm and wet mashed his lips. Will's eyes shot open to see Sam's closed eyes an inch from his. She was kissing him. Her tongue slipped into his mouth, searching for his. Will pulled away.

"What was that for?" he sputtered.

"Wakin' yeh up," she said, "and it worked. Now stay that way fer ten minutes while I get the doctor."

She was out of the door before Will could reply.

The gentleman doth protest too much, methinks.

The darkness came again and he tried to fight it. He needed toothpicks for his eyelids like in the old Bugs Bunny cartoons he watched as a kid. Of course, the toothpicks always ended up snapping.

Prob'ly made by ACNE, he thought. *Or was it ACME?*

"There he sits, Seamus," said Conor, "like a rock in the middle of a bay." Will craned his aching neck to see the two old men standing in the doorway, staring down at him. Seamus shook his head at Conor.

"Too soon, lad. Too soon."

"How're yeh feelin', Will?" asked Conor.

"Abandoned," Will replied. "Did you really just leave me on Sam's porch?" If he hadn't been so drained, he might have felt angry.

"Fer about a half a minute," said Seamus, nodding. "We brought yeh to Samthann's 'cuz it were closer than the doctor's. Then we set off to grab Fergus, but he was already on his way."

"By the look a' things," said Conor, "yeh're gonna need more'n a doctor."

"Tá," said Seamus, "an' time ain't yer friend today. C'mon, bye. Let's get yeh up."

The two men grabbed Will by the left arm and started pulling like he was a weed.

"What are.... Would you two—"

"We need yeh up and out before Samthann gets back with the doctor, else yer record-setting dive into Donegal Bay is fer naught. There's a time limit on these quests, bye."

"Right," Will muttered. "The quests." He nodded and winced at the grinding in his neck, rolled onto his side, and pushed to his knees with both hands, wanting to scream. His right shoulder throbbed and burned with cold fire. Conor pressed his walking stick into Will's left hand and put his arm around Will's waist.

"The blood," Will said, and the old man chuckled.

"Nothin' a little soap an' water can't fix," he said. Like a weightlifter, Conor picked up Will and set him on his feet.

Like Popeye, thought Will. He laughed. *Second cartoon reference in five minutes.*

"Stop the craic," barked Seamus, "and get the bye to the car." He walked ahead of Will and Conor, looking back every half a second, goading and encouraging. Finally, they managed to lay Will down in the backseat of the Pinto.

"You never gave the car back?" said Will.

Conor peeled out and turned right onto a small, two-lane highway. "In order to give something back," he said, "yeh have to have borrowed it. Ta be honest, Will, we sorta forgot to talk to Kevan before we...ummm, took it."

"You stole his car?"

"No, no," said Conor. "He said we could borrow it any time, an' we know where he keeps his spare key—"

"Frog in the front yard," said Seamus. "It has a head that comes off. There's the key to his cottage, an' he hangs the spare car key right inside his front door."

"Not very safe, fer sure and certain," said Conor. "A thief could just break the glass and take his car, were he inclined to. And if Kevan were away on a holiday or sumpin'...."

"Which he is," said Seamus.

"I'm an accessory to a crime," moaned Will.

"Do it matter, bye?" asked Conor. "If all goes well, yeh'll be quit a' this world in two more days, tá?"

Will relaxed as much as he could considering the amount of pain he suffered. Memory wandered to Samthann, and more specifically, to the kiss. He felt guilty, even though Cara had been gone almost ten months.

Too soon. The funeral baked meats did coldly furnish forth the marriage tables.

His laugh now was bitter, like cocoa. Was that him now? A darkly cloaked Hamlet meandering through life? Who was there to punish, then? No Claudius here—just faulty electrical wiring from a seventy-year-old house. In betraying Will and Cara and Sam, it had signed its own death warrant. No sword or poison could touch it.

Will's mind bent and curved and fell as thoughts of fire and Shakespeare jumbled together. If he could just fight fire itself, maybe he'd find some peace. He looked at his right hand. The skin was beyond pale. He was bleeding out.

The man came out of the water gasping for breath like a newborn baby. He blinked and pulled clumped hair out of his eyes. Two concerned-looking, elderly gentlemen stood in front of him, at the edge of the pool. He didn't recognize them, but they were staring at him as if he were a ghost.

"How are yeh, Will?" one asked. "Yeh were in there nigh on ten minutes."

Will? Was that his name? He didn't know the old man or recognize his strange accent. A soft...lilt?

"He's not all back yet, Conor," said the other. "Give him a tick."

The man closed his eyes and tried to find the name "Will" in his memory. In the dark, he heard it whispered—Will, and William. William McConnelly. The female voice was full of honey and velvet and...vanilla —warm and fragrant...unlike the water he stood in, which was cold. Overhead, the sun broke through a bank of gray-rimmed clouds and brightened even the darkness behind the man's closed eyelids.

"Will," he said. The spoken word was a key opening a box. Memories came tumbling one over the other. Millions of little moments flooded his brain, overwhelming his senses. Will opened his eyes.

"Conor?" he said, looking at one of the men. To the other, "Seamus?"

The men laughed and turned to each other.

"He's close. I'll give that to him."

"Tá, almost there now."

Will's forehead wrinkled. "Wait." He pointed at the first man. "No, you're Seamus, and"—he pointed at the other—"you're Conor."

Conor clapped Seamus on the back. "There we go! We got him back." And to Will, "We got ya back, bye."

"What happened? Why am I...Jesus, it's cold!"

"Get out then, Will," said Conor. "We have yer clothes over here in the car."

Will waded toward the bank of the shallow pool. The water was black and viscous, like motor oil, yet it didn't cling to his skin. He stopped and dipped his hand in it. Cold, thick, and not just black. Swirling in the depths was red maybe, or smoke, which wasn't even a color but...fit.

"Gonna stand there all afternoon, Will," asked Conor, "or do yeh remember that yer in the middle of a bleedin' quest?"

"Sorry." Will stepped clear of the pool. For some reason, he wasn't wet. Even his underwear was dry.

"I'm totally dry. How is that possible? How did I even get here? I can't remember that part, at all."

Conor handed him his jeans and shirt. "That's 'cuz yeh didn't get here. Seamus and I dragged yeh from the car and dropped yeh in the water. We didn't know if it'd work fer sure."

"We didn't," Seamus agreed. "Yeh were so close to gone that yeh were pullin' a Dullahan's ears."

Will stretched his shirt over his head, and Conor handed him his jacket.

"What's a Dullahan?"

"Death, bye," said Seamus, his face drawn and serious. "When the Dullahan calls yer name, yer time is up." He shivered. "The pool were the thing that saved yeh."

"C'mon, Will," said Conor. "Hop into the car and we'll talk on the way back to the village."

Will opened the rear car door.

"Be careful where yeh sit, though," Conor continued. "We tried to wipe the blood outa the seat, but there may be a few smears and splotches hangin' about. Don't want that on yer clothes. It's gonna be hard enough explainin' how yeh walked away from Samthann's house by yerself."

Will carefully slid into the seat, checking for droplets of blood, or sticky patches. He didn't see any. Seamus and Conor had done a good job with the cleanup.

"Why can't I just tell her you helped me?" asked Will.

Conor shook his head and glanced back over his left shoulder as he drove. "She'd like as not ta charge us with trespassin' if yeh tell her we just barged in an' stole yeh away."

"Wait, wait," said Will, grabbing his right shoulder with his left hand. "There's no.... It's not just the blood that's gone."

He tore his jacket off and looked at his right arm. No blood or wound, just smooth, pale skin. A little discoloration where his arm had been ripped open. Otherwise, it was like he'd never been injured. In fact —he took a deep breath—there was no pain anywhere. He felt better than he had since the fire.

"Guys?" he asked. "What the hell happened to me?"

Seamus, who wasn't driving, turned around fully. "A'fore that, why don't yeh tell us what yeh remember from the bay?"

Will's face puckered as he tried to recall—was it only yesterday? He stood on the cliff, terrified. Looking down. He couldn't do it, and then—

"Hey!" he yelled.

A surprised Conor swerved and almost hit a tree before squealing back onto the asphalt.

"Kill us, Conor," said Seamus, "and no fountain a' youth'll be there to heal our bleedin' bodies." He turned back to Will. "What're yeh tryin' to do, scare us all inta a meetin' with Jaysus?"

"That's the pot calling the kettle black!" said Will. "One of you pushed me off that cliff!"

"Ohhh," said Seamus. His bushy eyebrows rose so far they almost blended into his black and gray peppered hair. He slowly turned to face the windshield.

"Who was it?" said Will.

"Who was what?" asked Conor.

"Which one of you pushed me?"

The two old men glanced at each other, and then, at the exact same time, "Me."

"Bullshit," said Will. "I felt one person shove me over the edge."

"Yeh sure?" asked Seamus. "Yeh've been through the ringer, tá."

Will crossed his arms and pressed against the seat. Maybe it had been one hand from each man. He looked back and forth at the backs of their heads.

"C'mon, guys. Just tell me who it was."

Silence filled the air for a quarter of a mile or so. Then Seamus scooted around in his seat again. "Do it matter, Will?"

"Well, yes! You.... I wasn't going to jump."

"Yeh said yeh wanted to, yeh just couldn't."

Will heard the words in stereo. He realized that hearing had been restored in his right ear, as well.

Fountain of Youth? he thought, and said, "Yes, I did say I wanted to."

"Does it really matter then?" repeated Seamus. "Yeh jumped, with a little help. After that, what happened?"

Will sighed and told the Irishmen about falling and screaming and stopping a few feet above the surface of the water. He described the seal and the peeing and the race.

"We were diving down and down," Will said. "I don't know how long. At a certain point, I blacked out. The next thing I remember was waking up at Sam's. Or...it seems like I was on the shore for a moment and saw you two." He shook his head. "That part's a blur."

"That part we do know," said Seamus. "After yeh went into the water, me and Conor made our way down to the shore. That was a bit of a hike, fer sure and certain. When we got there, yeh were stretched out on the shore a-bleedin'. Conor bound yer arm with his favorite handkerchief."

"I don't have a favorite handkerchief," growled Conor. "Stop exaggerating."

"Fine, fine. His handkerchief that his mam gave to him when he was a wee lad that he has no emotional attachment to whatsoever."

"Me mam, really?"

"Will," said Seamus, "we bound yeh up and wanted ta leave. Yeh were woozy and weavin' like a punch-drunk prizefighter, but yeh insisted on swimmin' back out to the rock. Do yeh remember that?"

Will shook his head.

"Yeh grabbed a' rock from the bank and swam out into the bay. When yeh came back to shore, yeh were clutchin' this like it were a hunnerd-pound note." Seamus reached into his right pocket. "Ummm, I bet it's right...." He reached into his left. His face blanched. "C'mon now, Seamus. Don't be daft." He checked the right pocket in his jacket and smiled. "Tá, here it is."

He opened his hand and dropped a beautiful, white pearl into Will's. The memory came back to Will with the speed of a gunshot. "There were two piles of stones and pearls and things on the rock in the bay," he said.

Seamus nodded.

"I think the small one represented those who had won the race against the seal—"

"The selkie," said Seamus. "T'weren't no seal, Will, though it looked like one."

"Right," said Will. "The selkie. There were prob'ly eight or ten markers in the selkie pile for each stone in the other. I just wanted my race to count, I guess. After that, I swam back to shore, and then...everything goes dark again. How'd I get back to the car?"

Seamus's smile disappeared. "T'were the selkie, Will."

"What? How'd a seal—a selkie—get me back to the car?"

Seamus shook his head. "It were the damnedest thing. The selkie, he came ashore and disappeared around the edge of the cliff, and then this man, tall and muscled—"

"And naked," Conor added.

"Naked as Adam on his first birthday," Seamus agreed. "He came 'round the corner and grabbed yeh like a sack a' flour. T'were like he knew exactly where we was goin', fer he ascended the cliff as if it were nothin'. By the time we got to the car, yeh was already in the back seat, bleeding through the handkerchief."

"So, he's what," said Will, "some sort of wereseal?"

"Somethin' like that," laughed Conor. "A selkie can take off his fur coat and walk around as a man any time he wants. Or a woman, as may be. They hide their coats well, 'cuz if'n yeh find one, the selkie has to be yer slave as long as yeh keep the coat. Many a story's told of fishermen finding the coats of women selkies and marrying 'em."

"Huh," said Will. "At this point, I'd believe just about anything." *The water, though. The black, smoke-colored water.* "But what just happened at the pool? How did it heal me?"

"My voice is growin' dry, Will," said Seamus, "and Conor can barely drive, much less drive and weave a yarn. Yer healed, fer sure and certain, but yeh could prob'ly do with some rest. Why don't you lie back in the seat and catch some shuteye? We'll talk about the pool later."

Will started to protest but realized that he was tired, tired down to his very bones.

"All right, then," he said, yawning. "I'll catch twenty winks and we can finish up after that." Will closed his eyes, and suspected that his twenty winks might turn into twenty thousand.

Only two days left.

His eyelids struggled to open, then drooped closed again like an old-fashioned window blind.

Can I really afford to sleep?

As his consciousness faded, he realized it didn't matter whether he could afford it or not. He was going.

Chapter Ten

GOLD

"THE FOUNTAIN A' Youth," said Conor, lighting his pipe. Will's pipe sent white, fragrant plumes up to the low ceiling, and Seamus was pouring tea. "Though I never woulda called it that meself, 'cept that's what I heard it called in the history books. It were one a' them Spanish conquistadors went to yer country, Will, lookin' through Florida and Mexico. Who was it, Seamus?"

"Began with a C, I think," said Seamus.

"Ponce de León," Will said, laughing. He couldn't believe how good he felt, as if the waters of the pool had not only healed his wounds but made him stronger. "Maybe you were thinking about Cortés. He was an explorer too, but it was Ponce de León who was looking for the Fountain of Youth in America."

Seamus set teacups down in front of them. "Added a little milk this time," he said. "Hope yeh like it."

Will took a sip. It was like nectar. Warm, milk-rich nectar that danced across his tongue. Shakespearean text used to dance like that before he'd become a real-life tragic hero.

Hero, he thought, scoffing. *Some hero*. Aloud, he said, "Delicious. Thank you kindly."

Seamus smiled at Conor. "He said 'kindly,' Conor. We'll make an Irishman of 'im yet."

"Tá, if we get half a chance," Conor agreed. "But ta the fountain. Will, these places, they exist. Pocketed everywhere in the world, bubbling up from the ground. Some say they're the remnants a' God's grace. Others think it's magic. Whatever it is, that pool's been a fam'ly secret a' me and mine fer generations."

"Why a secret?" asked Will. "A real honest-to-God Fountain of Youth? People would pay millions...billions to bathe there. Think of all the people you could help."

"Mebbe," said Conor. "Or folk would come here and fight over it and end up dyin' fer ownership. And it's partic'lar the way it works, anyway. That's what I was meanin' about perception. Ponce de León may very well 'a found his fountain off in Florida and not recognized it. Ya see, it's not really about youth as such, Will. It's about healin'. It's...difficult ta explain." Conor paused, thinking.

Will saw an idea pop into the older man's head. His eyes widened. He smiled.

"Okay, bye. Look. One day in town, at the Forde Ian, there was a lad on a computer. One a' them small ones yeh can carry with yeh."

"Laptops," said Will.

"Fer sure and certain," said Conor. "An' it were causin' him all sorts a grief, workin' slow and not doin' all the things he wanted it to do. This fella with him, he says he should just...what was it?" Conor pulled on his pipe and rolled his eyes to the ceiling. "Reset the factory defaults," he said, excited. "That's it. Me mem'ry ain't what it used ta be, but it's there all the same. Reset the defaults. Make everythin' right again, so's I understood it. That's what the pool does, Will. It doesn't roll yeh back to when yeh were a babby drawin' milk from yer mam's breast. It just resets yeh. If there's illness, it takes it away. See what I'm sayin'?

"Even better," said Will. "If it can, like you said, reset our factory defaults, think of the people it could heal! You could bottle it and send it across the world. Cancer and AIDS and every sort of plague, just gone!"

Conor shook his head, his face carved with sadness. "Alas, that's not how it works, Will. If'n yeh just drink a bit a' the water, it'll set yeh right fer a time. Allow yeh health enough to live out yer natural lifespan. Last year, Seamus had his hunnerd and twenty-third birthday."

Will gasped. "Bullshit," he said, looking between the two of them, waiting for the joke. Neither laughed. "Bullshit!" he said louder.

"It's true, Will," said Seamus. "An' Conor's just behind me. We drank at that well long a'fore we understood what it was, 'cept that we were always in good health. An' a coupla times, when we were sick, we'd bathe there and feel better."

"And you don't call that a Fountain of Youth?" asked Will.

Seamus glanced at Conor and sighed.

"There's only so much healin' in the pool," said Conor. "Yeh were almost dead, Will, an' it brought yeh back whole. The pool won't be healin' anything fer a long time now."

Will remembered the water, the gray smoke and black liquid swirling. "The black water," he said.

"Death," said Seamus. "When we put yeh in there, the water was a brilliant blue-green, like grass and sky all swirled up together. It pulled the death right outa yeh, down to the very last part a' yer bein'. Now the pool is filled with it."

"Tá," said Conor. "It'll be a stretch a'fore the waters return to blue, if'n they ever do."

Will's face fell. "So, I ruined the water for anyone who might...." His breath caught in his throat. He looked at Conor and Seamus. "You two won't be able to use the waters anymore. To reset yourselves. To heal." His voice broke. What had he done?

Seamus reached over and put a small, wrinkled hand on Will's knee. "Bye, we've lived almost two lifetimes, and good ones, at that. We've seen loved ones come and go. That's mighty hard. It won't be so bad to visit 'em. Meet our Maker, as it were. See jus' what all the fuss is about."

Will took Seamus's hand and squeezed. The old man's hand might have been small, but it was certainly strong.

Seamus smiled. "I got a few years left in me yet. Me and Conor won't be rushin' off to see Jaysus this afternoon, which is good. 'Coz we need to get yeh goin' on that second quest, fer sure and certain."

"Fer certain and sure," agreed Conor. He grabbed the ancient book from their little table and opened it. Will stretched back into his seat, waiting for the fragrance of the pipe to work its magic. He held onto the guilt though, of ruining the pool for those who might need it. Another memory he'd be glad to shed when he stepped into the kingdom of the fairies.

"I inscribe these words upon the page. If yer readin' this and have up ta this p'int, yeh'll know that I've raced the selkie and won. My body is bruised and torn, and the distance between me and death in the race was the width-wise side of a horse's tail hair. I long to rest, to sleep, but there are only two days left to gain admittance to the kingdom. I set out at dusk to find a pùca and challenge him to a drinkin' match. If I can beat 'im, then I must complete the challenge he sets a'fore me."

"A pùca?" asks Will. "Seriously?"

"What is it, bye?" asked Conor. "Know the pùca, do yeh?"

Will laughed. "Know him? An American playwright named Mary Chase got a Pulitzer for writing about one. You've never heard of *Harvey?*"

"Harvey?" asked Seamus. "Who's he?"

Conor slapped Seamus on the shoulder with the front of his hand. "Seamus, lad. We know Harvey. He had a little place off the Diffagher River. Used ta fish a lot."

"Conor, that was Hagan. The two names don't even sound alike."

Conor laughed. "Tá, yer right. Hagan. He were a sight when he was blathered though. One night we caught him shoutin' at his fishing rod fer not workin' hard enough. Seamus p'inted out that there weren't no line on the reel. Hagan screwed up his eyes and lay right down beside that rod and stared at it up close. He says, 'Yer bluddy right, Seamus.' Then he grabbed the reel and threw it hard as he could in the river. 'Reel ain't no good without line,' he said. Then he boaked all over his shirt."

"So, who is this Harvey?" Seamus asked Will. He sat back in his seat and sipped his tea.

Will smiled. "*Harvey's* one of my favorite plays. They turned it into a movie eventually, with Jimmy Stewart." Will looked at them, expectantly. "You do know Jimmy Stewart, right?"

"Fer sure and certain," said Conor. "Moved to Dublin years ago. Bartender, I think—"

"Stop, stop!" said Will, laughing. "You know, there are more people in the world outside of Ireland than in."

"Not that we know," said Seamus.

"Oh, Seamus," said Conor. "We know a few, scattered here and yon."

"But they're all from Ireland, Conor. Every last one." Seamus relit his pipe. "We're gonna stop talkin' now, Will. Give us what yeh know about the pùca and this Jimmy Stewart, if'n yeh like. He has a good Irish name to 'im, so he's prob'ly got a story or two worth hearin'."

"I don't know that Jimmy Stewart is that important," said Will. "He was a good actor. From what I've read, he was a good person, too. But this movie—play and movie—*Harvey*, is about a nice guy with a drinking problem. He has this invisible friend named Harvey that everyone thinks is the result of his alcoholism. His sister even wants to have him committed to a mental hospital." Will took a sip of tea.

"What happens, bye?" asked Seamus. "Did they lock 'im up?"

"No," Will smiles. "The thing is, everyone likes Elwood. He's a truly kind soul. His sister decides if Harvey's the baggage that comes with her brother's huge heart, then she'll find a way to deal with it."

"I'd like to see that play, Seamus," said Conor. "If'n it ever came to Drumkeeran."

"Tá," Seamus agreed. "But the pùca, Will. Do yeh remember what it said about him?"

"It's one of my favorite plays, Seamus," said Will. "I can quote quite a bit of it."

"No need there," said Conor. "Just the pùca, if'n yeh please."

Will pulled on the pipe and tried a smoke ring, but no such luck.

"Like this, bye." Seamus took a long pull, blew a large smoke ring, then sent two increasingly smaller rings through it.

Will laughed. "That'd be a nice bar trick."

"Out here in the country, tá," said Conor. "They outlawed smokin' in the pubs in the cities. I guess it'd be a good outside-the-bar trick."

Will tried it again, unsuccessfully. "It doesn't matter," he said. "Okay, pùcas. In *Harvey*, one of the hospital guys reads something in the encyclopedia that says pùcas are fairy spirits in animal form, almost always large, and they're harmless but mischievous." He paused. "Oh, they also like alcoholics and crackpots, and...they can stop time. I remember thinking that'd be a nice trick. If nothing else, just to get a little more sleep."

"This Mary Chase," said Conor. "She seemed ta know a bit about the pùca. Then again, there are some things she's left out."

"Tá," Conor agreed. "A pùca *is* a fairy spirit that'll appear in the guise of an animal, fer sure and certain. They can be mischievous as the day is long, but sweet? They might help a farmer now and again, as they love things that grow and those that grow 'em, but a common man? Why, they'd make yeh believe yer walkin' through a garden when it's up on a cliff yeh be saunterin', a plunge ta yer death in front a' yeh, with the pùca all but laughin' as yeh fall."

"An' not 'cuz they hate men, yeh understand," added Seamus, "but in the name of a good prank. Yeh see?"

Will nodded. "How do we find one?" he asked. "Jumping into Donegal Bay was really specific. There aren't as many instructions here."

"That's 'coz everyone knows where to find a pùca," said Seamus. "If yeh be lookin'. Tell the truth, there ain't many Irish folk lookin'."

"Get yer cloak, Will," said Conor. He tapped his pipe ash into the little ashtray on the table.

"Where are we going?" asked Will.

"Why, our fav'rit place in the world, besides here."

"The pub?" laughed Will. Neither of them answered. "What? We can't go there! Samthann prob'ly thinks I'm dead in a ditch somewhere. If she sees me totally healed and I didn't check in with her, she'll break my nose again!"

"It's a chance we have to take, Will. Forty-eight hours ain't long in this world, but it'll be much longer before yeh get another chance to meet the faerie queen. Not in this life, fer sure and certain."

"Buck up, Will," said Seamus. "We're with yeh now, and if we don't carry the luck a' the Irish, why then...no one does!"

∾

SAMUEL CARRIES A SHOEBOX IN HIS HANDS AS HE SOLEMNLY marches out the back door and into Cara's small garden. Summer is creeping into fall, which will bring rain and humidity and Halloween soon. There might even be a cold snap sometime in November, but the heat will return soon after, and they will celebrate a balmy, eighty-two-degree Christmas.

Sam wears his church suit. At his insistence, Will and Cara also wear black. It's three weeks before his third birthday, and this morning before breakfast, he'd discovered his pet goldfish upside down in its small fishbowl.

"I told you he was too young for a fish," Will had said, but Cara'd shushed him and wiped away the beautiful little dewdrop tears scurrying down Sam's cheeks.

"Bury it?" he'd asked.

"Of course," she'd answered.

So here they are, dressed for the funeral. Sam is the lone pallbearer. Cara, with her garden trowel, will act as gravedigger. And Will? He's the minister who will officiate.

Sam sets the box beside the tomato plants. "Here," he says. Will wants to ask if he'd rather put the fish farther back, near the fence, but Cara instantly begins digging a hole.

She finishes her excavation and backs away. Sam places the shoebox in the hole and stands.

"Daddy?"

Will removes a small steno book from his pocket and reads the short sermon he's partially written and partially borrowed from the internet. "We are gathered here today to bury our friend, Sunshine, who passed away some time in the night. We know he was well taken care of by his best friend, Samuel, who fed him the exact right amount of food and talked to him daily. I'm sure that Sunshine was very happy for Sam's friendship. Sometimes, our friends leave us; we don't know why. Perhaps Sunshine knew that angels needed pet fishes, too. Maybe there was a little boy angel who was lonely up in heaven. Even Jesus couldn't make him smile, so they sent for Sunshine. Now he's up there and living in a place where fish don't even need water to swim, because they swim in the air, their fins like wings."

Sam reaches up for his mother's hand, and she takes it.

"Alas, poor Sunshine. We knew him well. A fish of infinite jest, of most excellent fancy. He hath borne Sam's joy on his back a thousand times, and his lips seemed to kiss the side of the fishbowl whenever Sam came near. We hope and pray that our good Lord in heaven will smile down on us and ease our pain, and that He will let Sunshine know we miss him here on Earth. We lay him to rest in this place of exceeding beauty, where he will stay in the sunshine, like his name, forever and ever. Amen."

"Amen," said Cara, and Sam added, "A-ben."

After they change, Cara sets the table with salads and sandwiches, paper plates, and plastic utensils. She'd convinced Will that they should go all the way, so that Sam won't be afraid when they have to attend an actual funeral in the future.

They fix their plates, and Will sits down at the table. Sam stands, plate in hand, looking at him quite seriously.

"What's wrong, Sam?" Will asks.

"Eat out dere?" Sam replies. He points at the backyard, almost losing his plate in the process. Will grabs the plate and looks at Cara, who nods.

"Sure, buddy." Will grabs Sam's and his plates and heads toward the back door.

"I'll get the drinks," says Cara.

"Thanks, babe."

Will leads Sam to the redwood picnic table near the garden. He sets the plates down, then grabs Sam underneath the arms. Will deposits Sam in his own, special picnic seat. He marvels every time he picks Sam up. He's so light, and yet so dense. Like the universe has packed so much potential into his little body that it's bursting at the seams.

Cara sets two glasses of lemonade and a sippy cup of apple juice on the table. "It's my special lemonade," she tells Will.

Sam reaches for her glass. "Dwink?" he asks.

"No," she says, laughing. "This is Daddy and Mommy's Special Adult Lemonade."

"That's a great title," says Will. "We should market it."

"I can do the graphics," Cara says. "Maybe a daddy passed out at the kitchen table while a mommy is pouring another glass?"

"Like you could ever drink me under the table."

"Oh, please. You're a lightweight when it comes to vodka."

"Vodka's my kryptonite," Will agrees. "But whiskey? I'll kick your butt any day."

"We'll have to wait until Sam's eighteen. No drinking games around our baby."

"Agreed," says Will.

"Shh," Sam whispers, his index finger across his lips.

"What, honey?" asks Will.

"Pway-er."

"Oh, of course." Will reaches out and takes his family's hands, making a little triangle. He starts to pray, but Sam interrupts.

"Now way me down sweep," he says. "Pway the Load my soul keep."

Will opens his eyes to see Cara gazing at her son, adoration resting on her like a crown.

"Angels gwide us fwew the night. Wake us in mow'ing night. A-ben."

"Amen," says Cara and Will in unison.

They drop hands to eat. There's nothing but silence and chewing for a few moments, and then Sam says, "Mommy?"

"Yes, my precious little boy?"

"Sunshine gone?"

"No, he's in the garden where we put him. Remember?"

"Oh." Sam continues eating, taking a bite of sandwich and then following it with a chip. Sandwich bite. Chip. Sandwich bite. Chip. He'll leave the salad for last, because—unlike most children—it is his "favwite."

"Mommy?"

"Yes, Samuel?"

"If Sunshine in gawden, why Daddy say...heaven?"

Cara glances at Will and grimaces. She's not ready for this discussion yet, but Will thinks, *Hey, you wanted a wake.*

"It's complicated, Sam," Cara says. "Hard to understand. Are you sure you want to talk about it?"

"Uh huh." Sam nods, shoving a chip into his mouth.

"Okay." She turns to Will again. "Daddy, you want to explain what you meant about heaven?"

Will's mouth falls open, and he glares at her. Then, he reaches up and physically closes his mouth, like in a cartoon.

Sam giggles. "Daddy's si-wee."

"Yes, Daddy is silly," Cara laughs.

"Mommy"—Will smiles—"I think Sam was asking you."

Cara shrugs. "Mommy made lunch. It's Daddy's turn to help, right Samuel?"

"Daddy?" says Sam.

Will gulps a mouthful of lemonade and vodka, stalling. It's difficult for him, because he hasn't gone to church much since his mother and father died. Of course, he and Cara are officially Catholic, for Aidan. They attend mass on Christmas and Easter, but Will's knowledge of scripture is lacking. "Hmm," he says. "Okay. You know how you can't see the wind, right? You can feel it on your face. You can see it blow leaves on the trees. Otherwise, it's invisible."

"Like Caspew, the fwiendwy ghost?" asks Sam.

"Like Casper," Will agrees. "Except Casper can make himself be seen sometimes. The wind, well...it's invisible all the time."

"'Kay," says Sam.

"There are other things like that in the world, too. Some people, Mommy and Daddy included, believe that we have an invisible part of us. It's call the soul."

"Like fwum Sunday Skoo?" asks Sam.

"Right. Just like they say in Sunday School. We're part body." He reaches over and tickles Sam under the arms.

Sam giggles and spits half a bite of sandwich out.

Cara laughs as Sam picks up the sandwich bite and sticks it back in his mouth.

"And we're part soul, which is invisible. But the neat thing about the soul is that when we die, like Sunshine, it separates from our body and goes to heaven to be with God and Jesus and all the angels."

"Sepawate?"

"Right. Your Legos come apart, right? That's like your body and your soul. So, when your body stops working, your soul just…pops off and goes to heaven."

"Hmm," says Sam.

Will stops talking and shoots Cara a dirty look. She pretend-claps, silently applauding his effort.

"So…Sunshine's weggo so' go to heaven," Sam says, matter-of-factly.

"Yes, that's it," said Will.

"An' he's happy?"

"Very. Even though I'm sure he misses you."

"Oh."

Sam finishes his sandwich and drinks some apple juice.

"Daddy? One mow queshun." He holds up one little finger, something he's modeled after his mother.

"Okay. What is your one more question?"

Sam looks at his daddy with his most serious face. "Can I haf a puppy?"

Will and Cara instantly crack up. Will tickles Sam again.

"Daddy, 'top!" More laughter. "'Top!"

Will stops, and Cara boops Sam's little nose. "Daddy and Mommy will talk about it," she says. "It's not the best time of year to get a puppy though. Next spring, that's the best time."

"'Kay!" says Sam, probably assuming that by "talk about it," Mommy means "yes."

WILL DUCKED AS SAMTHANN THREW A STAPLER AT HIS HEAD.

"How dare yeh, Will McConnelly! How dare yeh march in here lookin' as if yeh'd just visited a spa, and this mornin' leave a trail a' blood out me door! Yeh should be dead, yeh hear me? All yeh've been through! All yeh've put me through! What kinda devil are yeh, William McConnelly?"

Sam backed away from him, her face paler than normal. "Is that it?" she whispered. "Are yeh the devil, come to tempt me away from God?"

"No, Cara! Shit. Sam, I—"

"Who's this Cara, then?" Sam roared. "Some poor lass yer leadin' on when yer not eeking free drinks offa me?"

"Stop it!" Will yelled. Sam grabbed a pint glass from the extra stock behind the desk and went into a windup like a major league pitcher.

"Cara was my wife," Will said.

Sam slowly lowered the glass. "Wife?"

"Yes," said Will. "She and my son...my son, Samuel." *No tears, Will.* He stared at Samthann, waiting for the words to emerge. They refused. His mouth wouldn't open. Not without tears. Will's eyes filled then, and the words came. "They died in a fire last year. That's why I came here. My father-in-law's family is from Drumkeeran. He asked me to spread Cara's and Sam's ashes in the drumlin hills."

Tears fell onto his cheeks, but he didn't sob. At least, he could control that one thing.

Just breathe, he thought. *Breathe.*

"Will," said Samthann, her voice full of emotion and her eyes wet. "I didn't know." She paused. "I'm a right bitch, ain't I?"

"No." Will smiled. He almost lost it then. Almost broke down and cried. He kept it together, though. Barely. "You prob'ly won't believe me," he said, "but I have to get back out there. A pùca"—an involuntary bark of a laugh popped out—"a friggin' pùca, of all things, is coming to the Forde Ian tonight. I have to challenge him to a drinking game as part of this quest I'm on." He laughed out loud then. Really loud. "How crazy does that sound, huh? An honest-to-god, right out of the fairy tale books pùca."

"A pùca?" Samthann asked.

"Tá," Will replied. "Tá tá tá." Will slipped into a bad Scottish brogue. "And a coupla ayes fer good measure. So, call the looney bin, lass, coz Will is friggin' losin' it big time! What do yeh think about that?"

Samthann launched herself into Will's arms, crying huge tears that wet his shirt all the way through to his heart. She stood there, sobbing, her hands around his back pulling her even tighter into him.

"You don't think I'm crazy?" he asked.

Sam pushed away from his chest so she could look into his eyes. "I think yer daft as fishin' on Sundays," she said, "but there's truth in yer words. I know things sometimes. It's in me family." She slapped him hard on the arm.

"Ow! What's that for? You said you believed me!"

"That's fer invitin' a pùca inta me pub! If he tears up the place, yeh'll be wirin' back ta 'Oh Say Can Yeh See' fer the money to fix it. Now, get out there, a'fore yeh miss him!" She shoved Will toward the door.

"We're gonna need a lotta beer," said Will. "Plus, I don't know if he's gonna be invisible or not, so if you can keep people away from us, that'd be great."

"Can we just close down the whole bleedin' pub fer ye, Will? Maybe cater in some fish eggs and fairy cakes?"

Sam looked back at the pint glass again. He feared she might rethink her decision not to throw it, so he hurried out the office and back toward the floor of the pub.

"I remember it well, lad!" said the black-haired goat. His golden eyes shone brightly in the dim light of the pub. He and Will sat with Conor and Seamus at a table in the corner, as far from the main bar as possible. Sam had yet to approach the table.

Will thought about going to the bar, but he remembered Seamus's advice in the car on the way to the pub. "Don't be offering to buy any drinks before the contest has begun, lad," he'd said. "The pùca's a trickster. He'll have yeh drunk and the contest over before it's even begun. 'Ar stealladh na ngrást,' as we say here. 'Drunk as a lord.'"

Will was trying to make conversation with the pùca, which was difficult because he'd never talked to an animal before. Well, that wasn't true. He'd never talked to a man-sized animal that had the ability to talk back.

"I was down to Adare in County Limerick," said the pùca. His golden eyes cast toward the ceiling, as if he didn't quite remember the story and wanted to get it right. If the pupils of his eyes were off-putting—

they were like snake eyes but stretched horizontally instead of vertically—his voice was not. His rich baritone held a sweet Irish lilt, almost hypnotic. "There was an American, like yeh, an' he were visitin' an antique shop on the street. I just happened to be in the shop, fer it was owned by one Aengus McGregor. Oh, Aengus was a fine lad in his own way, but he'd have one up on the tourists when he got a chance." The goat pulled a tiny flask from the traveling bag hanging from his shoulder and drank.

"Ah," he said, "that's a fine Scotch. A seventy-five-year, and smooth as a river stone. Would yeh like some, lad?"

"No," said Will, "but thank yeh kindly."

The pùca turned to Seamus and Conor. "Polite for a Yank," he said.

The two old men nodded.

He turned back to Will. "So, where was I? Ah, yes. I was havin' a pint with me good friend, Aengus, when this American tourist came into the shop. He was lookin' at this and that, bag in hand as if he were there to buy the whole place out. So Aengus, he tells the lad that he has somethin' special behind the counter, and there's not a shamrock in Ireland if Aengus doesn't pull out the very skull a' Brian Boru. Have yeh heard a' Brian Boru, bye?"

"I haven't," Will confessed. "Who is he?"

"Why, he's only the most famous Irish warrior in history. United the entire island to fight the Vikings in 910 A.D., the year of our Lord. Beat one a' their greatest fighters at the turning p'int a' the war. An' Aengus, why he had the very skull a' Brian Boru fer sale, all authenticated an' everythin'. Well, this tourist reaches into his bag and pulls out another skull, a larger one. He says, 'Well, yeh sold me this skull as Brian Boru's yesterday and said it was authenticated as well. The people at the inn where I'm stayin' said that yeh were having me on. So, which skull is Brian Boru's? The one yeh sold me yesterday or the one yer trying to sell me today? They're not even the same size! Look at 'em!'

Aengus, he holds up the skull he'd sold the lad yesterday, an' it was a mite larger than the one he'd brought from behind the counter. He doesn't back down an inch, though, Aengus McGregor. He looks straight at the tourist, and says, 'Well, sir. To be perfectly honest, both of them are the skulls a' Brian Boru. Yeh see this one?' Aengus, he holds up the larger one. 'This one was when Brian was fifty, when he died. This one?' He holds up the smaller one. 'Well, that's his skull when he were a lad.'"

The pùca slammed both front hooves on the table between them, braying with laughter.

The joke wasn't funny, but the sight of the goat laughing and beating his hooves on the table was hilarious. Will couldn't help but join in.

"That's an Irishman fer yeh, lad!" brayed the goat. His black coat shimmered in the bar light, and his horns curved round and back between his ears. "They'll stand up fer a stranger in a bar fight and then borrow yer coat an' not give it back fer a winter."

"The Irish are amazing people," Will agreed. "And creatures, as well." He paused. "I'm not sure what to call you."

The pùca's eyes narrowed. "Well, you could call me a pùca, but that'd be like me callin' yeh Mr. Human, now wouldn't it?"

"Tá," said Will, sending the pùca into bellows of laughter again.

"He's half an Irishman already," the pùca said to Seamus.

The old man nodded.

"More 'n that," said Conor.

"So, why don'tcha just call me Billy?" said the goat. "It's as fine an Irish name as I know and'll do in a pinch."

"Billy it is, then," said Will. "Billy, I've never met a kinder people than here in Drumkeeran. Shakespeare said, in *Timon of Athens*, 'To set a gloss on faint deeds, hollow welcomes, recanting goodness, sorry ere 'tis shown; but where there is true friendship, there needs none."

"Here, here!" said Billy, once again tipping his flask to his mouth.

"Leave it to Shakespeare," said Will.

"I met him once," said Billy. It seemed the goat was smiling, but since Will had never seen a goat smile, he wasn't sure. "Smart feller. Too serious, but them playwrights often are. Even Oscar Wilde had a stick up 'is arse most a' the time, an' he were a good Irishman himself." The goat unscrewed his flask again to take another swig.

"The Irish are amazing," said Will. "The only thing that could make them any better is if they could hold their drink like we Americans can."

Billy was halfway into his pull, and choked and coughed. Seamus hopped out of his seat and started patting the goat on the back.

"Yeh okay, bye? Don't choke on a seventy-five-year! The windpipe's no place for good Scotch!"

The goat coughed a bit more, and finally got himself under control. He twisted his head at Will until he was looking at him sideways.

"Now, lad," said Billy. "Where did yeh hear that good Irish folk can't hold their liquor?"

"It's just something I've noticed since I've been here, though it's not really with liquor. The Irish are grand with whiskey, but give 'em a few pints of beer and they're under the table before the night's halfway done."

"Will Will Will," said the goat. "Now yer steppin' on national pride, don'tcha know? We Irish are the best drinkers on the planet, just slightly ahead a' the Germans. They start drinkin' as soon as they're tall enough to reach the bar. We start, if our mams are kind, with a nip or two in the baby bottle. No, no. The Irish hold their beer, liquor, whatever it may be, better than anyone on God's green earth."

"Really?" said Will. "I've never drunk with a pùca before, but if you're a true Irishman and I'm a patriotic American, what do you say to a friendly little drinking game?"

The goat's eyebrows rose, revealing more of his strange, sideways eyes. "I've heard yeh Americans think yerselves the best at everything, but yer gonna try to outdrink an Irish fairy?"

Will smiled. "I never said I'd try. I said I'd win."

The goat's laughter shook the rafters, though the rest of the bar patrons paid it no mind. The goat slammed his front hooves down on the table again, and his head shot out to within an inch of Will's.

"Well, bring on the ale!" he shouted.

Will waved at Sam, who'd been eying him from the bar. She ambled over, drying a pint glass.

"What can I do fer yeh?" she asked Will, totally ignoring Conor and Seamus.

"Do you have pitchers here?"

"Tá," she said. "We used ta have 'one euro pitcher night,' but no one was makin' it to work the next day and the mayor asked us to stop. Yeh want a pitcher then, fer the two a' yeh?"

Will started. He didn't know if anyone else could see the pùca. "Two pitchers a piece to start with," he said, "and two pint glasses and a large coin, if you have one."

"Oh, I've better than an English coin," said Billy, reaching into his knapsack. He pulled out a large silver piece and laid it on the table.

Will whistled. "That's perfect." To Sam, he said, "Just the pitchers and glasses then, please."

"Fine, but if the two a' yeh get pissed and fall on the floor, it's yer own damned faults." Sam stepped away from the table.

"She's a rare beauty, that one," said Billy. "Nothin' like a good Irish lass, Will. Especially when they're fiery."

"I didn't know if she would be able to see you or not," said Will. "No one else looked at you when you walked through the door."

"Folks see me if'n I want 'em to," the goat smiled. "And I'll always make an appearance for a pretty lass. A' course, she sees a black-haired gentleman with a strange hat and an unkempt beard. Yer seein' me fairy self, I believe, but yeh don't seem surprised."

"I've seen a lot of strange things lately," said Will. "Though you might officially top the list."

"Don't be tryin' to get on me good side, Will. I won't be takin' it easy on yeh."

The goat's right eyebrow rose high, his head cocked to the side a little. With the shadows of the lights in the pub, Will could easily see why people would be afraid of this strange creature, especially since it was rarely seen except at night. Will stood.

"I wouldn't insult such an amazing creature as you, Billy. I'm honored to share a table with you, and to engage you in a friendly game of quarters. Or whatever they call it here."

"I think we call it Drink the Yank Under the Table," said Seamus, laughing.

"Yer friend's a smart one," said Billy.

Sam returned with four pitchers of brown ale and two pint glasses. She set everything down between Will and Billy, eying one, then the other. Her gaze stopped on Billy. "I haven't seen yeh 'round these parts, have I?" she asked. "I never ferget a face."

The goat pushed his chair out from the table and stood on his hind legs, raising him well beyond six feet tall. "I've ne'er ventured much west a' Scal'd Hill...Sandymount, they call it nowaday, though I'll take a path a hunnerd mile outer the way to avoid Dublin. William Butler Yeats were born there. Yeh've heard of him?"

Sam planted her fists on her hips. "Tá. What good Irishman hasn't?"

"He said this once," said Billy, reaching out with his hoof and taking Sam's hand. "'But I, being poor, have only my dreams; I have spread my dreams under your feet; Tread softly because you tread on my dreams.' I think a lass like yerself could tread on many dreams, tá. Or raise them up into the heavens."

Sam barked a laugh as she jerked her hand back. "Don't be fresh, yeh mangy old muppet!" She laughed and walked away, with just a tiny bit more swing in her stride, Will noticed.

"Some women will tell yeh ta save yer compliments fer someone else," said Billy, "but in hunnerds and hunnerds a' years, I've ne'er seen a compliment wasted on a good lass."

Billy picked up the ancient coin and tossed it into the air, then balanced it on his hoof. It had some sort of very simple cross on one side, and when Billy flipped it over, a rudimentary face of some sort. It didn't look old; it looked ancient.

"Shall we flip ta see who drinks first, Will?" asked the goat.

Will nodded, and Billy sent the coin into the air, end over end, and then trapped it with his hoof as it hit the table.

"Call it, bye."

"Heads."

Billy took his hoof away to reveal tails.

Will sighed.

"Luck a' the Irish, Will," said Conor. "Here. Let us give ya some!" He picked up the pint glass in front of Will, spun it in his hands a couple of times, and then sat it back down. "There yeh go!"

Not that spinning a glass was going to do any good, but Will was happy for all the luck he could get. He filled his glass to the brim and picked up the silver coin. He tossed it into the air, caught it on the back of his hand, and made it dance across the back of his knuckles like a street magician.

"Here's nothing," he said. He set the coin on the table and thumped it as hard as he could. The coin began to spin. Will grabbed his pint glass, downed it, and was in the process of refilling it when the coin hit a notch in the table and collapsed.

"Ah, no!" cried Conor. "That's the table's fault, not Will's."

"Yeh picked the pub, not me," said Billy. He pushed the coin back to Will and smiled. "Start over."

Two hours later, Will's head was bobbing and weaving like an old video of Muhammad Ali he'd seen as a kid.

"Float like a butterfly, sting like a wheeeee!" he said to Billy, whose bearded chin rested on the table. Billy watched his coin spin and fall, not even trying to drink, at this point.

"Start over!" yelled Will, pointing to the ceiling as if it made him look more official. He giggled. The room was spinning, and Will took a couple of deep breaths. If he threw up, it'd be an automatic forfeit.

On the table beside them were thirteen empty beer pitchers, as well as four shot glasses.

Did we do shots? he wondered.

Seamus shook the rafters with his usual, late night snore. Conor's eyes were fixed on the coin Billy had spun again. The coin fell.

"Start over!" Will said. He yawned.

Billy looked hopeful for a moment, but Will shook his head and managed a somewhat steady gaze at the goat. Billy sighed. "Will, if I drink one more ounce, I'll leave it on the floor. I concede."

"There ya go, bye!" said Conor. His head hit the table, and he began snoring in time with Seamus.

"What'll yeh have 'a me then?" asked Billy. "What were this competition about this fair eve?"

"I'm looking for admission to the queendom of the frair...." Will reset. "The *king*dom of the faaaeries."

"Ah. Yer one a' those, are yeh?"

"One a' whats?"

Billy pulled his head off the table and attempted to hold it up straight, though it tended to twist to the side. "Melancholies," he said. "Black bile-filled, soul-aching poets who can't deal with life na more and seek respite in the arms a' the fairy queen."

"Tá," said Will. "You hit the nail on the thumb." He giggled.

Billy smiled his strange, goaty smile. "Ain't no respite there, bye. Only escape and nepenthe."

"Nepenthe?"

"'Wretch,' I cried," said the goat, "'thy God hath lent thee—by these angels he hath sent thee / Respite—respite and nepenthe from thy memories of Lenore; / Quaff, oh quaff this kind nepenthe and forget this lost Lenore!'"

"'Quoth the Raven,'" finished Will. "'Nevermore.'"

"You Yanks give us a poet now and again," Billy said.

"Then yes," said Will. "I want nepenthe from this world. Not in the arms of the queen, really, but a way out that doesn't come from the barrel of a gun."

The goat stared at him, then dismissed his mood with the wave of a hoof. "Gah, what need I fer humans and their silly emotions? I've seen gods born and kingdoms fall and a million sad faces walk by on their way from somethin' and on their way ta nothin'. 'When we are born, we cry, that we are come to this great stage of fools.'"

"*Julius Caesar*?"

"Indeed. I like the war and bloodshed."

"You should see *The Terminator*."

"Ne'er heard of it. One of 'is lesser plays?"

Will laughed. "Definitely not Shakespeare." He lay his hand on Billy's hoof. "If I were interested in this world at all, I would get a whole collection of Arnold Schwarzenegger movies. We'd find a television and DVD player and I'd sponsor us a marathon."

Billy cocked an eyebrow. "Ne'er seen a movie. Thought I'd give 'em a few hunnerd years to see if they hung about."

"Anythin' else, or are you two needin' to find a room now?"

Will realized that Sam was staring down at him. From her point of view, she probably saw him holding the hand of an Irishman with a shaggy black beard. "That's all, Samthann," he said.

"I'll get yer tab then." Sam turned to head back to the bar.

Quick as lightning, Billy gave her a sound slap on the ass.

She turned almost as quickly, eyes blazing, and slapped Will.

"What?" he sputtered. "I didn't do it!" His face stung and his cheeks heated.

"Well, yeh shouldn't be lettin' yer guest paw at me backside like I were a greased pig at the county fair!" Sam turned on her heel and stomped away.

"Oh, that one," Billy laughed. "She is lively! Why didn't yeh tell me she was yer cara baineann?"

"My what?"

"Yer lass, bye."

"What was it again? Car-uh what?"

"Cara baineann. A'times, things just sound prettier in the Gaelic, though e'en the good Irish folk don't speak it much anymore."

"Cara baineann," said Will, tasting the words. He laughed.

Even the Gaelic language knows I'm supposed to be with a "Cara."

Aloud he said, "You ever feel like you just can't escape something, Billy? Something that haunts you day and night and won't let you go?"

"Like I said, lad, human emotions don't interest the likes a' me anymore. Seen too many of 'em in me lifetime. But if I were interested in yer why's and why not's, I'd prob'ly tell yeh that the time yeh have here is but a minute, like Shakespeare said."

"True."

"An' if I were a creature such as yeh, with such a short life in front a' me, I'd take ev'ry pain and sorrow and joy and love...I'd fill my soul with it all and carry it 'round with me like a bindle." Billy shook his head. "Gah, I'm losin' me drunk. See if that gal a' yers can get us a couple shots a' whiskey a'fore we go. Make mine Scotch. I picked up a taste fer it when I went travelin' a couple hunnerd years ago, and me flask?" He uncorked his flask and turned it upside down. Nothing. "Dry as a slice a' soda bread."

Will wasn't sure he could handle another beer, much less a whiskey.

Then again, he didn't feel as drunk as he prob'ly should've. Sam strolled up to the table with his tab.

"Samthann, could we have two more Jamesons and two of your best Scotch? Just put it all on this." He handed her his credit card.

"It'd be my pleasure, Mr. McConnelly." She smiled. "We don't sell much of our 'best Scotch.'"

It wasn't until she returned with the receipt for him to sign that Will knew why she was smiling. Each shot of Scotch was €150, or about a hundred, sixty dollars American. Will woke Conor and Seamus, and they all toasted Samthann's health. Ten minutes later, Will and Billy walked out the door, arm-in-arm, Will's credit card a full seven hundred dollars lighter.

"There she is, bye," said Billy. He pointed his black, shiny hoof at a horse in the middle of a grassy field.

"A...kelsie?" asked Will.

"Kelpie," corrected the goat.

"Is it a shapeshifter, too, like the selkie?"

"Nah, bye. A water spirit. Sits in the middle of a field waitin' fer some lad or lass to try and ride 'im, then races fer the nearest lake or river an' drowns 'em."

Great. Another trip through the water.

"Then it gnaws through their bellies to get ta their innards. Likes the taste of 'em, so I've heard."

"Hmm," said Will. He decided that if Billy and he ever did have that movie marathon, he should add *Alien* to the mix. "So, I'm just supposed to ride it?"

"That's the normal challenge, ride it to a standstill. Might be a little more complicated tonight. Look."

"Where?" he asked.

"Over by the far fence. There, bye."

Will followed the pointing hoof and saw two children, probably no older than eight or nine, climbing over the fence. They slowly crept up on the horse—*kelpie*. The boy carried a looped rope.

"It wouldn't drown little children," Will breathed.

Billy laughed. "Why not? They're just miniature versions of yeh. Like cow babbies, right? Nice, milkfed calves yeh slaughter for veal?"

Will took a step toward them and shouted, "Get out of here! Run!"

The children whipped their heads toward Will, but rather than run away, they bolted for the kelpie.

"Ain't nothin' gonna stop those two," Billy said. "They be treasure huntin'."

Will turned, panic gripping his chest. "How do I keep the kelpie from the water?"

"Never seen it done, lad, so I can't tell yeh." The goat patted him on the back. "Yeh better hurry, though. The young 'uns are gonna beatcha there."

"Shit!" Will vaulted the rickety wooden fence and plunged through the grassy field. Ahead, the little boy tossed a slip-knotted loop over the kelpie's head. He pushed his little sister up onto the beast's back, then tried to climb up himself. The horse was too tall for him. The kelpie knelt, and the boy climbed aboard behind his sister. Will imagined that the creature's back elongated, as if inviting more people to the ride. Will was close now, but the boy grabbed the makeshift rein and settled into his seat. Will wasn't going to make it.

The horse stood, and the little girl lost her balance. She slipped sideways and almost fell. The boy grabbed her arm and saved her. He pulled her back into place just as Will jumped onto the kelpie's back. The horse's back elongated even more to accommodate him.

The little boy twisted around and began hitting Will on his arms and face with his small fists. "Get away from us!" he shouted.

Will blocked the blows as best he could while he scooched himself into position.

The kelpie's back curved up behind him, creating a hump not unlike a camel's. The beast wasn't interested in Will falling off. Oh, no. It wanted him on for the ride.

The kelpie turned its head at an almost impossible angle to stare at the three of them. It neighed softly, and the two children forgot about Will. They petted the thing's nose, and the little girl reached into her apron and withdrew some sugar cubes. The kelpie took them almost daintily. It chewed, then licked the girl's face with its long, slimy tongue.

"Can yeh be showin' us yer gold?" the little boy asked.

"Please," added the little girl.

"Please?" echoed the boy.

The kelpie looked at Will, nodding as if taunting him.

"Kids, you need to get down, now," Will whispered.

"Bugger off, mister!" said the boy. "We was here first!"

As if that were its cue, the kelpie whipped its head forward and took off like a shot. It reached the wooden fence in seconds and vaulted it as if it were a stone in the road.

The children screamed and grabbed for the rein. Will didn't bother.

This bastard's not letting us fall off until we're wedged under some log in the middle of a lake.

The kelpie plunged straight at a huge oak tree.

Shit!

At the last second, it veered left.

The children screamed again, clinging to the rope for dear life.

Will grabbed the little boy's hands and pryed them from the rope harness. He thought maybe he could toss the boy off into a soft patch of clover or grass. Then the girl.

The kelpie raced headlong through the forest, shooting past trees like a rocket. No empty fields here. Will screamed in pain as the boy clamped his teeth down on Will's fingers. Will released him. The boy grabbed hold of the rope again.

"You've got to get off this thing!" Will yelled. "It's going to kill you!"

The boy elbowed Will hard in the nose.

For the second time in a week, Will saw stars.

Focus on the horse.

He searched for a weapon and saw nothing. Moonlight pierced the trees, bathing the forest in skeletal white. Will could see how people might be entranced by the beauty of the ride and not realize that death lay ahead.

He wrapped his arms around the little boy's waist and heaved, but the boy was stuck, as if held with Super Glue. Will shoved against the horse's rump, straining for better leverage. His muscles trembled with effort, but he couldn't shift, either.

"Shit," he breathed. "Shit shit shit."

He grasped behind him for something, anything. The kelpie's tail swished away from his touch. Will grabbed it and jerked hard. The kelpie screamed a human-like shriek and cut left. A huge limb almost decapitated Will. Branches slapped his face and blood ran into his eyelashes. He dropped the tail and wiped blood from his eyes, but the flow persisted. He jerked off his t-shirt and tried to rip a makeshift bandage. The fabric stretched. His vision turned red. He tore into the t-shirt with his teeth. The fabric shrieked as it ripped. He tore the bottom off the shirt and bound his forehead.

As he worked, an idea flashed, then vanished. He grasped for a memory that hovered out of reach. Blood soaked through the bandage and trickled down his cheek. Ahead, moonlight glinted on something—a long, silver line past the trees. A river. A wide one.

Come on, Will.

Conor and Seamus invaded his head. *Bye, what's happened ta yeh? Step-by-step, jus' like yeh learned to tie yer shoes fer church.*

The kids stopped screaming. The little girl had gone limp and the boy held her, weeping.

Will wiped blood from his cheek. He'd deplaned in Dublin, gotten a ride to Drumkeeran. There was something before that. Will beat the side of his head with a fist, trying to dislodge the memory. What the hell was it?

Trees thinned as they plunged toward a clearing. Tree trunks shot past as if he rode an amusement park roller coaster.

The boy jerked his head around to Will. "Sorry I bit yeh!" he yelled over the wind. "I don't want to go to Jaysus with sin on me soul."

"It's...ummm, lad!"

The boy leaned against Will, crying. "I can't look." He covered his eyes with his hands.

The selkie burst into the clearing, two hundred yards from the river.

Alistair! From the flight.

When they'd reached Drumkeeran, the Scotsman had shared three words. The first was...tail?

Gripping the tail of the selkie had helped in the first quest. What was the second word?

The river loomed less than a hundred yards away.

The boy shifted, his hands pressed tight against his eyes.

"Yes!" Will shouted. He whipped the ripped t-shirt past the kids. The cloth slapped the kelpie in the forehead. As the beast roared, the shirt slid down over its eyes. Will caught the loose end of the shirt with his left hand.

Blindfold.

The kelpie bucked. Will hugged the children with his elbows and struggled to keep the blindfold in place. The monster bucked again, and Will lost his grip on the shirt. Wind pushed the fabric up around the kelpie's ears. The thing shot toward the water.

"Sonuvabitch!" he yelled. They were out of time. Will took a deep breath and tensed for another cold bath.

Two small hands grabbed the shirt and shoved it down over the creature's eyes. The kelpie swerved to a stop, shrieking, and bucked hard. Will pressed against the kids. The creature reared onto its hind legs, almost vertical. Gravity fought to wrench Will off the creature's back but the kelpie's magic held him in place. The creature dropped back to four hoofs, then tramped left. It missed the riverbank by a couple feet. Then, it veered right and cantered farther from the water.

The kelpie shook its head and screamed, then broke into a gallop, straight toward a weathered signboard. Crack! The beast's head hit the sign. A hundred pieces of shattered wood sprayed the air and struck the ground. The animal screamed again, this time in pain. It stumbled to a halt.

The boy slowly dragged his hands from his eyes. "Are we dead?" he asked.

The little girl released her deathgrip on the mangled shirt. She looked over her shoulder. "The bad horsie woke me up screaming," she said. "I helped the man cover the horsie's eyes."

Her brother threw his arms around her. "Yeh beat it!" he screamed. "Yeh beat the arsehole!"

"Not yet," said Will. "We still can't get off its back."

"Pluck three hairs from its tail," said the boy. He wiped tears from his cheeks with his shirtsleeve.

His confidence inspired Will to pluck the hairs. The kelpie growled and gnashed its teeth. Will handed them to the boy, who proceeded to wind them around the rope.

"We soaked the rope in holy water at church when no one were lookin'," said the boy. "But yeh need three hairs from the tail, too." He slapped the kelpie on the neck. "Yer ours now, ain'tcha?"

Before Will could shout "No," the boy yanked the shirt from the creature's eyes. The kelpie stood there, docile as a carthorse.

Will thought, *Well, at least you're not a sore loser*.

The boy clicked his tongue twice and tugged on the makeshift rein. The horse followed his direction.

"I'll be damned," said Will.

"Not now yeh won't," the boy said. "None of us will."

Thirty minutes later, the kelpie nuzzled a stone near the fence where they had begun the ride.

On the ride back from the river, the children had introduced themselves as Alannah and Padraig. Padraig had explained that the English translation of his name was Patrick. He was named after Saint Patrick who, according to legend, drove all the snakes out of Ireland. Will asked if Ireland was really snake-free, and Padraig looked at him as if he were crazy before he slid from the kelpie and helped his sister down.

"Well, surely there must be some rational explanation," Will said as he dropped to the ground.

Alannah watched Padraig grab a shovel hidden in the brush.

Padraig stood on the step of the shovel and forced the cutting edge underneath the stone.

"What is 'rational'?" Alannah asked Will.

"It means that something makes sense. Can be proved. Logical."

"Sir, we blindfolded a kelpie and he led us to his treasure. Does that make sense?"

Will looked down at the little girl and smiled. "You'd make a good college professor," he said.

"I want to be a princess," she replied.

Will knelt beside her. "Can I tell you a secret?" he asked.

"If'n yeh'd like," she said.

For the first time, Will noticed that she had a tooth missing, which made her smile just perfect. "You already are," he said.

Alannah laughed.

"Found it!" Padraig announced.

Will and Alannah turned as he lifted a small box from the ground. They held their breaths as he raised the lid. In the moonlight, old coins shone like silver-gold fire.

"We've done it," said Padraig. Tears filled his eyes. "Da will be so happy."

Alannah leaped onto her brother's back and threw her arms around his neck, almost choking him. The box of coins fell from his hands and spilled onto the ground. Will began to shove the coins back into the box, but Padraig pushed his hand away.

"I can do it," he said.

Alannah looked at her brother in shock. "Padraig!"

"It's ours!" he said.

"He saved us!" the little girl exclaimed. "He's not a thief."

Padraig looked at Will, then dug into the box and pulled out a handful of coins.

"Yeh want some, mister?" he said. "I guess yeh've earned 'em."

Will smiled and shook his head. "Keep it. Hide it away where nobody else knows, and just use a little at a time."

"Why?" said Padraig. "We could buy the whole village with this!"

Will gripped the boy's shoulder. "What would you do with a village?"

"Eat a lot more sweets!" said Alannah.

Will laughed.

Padraig strained to pick up the box, then nodded to his sister. "C'mon, Alannah." To Will, he said, "Thanks, mister."

Will smiled as Padraig stumbled through the field with the heavy box.

Alannah hesitated, then followed him, but halfway to her brother, she turned and rushed back. She leaped into Will's arms and kissed his cheek. "I'll bet yer a great da," she whispered. She pushed out of his arms and skipped across the field toward her brother.

I think I was, once, he thought.

Will teared up, but then he saw the kelpie staring. He sure as hell wasn't gonna give the demon horse the satisfaction of seeing him cry.

"You've lost your gold," Will said. "Why are you still here? Just go away."

"Yeh'll ask me fer nuthin' then?" the creature said.

Will stumbled back a step, surprised. "You can talk?" he asked.

"A six-foot-tall goat brings yeh here, an' yer surprised I can talk? Not the sharpest scythe in the field, are yeh?"

Will bristled. "At least, I don't go around eating children," he said.

"Yeh listen to pùcas and their blarney. I'd say that's almost as daft." The kelpie shook his head and neighed a laugh.

"So, you weren't going to drown us and eat us? Then why were you taking us to the river?"

"We're all on a path, bye. Mebbe mine was to free two good-hearted children from the bonds of poverty. Or ta help a sad Yank who can't do nuthin' but feel sorry fer himself most days."

Will clenched his jaw. His nostrils flared. "You don't know anything about me!"

"I know yeh want a meetin' with the Queen. Only sad folk are lookin' fer that. An' if yer gonna keep lookin', yeh might want to check in that hole a little deeper."

With that, the kelpie galloped back toward the river. Before it could reach the nearest copse of trees, it disappeared from sight like a popped bubble.

Confused and tired, Will wandered over to the hole where the children had found the treasure box. He knelt down and dug a little more in the wet soil. His fingers slid across something hard and smooth—a strange rock with a hole in the middle and a texture like glass. He dug a little more, but found nothing else. When he returned to the spot where he'd left Billy, he was gone, as well.

Will cleaned the stone off in the grass, stuck it in his jeans pocket, and headed back to town.

Chapter Eleven

CALM

WILL RETURNED to the bed and breakfast, famished and in desperate need of a shower. The clock in the lobby read 10:30. He crept into the kitchen to see if he might wrangle up some leftovers without letting anyone know he was there.

As he rounded the corner from the main dining room, Will saw a dim light in the kitchen. Maybe a nightlight, he reasoned. He took a deep breath and pushed the swinging door open just in time to see Robert pull a bowl from the stainless-steel refrigerator. The swinging door creaked a little, and Robert's head twisted around so hard Will thought the man might get whiplash.

"Oh, yeh gave me a fright, yeh did!" said Robert.

"Sorry," said Will. "I didn't think anyone was up."

"They're not, on most nights. That's why I like comin' in late, so's I don't have to relive me life's history with Meg. Bless 'er heart!"

"Don't worry. I'm not much of a talker. Whoops!"

The bowl Robert was holding tipped in his hands while he was talking. Will barely managed to grab it before its contents splattered the floor.

"Saints a' mercy!" said Robert. "Bye, yer quick as a sprite. I'll say that fer yeh."

"Thanks," Will said. He looked into the ceramic bowl. Various, indiscernible veggies and meat bobbed in a thick gravy. "What is this?"

"Stew a' some sort. I'm sure Meg tol' us, but Emma was talkin' about this and that an' carryin' on about what we were doin' today. To make a long story short, I have no idea. Looks like lamb though, or goat."

Will laughed. "Goat?" He pictured Billy floating around in a giant bowl of gravy with his flask of good Scotch. He laughed again.

"Bye, are yeh okay?"

"I was just thinking about something funny."

"No, not that." Robert stared at Will's forehead. "That's a mighty deep scratch yeh've got there. Yer forehead's all bloody, tá. I woulda seen it right away, 'cept fer the light's so dim. An' I were jugglin' stew."

"It's okay," said Will. "Head wounds bleed a lot, but they're not as bad as they look."

Robert continued to stare.

"But I'll see a doctor first thing in the morning."

"There yeh go, bye." Robert waved the bowl in front of Will. "Yeh hungry?"

"Tá," said Will.

Robert smiled. "Don't take long, do it? Slip into the manners a' the country?"

"No, it doesn't."

"Stay a while, bye, an' yeh'll be speakin' Gaelic a'fore yeh know it, though almost nobody'll understand what the hell yer sayin'. Grab a bowl, and I'll heat this up in the microwave."

Three minutes later, both men were dipping spoons into bowls of the hearty stew. Robert found some soda bread in the pantry and used it to sop up the gravy.

"Where yeh been, Will?" asked Robert. "Haven't seen yeh much, though Meg's been all a'twitter as to yeh bein' the most interestin' guest what she's had in years. Out all night drinkin' and borryin' her bicycle all hours. She's dyin' fer more gossip, but that's all she's got fer now. My advice, jes' say yeh don't remember where yeh've been. Blame it on the whiskey. It'll save yeh some time, though Meg'll be disappointed. By now, she has it in her head that yer some sort a' wild American spy here in Drumkeeran to sort out somebody fer doin' something somewhere. Like Liam Neeson but backwards, since he's actually Irish. Meg's not too specific, on account a' she's makin' everythin' up as she goes."

"Meg wouldn't believe me if I told her," said Will.

"Yeh never can tell. Irish country folk live in the midst a' crazy tales and legend most a' their lives. Me mam once said yeh couldn't scare an Irish country wife less'n yeh popped Ol' Nick out of a bottle. Then she'd rap on 'im a couple times with her wooden spoon to make sure he was real."

Will wondered what Robert's mom would've thought about Billy, with his polished horns and braying laugh.

Robert placed his bowl in the sink and grabbed a vase full of multi-colored flowers. He brought them to the table and started arranging them, spreading the colors out a little more.

"For your wife?" asked Will. "It's your anniversary, right?"

"Tá," nodded Robert. "She wore wildflowers in her hair at our weddin', so every year, I give her a bouquet a' these. One year I did roses up nice, an' she didn't speak to me fer an hour. 'I'm not a roses lass, Robert,' she said, an' if yeh loved me right and proper, yeh would know it!'" Robert laughed. "She's a wildflower lass, me Emma. That's some-thin' special, bye, if'n yeh didn't know it. I've had me share a' roses gals, married one once when I was young and thick."

Will's eybrows shot up in surprise. "Emma's not your first wife?"

Robert shook his head. "No, no. Emma and me, we got married when I was nigh on thirty. A' course, she were only twenty-three and fresh outa university. I'd been in the Irish Army fer about six years, ever since me first wife left me fer a fancy British bollix. A real gobshite that one was. So, six years later, I was in Lebanon with the United Nations peacekeeping forces. One a' me best buds were shot in the head by the South Lebanon Army. I took a bullet to the hip in the same attack, an' we both went home. It's jus' that I traveled on a gurney. Stephen...well, he returned to 'is family in a body bag."

"I'm sorry," said Will, meaning it.

Robert stopped fidgeting with the flowers and sat down.

"Seems all things happen fer a reason, Will. Not fer Stephen, I guess, but fer me. I came home an' sat around fer a few days feelin' sorry fer meself. Then some a' me udder pals took me to a disco in Dublin, wheelchair an' all. I wasn't walkin' yet, yeh see. There was this pretty lass in the corner with all her friends, an' me and mine across the room. The two groups jus' sorta mixed."

"And that pretty girl was Emma," smiled Will.

"Heaven's no, lad!" said Robert. "That was Orlaith! She danced with me all night. Wheeled me around the floor as it were, with that 'Dancing Queen' song playin'. We were havin' a drink after the dance, an' she said she really liked me, but—"

"Don't tell me," said Will. "She just wanted to be friends. You weren't—" Will used his fingers to make quotation marks—"her type."

Robert laughed. "Tá, she did indeed. Turned out that we both liked the same type. Women."

Will laughed. "She was gay?"

"Tá. Still is, as far as I know. We talk about once a week. Her partner died last year. Breast cancer, caught too late." Robert paused and crossed himself. "Anyways, she told me she knew a lass that was fer me if any lass were. I were about seven drinks in, so's I said, 'Call her up,' an' she did. Emma snuck outa her house while her da were sleepin'. I knew Orlaith was right the moment me and Emma's eyes met."

Will shook his head. "The first time I met my wife, it was right after sleeping with her roommate." He laughed.

"An' she still went fer yeh, eh?"

"We just talked. Had a pillow fight, of all things. I bashed my head that night, too." Will laughed. "Maybe that's a theme with me."

Robert laughed.

"It was so easy, Robert. Falling in love with Cara was the easiest thing I've ever done in my life."

"Where is she now?" the older man asked. "From the lack of a smile on yer face every time I've seen yeh, I'm gonna guess she's not back in America waitin'."

"A fire," Will said. The words came out easily, maybe because he'd said it so much lately. To Seamus and Conor. Samthann. Even Billy.

Robert nodded. "How long ago?"

"Almost a year. My son died, too. Samuel."

"Ah, bye. Sorry to hear it."

"Thanks."

"I'd not be tellin' Meg, though. Yeh'll have every single lass in town tryin' to chat yeh up at dinner tomorrow night. She'd prob'ly sell tickets."

Will closed his eyes and shook his head.

Ridiculous.

Something brushed his hand. He opened his eyes to see a flower on it.

"Bluebell," said Robert. "We use it to comfort those left behind."

Will picked up the flower—a stem of four, purplish-blue flowers with cream-colored anthers.

"I have never seen anything more beautiful than the bluebell," said Robert. "I know the beauty of our Lord by it."

"That's nice," said Will. "I didn't know you were a poet."

Robert burst into laughter. "Me, a poet? Bye, yeh must be daft. I'm just readin' the card here. I bought it fer Emma coz a' the flowers on the front."

Robert held up a greeting card that had a field of bluebells, with "On Our Anniversary" inscribed over it.

"I must have a little mousie up fer cheese," a voice said in the dining room.

"Oh, shit," whispered Will. "It's Meg."

Robert grabbed Will's bowl and stuck it in front of himself.

"Go, bye! Through that other door, and quick!"

Will rushed to the back door and shoved it open. He burst into the night, then snuck back in through the front door while Meg was still talking to Robert. He shot upstairs for a shower and a change. Then he lay down for, hopefully, a few hours sleep. Tomorrow was the last day he had to complete his quest. He would need every bit of rest he could get.

Will woke to his phone alarm at 5 a.m. He washed his face, brushed his teeth, and was downstairs before even the early risers. He was just sneaking a piece of strawberry pie from the refrigerator when a familiar voice said, "William McConnelly, as I live and breathe."

He turned to see Meg in her nightdress. Her hair stuck up at different angles where it had popped free of the huge rollers she wore.

Women still wear rollers? he thought.

"We all feared yeh'd died, Will," she said.

"I'm still kicking," he replied. "Is it okay if I get a piece of this for breakfast?"

"Well, a' course! Yer welcome to anything we have. Lord knows, yeh haven't eaten enough here to feed a fly. I was afraid yeh'd ask fer the breakfast part a' yer bed and breakfast fee back! Can I get yeh some coffee?"

Will started to say no, that he didn't have time for coffee, but— "Sure," he said.

Meg's face blossomed into a smile. "Good," she said. "Then we can catch up on yer adventures in the beautiful hills a' Drumkeeran."

She made a pot of coffee, and they sat down at a table. Will dug into the pie.

"Yeh must be havin' a right wild time of it, Will," said Meg. "We've seen neither hide nor hair of yeh around here. Some a' the folks think mebbe yeh met someone special. Mebbe even that bartender what knocked yeh up a coupla days back to take yeh to the fair."

Will choked at the words "knocked yeh up."

Meg rose and patted him on the back. "C'mon, Will," she said. "Get it up. There's a lad."

"Knocked me up?" he sputtered.

Meg returned to her seat. "Yeh know. Knocked on yer door and woke yeh up. Yeh *did* go to the fair with the lass, didn't yeh?"

Will remembered Robert's advice from the night before. "I think so," he said, "but my memory is a little hazy. I've been enjoying the pub a little too much since I've been here."

"Oh, yeh've been carryin' on like a stallion in a field a' mares!" said Meg. Then she realized the connotation of her words. Her face turned beet red. "Well, not like that, Will. I just meant...ummm."

Will put his hand on hers. "I know what you mean, Meg." He sighed.

"You're right. I've been having too much of a good time. The thing is, I'm about to go on this...outing?" Will couldn't say quest, because that would make him sound crazy.

"Do yeh need some things to take with yeh?" asked Meg. "I could put together a sammy, and I've a nice salad I made fer lunch today. I could put some in a Tupperware round fer yeh."

"I'll be fine, foodwise," Will said, smiling. "It's just that, I'm a bit of a"— *what's a good word?*—"ummm, a thrillseeker?"

"Thrillseeker?" Meg said. Her eyes opened wide, and her hand crept out from beneath his to cover her heart. "What do yeh mean?"

"I...I ride motorcycles through fiery hoops."

Meg gasped.

"Well, not really. But stuff like that. Ziplining and mountain climbing. Uh...cliff diving! I dive off cliffs."

"Oh, Will! Why would yeh do things like that? Yeh could get yerself killed, couldn't yeh?"

"It's possible, I guess." Will chose his next words carefully. "The thing is, I leave instructions in my room any time I go on one of my adventures. Just in case something bad happens, you know?"

"Yer goin' out now, aren't yeh? To do somethin' crazy, as yeh say."

"Yes," Will said. "I was gonna leave you a note, but—"

"Oh, dear!" Meg yelled. She jumped from her seat, her chest bouncing so much that her bra almost gave up the ghost. "Speakin' a' notes!" She rushed from the dining room and returned with an envelope and a flower. "Here." She handed him the envelope. "Someone left this at the front desk fer yeh last night. And Robert asked me to give yeh this." She handed Will the flower. "He was up late grabbin' a bite a' stew an' gave it to me in case I saw yeh. That's one a' the reasons I'm up so early this mornin'."

Will took the flower, another blue one, this time with small, golden anthers in the center.

"It's a blue violet, Will. Protection against evil and bad luck. Oh! Did Robert know yeh were a...a thrillseeker?"

"I may have mentioned it," Will said, twirling the flower stem between his fingers.

"Well, maybe that's why he left it fer yeh. Thrillseekers should avoid bad luck with all four legs, I suppose."

Will laughed. "You're probably right." He dropped the flower into the pocket of his hoodie. Then he tore open the envelope, which had a scrap of paper inside, and a scrawl in cursive. He angled the paper toward the light to see better, or, at least, that's what he hoped he appeared to be doing. Really, he was trying to make sure that Meg's straining neck didn't give her the angle she needed to read over his shoulder.

"Will," he read silently. "Left the book with Samthann at the pub and this note with the proprietor of this establishment. Seamus has developed a case a' the scoots. He ain't wanderin' far from the loo today. Yeh've one day left, lad. Good luck ta yeh! Can I say, we hope ta never see yeh again? Go find yer Fairy Queen. Conor, with Seamus."

"Is it bad news?" asked Meg, still trying to steal a peek. Will folded the note and stuck it in the envelope.

"Kind of," said Will. "I've got to get going. If I'm not back in two days, please contact my father-in-law, Aidan Brady. He's the one who made the reservation." He strode to the door, then looked back at Meg. Her face was flush, her eyes watery. She was truly worried about him. A stranger she barely knew.

She's sweet, he thought.

Will returned and gave her a small kiss on the cheek. "You're an amazing hostess," he said. "Thanks for everything."

"Bless yeh, Will McConnelly," Meg said, breathless. "Yeh come back with all yer limbs attached, if'n yeh please."

"I'll try."

Though it was only six in the morning, Will took a right on the sidewalk and headed for the pub.

There's no way Samthann would be there this early, he thought. *Or this late.* Whichever it was, he had to hope she was there. She had the instructions for the final quest.

Overhead, lightning forked through the air, preceding a huge thunderclap. Will stopped to look at the sky, at the dark clouds moving in on the morning sun. He remembered that Conor had promised a storm, and he thought to himself, *It's almost here.*

"GODDAMMIT, WILLIAM MCCONNELLY," SAYS CARA, throwing her purse on the couch. "Why do you have to be so arrogant?"

Will almost chokes on his water. They've just come from a party for one of Cara's artist friends. Will knows that something is wrong because Cara hasn't spoken the entire car ride home. Still, he wasn't expecting an attack.

"Arrogant? What are you talking about?" He screws the cap back on his water bottle and sets it on the dining room table.

"The way you talked to Denise!"

Will rolls his eyes toward the ceiling, trying to remember what he'd said.

"And don't roll your eyes at me like I'm stupid!"

"Seriously?" he says. "I was just trying to—"

"You do it all the time, Will. Every time you think—"

"I do what?"

"Every time you think I'm—"

"I was trying to remember—"

"It's like you think I don't—"

Will slaps his hand on the table. It stings…a lot.

"Can I finish a thought?" he shouts. "Please?"

Cara gets right in his face. "Because your thoughts are so goddamned better than mine? Because you're so smart you're the only person in the room worth listening to?"

Will doesn't push her hard. He's just trying to get her out of his face. Her heel catches in the carpet, and down she goes, slamming her elbow on the edge of one of the wooden dining chairs as she falls.

She screams and rolls over, grabbing her arm.

Will springs to her side. "Cara? Shit! Are you okay?"

She rolls back over and slaps him as hard as she can with her left hand, the one connected to the forearm connected to the elbow that hit the chair. The slap stings worse than his slap on the table.

"Well, I guess you're okay then," he says.

"You shoved me down!" she cries.

"I pushed you away because you were screaming in my face, and you tripped." He takes a breath and realizes that he's scared. Really scared. "But it was my fault. I'm sorry."

Cara gets up, still cradling her elbow. Tears pour down her cheeks. "Fuck you!" she yells. She darts for the bedroom and slams the door behind her. Will sees the doorknob jiggle as she locks it.

"What the hell?" he says. He waits for a moment, to see if she'll return. "Fine!" he yells at the door.

He heads for the fridge and opens the freezer door, retrieving the bottle of Rumple Minze he and Cara keep there for emergencies. Normally, that entails a shot or two to relax after a rough day. Last week, they'd toasted their eighteen-month wedding anniversary. Tonight is the first time in their marriage he's actually considered the bottle an emergency resource.

Will pours a shot in a cocktail glass. Since the shot looks so small in such a big glass, he doubles it. He plops down on the couch and sinks into cushiness.

Okay, he thinks. *Cara said "Denise." Denise is the one who...oh. Denise.*

She was the one who talked on and on about Dali.

Droned, he thought. *Not talked.*

Denise, one of Cara's professors, is a Salvador Dali fanatic. Earlier, she got on a soapbox about how Dali took cubism and elevated it into his own style of surrealism...blah blah blah.

Then she misstated a fact about Dali's time with Disney. Being a huge entertainment trivia nerd, Will explained that she was wrong.

Explained?

Will's own thoughts are skeptical.

"I threw her under the bus," he says aloud. "In front of her friends." He sighs. "In front of Cara."

Shit.

Will polishes off the Rumple. If it had been Cara drinking it, she would have exhaled a minty blast of breath. She says that Rumple makes her feel like an ice dragon. Of course, she only says that when she's high. Will laughs.

I love that girl so much.

He grabs another glass and pours two more shots in each, then heads for the bedroom.

"Cara?" he says. He presses his ear to the door just as something slams into it. That something hits the floor and shatters.

"What did...? Did you just throw a glass at the door?"

"I'd rather throw it at your stupid face!" she screams.

Will fights back the urge to react in anger. Where has that gotten them?

He breathes and counts, in to four and out to eight, until his heartbeat slows.

Stay calm, he thinks.

"I'm a dick," he says, trying to push his voice through the wood of the door.

Something else hits the wood. This time, nothing shatters.

"Shoe?" he asks.

"Shoe!" she yells.

"Honey, I'm a dick! I didn't realize it at the time, but I do now. I'm a giant, first-class dick!"

He hears nothing at first, but then a tiny bit of laughter eeks to him through the door.

"You're not a giant dick," she yells. "You're a...a tiny...small-minded dick!"

"Maybe not...tiny!" he says. "But I'll accept average on the standard European scale."

She laughs a little louder. "You're not supposed to make me laugh when I'm pissed at you. I need to be able to express my emotions."

"I want you to express your emotions," he says. "But I love hearing you laugh."

Something thumps the door.

"Is that your head?" he asks.

"Yes."

"Here's mine." Will taps his head against the door. "Now it's like we're together, except one of us has a giant piece of wood glued to his forehead."

Cara laughs.

"Back up," she says.

Will does, and she opens the door. He hands the glass of Rumple to her.

She sniffs it. "Emergency Rumple?" she says. "Good idea."

They clink their glasses and shoot. Cara breathes out a long exhalation. "I just burned you with my ice breath," she says.

"Thank God I have my shield of douchebaggery," Will replies.

Silence.

"Babe, I really am sorry for tonight. It was wrong, what I said."

Cara opens the door and grabs his hand. "Come on." She leads him to the bed, where they sit on the edge staring at one of her paintings. Cara takes Will's glass and sets both glasses down beside the bed.

"It's not that you were wrong, Will."

"I was wrong." He pauses. "Well, what I was saying wasn't wrong, but I—"

"You—" she says.

"Shouldn't have said it," they say in unison.

"I mean, Denise can be way too much," Cara says.

"Tell me."

"But so can you."

Will pretend-chokes, then looks down at his chest. He removes an imaginary dagger from his heart and falls backward onto the bed.

"I'm serious," Cara says. "Let people start talking about anything you know and you immediately usurp the conversation. You're a...a...trivia Nazi."

"Whoa whoa," says Will, a little hurt. "I'm not that bad."

"Honey, I love the fact that you're one of the smartest men I know, but loving a fact and loving a person are two different things. You don't have to be a teacher all the time, you know."

"Professor," he says.

"What?"

"Ummm…I teach college, so I'm a professor."

Cara jumps on top of him and play-slaps him on the chest.

"That's exactly what I'm talking about!" she says. "It's like you're better than everybody else." She slips into a bad German accent. "You vill listen to me becuz I am your professor. Zo shut up and learn, you little theatre svine."

"Stop it," he laughs.

"You stop it!" she says. "Stop being a dick."

Cara reaches around Will and tickles him in his back ribs, the only place he's still ticklish.

"No no no!" he howls. He pulls her face to his. She opens her mouth and kisses him. The tickling stops.

After a few minutes, Cara rolls off. They lay side by side, catching their breaths. Her hand finds his.

"Didn't we promise we were never going to fight again?" Will asks. "That night when you painted all the little one-letter signs?"

"Yes," Cara says.

"How long ago was that?"

"Six months."

Will pauses, thinking. "How many arguments have we had in those six months?"

"About twelve…maybe."

Will's eyes narrow, and he cocks his head at Cara.

"Okay," she says. "Twenty? Thirty? We're artists, Will. Did you really think we'd never fight?"

"I just want us to be the perfect couple," he replies, a little sad. "I love you more than I ever dreamed I could love. I don't want to hurt you."

"Then love me, no matter if we fight or not. Then we can be the little old couple on the cruise ship."

"Cara McConnelly, I love you."

"William McConnelly, I love you."

Cara pops up from the bed and rushes across the room.

"What?" Will asks.

"I have something to show you."

She grabs a little plastic stick from the top of their chest-of-drawers. It's a pregnancy test.

Will sits up, then stands.

"Are we...?"

She turns it over. Will examines it closely.

"It's a blue line," he notes. "A little, horizontal blue line."

"It's supposed to be vertical for a baby." Cara gives him a half-smile. "I didn't want to look at it alone. Sorry if I disappointed you."

"You didn't," Will says, "and don't worry. It'll happen. When the world is ready to meet the most amazing baby of all time, it'll happen."

Cara tosses the stick in a little trashcan beside the bed, then sits.

"It could happen tonight, if you're lucky." She pats the bed beside her, and Will sits.

"Well, we've already had some emergency Rumple Minze," he says.

"True."

"So, if you're really an ice dragon...." he begins, then pauses. He kisses her ear and her neck and eases her back against the pillow.

"If I'm really an ice dragon, what?" Cara asks.

Will traces her collarbone lightly with his tongue. He moves to her breasts, then to her belly button. He rests his chin on her belly and looks up at her.

She returns his gaze. "Why did you stop?"

"If you're really an ice dragon," he continues, "we're gonna have to redo our bedroom ceiling tomorrow."

"Oh," Cara says. She lays her head back on the pillow. Will kisses lower, and lower again. The "oh" becomes a moan, and after a few minutes, the moan becomes a scream.

SAMTHANN SAT ON THE STEPS OF THE PUB WHEN WILL GOT there.

"I'm not surprised you're here," he said. "But I'm curious. As to the how and why."

Without a word, Sam handed him a folded note.

Will unfolded it and read, *Dear Sam. I need to explain some things to you, and to apologize and maybe even ask for your help. Not that I deserve it. Can you please meet me at the pub early in the morning? Will.*

Will looked up from the note. "Where did you get this?"

"It were waitin' on me at home after work, about two hours ago. If the explanation can wait ten minutes, I'm gonna be needin' a cup or three a' coffee."

"Did they...did I leave a book with the note?"

Sam shook her head. "No book." She stood. "Coffee."

"Coffee," Will repeated.

Sam unlocked the pub and he followed her inside. She flipped the light switch.

"Mary, mother a' God," she whispered.

On a table between the main bar and the door sat the book, and behind it, an ancient-looking scabbard.

Will shuffled to the table and picked up the scabbard. He looked at Sam and shrugged.

She shook her head as if to say, "Don't ask me."

Will unsheathed the sword. A spark of blue light shot through the blade, and the grooved metal grip buzzed in Will's hand with an electric-like charge.

"Shit!" said Will.

"It can't be," Samthann said.

"Can't be what?"

"The Claidheamh Soluis," she whispered.

"The Clive-what?" he asked. His eyes were glued to the weapon as light continued to play across the blade.

"The Claidheamh Soluis," she repeated. "A mystical weapon, if'n yeh can believe it. It's from Gaelic mythology. Thousands a' years ago, the Tuatha Dé Danann, the tribe that followed the goddess Danu, brought four treasures from the Otherworld. Magical treasures to help mankind. The Claidheamh Soluis is the sword of light brought from the island city of Finias. Accordin' ta legend, a famous warrior named Lugh killed a huge, one-eyed giant with it." Sam shook her head. "But it was a spear in that legend. Jaysus, I need coffee. I'm either daft or dreamin'."

Sam stumbled behind the bar and grabbed the funnel for the large coffee maker. She opened a metal can and filled the funnel with strong, fragrant coffee, then placed it inside the urn and pushed the "on" button. She struggled to keep her eyes open as she crawled on top of the bar like a cat and collapsed.

Will sheathed the blade. For some reason, holding it was more real to him than anything else that had happened the last three days. He was a certified stage combat instructor, trained in falls and lifts, tumbling and fight choreography. Sword fighting had been his specialty in college, and he'd maintained his skills since, at least until the fire. He supposed he was a little rusty, but the sword felt good.

Will lay the scabbard down and picked up the book. He opened it. "What the hell!" he said.

"What?" asked Sam, eyes still closed. Behind her, the coffee began to pour, an aromatic stream that scented the room.

"This doesn't make sense," said Will. He closed the book and looked at the cover. "It's the same book." He opened it again.

Sam sat up. "What are yeh blatherin' about?"

"Look." Will shoved the book into her hands. "What do you see?"

"A title." She flipped through a few pages. "Words, pictures...it's a book, Will. What's it s'posed ta be?"

"A book in English, right?"

"Tá."

"But it wasn't in English two days ago when Conor read it to me! It was in Gaelic. That's why I couldn't read it myself." He set the book on the bar. "Sam, I didn't leave a note at your house last night."

"Bollocks," she muttered.

"I didn't. I didn't even write it."

"What do ya mean yeh didn't write the note? I'm here on not even two hours a' sleep 'coz yeh said yeh needed help. Don't tell me yeh didn't write the note."

"I do need help," Will said. He tried to shake the cobwebs from his head. "Look, I have a long story to tell you. If you don't call me a liar afterwards.... I don't know. Maybe you *can* help."

Sam rubbed her eyes and yawned. "Will, have yeh never wondered why I've been so nice ta yeh?"

Will laughed unintentionally and stifled it as soon as he could. "Sorry," he said.

"What?"

"Nice to me? You...you say...." Will laughed again. "You've broken my nose, slapped me, thrown a stapler at me." He threw up his hands. "And then invited me to a fair and wanted me to dance. Ever heard of mixed signals, Samthann?"

Sam stared at him, looking almost confused. "Mebbe I've seemed a bit mental...once or twice."

"Or every time we've been together."

"But Will. It's hard ta meet the man a' yer dreams."

The words hung in the air like breath on a wintry day. Like an ice dragon's breath. Will blinked a couple times, as if that could help him make sense of what she'd said. "Pardon me...uh, what?"

"Sit down. What do yeh like in yer coffee?" Sam swung her legs around to the other side of the bar and grabbed two cups.

"Ummm...two teaspoons of sanity, please?" he said, sitting. "And a little milk if the coffee's strong."

"We're all outa sanity"—she laughed—"but the coffee is most certainly strong."

Sam snagged cups, a glass of ice, and a little pitcher of milk. She placed all that and a spoon in front of Will, then sat across from him. He sipped his coffee, then added milk. Quite a bit of milk, because the coffee was really strong. The old ritual felt good. For the last ten months, more often than not, he'd had a beer first thing in the morning.

Voluntary alcoholism.

It wasn't, after all, the alcohol that had enslaved him. He'd given himself to it, and to despair. He glanced at the sword again, at the scabbard. Maybe he was almost done with despair.

Sam dumped four chunks of ice into her coffee and stirred, then drained half the cup. "It'll take a minute," she said, "but the coffee'll set me right soon enough." She smiled and looked at her hands. She seemed almost shy now.

A shaft of morning sunlight reached through the window and caressed the side of her face. Even exhausted, Will found her beautiful.

Sam raised her head and looked at him. "I started dreamin' about yeh eight months ago," she said. "There yeh were, in a field a' clover at dawn. There were a look on yer face that made me gasp when I woke. It was as if yeh were seein' the sunrise fer the first time in yer life."

Will frowned. "You mean...you dreamed of someone who looked like me, right? Not me."

Sam shook her head. "No, it was yeh, as sure as it'll rain in the hills some time today. It was the first dream, but not the last."

She reached out and took Will's hand from the cup he was holding. Her fingers were warm from her coffee, and they were smooth and pale. The handclasp seemed strange, because Will's hands had been empty for so long.

Cara's hands had always been tinted because of her paints, reds and blues underneath her fingernails. Samuel's fingers had been so tiny. He and Will had played the "look whose hand is bigger" game all the time. Sam's little hand barely covered half of Will's. Those were the last hands he'd held. He struggled to not jerk his hand away from Samthann's. For all of the wrong he felt, there was right there, too.

"Me seanmháthair—my grandmother—had the sight," Sam said. She absently ran her thumb over Will's knuckles. "She ne'er talked about it much, but she would tell people things that helped 'em, when they'd listen. My cousin Bartley, fer instance. One day, he's heading ta Dublin fer a big music festival. Máthair Mhór says ta him, "Leave now, bye, or yeh'll ne'er get there in time." It weren't but two hours there, Will, an' it were eight in the mornin'. The festival didn't start until sundown. Bartley, he ain't one fer listenin', totters around town doin' nuthin' good. He leaves at noon. Well, there was a big truck that loses its chemical tanker five miles outa Navan, and they shut everythin' down. Bartley's three hours late to the festival and misses the whole first night a' bands."

"Huh," said Will. He pulled his fingers away from hers under the pretense of adding more milk to his coffee. In truth, her touch felt too good. He didn't want his fingers to get used to it.

"She saved me da's life one time, too," Sam continued. "She told him ta stay home from work. There was a mining accident that day—he worked in the zinc mines—ten of his mates were buried in a cave-in. Only three came out alive." She looked back down at her cup. "If me seanmháthair had still been livin' two years ago, me parents wouldn'ta gone to the games in Paris. Me aintín had bought them tickets to the football finals for Christmas. Me da loved the games, and me mam had always wanted ta go to Paris."

"What happened?" asked Will.

"Yeh don't remember?" she asked. "The ISIS bombin's?"

"Jesus," he said. "I didn't think about the timing." He was the one who reached out this time. He took her hand in his.

"It were first time me mam had been outa Ireland since she were six. Her parents had taken her ta London ta go ta the museums and see where the Queen lived."

"I'm sorry," Will said.

"Everyone was sorry. The truth is, what does it matter? No amount a' sorry can bring 'em back, yeh know?"

Will nodded. "It's the same with my wife and son."

Her hand squeezed his. "How long ago?" she asked.

"Ten months, but it feels longer. Time's a funny thing when you're...when you're, what? Going insane? Drinking too much and ignoring everybody who cares about you?"

Sam nodded. Silence, then, "How did it happen, if yeh can talk about it?"

"Bad wiring in our house," said Will. "I was at a rehearsal at the college where I teach...taught. It was late when I headed home. Cara and Samuel were already in bed. By the time I got there...." His words hung in the air, unfinished.

"An' yer son's name was Samuel. Sam."

"Yes."

"And Cara?"

"Caralin," said Will. He pulled away and leaned back in his seat. "Her father and mother were from around here, but she'd never been to Ireland. Aidan, Cara's dad...he felt guilty for never bringing Cara and

Samuel to see their homeland. He asked me to spread their ashes here." He paused. "They're in my room at the bed and breakfast."

"Still?"

"I...I got busy."

Sam laughed. "Yeh got busy drinkin' in me pub," she said. Her smile softened. "Yeh didn't want ta leave 'em yet."

"I guess not," said Will. It was more complicated than that, but she was close enough.

She rose to get refills for their coffee and more milk in Will's little pitcher.

"It's funny," she said. "I've dreamed yeh fer so long, and everything in me dreams were in sunshine and laughter. Sometimes we were at the fair and...there was always dancin'. Yeh would grab me around the waist and twirl me until I couldn't catch me breath. Can yeh understand what a shock it was to meet yeh...so sad an' such?"

Will smiled. "A week ago," he said, "I would've thought you were crazy. Ten minutes ago, I unsheathed a sword that slew a giant. 'There are more things in heaven and Earth, Horatio, than are dreamt of in your philosophy.'"

"Hamlet," said Sam.

"Shakespeare loved ghosts and fairies," said Will, adding milk to his fresh cup of coffee. "I wonder if he saw them, or if he was just writing about things he'd heard. Like I said, a week ago...."

"A week ago, I wouldn'ta had me hand kissed by an old, black billy goat," said Sam.

"You saw him?"

"I did. Outa the corner a' me eyes. He looked like a vagabond from the front, but me grandmother always said if'n yeh want ta see a pùca, yeh have to look at 'em from the side." She added more ice to her coffee, then drank. "So, how did yer adventure finish up last night? Did yeh win yer contest? I feared yeh might have a heart attack in the middle a' the pub when I brought yeh yer bill."

"I have no clue what my bank account looks like right now," said Will. "I really didn't think it mattered. I guess I still don't, if I have a shot of getting into the fairy kingdom."

Sam stopped drinking in mid-sip. "What did yeh say?"

Will grabbed the book and pushed it over to her.

"It's in the book. The other night, my second night here, I saw the castle of the Fairy Queen. Here."

He opened the book to the beginning of the last chapter, where Conor had begun. "Read."

Twenty minutes later, Sam closed the book. Her tired eyes met Will's. "Yeh raced a selkie?"

"That was how I got so bruised and bloody, the day you found me on your doorstep. I don't remember if I ever apologized about that, by the way."

"Yeh didn't, but I mighta been heavin' a stapler at yer head, so I won't hold it against yeh."

"Thanks."

Sam pushed the book back to the center of the table.

"Yeh were on the verge a' dyin', and now yeh barely have a scratch on yeh. How?"

"Well, there was this magic pool, kind of a Fountain of Youth thing that doesn't make you young but heals you."

"Really?" Sam asked.

Will laughed. "I'm gonna wake up in a nut house and you're gonna be the girl next door, I swear." He shook his head. "How can any of this be real? I mean, you think you know how the world works, and then a six-foot-tall black goat with creepy eyes tells you to go ride an Irish water spirit that looks like a horse."

"A kelpie?"

"Yep."

"Yeh rode a kelpie?"

"Me and two Irish kids. Padraig and Alannah. Then we dug up gold. The kids kept that, but I got this." Will reached into his pocket and retrieved the stone with the hole in its center. He handed it to Sam.

"An adder stone," she breathed. She looked through the hole at Will. "Nope, yer not a fairy."

"It's magic?"

"Tá. It lets yeh see fairy magic. If yer babby were taken by the fairies, say, an' replaced with a changeling, then yeh could tell. Yeh'd look through the stone an' see this ugly, deformed thing."

"Fairies do that sort of thing?" Will asked. "Steal babies?"

"Accordin' to legend. The changeling is a fairy that's the spittin' image a' yer child, so's yeh never know they're gone."

"But the adder stone can help you get your baby back, right?"

Sam shook her head. "It can show yeh the changeling, but yer child would be gone by then. Once yeh enter the fairy kingdom, yeh can never return." Sam's eyes grew wide, and then her shoulders slumped. "Which is what yeh want ta do, tà? Disappear?"

Will looked away. "It's too hard here," he said. "A week ago, I just wanted to kill myself. Let the depression win. Then I saw the fairy castle and found out that I could go there. Live in a place with no pain."

Sam opened Will's hand and placed the adder stone on his palm. She curled his fingers around the stone, then covered his hand with both of hers. "Will, if there's no pain, what is there? Can yeh have joy without sorrow? On Sundays, the priest talks about heaven bein' a place a' pure happiness in the light a' God, but ain't that why we spend so many years here on Earth? If we don't understand how hard life is, would bliss mean anythin'? What will an eternity a' happiness be like without a nice fight every now and again?"

Will laughed. "You do like to fight, don't you?"

"Nothin' gets done if there's not some discussion. How's a mountain born, if not from of a volcano?"

"I guess." Will squeezed her hand. "But I'm tired of mountains. I'm not strong enough to keep climbing."

"A man who raced a selkie, outdrank a pùca, and beat a kelpie," said Sam. "Not strong enough?"

More silence. How could Will explain any more than he already had?

Eventually, Sam sighed and pulled her hands away from his. "All right, then. It looks like the last part of yer quest is...what was it?" She opened the book and flipped to the back. "Yeh have ta...gain the key to the barrows from the Leanán sídhe and then take the head of the Questing Beast." Her face grew troubled.

"What is it?" asked Will.

"If this is real," she said, "and if I can accept selkies and kelpies and pùcas, then why wouldn't I believe?" She laughed.

"Samthann?"

She shook her head. "All these things yeh've done so far, they're nothin', Will." She tapped the book. "Accordin' ta this, the third quest will lead yeh straight ta Hell. Yeh'll take that sword and challenge the son a' the devil himself."

She turned the book around so that Will could see the picture of a dragon-like creature with the head and neck of a serpent and the body of a leopard.

Will touched the picture, and a bolt of lightning flashed outside the pub. A thunderclap roared.

He jumped.

"Oh, tà," said Samthann, nodding. "Yeh'll make a right fine warrior, Will. Unless it rains."

Chapter Twelve

STORM

WILL and Sam were soaked to the skin during the first half of the trip to Boyne Valley and the Newgrange burial mound. Newgrange, a five-thousand-year-old passage tomb was, according to Sam, the most likely place to begin the third quest. Just getting to Sam's car, however, left them drenched.

"We'll take the tour," she said. "Mayhap yeh can use yer adder stone to find a way farther inside, to the Leanán sídhe."

The torrential downpour followed them on the road. Luckily, Sam had recently replaced her wiper blades, and the heater blew toasty warm air. Eventually, they dried out.

"Will they run tours with all this rain?" asked Will.

"If they stopped takin' guests because a' rain, the tourism board'd throw a banshee fit," said Sam. "A flood like this now, I don't know. We have a while a'fore we get there, so maybe we'll get a wee break. Lord willin'."

Will opened the book to the drawing of the Questing Beast. "Before we left," he said, "you were telling me that the Questing Beast was the son of the devil."

"Son or daughter," said Sam. She swerved a little to miss a chunk of tire tread in the road, then immediately braked. The driver ahead of her was doing half the posted speed. Sam waited until she topped the upcoming hill, then passed him.

"Seems like you're a good driver," Will noted.

"Oh, no," Sam replied. "I've been in seven accidents the las' three years. The Road Safety Authority threatened ta take me license, but one a' me best customers is a manager there. He got me off with a warnin'."

"That's...comforting." Will focused on his breathing. In with the light and out with the dark.

Think good thoughts. No car crashes today.

"So, yeh want ta know more about the Questin' Beast, do yeh?" Sam asked.

"You can just focus on the road," Will said. "We've got plenty of time to talk later." He checked his seatbelt.

Sam laughed. "C'mon, Will! A week ago, yeh were suicidal. Now yer worried about a car wreck that prob'ly won't happen?" She patted his knee.

"Look out!" he yelled.

Sam jerked her head back around to the road just in time to see a rabbit staring at her car.

Bump!

Will took a huge breath and held it as Sam pulled the car to the side of the road. Neither of them spoke for a good two minutes.

"Should you...go back and check on it?" Will asked.

Sam shook her head. "I hit it goin' sixty kilometers an hour with the driver's side tire. It's prob'ly at the pearly gates right now complainin' about the dumb bitch in the Ford Focus."

A horn honked, and the slow-moving car passed them on the right.

"I guess we should...get back on the road," said Will.

"All right, then," said Sam. She pulled back onto the road, passed the slow-moving car again, and sped on toward Boyne Valley.

"So, this son of the devil," said Will a few minutes later. "Is it a biblical thing? The Anti-Christ or whatever?"

"Oh, no," said Sam. "This pre-dates Christianity by hunnerds a' years. Celtic mythology ran along the same time as the Greeks an' Romans, though it weren't as organized. We borrowed a lot from other peoples. It fascinated me as a lass, so me da gave me a book about the Tuatha Dé Danann an' the gods and goddesses. The Tuatha Dé were the forces a' good in the world, the warriors and builders and growers. They were opposed by the Fomorians, who loved only destruction and death.

"This next part weren't in the book me da bought. That were a picture book fer wee lads an' lasses. Accordin' ta the more adult legends, there once was a woman who was in love with her brother. It were an evil thought to lie with one born of the same mother, even in the oldest days. So, she went to one a' the Fomorians, a death god named Crom Cruach. She pleaded with him to make her brother fall in love with her. Crom Cruach offered to do this only if she would lie with him, which she did. Then he refused to keep his part a' the bargain.

"Nine months later, she gave birth to a monster that burst up through her innards with the roar a' thirty wild hounds. After devouring the midwife and its own mother, it disappeared inta the woods. Next time it were seen, it was the size of a dragon. Head and neck of a snake, body of a leopard, haunches of a lion, an' feet of a hart."

"That's a lot of animals for one creature," said Will.

"Tá. The legends, they go on sometimes. Maybe they exaggerate. Yeh can tell me if'n yeh find it, and yeh have time to count all its parts while it's tryin' ta tear yer head off." Sam laughed a little, then stopped. "I thought that'd be funnier." She took his hand. "If yeh really do meet it, don't let it tear yer head off, okay?" She tousled his hair, then gripped the wheel again.

Will closed his eyes, feeling her touch even after her fingers were gone. He wished her touch could be enough to wipe away all the bad things in his head. Nothing could do that, though. Except maybe a fairy queen.

The rain had slowed by the time they arrived at the Brú na Bóinne Visitor Centre. Huge glass windows fronted the beautiful building, and giant rocks dotted the landscape. Inside, a handful of people stood in line for the tour. Will checked the clock on the wall. 9:00 a.m. The centre had just opened, according to the hours posted beside the front entrance. Whatever this quest was, he needed to get started. He had to finish and return to the hills of Drumkeeran by dawn tomorrow morning.

"Not a lotta time," murmured Sam.

"What did you say?" he asked. *Did she read my mind?*

"I said, not a big line. Normally, this place has tourists out the door year-round. The storm was a godsend. Fer us, at least."

"Hmmm."

The short line moved at a good pace. After Will passed twelve Euros to the clerk, he and Sam crossed the pedestrian bridge and boarded a tour bus. As they drove up through green and brown patches of grazing land dotted with sheep, an elderly tour guide spoke through the bus microphone. "Top a' the morning to ya, visitors and friends alike."

Various greetings came from the passengers, amiable people fresh off their morning coffee.

Will marveled that no one asked what he had strapped to his back. He'd intended to try to hide the sword somehow, but Sam disagreed.

"Hide it in plain sight," she'd said. "If they ask, it's just a fancy walkin' stick yeh brought with yeh."

So, he'd strapped the scabbard on his back, the handle partially obscured by the hood of his hoodie.

"Well, if'n yeh've been here before, this speech'll be nothin' new. An' even though the word 'new' might be the beginning of the place we're visitin', I promise yeh the mound is not. No, friends. Newgrange was here well before the birth of our Lord on December 25th, 0000."

That elicited a few laughs from the crowd, which seemed to please the old man.

"Tá. The Newgrange was first owned by the monks a' the Cistercian Abbey, the order a' Saint Malachy. There were about a hunnerd or so good Catholic byes that lived in Mellifont in the year 1142. They acquired the land around the monument we now call Newgrange. The name 'grange' refers to a farm, an' that's how the mound got its name.

"Now, that's in the year of our Lord, a' course," he said. "Way before then, the name given the tomb was Sí in Bhrú, which means 'the fairy mound of the Brú.' Supposedly, they were built by Tuatha Dé Danaan, the People of the Goddess Danu. The Celtic people worshiped a collection of over three hundred Celtic gods, one a' the largest pantheons of its day. When man began overpopulatin' the earth, the Tuatha Dé Danaan disappeared. Legends say that they moved inside fairy mounds and forts such as Newgrange and, just down the road a tetch, Knowth an' Dowth."

By now, the bus was pulling up to the front of the monument.

"Right there in front a' the tomb, yeh can see a series a' standin' stones. Those've been carbon-dated as much as seventy-three hundred years old, which is even older than some a' the lasses I've carbon dated." He waited for laughs.

There were a few, along with some groans.

"Fine, fine" he said. "At my age, I'll take a weak laugh or a strong pint any day. Now, when yeh get out a' the coach, yeh can stop an' look at the standin' stones if'n yeh have a mind to. Otherwise, jus' go straight up the wooden stair over the great stones of the entryway. One a' the things yeh'll notice is all the swirls carved into the stones and in the tomb itself. They're called triple spirals, and they're from Celtic and pre-Celtic times. Professors at the university say they have religious significance a' some sort, but me? I think back in olden times it meant something like 'Aidan + Betha 4ever.'"

Will stopped breathing.

Sam cupped his chin with her hand. "Will, yeh've gone pale as a ghost. Are yeh okay?"

The tour guide was still talking, but Will couldn't hear what he said over the roar inside his head.

"Aidan and Betha," he whispered.

"What the tour guide said?" asked Sam. "It were a joke, Will."

He turned to her. "They were Cara's parents, Sam. Betha died of cancer over four years ago."

"Fuck me," Sam breathed.

"I'm where I'm supposed be," Will said. He pulled Sam into a huge hug, then took her face in her hands. "This is where it happens. Thank you, Sam!" He kissed her—a quick peck on the lips. "Let's go!"

The door opened, and most everyone applauded. Many handed the smiling guide a Euro or two as they stepped off the bus. As Will passed by, he gave the man ten Euros.

"Thank yeh kindly," the guide said, surprised.

"Thank *you* kindly," said Will.

When he and Sam stepped off the bus, she said, "He wasn't lookin' ta get rich, Will."

"I paid seven hundred Euros to drink with a goat last night. Ten isn't gonna kill me." He adjusted the strap on his sword. "Besides, if I manage to get into the fairy kingdom, I don't think I'm gonna need a bunch of cash." He headed for the wooden stairs.

She didn't start away with him. "Well, yer certainly welcome ta leave the rest ta me!" yelled Sam. "An' yeh shouldn'ta kissed me like that, William McConnelly, what with yeh runnin' off ta yer death and such. It's rude!"

He turned. "C'mon, already!"

"Don't get up," Will whispered as Cara slid off him.

"I'm not," she smiled. She slid into the warm, perfect spot in the small space between his upper arm and chest where it seemed her cheek fit perfectly. Will pushed his hand into her hair like a decorative comb.

A shudder ran through him, a kind of post-orgasm muscle release. The sweat rolling off him was already giving him chills. He liked turning the a/c down to sixty-five when they made love.

"God, I love make-up sex," Cara breathed.

"I love sex with you any way I can get it," Will replied, "but I kinda hate going through the whole argument thing to get to it."

She slapped him lightly. "Hey, it's not like we only have sex when we argue."

"I didn't say that."

"'Cause that would be an asshole thing to say, and I might have to get mad at you just so we could do it again."

"Are you ready to go again?" he asked. "Cuz I can prob'ly—"

"Not yet," she said. "I want some snuggle time first."

"Good. I need to catch my breath."

They lay there, arms wrapped around each other. Will's eyes closed, and he was just drifting off when—

"Of course, if you'd decided where you wanted to go for dinner instead of pushing it off on me," said Cara, "we could've had regular sex instead of makeup sex. Though in my book, makeup sex is hotter."

Will's eyes popped open.

"That's what the argument was about?" he asked.

"That's how it started," she said. "Then it went into all sorts of little things—how I leave splotches of paint all over the kitchen sink, how—"

Will sat up, dislodging Cara from her happy spot.

"You do, all the time! And I have to clean it up, along with most of the dishes, 'cuz, god forbid, you load a dishwasher every once in a while! Why don't you just go to the sink in the garage? You know, the one within two feet of your painting room?"

Cara's mouth hung open in shock.

Will relaxed and smiled. "Was that kind of how it went?"

Her eyes widened, and she slapped him harder. "Asshole!"

She rolled off the bed and strode toward the door, with Will close behind.

"Wait, I was just playing!"

Cara reached for the doorknob. Will pushed his hand against the door.

"Please don't," he said.

She stood there, back to him, then turned with a smile.

"Huh?" said Will, confused.

"What?" Cara said. "You think just because I'm an artist I can't act?"

"You bitch!" Will grinned through the expletive.

Cara slid her hands around his waist and pulled him close. Then she lowered her hands to his hips and pulled their private parts even closer. She jumped and wrapped her legs around him.

"You've gotta admit," she said, "fighting gets you a little horny."

Instead of answering, Will repositioned his hips and thrust himself inside her. She gasped and bit his shoulder hard.

"Maybe more than a little," she moaned, and then Will's mouth found hers.

The next morning, Cara woke with bruises on her back from the router work on their bedroom door. She told a very concerned Will that the bruises were totally worth it. He wouldn't show her the bite mark on his shoulder for weeks, and by then it had become a tiny scar.

WILL AND SAM STROLLED THROUGH THE ENTRYWAY OF THE passage tomb. Once inside, he was amazed by the architectural genius who had designed the walls and ceilings around him. Huge rocks that didn't quite fit together were interspersed with smaller rocks and white quartz cobblestones, along with gravel and flat, striated rock. The structure was crafted so well, that the walls had survived over seven thousand years. What was man even like seven thousand years ago? How were these huge stones moved to this location? Ireland had no large slave population during the…what?

Neolithic period?

At least, not that he'd read in his college history texts. They weren't like the Egyptians, whose magnificent pyramids were built over centuries on the backs of the Israelites. Sightseers were beginning to return from the far end of the passage, forcing Will to hug the wall as he walked. His stomach turned over, and he stifled a belch.

"I know this is called a passage tomb," he said. "I just wish they'd made their passage a little wider."

"Yeh're not claustrophobic, are yeh?" Sam asked.

"Just when other people crowd around me."

An elderly couple shoved past them on the right, headed back to the entrance of the tomb.

"Beggin' yer pardon," smiled the older lady.

Once they were past, Will whispered, "Like that."

He examined the walls around him, and the smooth, rafter-like stones directly overhead, positioned every few feet.

"Why is the inside so popular?" he asked. "I think the outside was a lot more interesting."

"Down here is where they buried the bodies," Sam replied.

"Makes sense, I guess."

The passage, about sixty feet long, ended in a large chamber with three smaller, adjoining chambers branching left, right, and ahead. Will and Sam stepped into the larger chamber and, instantly, his nausea diminished. He could even see the sky through a hole in the ceiling of the main chamber.

"Interestin', idn't?" asked Sam. "At the winter solstice, the sun beams directly down that hole, right ta where we're standin'."

"For what purpose?" Will asked, staring at the hole. A few drops of rain struck his face and he backed up a little.

"No one knows. Jus' a bit a' trivia, I suppose."

"What are we looking for exactly?" asked Will. "And if we find it, how do we make it past the other tourists to get to it?"

"If there's anything here," Sam whispered, "it'll prob'ly be in one a' the inner chambers."

They peeked over and around other tourists. Everyone was trying to get a glimpse at whatever was cordoned off by ropes at the end of the passage. Will glimpsed a huge pot in one of the side rooms.

"Cremation vessel," someone said.

Will's stomach churned again. Four thousand miles away from home, and he still couldn't escape the thought of burning bodies. He leaned against the wall for support.

"Yeh okay?" Sam asked.

He shook his head.

A small Asian man with a huge digital camera shoved past Will and through the crowd. He clicked away at the chambers, his flash illuminating every crevice of the walls like a strobe. Will thought he might vomit. He looked back toward the entrance, a rectangle of light sixty feet away, just as a huge outside flash lit up the inside of the tomb.

"What the—" Will breathed. Before he could finish, a deafening thunderclap crashed through the monument. The explosive sound echoed off the walls like artillery fire in a canyon. All activity stopped as tourists looked overhead and toward the distant entrance. Several older visitors headed down the passage toward the bus. The docents on guard near the cordoned-off areas tried to help them.

"Now, Will!" said Sam, grabbing his arm. "The adder stone!"

The crowd thinned rapidly. Will grabbed the adder stone from his pocket. It seemed to shimmer in his hand. He held it up to his eye like a monocle.

"Bloody hell." An elderly man lurched into a wall as a British couple shoved past him. "Feckin' gobshite!" the old man said.

Sam giggled, but Will barely heard the expletives. The lens of the stone's small hole had turned his world upside down.

The tomb passageway was lined with huge sections of carved bones, as if this place had become a tomb for giants that had roamed the earth before men. Was this what had happened to the Tuatha Dé Danaan? Had they disappeared into the fairy mounds, or had they themselves become the fairy mounds? To his right, a full leg bone, complete with knee joint and cap but no foot rested atop similar bones of different sizes and variations. The ceiling of the passageway was a column of vertebrae. The back section of ribs shot over Will's head like a bony cage. Filling in the holes, instead of gravel and striated stone, were finger bones, toe bones, and fragments of ribs.

"What do yeh see?" asked Sam, resting her hand on Will's arm.

"Hold on," Will said. He walked over to the small chamber at the end of the passage. He looked first without the adder stone, then with it. Both views were the same. Just another cremation vessel and a few bones that looked human. Will laughed.

"What?" asked Sam.

"Everyone was so interested in the chambers, that they missed the real secret of the passage tomb."

"Which is?"

"The passage itself. Look." He handed her the stone.

Sam placed her eye against the hole and gasped. "Jaysus, Will!"

"I know, right?"

She took the stone from her eye and said, "Yer feckin' with me, ain'tcha?"

"What?"

Sam put the stone in front of her eye again. "There's nuthin' there, Will!"

She shoved the adder stone back into his hand. Will raised it to his eye and saw the bones.

"You really don't see anything?"

"Ah, sure," Sam said, voice dripping with sarcasm. "I see a bunch a' rocks and gravel an' a lot a' smart people makin' their way back to the coach." She sighed. "We should go."

Sam headed for the entryway. She stopped and turned. "Are yeh comin', or is there another car yeh'll be takin' back to Drumkeeran?"

"Samthann," said Will. "What exactly is the Leanán sídhe?"

Sam's hands shot to her hips.

"An' what do that matter, Will McConnelly?"

Through the adder stone, a tall, red-haired woman floated up behind Sam. She wore a white, half-sleeved garment similar to a chemise except it hung open in the front, like a robe. She stopped and kissed Sam gently on the cheek, all the while staring at Will. Sam's eyes seemed to go out of focus, as if she were in a waking dream. Sam closed her eyes, and her lips parted as if she were about to kiss a lover.

The red-haired woman's chemise gapped a little, providing a momentary glimpse of a breast and, lower, a small patch of red hair. The woman said something in a language Will didn't understand.

"I'm sorry," he said. "I don't speak Gaelic."

The woman smiled. "Gaelic?" she said in perfect English. "That was Welsh. But I do know the Irish tongue quite well, William...Bradford... McConnelly."

She bent her head to Samthann and kissed her. Though lost in a trance, Sam opened her mouth wider to accept the woman's kiss. The woman ended the kiss, gently pulled Sam closer, and rested Sam's cheek on her breast. "Do *you* know the Irish tongue?"

Anger replaced Will's nausea. "Leave her alone," he breathed.

The woman laughed. "Very well." She brushed a hand across Sam's cheek.

Sam woke, eyes wide and confused. "Will?" she said.

"Let's get out of here, Sam," he replied. He stepped forward, meaning to put his arm around Sam and direct her to the passageway's entrance. Images and feelings shot through him like fireworks.

a child sits in a swing while other children play

a teacher scolds someone for stealing a pencil

a cat eats a dead bird

sitting in the lap of an old woman who smells like cinnamon

people laugh at a picnic

a bomb explodes in an arena; people scream

mind-numbing sadness

quiet loneliness, ever-present, always there

Will passed through Sam's body, whirled, and found himself facing her back.

Sam looked around the passageway. "Shite," she said. "The bastard snuck out without me."

She stomped through him, and more memories flooded his mind. "William McConnelly! Yeh'd better not've left me!"

"I'm right here," Will called.

"You're not in her world anymore," said the red-haired woman. "Judging from the adder stone, you must be here to gain admittance to the lair of the Beast Glatisant. Is that right?"

"The Questing Beast?" asked Will.

"Yes. The French name is more descriptive, don't you think? 'The barking beast.' It's the sound he makes as he tears into your stomach and devours your entrails. You're still alive, of course, for a time."

"And you're the Leanán sídhe?"

She straightened. "I am she."

Will's confidence faded. He reached over his shoulder and touched the scabbard on his back. What had Sam called it again? The Claid-heamh Soluis?

The Leanán sídhe glided toward him. She stopped inches from his face, so close that he almost couldn't focus on her forest green eyes. She closed them and inhaled deeply.

The hair on Will's arms prickled, as if she drew his very essence from him.

She opened her eyes. "You're an artist."

"An actor. Or I was, once. And a teacher, and a husband and a father. I was a lot of things once."

Her smile crinkled her cheeks and elongated her face, giving her an elvish look. "You could be so much more," she whispered. She caressed the side of Will's cheek.

Suddenly, it wasn't her hand, but Cara's. Will's eyes widened as her face lost its form and became the face of his dead wife.

Will wanted to call the Leanán sídhe a liar, but she closed the distance between them with a kiss. Her tongue slid over his as naturally as it had the first time he had kissed his wife.

Cara pulled him close, her smallish breasts flattening against his chest. She jumped onto him, wrapping her legs around his waist.

"Are you really here?" he asked, kissing her neck. He inhaled her vanilla and lavender scent.

"You know me, Will McConnelly. Doesn't this feel like me?"

Cara kissed her way from his mouth to his ear, then nibbled at his neck. She was driving him wild. Will tugged at his belt and eased her against the stone wall, ready to push himself inside her.

But it's not a stone wall, he remembered. *It's not really a wall at all, just...*"Bones," he said.

"What's wrong, my love?" Cara asked.

Will smiled. "You never called me 'my love.' Pooh Bear, Silly Willy"—he laughed—"drama Wookie."

He gently lifted Cara and pushed her away. She unwrapped her legs and allowed him to lower her to the stone floor. Cara's face melted into that of the Leanán sídhe.

"Did you love your wife so little," she asked, "that you wouldn't give eternity to spend five more minutes with her?"

"You're not her," said Will. "Her bones are ashes, and her ashes are in my room in Drumkeeran."

"I was her very essence," she replied. "I pulled her from your memories. Her smell was still in your nostrils and her sweat on your chest."

"I feel like I should be pissed off about this, but I'm not." He reached down and lifted the Leanán sídhe's hands in his. "Thank you for giving her back to me, if only for a moment."

"I can make you happy again, Will," she said. "Help you find the art that lives inside your heart."

"As Cara?"

"As whoever you wish. A waitress, a student, a Hollywood actress. I've inspired men for thousands of years. Mozart and his requiem, Van Gogh and his ear. I've been by the side of many great men, and I feel your greatness"—she placed her open hand on his chest—"here."

"I wanted to write a play someday," he confessed. "Something that would move people to love and weep and confess things to their priests. All the biggies."

"You could," she said, moving closer once again. "With me to inspire you."

Will shifted a stray lock of hair from her face and gently kissed her forehead.

"Thank you for the offer, Leanán sídhe, but I think I have a dragon to slay."

Her smile faded a little.

Will bet she wasn't used to rejection.

She shed her drape to reveal her naked self, as if to taunt Will with what he was turning down.

"Very well, William McConnelly. As you have refused my love, I am your servant and can open the door you seek. However, you must answer three riddles in order to pass through that door. If you cannot answer one of them, your life will be forfeit. Do you still wish to pass?"

"That isn't fair," Will sputtered.

"What?"

"I'm supposed to fight a dragon that I probably can't beat. But before I can kill myself that way, I have to answer a bunch of riddles, and if I miss one, I die anyway." He snorted. "I thought the odds in Vegas sucked!"

"You could've had this," she said, gesturing to her perfect body. "So, answer the riddles or go home a fool."

Will laughed. "I'm a fool either way, but I guess I'll try the riddles. Cara once called me the trivia Nazi, so hey! Maybe I'll get lucky."

"That is your decision?"

Lightning lit the outside entrance. Its thunderclap rocked the tomb. Samthann reappeared at the entryway.

"Last chance, Will! If yer not to the coach in five minutes, yeh'll have to find another ride home!" She disappeared down the steps.

Will felt the Leanán sídhe's cool hands on his chest.

"You could go with her," she said. "Haven't you both faced enough dragons for one lifetime?"

Will stared into her green eyes. He could, he realized. He could walk away and take Samthann into his arms and...what? Dance? Whirl her around as she'd dreamed? That part of him was dead, wasn't it? Cara and Sam still lay in ashes.

Will felt something new. Anger. Not at the fire or God, but at them. They'd left *him*, hadn't they? Why hadn't Cara stayed up and smelled the smoke? Why hadn't Sam snuck out of bed to wait up for Daddy, like he'd done so many times on late rehearsal nights? For the second time in a week, the same verse from Macbeth popped into his head.

She should have died hereafter.

There would have been a time for such a word.

Tomorrow, and tomorrow, and tomorrow,

Creeps in this petty pace from day to day

To the last syllable of recorded time,

And all our yesterdays have lighted fools

The way to dusty death. Out, out, brief candle!

Life's but a walking shadow, a poor player

That struts and frets his hour upon the stage

And then is heard no more. It is a tale

Told by an idiot, full of sound and fury,

Signifying nothing.

Will had performed the monologue for Seamus and Conor, but he'd forgotten the first line. *She should have died hereafter. There would have been a time for such a word.* It was Macbeth's response to the messenger telling him that his wife had died. Even a proud warrior sucked into the machinations of deceit and usurpation could stop to grieve for his wife.

"William?" said the Leanán sídhe, "the time draws nigh. Will you do the intelligent thing and leave, or play the fool and stay?"

Play the fool? Will thought. *Isn't that what I'm good at? I'm always cast as the clown.*

More words from Macbeth came to his lips, "Arm, arm, and out!—If this which you avouch does appear, there is nor flying hence nor tarrying here. I 'gin to be aweary of the sun and wish th' estate o' th' world were now undone.—Ring the alarum-bell!—Blow, wind! Come, wrack! At least we'll die with harness on our back."

The Leanán sídhe stared at him.

Will sighed. "I'm doing the stupid thing. So...riddle me this."

Her eyebrows wrinkled. "Macbeth *and* Batman? You are well studied."

"Just give me the riddles."

She said nothing.

"Please?" he added.

Her hands shot into the air.

"Oscail an doras!"

Lightning shot through an opening in the top of the tomb. The thunderclap that followed knocked Will off his feet, and a fire exploded in one of the inner chambers. Walls slid back, and a stone staircase revealed itself, descending into darkness. Vines shot through cracks in the floor and twined around Will's arms, legs, chest, and throat. They bound him flat against the floor until he couldn't move.

"What has been opened," said the Leanán sídhe, "cannot be closed 'cept through word or blood."

Her body fell forward and stopped in mid-air, hovering over his. Her breasts grazed his shirt. The Leanán sídhe's eyes were no longer green but black. Rivulets of blood trickled from her pores. Will squeezed his eyes shut to prevent the blood from pouring into them, but whatever magic held the Leanán sídhe in place created some other gravity for her. The thick, red liquid flowed down her face as if she stood upright.

"Answer this, mortal," she hissed. "Rigid with curved bronze, I am fashioned in the form of a wide-mouthed circle. Within is the nimble likeness of a tinkling tongue. Set down, I make no sound; when moved, I often speak out."

Will fought the panic caused by the vines coiled tightly around his throat. He pictured a wide mouthed circle, curved, with a tinkling tongue inside. When moved, it made sound. Was it really that simple?

"A bell," he said.

An almost painful heat burned his face. He opened his eyes to see that the Leanán sídhe had changed again. Her skin was ashen now, as if she had passed through fire. Rows and rows of thin, needle-sharp teeth jutted from her wide mouth. Her eyes, still black, had thinned and widened as well. They stretched back toward her ears, which had lengthened into points.

Was the cute young woman just a façade? he wondered, his breath coming faster. *Is this her true form?*

"Holding the name of a human being," she said, "after death I am left behind. The empty name remains, but sweet life has fled. Yet life outlives death after life's course is run."

Will didn't even have to think. His jaw grew rigid. The answer could barely squeeze its way through his clenched teeth. "A gravestone." He glared at the thing above him. "If you want me to fail your game, you should probably avoid the subject of death. I have a Master's degree in Shakespeare, but death? I've got my fucking PhD."

"Harder then, for thee," the thing said, a string of thick bile defying her gravity and oozing from her mouth. It pooled on Will's cheek like a cancer.

His anger cut through his disgust. "Bring it, bitch," he said.

The Leanán sídhe paused, her nostrils flaring as if she smelled prey. "No snares I fear from lurking fraud; for a god has bestowed upon me this gift of form, that no one moves me, unless he himself first be moved."

Snares. Traps...fraud.

Was that it? Or was it about movement?

No one moves me unless he's moved first. What can't be moved without something else?

Will opened his moutht to speak, but no words came. No answer popped into his head. The Leanán sídhe smiled, revealing even more teeth. Will's anger melted into frustration and frustration into panic.

Traps. Snares. Shit!

He was good at riddles because he was good at thinking.

So think, asshole!

"End this," the Leanán sídhe whispered. "Utter a word, and it will all be over." A thin, wet tongue snaked between her lips and crept across his cheek.

A word popped into his head, and without thinking, he said, "Tail."

The Leanán sídhe appeared confused. Then her head rocked back and she roared in triumph. "Wrong!"

"Blindfold," said Will. As the thing looked back at him, he smiled.

"You don't get two guesses," she hissed.

"Those weren't my guesses," he said. "I was remembering three words that would keep me from harm. Tail, blindfold, and... What is it that someone cannot move unless he himself first be moved? That would be...a shadow."

Instantly, the Leanán sídhe shimmered into the beautiful, red-haired woman he'd first encountered. She smiled and placed something on his chest.

"Admittance," she whispered. The Leanán sídhe lost her shape and melted into a silver liquid that poured over his body, dissolving the vines holding him. She seeped into the cracks in the stone floor and disappeared.

Will took a deep breath and screamed, relief and triumph pouring out of his body through sound. Tears pooled in the corners of his eyes and dampened his temples.

He reached for the object on his chest and turned it over. It was a large, dull silver coin with a strange face on one side and words on the other.

The price of admittance? he thought. *A coin for the ferryman?*

Will stood. Darkness stared up at him from the abyss into which the stone staircase descended. He flipped the coin in his right hand and turned it over onto the back of his left.

"Heads," he said. "We move on."

Even though I would have moved on with tails, too.

Will put the coin in his pocket and stepped through the opening that went down, down, into the darkness.

Chapter Thirteen

HELL

WILL TOOK his time easing down the steps. The dark was palpable...thick. He literally couldn't see his hand six inches in front of his face. He'd tried. He dragged his feet across every step to avoid uneven places and his right hand across the wall for support.

At first, he'd counted the steps. That made the journey seem interminable, so he'd stopped after the first four hundred or so. Instead, he tried to write the scenario of what would happen when he fought the Questing Beast and won, because...why not? He'd made it this far. No more help would come from Alistair McCulloch. The three hints, like genie wishes, were used up. The rest was old-school knight work. Find the dragon, kill the dragon, save the princess...except for the princess part. Unless Will himself were the princess. He laughed.

"That's it, ladies and gentlemen," he said aloud. "Will McConnelly has officially lost it. He's stepped off the deep end, gone nuts, is mad as a hatter...I'm sure there's more, but it don't even matter! Hatter...matter! I made a rhyme. Gimme a dime!" He ran out of phrases, then remembered one from *The Princess Bride*. "Stop that right now, and I mean it! Anybody have a peanut?"

Tired of the sound of his voice, Will shut up for a while. He wished for a little light, because the air was getting cold enough that he thought he might be able to see his breath. Eventually, he made up a number, 957, and began counting from there. That lasted for awhile, but at 3,115, he gave up again. His feet were cramping from the constant sliding. He thought about turning around, but what good would that do? All this work for nothing. So, he continued down the steps. One at a time. Then another. Until he thought he might actually go insane.

Will slid his foot forward, and it didn't go down a step.

"What?" he said.

He slid it a little farther. Still no step. He found his footing on the flat surface and moved forward, continuing to drag his feet one at a time. Just in case. The air seemed a little warmer here, and the black slowly turned gray. Will raised a hand and wiggled his fingers. Perhaps it was just his imagination, but he thought he could see movement.

He came to a place where the wall ended at an outfacing corner. He couldn't see a light source yet, but it was bright enough now to make out the stonework on the floor. He rounded the corner. Maybe a hundred paces ahead rose a huge door nested in a wall that blocked the passageway. The door was bolted from the outside, as if whatever giant had set it in place was more worried about something getting out than anyone getting in. The wall and door bore cracks, which allowed beams of light to shine through. The light illuminated the path well enough that Will could finally walk with some confidence.

"Once more into the breech, dear friends," he muttered.

Will continued walking until he stood before the massive door. He craned his neck to see the huge drawbar dropped over two giant, L-shaped pieces of metal bolted into the stone. The drawbar rested four feet above Will's head.

"How the hell am I supposed to move that?" he said.

"Yeh could jus'—" a voice said.

Will jumped. "Shit!"

He reached around his back for the sword. The scabbard shifted and the sword slid out, struck the floor, and rang like a bell against the paving stones.

"Sorry, lad," a voice said from the shadows. "There ain't no good way to warn a person, 'specially when he appears outa nowhere. Yeh caught me nappin'."

A pair of boots marched from the shadows. Will was shocked when he saw that the boots were not attached to legs.

"I know, lad. It's passin' odd, but when yer a ghost, yeh just haf ta be happy that yeh can make a pair a' botes move with yer spirit feet. Otherwise, yer jus' a voice billowin' in the dark. If'n a pair a' botes movin' without feet give yeh the frights, well...think if there weren't any botes at all."

"You frightened me enough, thanks," said Will. "I appreciate the boots. Uh, botes?"

"Yer voice is passin' strange, lad. Yer raiment, too. It's been a century and a half since a hero made the journey down the steps. Has time changed so that yeh've abandoned the waistcoat fer...is it a tunic, now? An' pantaloons? Are yeh in a commedia troupe then, traveling the country? If so, yer awful young ta be a Pantalone. Mayhap too old for a Tristano, but Arlecchino might fit yeh well."

Will laughed, put at ease by a familiar topic. "You sound like my theatre history class notes," he said.

"It's a simple question, lad. Unless yer daft or rude, in which case, I'll return to me corner and leave yeh to bang on the door there until yer arms fall off."

"No, no!" said Will. He took a quick step toward the boots, which took a step away from him. "My apologies. You brought up commedia, and I'm a huge fan of Renaissance theatre. I teach it, actually. Ummm...my jacket is called a hoodie, and the year is 2021. We don't wear waistcoats much anymore, unless we're doing a period play. These are jeans, not pantaloons, although that's where pants got their start. Lots of people wear pants now, even women. Not just old men. Uh...oh. Men don't wear tights anymore, unless they're dancers or really like Renaissance fairs. Does that make sense?"

"A little," said the ghost. "What about yer voice, then? From whence do yeh come?"

"The United States of America. Have you heard of it?"

"I'm not daft, lad. Jus' outa tetch. Last I heard yeh was fightin' a war
. Who won?"

"Which war? Vietnam or...?"

"The War Between the States, bye. The last lad who came down the
stairs had news that the southern states of America were winnin'. I
didn't support 'em a' course, 'coz a' the slavery issue. So, what
happened? Did the slaves get freed?"

"The north won, so yes. The slaves were freed. There's still a lot to
do, though. Black men in America are still persecuted. Minorities overall
aren't given the same opportunities as white people. Women have
rights, too, now, so that's good. But they don't get equal pay for doing
the same jobs. Oh, someone invented a bomb that can destroy whole
cities now. In a nutshell, America isn't the land of the free as much as
we'd like to think. It's still better than most everywhere else in the
world."

"That's too much, lad. What, women are workin' now? Outside the
farm? An' what's a bomb?"

Will sighed. "I think maybe too much time has passed for you to
understand the world today. We've had a few ages of enlightenment over
the past seventy-five years or so. You'd think that would make us better
people, but...no. We're still the same assholes who picked up rocks and
beat each other to death when we were monkeys."

"We...were monkeys?" said the ghost. "Now yer pullin' me leg. An'
yeh can't even see it!"

Will changed the subject. "So, you're a ghost?"

"Indeed! Kagan is me name, an' I'm the guardian a' the door to the
Hall a' Fire. Which yeh be standin' in front of as we speak."

"The Hall of Fire?"

"Tá. Yeh'll see why. But I have three questions fer yeh before I can
open the door."

"More questions?" asked Will. "I've already answered the Leanán
sídhe's three riddles!"

The ghost laughed. "Not riddles, bye. Don't worry. I'll have yeh on
yer way in a horologist's minute. Now, have yeh made yer peace with yer
Maker?"

Will was taken aback a little. Made peace with his Maker? He shook his head. "God gets no peace from me," he said. "If he even exists, he's a cruel being that gave me a perfect family and then stole it back. He deserves no peace from me."

The boots in front of him shuffled a little.

"Yeh've had a time of it, then. More's the pity fer yeh, bein' here ta face the beast without a God. Ah, well. The second question is this—have yeh delivered yer farewells to all above in the almost sure event that yeh never return?"

Will paused. He hadn't said goodbye to Aidan, but there was nothing he could do about that now. At least, he'd left a message for him with Meg. He hadn't said goodbye to Samthann, either. He'd been hidden from her before he even knew it. There was a tinge of regret in that. She'd tried to help him, though at times her help was a battle in and of itself. If he failed, she'd never know what happened. He silently promised himself that if he did make it out of this alive, he would try to visit her before he returned to the hills. If there was time.

"I've said goodbye to everyone I can," said Will.

"Well then, only one question more an' we'll get yeh on with yer quest. Do yeh have the coin? From the demon lass?"

Will reached into his pocket and held it out. He had no clue where Kagan's face might be, so he guessed based on the boots.

"Do you take it?" asked Will. "Is it for admittance into the Hall of Fire?"

"Tá, it's fer admittance, bye." The ghost paused, and then his voice was gentle, almost sad, "Yeh know bye, yeh really have all yeh need. Not one warrior has conquered the Beast in the three thousan' year I've watched the door. Why feed yerself ta death as if yeh mean nothin'?"

"Because I do mean nothing," said Will. "I mean nothing to myself." That was it, right? He had people who cared about him. Quite a few, actually. Somewhere after the fire, he'd stopped caring about himself. It was the first time he'd said so out loud.

Enough.

If he was going to fight this thing, this beast that no one had ever beaten, he needed to focus.

"Please open the door," he said.

Kagan sighed. "Fine, bye. Die if yeh must."

The shoes turned and meandered to the wall, just to the left of the giant door. Will followed and discovered another, much smaller door there.

"That's crazy," he laughed. "I didn't even see it. I wondered how you would move that giant drawbar!"

"That's why I'm the Guardian," said Kagan. The boots turned. "Okay, bye. This is farewell, e'en though I may see yer spirit glide by me on the way outa this hellish place."

"How did you become the guardian of this place anyway?" asked Will.

The ghost laughed—a bitter sound. "Once upon a time, I fought the Beast meself," he said. "Mayhap yeh'll take my place."

The boots disappeared into the gloom, and the ghost said no more.

Will lifted the handle, and some mechanism released a hidden latch. The door swung open of its own accord. He grabbed the sword from the floor and sheathed it.

"Into the breach," he whispered. His Timberland hiking boots, the twenty-first century version of Kagan's botes, took him into hell.

"I may be late tonight," Will said, kneeling in front of Samuel as he ate his SpaghettiOs. Will had given his classes a walk that day because he wanted to spend a little extra time with his son. Show week meant dress and technical rehearsals until eleven or twelve every night. Then there was the opening night reception, the shows themselves, and strike, where they would disassemble the set.

"Daddy pway," said Sam, bright orange pasta drooling down his chin.

"We've been playing all day, buddy," said Will. He picked up a napkin and dabbed at the mess.

"Pway mo-uh!" Sam thrust his plastic Scooby Doo spoon into the air, a three-year-old Don Quixote ready to lead a charge at the windmill of his father's giant of a job.

"Okay," said Cara. She strode into the room with a laundry basket full of folded clothes. "Who's ready for a bath?"

"Daddy!" said Sam, waving his spoon in the air.

"No," said Will. "Daddy doesn't have time for a bath." He stood, his knees aching a little but otherwise, itching to have this show in the books. He needed more time at home, for his own sanity.

"Daddy baff!" screamed Sam.

Will felt SpaghettiOs hit his shirt even before he saw them.

"Samuel Aidan McConnelly!" yelled Cara, sounding more surprised than angry.

Sam had celebrated the end of his terrible twos by starting his terrible threes. They needed to figure out how to deal with his tantrums soon. In seven months, their attention would be split between Sam and the little bean growing inside of Cara.

"That wasn't very nice," said Will.

Sam immediately burst into big, loud, screaming tears.

"Shit," said Cara. She grabbed the spoon and pulled Sam out of his booster chair.

He screamed louder, "DADDY!"

Will grabbed a dishtowel from the table and scooped the pasta and sauce off his shirt, and then off the floor.

Should've worn my burnt orange Longhorns shirt.

"Daddy!" Sam screamed from the general vicinity of the master bathroom.

Will pulled off his shirt as he walked toward the bedroom and tossed it into the laundry hamper there. He sifted through shirts in his closet, then remembered that Cara had just laundered the one he wanted. Three minutes later, he was ready for work again.

"How're we doing?" he asked, peeking into the bathroom. The tub was about half-full, and Sam was already naked and playing with the bubbles.

"Daddy!" he yelled.

Will laughed. "Is it possible our son is bipolar?" he asked.

"That's not even funny right now," Cara said. She squirted children's bath soap into a washrag and scrubbed the tears from Sam's face.

"Sorry." He stepped in behind her and massaged her shoulders. "You know all kids are crazy, right?" he asked.

"I know," she said, laying her head back against his knees.

"And ours is pretty damned cool most of the time."

"Dam coo!" said Samuel.

"Thanks, Will," said Cara, turning. "Now he can take some colorful words to his playdates."

Will stepped back. "He can't even do his l's and r's right yet! How am I supposed to know his expletives kick ass?"

"Kick ath," giggled Sam.

Cara glared at him. "You're lucky his esses aren't great yet."

Will shook his head and threw up his hands. "I'm doing my best, honey."

"Is that good enough?" she asked, standing. "Seriously, Will. What the hell are we doing? I mean, we're pretty good at lots of stuff, but this parenting thing gets harder and harder. What if one is my limit? What if I can't handle two?"

"Sweetheart," said Will. "You can handle the whole world." He tried to pull her close, but she shrugged him off.

"Don't patronize me!" she said, eyes flashing.

"Whoa whoa. You know I don't do that."

Cara didn't answer.

Will knew she wanted to be pissed off, but the only person she could really be angry with was looking up at her with wide eyes from a bubble bath. How could you get angry at that amount of adorable?

She sighed. "I don't know, Will. This is a lot. Two will be double the crazy."

Will pulled her into his arms. "Cara, we're not perfect, but who is? We're human and stupid and crazy, but I'm so freakin' in love with you and Sam that I wouldn't trade this life for anything in the world. Anything."

She looked up at him. "Nothing?"

"No," he smiled.

"Not even to go back in time to see Shakespeare play the ghost in *Hamlet* at the Globe?"

Will grabbed her shoulders. "Hey, that's not playing fair."

"I'm your wife. I don't have to play fair. And you didn't answer the question."

"Would you leave me to watch Michelangelo paint the Sistine Chapel?"

Cara wrinkled her face. "Ew. Michelangelo was gross. You know he wouldn't take his boots off for such long periods of time that his skin would come off with the boots?" She made a choking noise in the back of her throat.

"So...you wouldn't go back to watch him paint?"

Will waited.

She finally shrugged. "Fine, I might go back, but only if I could take him some Odor-Eaters."

They laughed.

"And I might have to check out Shakespeare," said Will, "though I'd rather see him in one of his comedies. But I still don't think I'd trade my family for a few days of Elizabethan England. I'd be miserable."

"What if you'd never met us? What if you could live back then and were part of the King's Men or whatever? What if you could forget we had ever existed?"

"We'll never know," said Will. "I was born to meet you, and I was meant to fall in love with you, and I am blessed to get to spend the rest of my life with you. That's the path I'm on, and no. I wouldn't trade it for anything in this world." He kissed her forehead.

"I love it when you direct Shakespeare," Cara said. "You're all poetry and pretty words for at least a week after." She kissed him.

Their mouths opened and tongues met. Will pulled her in close, enjoying her breasts pressed against his chest. Maybe he could start rehearsal fifteen minutes late.

"Damn coo!" yelled Sam. He slapped the water, sending little tidal waves over the edge of the tub.

Will released Cara. "Shit, sorry."

"Thit!" said Sam.

Cara grabbed her head. "What are we doing having another one of these little monsters?"

"Mommy, pway wif me!"

"The monster calls," said Will.

The first chords of Beethoven's *Moonlight Sonata* began to play in his jeans pocket. He pulled out his phone. "And so does my stage manager. I've gotta go."

"Hurry back," said Cara.

"I'll try, but things haven't been going too well. And if we screw up this play, I'll be the embarrassment of the faculty. They'll inscribe it on my tombstone: 'Here lies William McConnelly. He couldn't even direct *Midsummer Night's Dream.*'"

"You'll be fine, Cara laughed. "Get going."

He kissed her one last time on the cheek and headed out.

"Say hello to all the fairies for me," she said. "Especially that cute senior. What's his name?"

"Ian. And he's not interested in women."

Cara laughed. "If I'm asleep when you come home, wake me up. Maybe we can continue what we started."

Will smiled. "I will. If I have enough energy to make it to bed."

THE DOOR SCRAPED CLOSED BEHIND WILL, AND A METAL bolt squeaked into place. Apparently, this was only the entrance, not the exit. Sulphur hit his nostrils almost as quickly as did the wave of torrid humidity. Will choked, trying to inhale the thick, rancid air. Eyes stinging, he blinked up at the massive edifice before him.

"Holy shit," he whispered.

The ancient hall towered over him fourteen or fifteen stories. No windows were visible, though time and erosion had created irregular cavities and fissures in the walls. Rough-hewn stone, much the same as outside the gate, paved the floor of the hall. Molten lava bubbled up through craters in the stone. The bubbling lava cast a reddish-yellow glow throughout the hall, while patches of luminescent fungus growing on the stone added a baleful, green tint.

A hissing drew Will's attention to a crack in the wall, where a steady stream of water flowed. It poured into the lava and turned to steam.

"It's not the heat that'll getcha," his dad had said about the Texas summers. "It's the humidity."

No shit, Sherlock, Will thought, and smiled. That was another of his dad's favorite sayings.

Through the heat, Will felt a brush of fresh air. He followed the draft to a rectangular crevice cut into the stone wall and discovered the source of the cool breeze. Of course, there had to be some sort of ventilation entering the room. Otherwise, the sulfuric gases rising from the lava would have killed him.

Throughout the hall, crumbling stone walls intersected to create barely recognizable corners, as if many separate rooms had once filled the space. Most were rubble now. Scattered amongst stone chairs and tables in various phases of deterioration lay thousands of human skulls and ribcages and femurs—every kind of bone—strewn haphazardly alongside swords and spears and suits of armor.

Will wondered what this place had been before lava had burst through the stone and transformed the majestic hall into a place of destruction. Was this edifice like the mines of Moria from *The Lord of the Rings*? Had someone dug too deep and accidentally invited hell itself to invade?

Will crept across the cobblestones, slowly reaching over his shoulder for the sword. A scuttling near the door caused him to wheel around just as a foot-long scorpion-like arachnid rushed across the rock.

A black tentacle shot out from a crevice in the floor and wrapped itself around the creature.

Will stepped back as the scorpion furiously tried to free itself from the tentacle's grip. Both disappeared into the crevice, and a crunching snap followed as the thing's carapace cracked. Mewling followed, along with the unmistakable sound of teeth ripping flesh.

Hell could look like this.

He pulled the blade from its scabbard. The polished metal seemed to glow in the flickering firelight and the fungus's green luminescence.

Another Tolkien reference popped into his head—Bilbo Baggins and Sting, the sword that glowed when evil was near.

Will felt a presence grow behind him before the area in his periphery darkened. Then another shadow, wider and taller, enveloped his own. A strong, musky scent hit his nostrils, overpowering even the stench of sulfur. Will turned slowly, his heart pounding against his chest as if trying to escape its ribbed prison. A broad body, at least ten feet tall, continued to rise onto its haunches before him. A thick, scaled neck and triangular head snaked another six or eight feet beyond the shoulders. No fire or fungus glowed high enough in this area of the hall to light the thing's face, so the beast's features were dark and ill-defined. His arm shaking, Will raised the Claidheamh Soluis. Was it just an hour ago that he'd been positive he could win this battle? He might die of a heart attack simply standing in the presence of the creature.

The beast arched and its front hooves hit the cobblestones with a crash. The shift reduced the creature's height by four or five feet, but elongated the beast, like a monstrous crocodile.

"Jesus Christ," Will breathed.

The thing whirled and a whistle rent the air in front of Will. A powerful blow hit the sword, wrenching the weapon from his hand. It clattered onto the cobblestones several yards away. Will gripped his wrist, trying to counter the sting from the force of the attack.

Had the tail hit the blade?

Will leapt aside and rushed toward the sword.

The beast continued its turn. As its head swung toward him, Will tried to duck, but the creature's neck wound around Will's body so quickly that he had no chance to dive out of the way. As the coils tightened, Will struggled to breathe. Was this it? Before he could even offer a single blow from the famed sword? He wanted to laugh at his idiocy. No armor, no real combat training—what did he think would happen?

Effortlessly, the dragon lifted him, then lumbered across the cobblestones. The lurching gait made Will seasick. The creature finally stopped and dropped Will on the floor before an ancient, stone bench.

Am I supposed to sit? he thought. *I've already lost. Why didn't it crush me?*

Will sat on the bench and faced the creature. It rested on its haunches several feet away, studying him. The fire in this part of the room burned brighter, so Will could make out more of the Questing Beast's features. Its gold and black body fur was dappled like a leopard's, the spots ranging from polygonal black blobs to arcs encircling orangish centers. The colors disappeared into white, matted chest fur, and faded down the golden legs. The beast's hooves were the size of Will's head. The shoulder fur gave way to greenish black scales that followed the neck up to the head.

Behind thick, golden haunches, the tail lashed like a whip.

The beast rumbled somewhere deep in its abdomen. The thing's nose lowered to within inches of Will's head. Keyhole-shaped pupils stared at him from the sides of a reptilian head. The mouth opened, revealing huge fangs that dripped viscous saliva.

Poison?

"Taispeáin dom an bonn," it whispered. The words echoed up the long throat as if spoken in a well. Goosebumps rose on Will's arms, and the rumbling grew in volume.

Maybe it's hungry, he thought, *and I'm lunch.*

"I don't suppose you, uh, speak English, do you?" Will asked.

The creature's eyes narrowed. "American," it hissed. Its accent matched Will's, though the timbre of the voice remained the same—deep and resonant, like an open tomb.

Will nodded.

"The...Headless Horseman," the thing growled. "Jersey Devil. Your people still fear them?"

What?

Will almost laughed. "No...not really. They're myths. Folklore."

The Questing Beast smashed Will in the chest with its snout and sent him flying backward over the bench. The creature was on top of him in an instant, its face so close that Will saw only rows of razor-sharp teeth and a scaly jaw.

"Folklore?" it hissed. "Like me?"

Will's mind raced at the connotations. What if the Jersey Devil and Headless Horseman and chupacabras were the fairies of the United States, as real as the thing slavering over him?

"I don't know," Will croaked, his chest throbbing from the blow.

The thing seemed to ponder Will's ignorance, then shook its head as if to clear its thoughts. It returned to its haunches, allowing Will to stand.

"Do you have the coin?" it asked.

Will fumbled in his pocket and pulled out the piece of silver, which he held in two fingers in front of the beast's face. It stared at the coin, then backed away.

"You have all you need then," the thing said. "Leave and you need not die today."

Will shook his head. "I seek the Fairy Queen," he said. "I must take your head to gain admittance into her kingdom."

Looking at the creature's huge head, Will had no idea how he would get back up the stairs, much less carry (drag?) it cross-country to Drumkeeran.

"Foolish." The beast's hiss echoed with disappointment. "Like all others before you, your first instinct is to kill. How do you survive as a species?"

"How have you survived down here?" Will looked around the floor. His sword lay a few feet away. He cautiously retrieved it while he spoke. "You stand on the bones of those you've killed."

The creature shook its head, as if annoyed by an itch. The rumbling grew louder and began to take on different tones, different voices.

"I have never taken a life that did not aim a sword at my heart," said the Questing Beast.

"Then why are you here?" asked Will. "Why do you wait for men to come to you to die?"

"I am where I'm supposed to be, William McConnelly."

"How do you know my name?"

"Knowledge of you began to seep into my pores as you entered this place. It's taken a few minutes, but I know your entire path. From your birth to the death of your parents to the late night at work that left your family beneath a mound of ash."

"What?" Will sputtered.

"You seek the Fairy Queen and respite from...what? The pain of living? That stale shibboleth?"

Will said nothing.

"If it's respite you seek, then raise your sword and leave your blood here in hell."

"This *is* hell?" asked Will.

"For you, yes. Don't you Christians define hell as a place of fire and suffering?"

Will flashed a bitter smile. "Fire and suffering brought me here. So I guess I've been in hell for a while."

The huge head nodded. "Now you begin to understand."

Will raised the sword.

The Questing Beast smiled, then shivered. The roar in its belly grew louder and louder. Its snake-like face contorted in pain and anger, and its viper eyes shut as its mouth unhinged to roar. Will dropped his sword and fell to the pavement, covering his ears with his hands. The roar exploded in his senses, burrowing like worms through gaps in his fingers. Trembling, he saw the Questing Beast's neck grow rigid with pain. Its mouth opened in a blast that might have been Gabriel trumpeting the end of the world. To Will, it looked like the roar wasn't anything the beast wanted or could control. It was like a violent, painful belch.

The giant mouth closed, and the creature's face dipped toward Will's again.

"Get up, boy!" it said. "Get up and die."

"Have at thee then," said Will, trying to mask his fear. He retrieved the sword and raised it.

The beast reared its head back and lunged at Will's chest, jaw unhinged and fangs dripping venom. A killing blow to begin and end a fight.

Chapter Fourteen

EPIPHANY

WILL LEAPS INTO A SIDEWAYS ROLL, using his right arm and momentum to spring back to his feet. There's no time to recover from the move. The Questing Beast's head lunges again, six-inch fangs targeted at Will's shoulder. Instinct and years of stage combat kick in. Will pinwheels the blade from his feet to his chest, parrying the attack. The heaviness of the beast's head knocks him to the left. Rather than try to stop himself, Will lets his body go with the blow. He falls into a shoulder roll, blade safely to the left of his body as he spins forward and back to his feet again. He ducks behind a large stone chair, trying to catch his breath.

Crack! Two huge hooves burst through the chair, sending chunks of rock flying. The Questing Beast rises on its huge, lionesque haunches and aims its hooves at Will's head.

Will dives forward underneath the creature just as the hooves crash into the spot where he'd crouched milliseconds earlier. He rolls onto his back and pulls the Claidheamh Soluis across the soft underbelly of the Questing Beast. The ancient sword slices through the creature's flesh as if cutting a sheet of paper.

A howl of pain erupts above Will, joined by an ear-splitting roar from the creature's abdomen. The beast's body shakes with the barking, blood-curdling blast. Will fears that, at any moment, brain fluid will leak through his broken eardrums.

The Questing Beast leaps, taking the skull-crushing scream with it. Will grabs the sword and hops to his feet, searching for cover. A tentacle shoots out from another crack in the stone floor. Its suckers attach to Will's pants leg for just a moment, but he manages to rip himself free and not lose much of his stride. The ground shakes. Will feels the presence of the Questing Beast behind him, its hot, pungent breath on his neck.

Will darts right, managing to stay clear as the beast pounces. He runs a few more paces and turns, sword held in an en garde position. The beast takes a couple more steps toward him, then smiles. "You took first blood."

Will says nothing.

"A blade hasn't touched my flesh since Pellinore of Listenoise pursued me through the forests near Camelot a thousand years ago. He claimed royal descent from the line of Joseph of Arimathea. Are you of that lineage, William McConnelly? Or are you just a very lucky college theatre teacher?"

"Professor," Will says.

"What?"

Will swings the sword from the en garde position to behind him and lowers the tip of the blade to the stone floor. "I have a Master's degree and I teach college, so I'm a professor."

Will yells and leaps, swinging the Claidheamh Soluis in an arc over his head, aiming at the thing's long neck. It dodges easily, although it barely moves.

"What's the difference?" it asks. "Teacher? Professor?"

Will barks a tension-filled laugh. "That's exactly what my wife would ask."

The Questing Beast slowly circles Will counterclockwise.

Will spreads his feet, ready to run or fight, whichever opportunity presents itself.

"You know little of your heritage," says the Questing Beast, "but it matters not to me. Eight, nine hundred years ago, I'd have a hero every two weeks. I was a fat thing then, dragging my belly across the floor for my next meal. But two hundred years? That'll make a chimera more than a bit peckish for a nice, cooked meal."

The Questing Beast emits a coughing noise. Its long neck expands and its jaw unhinges. A flame jets from its mouth. Will jumps back with a yell. The beast laughs.

"You've a mighty sword there, boy. I wasn't expecting to see such a weapon again, not after the deaths of Arthur and the Round Table. How did you get it?"

"It was a gift." Will backs away, turning to keep the Questing Beast in front of him.

"From whom? Ancient swords forged by gods aren't sold in shops, are they?"

"What does it matter?" asks Will.

"It doesn't. I was simply...gaining the land advantage, you might say."

Will's head jerks right and left and he realizes he's been cornered. To his back and right are large pools of burning lava, and to his left, a broken wall before which lies a huge pile of bones. Will's mouth sweats and then goes dry, as if he's about to vomit. Can he hide behind the bones? Jump the pools?

"Do you feel it, William McConnelly?" asks the Questing Beast. "Surrounded on three sides by fire and on the fourth by an impenetrable wall?"

Will scans the bones again for anything he might use. The beast's head inches toward him. He crouches, ready to strike one last blow before the creature crushes him in its mouth or claws.

"Do you think that's how she felt?"

Will slowly rises out of the crouch and faces the Questing Beast. "What did you say?"

The thing's neck cranes toward Will. He can smell the sulphur on its breath.

"Your wife," it replies. "Cara Brady McConnelly. Did she wake to the heat of the fire surrounding her, feeling as lost and trapped as you do now?"

Will's upper lip slides into a snarl. "How...?" he asks. His grip on the sword tightens. He struggles for words, for breath, but they escape him.

"I was there that night." The Questing Beast lowers itself to its haunches, relaxing before Will as if to ask for a pint at the pub.

Will's mouth opens and shuts. He grinds his teeth, and tears burn his eyes.

"I'm there in all fires, William McConnelly," says the beast, its tail swishing forward and relaxing on the stone. "I came to life in the wall of your office when two wires sparked. They burned through the sheetrock and into the shelves on both sides of the electrical panel. The first book I took was so poetic I almost laughed—Marlowe's *Doctor Faustus*. It was old and dry, like most of your tomes. I fed on them and grew, bubbling the paint on the ceiling of your office. I burned my way into the room above it. You know the one?"

Will doesn't respond. The home's floor plan was one of the things he'd loved about the house. Samuel's room was directly above the office. When Will worked late at night, he could look up and know that his little guy was directly above him, floating in perfect, dreamless sleep.

"It wasn't a long journey to your bedroom," the Questing Beast continues. "Your wife woke to the flames. She screamed for your son first, and then for you."

Will closes his eyes, sees Cara in their bedroom, engulfed in a raging inferno. He tries to block out the images, but they come anyway.

"She ran to the window beside your bed and opened it, but she couldn't leave. Not without your little boy."

"Samuel!" Cara screams.

Will's eyes shoot open. It's her voice, Cara's own terrified voice, echoing up from the Questing Beast's throat. Flames dance inside the creature's mouth, and Cara's voice rings through the fire.

"Sam! Get out of the house!"

Will staggers to his knees.

"Will!" Cara's scream rips through his heart. The scream breaks into sobs and then fades as the Questing Beast speaks again. "The open window brought fresh air into the room, almost like an invitation to the burning." The creature paused, and then whispered, "And I took it."

Something breaks inside Will, like a dam in an earthquake. Except the water's not wet, but cold. Burning, fiery, and cold. With a roar, he shoots to his feet. He takes three steps and leaps at the Questing Beast. He swings with a strength and speed he doesn't understand or care to understand.

His sudden fury surprises the creature, and its reaction is too slow. The beast jerks its head in time, but Claidheamh Soluis's tip slashes deep into its thick, meaty shoulder. Blood shoots from the wound, and the Questing Beast roars. It stumbles back, freeing Will from the lava pools and the stone wall behind him.

Will sees everything with new eyes. After a year of helplessness, he finally has an enemy. He looks again at the pile of bones and sees a ribcage clinging to its breastbone, shoulder blades, and a partial column of vertebrae. He thrusts his left hand through the opening at the bottom of the ribcage and grabs the top of the sternum, lifting it as a shield.

The Questing Beast whips its head toward Will, and Will leaps, ready to plunge the Claidheamh Soluis into the creature's heart. The beast slams its head into the makeshift shield just as the sword descends. The bones shatter and deflect Will from his attack. He hits the stone floor and rolls to his feet. The beast roars once more. A broken rib from the shattered ribcage juts from the side of the creature's cheek.

Will advances and, for the first time, sees panic in the beast's eyes. It backs away, then whirls and retreats with huge strides.

"No!" Will screams. He leaps after the beast, barely aware of the exhaustion that saps his strength. He stumbles from a fast walk into a trot and then a full-on run. His lungs inhale heat and fire from the room and exhale frost from the hatred frozen inside his heart.

The Questing Beast stumbles over a crumbling wall and tumbles end-over-end, giving Will the chance to close the distance between them. The creature regains its feet and lunges for a large pool of molten lava. It plunges into the pool as Will swings the Claidheamh Soluis above its disappearing tail.

In his head, Will hears Cara shout his name once more. This time, her scream rises from the pool of lava. Without a pause, he closes his eyes and dives into the pool, following the Questing Beast down into fire and pain. His skin begins to burn.

WILL AND CARA SAT ACROSS THE TABLE FROM EACH OTHER, along with Richie and Tammy and another theatre couple, Brett and Sarah. They were playing Clue with a drinking game. Whenever one of them rolled a double, everyone had to take a drink, and when anyone said "with the candlestick" or "with the knife," they had to take a shot. Cara had also made it a rule that whenever a character token entered the Ballroom, the couple had to go into the kitchen and make out for two minutes. It sounded like a great idea at first, but Cara had guessed Ballroom six times already. The game was threatening to last forever.

Tammy rolled a twelve, and everyone took a drink. Counting by 2s, she moved her red token to the Conservatory. She looked at her cards. "I think it's Ms. Scarlet in the Conservatory...with the knife."

She grabbed a bottle of Jägermeister out of an ice bucket and poured shots. They cheered and downed them.

Brett, seated to the left of Tammy, said, "I got nothin'." He turned to Cara.

"Zilch," she said. They looked at Richie.

"Lookin' good, babe."

Sarah checked her cards, and then checked them again. She sighed.

"Jesus Christ, Sarah," Richie said. "You're not on stage. Just tell us if you have a card."

"I'm always on stage." Sarah smiled. She turned to Tammy. "But no, I don't have a card."

Will scanned his hand and placed his clue cards face down on the table. "Like Caliban at the end of *The Tempest*," he said, "I got nothin'."

Tammy smiled and wrote on her sheet. "I think the murderer is"— everyone leaned in a little—"still unknown. But I rolled a double, so I get to go again."

"Sonuvabitch!" Brett threw his cards down in front of him.

Tammy laughed and held up her hand for a high five from Will.

He liked the way she played. It was a good trick, guessing some of the cards in your own hand in order to eliminate certain clues.

"That's cold, baby," said Richie, erasing some of his notes.

"That's why you love me," Tammy replied. She rolled an eight and moved her token out of the Conservatory, then right back in.

"Seriously?" said Brett. "Is that even legal?"

"I'm gonna guess it's Colonel Mustard in the Conservatory...with the knife," she said, grabbing the bottle of Jäger again.

She poured shots and they drank.

Thirty minutes and two shots later, Tammy declared, "I want to make an accusation."

Four of the five players dropped their cards.

"It's about goddamned time," said Brett.

Will held onto his. He wasn't sure if Tammy was going to say "Just kidding" or would actually reveal her guess.

Cara's head lay on the table in mock inebriation. Or maybe real inebriation. Will wasn't sure exactly how many shots they'd had, but she'd started on her second bottle of red wine.

"I'm accusing Colonel Mustard in the Ballroom, with the...candlestick?"

Tammy picked up the small envelope in the center of the game board and opened it. She squealed and threw her cards down. "That's right, bitches! I won, and I did it in the Ballroom. We're takin' a shot because of the candlestick, and Richie's taking me to the kitchen for two minutes a' heaven!"

Cara lifted her head. "Shot?" she asked, smiling.

Tammy grabbed the Jäger and picked up her glass to start pouring. A small drizzle oozed from the dark green bottle.

"Shit," she said.

"Shot...shit," Cara said, giggling.

"I've got a backup bottle," said Will. "It's in the freezer, if y'all are going to the kitchen."

Richie and Tammy brought the new bottle back a couple minutes later.

Richie raised the bottle into the air. "For this sweet elixir, Dionysus, we give thee thanks!"

"Amen," said Will.

Richie poured the shots.

"Sláinte mhaith," said Cara.

The others repeated the toast and drank.

"No more Clue," said Brett, banging his shot glass on the table. "I'll end up slitting Tammy's throat, and then Richie'll be pissed 'cause he'll have to find a new gal."

"After the compulsory three-day waiting period," added Will.

"Come on, assholes!" said Tammy. "You don't think I'm worth a week? Or maybe a fortnight?"

"I could do a fortnight," pondered Richie, "as long as I can collect digits at the funeral. Tears bring out the babes, ain't that right, fellas?"

Richie high-fived Brett with one hand and Will with the other, which went about as well as a drunk, two-handed, three-person high-five can go. He smacked Will in the face and slapped Brett on the elbow.

Tammy gave Richie a playful shove. "You get numbers at my funeral, I'll haunt you the rest a' your life. Every time you try to have sex, I'll be there, hovering over your shoulder."

"Ooh," said Richie, "why can't we do that now? What good's a three-some after you're dead?" He laughed and held up his hands for more high fives. Will and Brett backed away to avoid injury.

"What do you think, Sarah?" asked Tammy. She finished putting the Clue pieces back into the box and positioned the lid. "Period of mourning for Brett if you die in a horrible accident next week."

Sarah replied immediately. "Six months."

"That was fast," said Richie. "Have y'all talked about this or something?"

"No, but I've thought it through," she said. "Two weeks of seclusion, then a month-and-a-half of not returning phone calls but still doing day-to-day stuff. Like going to the grocery store. Then a month of feeling a little better but still missing me." Sarah smiled and dug into Brett's ear with her fingernail.

"Seriously?" he asked. "Here?"

"You get wax, babe," she said. "I'm OCD. Sorry."

"Just threw up a little in my mouth," said Richie.

"Moving on!" said Brett.

"Okay," Sarah said. "Two more months of remembering how happy we were. Then a month realizing he wants to be happy again."

"Nice," said Tammy.

"That's only five months," said Will. "You said six."

"The last month is him getting over the guilt about dating again and realizing that I would never want him to be lonely." She gave Brett a peck on the lips.

He pulled her onto his lap and kissed her deeply.

"Get a room!" said Richie.

"The kitchen's nice," offered Cara.

Sarah ducked away from Brett's lips and rested her head on his shoulder.

"And that's why I'm marrying this girl in two months," Brett said. "She thinks things through like that. House, money, jobs—"

"Sex?" asked Richie.

"Definitely sex," Brett agreed.

"Liar!" said Sarah. "I like to be spontaneous sometimes."

"What about you, Will?" asked Richie. "How long would you wait to go out again if this one kicked the bucket?"

Will and Cara had been dating a few weeks, but Will's answer was just as immediate as Sarah's. "Never."

"What?" said Richie.

Brett chimed in with, "Bullshit!"

"Seriously," said Will. "This is it. The rest of my life."

Tammy punched Cara lightly on the arm. "Girl, you didn't tell me you were engaged! Where's the ring?"

Cara hiccupped, then laughed. "There isn't a ring, 'cuz he hasn't asked me yet."

"Awkward," said Richie.

The others laughed.

"A ring?" said Will, standing. "I need a ring to profess my love to this fair maiden?"

"Oh, shit," said Brett, "here comes the Shakespeare."

"It's the go-to, brah," said Richie. "The bard makes the panties drop."

"Shut up, Richie!" laughed Tammy.

Will knelt beside Cara.

"'O heaven, O earth, bear witness to this sound and crown what I profess with kind event if I speak true! if hollowly, invert what best is boded me to mischief! I beyond all limit of what else i' the world do love, prize, honour you.'"

"Damn actors," said Tammy. "Is there anything real behind all the fancy words?"

Will reached into his pocket and pulled out a ring box. "Is this real enough?" He opened it.

"Shit, man," said Richie.

"Panties just disappeared," said Brett.

Tammy and Sarah arrive beside Cara so quickly they might have teleported.

"Omigod, Cara," said Tammy. "Look at that shit!"

"It's beautiful," said Sarah.

Cara didn't speak.

"Say something, honey," said Tammy, "before he takes it back."

"She already said yes," said Will, "in her heart. But she knows I can't officially ask her yet. I have to talk to her dad first."

"It's so soon, though," said Sarah. "You've only been dating a few weeks."

"When you know, you know," said Will. "And I know."

Cara didn't say a word, but her smile spoke volumes. She stood and pulled Will to his feet.

"Kitchen?" she asked.

"Kitchen," he replied.

He picked up Cara and carried her into the next room.

"Damn," said Richie. "I think *my* panties just dropped."

WILL KICKS AS HARD AS HE CAN AND SHOOTS UP, UP through freezing water. He reaches for the surface, feels air on his hand, and breaks the surface.

"Oh...my God, he sputters. He fills his mouth with water to cool his burning tongue, then spits it out. Taking short breaths, Will tries to feed oxygen into his lungs without hyperventilating. Water coats his eyes, so the world seems faint and fuzzy.

"Where...am? Where am I?"

"Give yourself a moment," says a familiar voice from somewhere behind him. "It'll come to you."

Will turns. The Questing Beast lies on the bank of a river. They're underneath some sort of bridge. Everything seems dull in the dim light of the sodium lamps that illuminate the bridge. Rain shimmers in the yellow glow, not a storm anymore, but a gentle wash. Something heavy pulls Will's right arm down into the depths. He peers through the dark water to see the Claidheamh Soluis.

Swimming with one arm and kicking with both feet, Will struggles toward the bank. His feet find purchase, and he stands, only to teeter backward toward the river. He thrusts the sword into the bank and uses it to pull himself into the chilly, Irish morning. A gust of wind hits him. That's when he realizes he's naked.

"Were I in better humor," says the Questing Beast, "I would offer that the river must indeed be cold."

The dragon lies on its side, its huge, reptilian head resting on its own neck. The skeletal rib sticks cruelly out of the thing's cheek, and blood oozes from its shoulder where the Claidheamh Soluis bit. Curiously, the anger in Will's heart seems quenched by the icy river, and his fear of the creature has disappeared. He lays the Claidheamh Soluis on the mossy ground and approaches the Questing Beast.

"Careful, mortal," groans the beast. "Things inside me still yearn for battle, though these wounds have cost me dearly."

"Hold still." Will grasps the end of the jutting rib. "This will prob'ly hurt." He pulls the rib hard at a ninety-degree angle. Blood sprays Will's naked body as the rib comes free. The creature roars, shaking the bricks in the overhead bridge. It makes no move to strike at him, though. Will tosses the rib into the river.

The Questing Beast uncoils, leaving its long neck open and unguarded. Will retrieves the Claidheamh Soluis. The blade shines faintly with the same yellow glow as the sodium lamps. Will drops it in the grass.

"What's wrong, human?" the thing asks. "You battled for my head. Take it."

"Yes," breathes Will. His vision fades into that unfocused realm of imagination. "Your head."

Absently, Will kneels beside the creature and caresses its shoulder with the soft stroke one would use on a kitten. The fur is short and smooth, and the leopard spots, up close, are like Rorschach tests—each one slightly different. Will slides his hand up the neck to where fur blends into scale, the smooth skin of a snake, but warm. The Questing Beast closes its eyes, and a deep rumble comes from its neck. Not angry this time, but...

contented? pleased?

Welcoming.

Cara and Samuel burst into his thoughts. Their voices cry out to him from the fire, and Will's facial muscles harden. He grabs the sword. Their deaths cannot remain unavenged. This is it, the last key to unlock the Kingdom of the Fairy Queen.

Will raises the sword high.

Clenching its muscles, the dragon prepares for the attack.

Will's arms freeze as if rebelling against the act of killing the beast. He screams with anger and indecision. With all his strength, he regains control of his muscles and swings the sword down toward its mark. At the last moment, he turns the blade sideways and slaps the side of the Claidheamh Soluis against the creature's neck.

The Questing Beast screams. Then, as if realizing that its head is still attached to its body…"Ouch," it mutters.

"Sorry," says Will. "I don't—"

"Please, William McConnelly! Offer no apology. My life was yours to take, and you refused. I'm in your debt."

Will drops the sword and falls to his knees, choking back sobs. "It's over," he whispers.

Warm breath wafts across his face.

"Why?" the beast asks.

"I don't know," says Will. His voice sounds far away, as if he's hearing it through a long, cardboard tube. Far away and dull and barely there.

The beast's nose bumps Will's forehead. "Tell me."

"You're…innocent."

The thing laughs. "I'm far from innocent, boy. Today, you stumbled over the bones of those I've killed."

"You never hurt me," Will says. "You said that you've never fought anyone who didn't raise a sword against you first."

"What about your wife and son? I watched them die."

Will shakes his head. "Did you?" he asks. "Or was that hyperbole and metaphor?" Will wipes his nose. "Be honest. You were no more there that night than I was. Except, I should have been there. You simply took my regrets and used them against me in battle. Not totally fair, but not worthy of death."

Will stands.

"So, you find the son of the devil innocent," says the Questing Beast. "You may be the strangest man I've ever met."

Will runs his hand absently over the beast's smooth brow, then over the jagged ridge of small horns behind it.

"If the devil is your father, I hope you bless him with all the love my little Samuel did me."

A groan begins in the throat of the beast, and its eyes close, then clench. Pain shoots across the thing's face and it rolls onto its back. Another ear-splitting roar explodes from its throat.

Will backs away, fearing injury from the lashing tail and legs.

"What's wrong?" he shouts. "Why do you do this?"

The beast draws another breath and roars again. Movement along the creature's abdomen catches Will's attention. Its belly pulses in a dozen places, as if invisible hands push from the inside of its stomach. The revelation hits Will like the proverbial ton of bricks. The Questing Beast is not an it—she's a she.

Will grabs the sword and springs for the distended abdomen. Between the beast's legs is a pink, bulging...*vulva? dragon vagina?*

He almost laughs with incredulity, but the pulsing in the Questing Beast's abdomen and the accompanying roars grow more violent.

Holding his breath, Will waits for the vagina to open, to fulfill its function in childbirth—

dragonbirth?

The opening, as if to defy its own definition, remains stubbornly sealed.

Will looks at the sword in his hands.

"Shit," he breathes.

The dragon's tail almost bowls him over, and he shouts at the beast, "Stop swishing your tail!"

The tail slows, though the beast can't stop its—*her*—legs from twitching as the pain continues to tear at her insides.

Will places the tip of the blade at the top of the vulvic opening.

"Not too deep," he tells himself.

He plunges the sword gently into the valley between the two swollen ridges, expecting the beast to roar louder. She doesn't. It's as if she can't feel the blade in the midst of her agony.

Will pushes the Claidheamh Soluis a bit deeper. Blood and a thick, yellow fluid pour from the puncture wound. Carefully, he withdraws the blade, slicing through the skin. The canal opens to the cold night air.

The roar immediately softens. Will tosses the blade aside as a huge reptilian head emerges from the opening, followed by a long neck and two Clydesdale-sized hooves. A viscous, translucent goo and thin, shredded placental sac cling to the newborn's body. The Questing Beast snakes her long neck around to witness the birth.

"Push!" shouts Will.

"What?" the beast sputters, trying to catch her breath.

"It's...it's like when you're.... Jesus."

Will wipes sweat from his face with his semi-clean forearm.

"Like when I'm Jesus?" yells the dragon.

"Not that!" shouts Will. "It's like...when you defecate, expel waste from your body! I don't know your anatomy. Just tighten up your abdomen and grunt!"

"They're tearing me apart," the Questing Beast screams. She opens her mouth and releases another roar. "Ahhaaa—"

"Don't," Will shouts. "Hold that sound in your throat and use it to push down with your stomach. PUSH DOWN AND OUT!"

The beast shuts her mouth, and her body tenses with effort. The baby shoots from her vagina like a small-load cannonball, landing on top of Will with a thud. It begins to scream, a small echo of its mother's voice.

"Get...off," Will struggles to say.

The baby dragon lies flat on top of him, unwittingly compressing his lungs. It rolls over and off, then tries to stand and fails. With another mighty effort, it manages to get its legs underneath its body and waddles off into the grass.

Will has no time to appreciate the beauty and wonder of the birth, as another head shoves its way into the world. He scuttles to the river to rinse some of the blood and fluid off his hands so he can get a tighter hold. Then he's back between the dragon's legs.

"Okay, Mom," he bellows. "We're gonna do the pushing thing again, on three. One. Two. Three!"

WILL LIES ON THE GROUND NEXT TO THE QUESTING BEAST, both of them exhausted yet happy in the aftermath of new motherhood.

"Son of the devil?" asks Will.

"Metaphor," the beast replies, yawning.

As the last of her babies were born, several large teats had emerged on the Questing Beast's abdomen. The dragonlets had suckled her dry, then fell asleep in a mound against her. All except one little whelp, whose warm head lies on Will's bare stomach. It feels good, because it's cold in the Irish night and Will has no clothes.

"Your children are beautiful," says Will, "and warm."

"Much nicer now that they are born," the Questing Beast says.

"How long have you been pregnant?"

"Thousands of years, I suppose, though I never understood it. I thought it was just part of being a chimera."

"Why didn't you just ask someone to help you give birth?"

"Who, Will?" she says, her voice as soft now as the new baby's scaly face. "All who've visited me have come to kill, as did you. At least, until you came through the fire."

Will lost his smile. "At least one of my family came through unscathed."

"Not unscathed, Will. You bear my mark now, on the inside of your right arm. Look."

Will turns his arm over, and there is, indeed, a mark burned into his skin. It's a familiar pattern, the swirl he'd seen carved in the rocks at the entrance of the fairy mound.

Aidan + Betha 4ever, the tour guide said.

Curiously, it doesn't hurt, even though the pink ridges of burn are still slightly charred.

"The fire will follow me then, the rest of my life."

"Scars heal, Will. What is red and painful now will eventually just be a memory, disfiguring only a very small part of your life."

"The scars are on my heart," Will replies, "and those will never heal. I can't even ask for admittance to the fairy kingdom."

"As for that," says the Questing Beast, "who told you that you needed my head to present to the Fairy Queen?"

"It was in a book written by a man trying to accomplish the same thing. Three quests. The third was to acquire your head. Since you're still here, I guess he didn't make it to the Fairy Queen. Like me. Except you probably ate him."

The Questing Beast laughs. "Look at your feet," she says.

Will glances over the prone body of the sleeping whelp. Something shines in the grass. It's the coin he'd won from the Leanán sídhe.

"How did that get here?" Will asks. "I had it in my pocket, but...no clothes."

"Sometimes magic follows you no matter what you wear," says the Questing Beast. "Look at it."

Will gently moves the whelp's head off his stomach to retrieve the coin. The whelp whines a little, then scooches closer to its mother.

"Just a bunch of words in a language I don't read."

"Turn it over."

Will does so. "Heads, yeah. And the other side is tails."

The Questing Beast nudges Will's shoulder with her giant snout. "Look closely, Will. It's old and worn, but look with fresh eyes. See what's there."

Will tilts the coin into the light, and his brow rises. "I'm an idiot," he groans. In his hand, on the face of the coin, is the head of the Questing Beast. "It was there the whole time."

"Yes."

Will laughs again. "Kagan...the ghost. He said I had all I needed for admittance. I thought he meant through the gate to fight you."

"That's the trouble with you humans," says the Questing Beast. "You're so involved in solving the problem that you cannot see the solution that has been there the whole time."

Realization surges through Will like an electrical charge. He shoots to his feet. "I can still make it!"

His shout wakes a couple of the little dragons. They stretch their necks and bark half-heartedly before settling back into their naps.

"What time is it?" Will asks.

"I have no timepiece," says the Questing Beast, "yet I believe it is three hours until dawn."

"Three hours," spits Will. "There's no way I can make it in three hours. Even if I could get a ride, I'm... Shit! I'm naked! Who's gonna pick up some weird naked guy with a sword in the middle of the night?"

"Will?"

"Goddammit!"

"Will!"

"What?"

Will whirls on the Questing Beast, barely able to control his disappointment and anger.

"Clothes," the creature whispers.

A rush of fiery wind envelopes Will, whirls around him like a dervish. The wind lifts him into the air, and tongues of flame dance across his skin but do not burn him. The gale disappears as quickly as it came, and Will drops to the ground, no longer naked. He wears a pair of simple drawstring pants and a white, collarless, long-sleeved shirt. On his feet are a pair of brown leather, buckled shoes. He gasps.

"Come, William McConnelly," says the Questing Beast. "Surely, magic is no surprise to you now."

"I guess it shouldn't be," Will says. "Of course, I look like I'm set for a Renaissance fair."

"I thought the Renaissance had ended," says the Questing Beast.

"How do I get back to Drumkeeran?" Will asks. "Do you have magic for that, too?"

The dragon smiles. "I might," she says, "but I believe you'll need no magic. Follow the path back up the riverbank to the stones. You'll find your way."

Will lays his hand atop the Questing Beast's head. "Thank you," he says.

"Thank *you*," says the beast. "You came to take life, yet you brought life into the world. You are truly unique, William McConnelly."

"What will happen to them?" Will asks, looking around at the whelps. "Where will they go?"

"We'll return to my world," she says. "One or two may venture out someday, but they won't travel far. This is our home. Now go, and take your hero's sword. Perhaps you will find a worthy lord to pass it on to."

Feeling clumsy, Will bows to the dragon. She returns the gesture with her scaly head. Strapping the sheathed sword onto his back, Will turns to leave. He immediately falls. Behind him, a little whelp has wrapped its tail around Will's legs.

"I have to go," Will says.

The little guy whines, a sad, sonorous voice. It barks once.

"Maybe we'll see each other again someday," Will says. He unwraps the little tail from around his legs and scratches around the whelp's ears.

"Perhaps," says the Questing Beast. "Stranger things have happened."

With a final pat on the little one's nose, Will sets off along the path and the rock mounds beyond.

Chapter Fifteen

CONVERGENCE

WILL peers through the driver's side window of Sam's little Focus. After a week in Ireland, it doesn't feel strange that he's standing on the right side of the car. Sam has reclined her seat to an almost horizontal position. Her face looks soft and pure and blue in the half-moon light shining through the windshield. No wrinkles...no scars. No pain. Every little muscle relaxed.

A shadow passes over Sam's face, and a brilliant light hits Will straight in the eyes.

"Ow." Will jerks upright.

"Yeh wouldn't be thinkin' a' breakin' inta that nice young lady's car now, wouldja?" says a voice.

Will lifts a hand to block some of the light. "No, sir," he replies. "Actually, she's my ride back to Drumkeeran."

The light lowers and illuminates the gravel. Through multi-colored spots popping in front of his eyes, Will sees a white-haired security guard holding a flashlight.

"Do yeh haf any proof a' that, bye?" asks the guard.

"Can we just knock on the window?"

"She looks a bit knackered," says the guard. "No reason ta wake her just ta find out yer some homeless actor lookin' fer a handout."

Looking down at his outfit, Will thinks that yes, homeless actor probably fits. He laughs.

"Yeh havin' a laff now, are yeh? Easy target, me, an old man makin' what income he can now that they've closed down the cannery. Fine lad yeh are, eh? Maybe I'll be callin' the Garda Síochána and they can sort this out."

Will knocks on Sam's window. She sits up so quickly that, were she taller, she'd have bashed her head on the roof of her car. She blinks and rubs her eyes.

"Sam," Will shouts, projecting his voice through the window.

Still rubbing her eyes, she opens the car door and almost falls out.

"Ah, me leg," Sam mutters. "It's asleep." She rubs her calf fervently, looking up at Will. "What the hell are yeh wearin', Will? What happened ta yer clothes?"

"Long story," he replies. "I can tell you on the way back. Can you please let this gentleman know I'm not assaulting you or trying to make you buy me drinks?"

"Oh, he tries ta get me ta buy him drinks, all right," Sam says to the old guard. "Don't yeh worry though, Athair. I charge 'im fer every one."

Sam winks at the old man, who smiles.

"Yeh'd best be on yer way then, lass, if yeh don't want the sun bitin' yeh on the arse a'fore yeh get back home."

Will's breath catches in his chest. "What time is it?" he asks.

"Oh, it's goin' on 2:45, I'd say, judgin' by the stars."

Sam grabs her phone from the car and looks. "Yer right as a plump goose," she says.

"Me father were a sailor," says the old man. "Taught me to read the stars a'fore I could drive a car."

"We've gotta go," says Will. He gently nudges Sam back into her seat and hops into the left-side passenger seat.

"So yeh got what yeh came fer?" she asks.

Will holds his finger up to his lips. "Shh," he breathes, then yells, "Good night, sir! Thanks for your help!"

"Godspeed," the old man says. He ambles back toward the lighted guard house a few hundred feet away.

"If yeh've got a dragon's head on yeh," says Sam, "it must be a wee one."

Will opens his hand, and Sam turns on her phone flashlight to see the coin.

"Is it silver?"

"Maybe."

Samthann pushes her key into the ignition and starts the car. She cocks her head at Will. "So, yer really gonna do this," she says. Not a question—a statement.

Will nods.

"Yer a dim-witted git."

Before Will can fasten his seatbelt, Sam throws the car into gear and peels out of the parking space.

Will hits the side of the car and struggles to grab the seatbelt. "What?" he asks.

No answer.

"That's why we're here," he says.

No answer.

Sighing, Will leans back into his seat. Sam turns out of the parking lot and onto the road.

Ten minutes later, Sam turns to Will. "Where'd yeh go?" she asks. "I was right there in the middle of the hall an' yeh jus' left without so much as a 'be seein' yeh.'"

"You mean in the—"

"An' yeh were gone half the night. Where'd yeh get those weirdo clothes?"

Will draws a breath. "I—"

"An' now we're racin' back to the hills ta meet a Fairy Queen so's yeh can disappear? An' here I am like yer bloody tour guide. 'Get me drunk, Samthann.' 'Take me to the doctor, Samthann.' 'Drive me to my destiny, Samthann.' Then, 'Forget the hell yeh ever met me!'" Sam punctuates her last syllable by hitting both hands on the steering wheel.

"Sam," Will says, but once again, he can't get another word out.

"Don't even talk ta me, William McConnelly! Yeh'll be gone in two hours. I might as well start getting' used ta bein' without yeh right now!" Samthann's eyes shine in the glow of the dashboard lights, but she doesn't cry. She exhales a small scoff.

Will wonders if the scoff is for the fool she thinks she is or the fool she knows Will is.

It doesn't matter.

Will turns his attention back to the road and the night.

I'll be gone soon, and this stupid place of death and madness will be a memory.

Lost in his thoughts, it takes Will a minute to feel Sam staring at him again. He glances over.

"Well?" she says.

"Well, what?" says Will.

Sam sighs with exasperation. "Are yeh gonna tell me where you went in the tomb or ain'tcha?"

Will shakes his head, confused. "I thought you didn't want to know."

"A' course I want ta know!" she replies. "Yeh disappeared right in front a' me eyes. Yeh think I want ta take that mystery ta me grave? It'll drive me mad."

Will laughs.

"Oh, an' now I'm funny, am I?"

"I think you're mad already," the words pop out like a fart in church.

Sam's eyes narrow, and then she smiles. "That's the first intelligent thing yeh've said all night."

The smile makes Sam's face glow like a Snapchat filter. If this had been another life, Will could see himself falling in love with her.

Like she did with me, in her dreams.

Sam twists around in her seat. Her back pops loudly.

"We've got a drive ahead of us, an' yeh've got a story inside yeh. Let's put the two together, as me da used ta say, an' take a trip down memory's lane."

"Okay," says Will. "What's the last thing you remember?"

"Yeh told me ta look through the adder stone, but there weren't anything there. I said, let's leave, and yeh asked me if I knew what the Leanán sídhe looked like. Then yeh disappeared."

"So, you don't remember feeling a kiss on your cheek?"

"I think I'd remember if yeh'd kissed me cheek, Will," Sam scoffs

"It wasn't me," he says. "It was the Leanán sídhe."

Sam's eyes grow wide. "Bollix!"

Will's smile turns into a grin. "Yep. And she was naked, too."

Sam gasps, then slaps Will in the chest with the backside of her left hand.

"Ow!" he says. "What was that for?"

"Havin' dirty thoughts! Were it Sister Rose at me primer school, yer hands'd be nigh fallin' off from the whacks yeh'd get with a ruler! Talkin' about me with some nekked hussy like I'm some kinda hoor!"

"So, you don't want to hear the story?"

"Of course, I want ta hear the story!" Sam roars. "Why do I have ta keep tellin' yeh I want to hear the goddamned story?" She crosses herself. "Forgive me Mary, mother a' Jaysus."

WILL AND CARA STOOD IN FRONT OF THE COFFIN, UNABLE TO move. Before them lay one of the most jovial people Will had ever met—Cara's mom, Betha Caoimhe Brady. Will hated bodies in a box. That thing dressed up in Betha's clothes was not his mother-in-law. Betha had been laughter and food and comfort, not this room-temperature shell.

Cara's hand tightened, threatening to cut off Will's circulation. She began to whisper, "I can't. I can't." A few tears escaped eyes too dry to weep.

"We need to sit down," Will whispered. "They're ready to start the service."

"I can't move, Will," she said.

"I'll help you."

"No!" Cara's voice was loud enough for the whole congregation to start whispering.

Will turned and offered a regretful smile to them. He looked for help from Aidan and saw that his father-in-law's hands covered his face. His suit jacket had bunched across his shoulders like a shroud. Grimacing,

Will returned his attention to Cara. "Honey, we have to take our seats. The priest is waiting."

"We can't," Cara said. "If we move, they're gonna put my mom in the ground and I'll never get to see her again."

Cara pressed the side of her head against Will's shoulder, refusing to take her tear-stained eyes off her mother.

Will felt helpless. Betha was the second mother he'd lost. He wanted to believe as Cara did, that Betha was still here somehow, but— "That's not her," Will said.

"What?" Cara breathed.

"It's not," said Will, suddenly angry. "We put this...this thing in a box, but the spirit is gone and the laughter is gone. Everything that made it her. She's gone, Cara."

Will's tears drizzled down his face and into Cara's hair.

"No," Cara said.

"She's not here! If there is a heaven, she's there, and all the angels are happier because of it. And if Jesus has never had shepherd's pie, he'd better learn to like it. He's gonna get it at least once a week now."

Laughter bubbled out of Will's nose, with some snot bubbles immediately behind.

Cara giggled a little, and then she began to wail. She turned away from the coffin and pushed her face into Will's shoulder so hard that he thought she might asphyxiate.

Looking embarrassed, two ushers trudged up the aisle to Cara and Will. One gently placed his hand on Cara's shoulder as if to pull her away. "Miss?" he said.

"We're almost ready," said Will.

"We have to start," said the usher, a middle-aged man in a black suit. "There's another mass scheduled here in less than an hour."

Anger sting the back of Will's throat. "This is the only mother she's had or ever will have."

"I'm sorry, sir," began the usher, but he was cut off by a strong hand on his left shoulder.

"That'll be enough," said Aidan Brady.

"Sir, I don't mean to be crass," said the usher, "but she's been standing here for half an hour."

"Bye," growled Aidan, "if yeh don't leave me daughter alone with her grief, I will end yeh, an' there'll be no body to weep over because they'll never find it."

Shocked, Cara looked up from Will's chest. From her wide-eyed stare, Will believed she had never heard her dad speak like this. Will himself could never have imagined such a staunch Catholic threatening someone's life during mass.

"Dad," Cara whispered, "it's okay. Let's go sit down." She grabbed Aidan's arm, but it was as if the man had become a tree rooted in the floor of the church.

"Da," she said. "Is breá liom tú. Suigh síos."

Will did a double take. He'd never heard his wife speak Gaelic; didn't even know she could.

The words of Aidan's homeland seemed to reach him. He released the usher.

"It's all right, Da," she whispered, caressing his cheek. "We're okay."

"We're not, lass," Aidan said. "She's gone."

Cara's hand left her father's face and found his chest. "She's here," she said, tapping Aidan's chest. "She'll always be there. And here."

She took Aidan's hand and placed it on her belly. A tiny paunch had just begun to develop in her fourteenth week of pregnancy.

"She'll live in the heartbeat of your grandbaby," said Will. "And in the heart of his grandchild, and then his and hers forever and ever."

Aidan smiled at that. "Let's have this over then," he said.

The three of them took their places in the pews. The mass was a bit rushed and the burial, a bit soggy—it rained all afternoon. Many of the mourners brought food and sympathy to the wake at Aidan's house. It was a traditional Irish wake, where laughter, tears, and whiskey poured generously throughout the evening.

That night, lying in each other's arms, Cara thanked Will for his strength and patience.

"You're my Betha," said Will. "I don't know what I'd do without you."

Cara snuggled closer. "I do."

"I do what?"

"I know what you'd do without me."

Will laughed. "You do? Well, wise prophet. Tell me my future."

"Don't make fun of me. I do know what you'd do."

"Okay," said Will. "Tell me."

Cara whispered into his ear, a long whisper.

"I don't think so," he said.

"You would."

He thought about it a few minutes, while Cara's breath grew slower. She began to snore. It was just him and the night now. As much as he wanted to disagree with her, he thought she might be right.

Will closed his eyes. Yes, he would do that. It would be difficult, but he would.

SAMTHANN SLAPS WILL ONCE MORE AS HE DESCRIBES THE encounter with the Leanán sídhe. Perhaps he added a little too much detail of the fairy's open-mouthed kiss with Sam in her hypnotized state.

After that, she lets Will settle into his storyteller mode, illuminating each detail of the riddle game, the endless staircase, the ghost at the door, and the birthing. The story ends with Will and the security guard arguing over waking Sam in her car. Finally, all the words have been said. Will looks at the clock on the dashboard. His tale has taken over an hour.

"Samthann?" he asks.

Sam sighs. "Yeh make a good audiobook, William McConnelly. That yeh do, fer sure."

"Fer sure and certain," he adds.

"So," she says.

Will echoes her. "So."

"Yeh have yer coin. Yeh have yer plan, and nothin's changed fer yeh."

"Right. Nothing's changed."

Sam angles her head toward him, a sad smile pulling at her lips. "It's butter from a cow, then."

"Huh?" asks Will.

Sam's smile disappears. "It's done." Her attention returns to the road, and an uncomfortable silence builds a wall between them. As chaotic as the journey to the tombs was, the return is the exact reverse. It's as if a giant remote control has paused the world, all except that little space that holds Will, Sam, and her Ford Focus.

Will tries to sleep, but he tosses and turns in the small car seat. The determined misery resting on Samthann's face screams at him to say something. Finally…"Sam?"

"Don't," she says. "Don't speak ta me again ever in this life." If Sam's voice shakes a little, her features do not.

After another hour of deafening, accusatory calm, the Focus rolls into Drumkeeran. Sam stops behind the pub, shifts into Park, and shuts off the engine. Her hand pulls the key from the ignition, and she palms the set of keys.

They sit in the car, both of them staring at the floor mats. This is a different silence, Will thinks, like after the credits at a movie, when you're waiting to see if there's an Easter egg, or a teaser for the next film in the series. Sam and he are both waiting for the lights to come up.

"Yer an eejit, William McConnelly," Sam whispers. "I can't pretend to know yer pain, 'coz I barely know me own. But yeh have feet, and they danced once. They're not broken, neither; that's just yer heart. Sometimes in life…sometimes, yeh just have ta follow yer feet." She looks at him and sighs. "I'm gonna get the pub ready fer lunch service, 'coz there's beer an' whiskey ta be poured. Tonight, I'll drink and carouse with the fine folk a' Drumkeeran, and mebbe even some out-a-towners, mebbe as far away as Texas, even. I'll dance with the lads and lasses who'll dance, an' yer face'll be in my dreams fer a while, but I'll get over yeh someday. Not by traipsin' off ta live with the fairies. Nuthin' fancy like that. It'll be gettin' up in the mornin' and goin' ta work and goin' ta bed every night, and ta church on Sundays. It'll take time, Will, and that's fine, coz I'm not afraid a' time like yeh are."

"I'm sorry," Will says again. He hopes it's the last time he ever has to utter the words. He waits for Sam to yell at him, or more likely, hit him.

Instead, she smiles. "Go on," she says.

She pops the door open and hops out of the car. Will steps out on his side, but there's no time to say goodbye. Sam's already inside the pub. Will shakes his head at the abruptness of it all, but out of the corner of his eye, he sees the first glint of dawn.

He slams the car door and heads toward the bed and breakfast, thinking he can borrow the bicycle and leave a note and some money for Meg to have someone retrieve it. He'll have to grab the urn too, if he's going to—

"There he is, Conor, fer sure and certain."

"Fer certain and sure!"

Will almost trips over his own feet trying to stop as he passes Conor and Seamus. They stand in the alley next to an old, rusty bike with a basket and a rubber horn.

"Where did you come from?" Will sputters. "Are you two following me?"

Conor loads his pipe and leans in to Seamus. "Don't seem like he has time fer all these inquiries, do it, Seamus?"

"No Conor, it don't. If the bye is gonna be greetin' the Fairy Queen at dawn, I think he'd best take his dragon's head coin and get up into the hills."

"Dragon's head coin?" Will asks. "How did you know it was—"

Conor squeezes the black bulb on the bike horn. "Action, bye!" he shouts. "Action! There's no time fer hesitation now! Ta the hills and yer destiny, or stay and fill yer life with days an' weeks an' moments like the rest of us!"

Conor pushes the bike, and like magic, it floats to Will without a bump or waver. Will slides onto the seat and seamlessly begins to pedal, pumping faster and faster, pushing everything he has into gaining speed and then more speed. He pedals through the steadily increasing incline. Somewhere near, a rooster heralds the break of day.

The mindless pedaling gives Will a moment to think.

How did Seamus and Conor know about the dragon's head coin? Did they tell him it was a coin? It was their book, after all.

No, I found out about the Questing Beast with Samthann.

"Samthann," he breathes, feet pumping. He's never known a woman whose fist was as fast as her smile.

Will shakes his head. Why is he thinking about her now? Is she right? Would he be better off here, with her and her kiss that...?

No. Samuel's and Cara's deaths and Will's happiness cannot coexist in the same world.

The image of two gunfighters from some old western pops into Will's head. "Ain't room in this town fer the both of us," one of the gunfighters says. Will laughs a little.

You're right, pardner, he thinks. *Ain't room in town for the both of 'em.*

"Shit!" Will shouts. "The ashes!"

He almost pulls the bike over and wheels it around, but he realizes even as he's braking that he doesn't have time. He can either spread the ashes or meet the Fairy Queen.

Meg has Aidan's number, he thinks. *She'll call him when I come up missing, and they'll take care of the ashes somehow. Still, it was the one thing Aidan asked me to do.*

Will shoots into the field where he'd tried to kill himself five days ago. He's almost died four times since then.

Will realizes he won't be sneaking up on the fairy kingdom today. He veers right, and suddenly the bike's barreling downhill at twenty, thirty miles an hour, rocketing toward the gold and silver ball in the field below. As the colors of the ball grow transparent, revealing the ancient castle, Will plows into the field. He tries to brake going full speed. The bike twists and falls. Will flies over the handlebars and crashes into the clover. The castle grows solid, and the drawbridge falls open, burying itself into the grass three feet away from Will's head. The fairy folk pour out of the castle.

They fly toward him, weaving the carpet for the Fairy Queen. Up close, they look nothing like the fairies from picture books or movies. Disney has prepared Will to see tiny humans with wings, but they're more animal than human. Here's one with a pig-like head and six legs, colored blue like a berry and flitting about on veined, dragonfly wings. There's one like a prawn, with green, glistening tentacles that hold three separate ribbons. A third doesn't even seem organic, but rather a prism of light that doesn't stream but oozes and pools and stretches her strip of ribbon into place.

Hundreds of other creatures exit the castle.

Will stands and backs away as they continue to weave the carpet. The fairies take no notice of him at first, but when they realize they have an audience, a group of insectile fairies begin coaxing the clover to flower. Delicate blooms open amidst the green. The fairies then change the flowers to all the colors of the rainbow, in reverse order. Overhead, two oozing blobs launch themselves at each other. At each collision, purple thunderclouds emerge and begin to rain, the droplets rising up and away from the ground as if gravity no longer works.

The fairy guard marches out of the castle double time. Apparently, word of the interloper has made its way through the ranks. They line up on either side of the carpet and wait for instructions. Hand on his mace, the Captain of the Guard glares at Will and licks his lips.

Music rises, the same magical tune that had captured Will's imagination days ago. The powder blue light appears again, and the Queen emerges.

Her opalescent, horse's mane hair flows across her shoulders and down her back. It gently blows in the soft breeze. The Queen's elongated eyes, opened wide, are focused straight at Will. Something happens, because he feels every thought in his head pour out through the soul of his eyes and into hers.

The Queen shimmers into place in front of Will, at the end of the carpet. He feels naked in front of her, and embarrassed, even though it is she who is unclothed. Unsure of what to do, Will kneels in front of her.

"Your Majesty," he whispers.

The coolness of the first autumn wind brushes the side of his face. Will understands that this is the touch of the Queen's hand.

"Rise, William McConnelly," she breathes, and the entire meadow blooms at the music of her voice.

He stands carefully, so as not to look directly at her nakedness, but is still too shy to look into her eyes.

"What have you brought me, Will?" she asks.

He reaches into the little pocket sewn into his strange garments, garments that now seem apropos for the occasion, and locates the coin. He places it on the Queen's palm, where it hovers as if part of a magic trick.

The Fairy Queen raises her hand. The coin spins faster and faster until, with a slight pop, it disappears. The Queen takes a step backward, leaving room on the carpet.

"Enter into my kingdom, William McConnelly," she whispers, "and forget everything that it is to be human."

Will's eyes gravitate to the carpet, the edge of which rests a mere six inches from the toes of his buckled shoes. His breath catches in his chest. This is it. Nepenthe, as Edgar Allan Poe wrote in "The Raven." Forgetfulness.

His lips curl into an unbidden smile, and Will shakes his head. After months of misery and despair, he stands mere inches from relief.

Unbidden, Will removes his shoes and places the bare sole of his right foot on the carpet. Warmth pulses through the ribbons and into his leg, through his leg into his stomach, and into his chest and arms and head and....

"So," says Samuel, clear as day, "Sunshine's weggo so' came off his body an' went to heaven?"

Will sees himself beside his son at the funeral of his goldfish, Sunshine.

"Yes, that's it," says Will.

"An' he's happy?"

"Very. Even though I'm sure he misses you."

The vision disappears from behind Will's eyes. The memory pours down through his body and is sucked away, into the carpet.

What's going on? he wonders.

Another memory appears.

"Penny for your thoughts," Cara says, her voice a beautiful, sweet-toned bell in Will's ear.

Will says nothing, because it's a perfect moment, and he doesn't want to ruin it.

"Will?"

He pulls her closer, if that's possible, as they lie side-by-side in the park on their picnic blanket.

"I don't sell my thoughts for anything less than a quarter," he says.

She smiles against his cheek.

"That's kind of expensive."

"They're good thoughts."

"Okay. Give me one."

He turns his face toward her, his eyes opening the tiniest bit. "On credit?"

Cara grins and nuzzles her nose into the crook of Will's neck. "I'm good for it."

The memory is pulled from Will's mind and down into the fairy carpet.

"What's going on?" he asks.

"The passage of time," says the Queen. "From your mind into our ribbons. They will be released into the wind and you will join us, dancing and whiling away eternity just as innocent as when you first came into the human world. This is your rebirth, William."

"The fire," Will whispers.

He sees the house burning, flames exploding through windows. The rain pounds against him as the neighbors gawk. The horror disappears into the carpet. A weight lifts from his soul, and he takes an honest to God, lungs-filling breath.

The memories come faster now. The first time he and Cara made love. It appears and is gone in the blink of an eye. Will's mom making him a carrot cake, his childhood favorite, for his thirteenth birthday. Gone. Betha's beautiful, unrestrained laugh as Aidan makes a rare joke. Gone. The weight of Samuel's tiny body resting on Will's chest the first night they bring him home. It's gone, too.

As the memories continue to flow into the carpet, Will can no longer picture Cara's face, how her mouth looked when she smiled, and the color of her eyes. Samuel's name is like a prairie dog, popping in and out of memory until it vanishes. He'd once had a child, right? A boy, or a girl? It's going, going, gone in a few blinks of Will's dazed eyes.

The man's own name is hard to speak now. The syllables are on the tip of his tongue, but...where is he? What's going on? He looks down at his feet, but he can barely remember the word—feet. He sees a woman with a baby in a hospital. The woman looks at him with kind, tired eyes. The eyes elongate into the eyes of the Queen. Will hears a name far, far away, as if underwater.

"Cara. Caralin."

The man panics and loses his balance. He stumbles off the carpet and back into the grass. His head clears, and he sees the color of Cara's eyes —*green*—and the curve of her smile.

Not the heart-shaped smile of the Fairy Queen, but a heart, nonetheless.

"William?" says the Queen. "The sun rises, and we with it."

"My memories," Will stutters. "All the good ones—"

"Good. Bad. They carry with them the emotion of being human. As you can surely see, we are not of that species. Nor can you be, if you are to come with us."

"Why?" Will asks. "You smile, you laugh...surely you have emotion in your world."

The Queen's smile grows warmer, yet less merry. "We smile with the changing of the seasons and laugh as the world turns on its axis. The eternal cannot find joy in the small victories and defeats of your world. We must be clear-eyed for the passage of time that, millions of years from now, will claim even our lives when the sun turns to ash. Until then, we help the earth grow, and if we cavort with you, it is but the space of a dream for us."

"You have but slumbered here," Will quotes, "while these visions did appear."

The Queen nods.

"Shakespeare was talking about you," Will says. "Not humans."

"I offered him solace once, the man to whom you refer. He refused. He's ashes now himself, and soon his words will join him, in the blink of a fairy's eye."

The weight of the world once again presses on him. "So, if I stay with you, I will lose all my memories, everything I loved in this life."

"And everything you hated."

A ray of sunshine hits the castle, and it begins to dissolve.

"Just a moment more," says the Queen, "and we fly home on the wings of true dawn, leaving only the dew. Make your choice."

Will feels her imposing her resolve on him. The Queen wants him to join her, to serve her, become another fairy in her legion. She offers him what he's been begging for, a release from his pain.

"William?" the Queen says. Her voice begins to waver and her form grows translucent.

Will can see right through her and yet, it's as if her form is a projection screen on which he sees his own life unfold. Pain and happiness twine around her like two vines running up the same tree.

Will sees Cara's smile, and he hears Samuel giggle. The crackling flames devouring his house and family. Cara's soft moans as Will kisses her hair. Aidan's pounding on the table with his fists. The roar of the tornado as Will faces it, screaming into the face of God Himself. The sounds and images in Will's returning memory weave together, making a carpet of another color—the color of Will's life.

Will stares into the Queen's eyes as she disappears. She reaches out to him one last time, her hand brushing through his face like forgiveness. She whispers a word once, twice, and then she's gone.

"Wait," cries Will, not understanding her, but then he hears the word again on the wind.

"Live," she said, and again, "live."

Will is carried back to the day of Betha's funeral, later in bed when Cara whispers to him, "Here is what you would do if something happened to me," she says. Cara's words, even in memory, tickle Will's ears. "You'd live, Will. You'd have to, because I'd never forgive you if you didn't." Cara stops whispering and kisses Will on the cheek.

"It only takes a moment to heal," she says. She snuggles into Will's shoulder and drifts off with little snores.

A moment, he thinks, both in the past and the present.

In the present only, *When is healing finally going to come?*

In memory, Samthann's lips brush Will's. That was a moment, wasn't it? Or, at least, the beginning of one. While Sam's lips touched his, the pain and anger had vanished, just like the Fairy Queen.

Will looks into the green hills and sees the sun going down, and—

"Wait a minute," he says.

That's not right. The sun was just rising.

Will takes a step and falls.

"What the hell?" he says.

His legs are as stiff as boards.

What's going on?

The sun sinks lower, moving into night. Will realizes that time, in this field, is passing differently than outside of it. In his head, he's only been there a couple minutes, but a whole day has passed. He remembers the story of Rip Van Winkle, the man who slept a lifetime away in a night. Maybe the old man had stumbled upon a field like this somewhere in America.

Maybe he'd even met a chupacabra, he thought.

Will stretches his legs and stands. Grabbing the bike, he quickly trots out of the enchanted field. He pushes the bike up the incline and into the meadow above, then hops on and pedals toward the road. He realizes something and stops.

"No tears," he says, reaching up to his dry eyes. "They're gone."

Will reaches for the memory of the fire, the despair of watching the flames consume his everything, but it's as if those memories are far away. The memories he loves, with Cara laughing and painting his nose and Samuel pushing him into the flower beds, those are almost fresher than they were before.

Will smiles and looks back toward the fairy field, now a shade of gray under brightly glowing stars.

"Thank you," he whispers. "Thank you, Your Majesty."

He points the front bike wheel toward Drumkeeran and pushes off into the night.

Chapter Sixteen

DUST

"C'MERE, LUFF!" shouts an old gaffer in the middle of the pub. "I'll give yeh a kiss fer a pint!"

Samthann shakes her head and throws a towel at his head. "Yeh'll be gettin' no kisses from me, Coilin!" she says. "An' no pints either, if yeh don't pay yer tab from last week!"

The pub patrons roar with laughter as Coilin pulls the towel from atop his bald crown. "Ah, yeh used ta be a laugh," he says. "Now...now—"

"Now now now!" says Samthann. "We don't listen to vinyls anymore, Coilin, but if we did, I'd say yer a broken record and it's time to throw yeh in the waste bin. Not the green one, either. Jaysus knows, we don't need to recycle any more bollocksed old muppets in this town."

The pub grows quiet...or quieter. A few old sots whisper to each other, but most give their attention to Samthann or Coilin.

"Yer right scundered today, ain'tcha?" says Coilin, his voice a mixture of hurt and wonder.

"Well, yer a right arse!" Sam yells. She turns away from the crowd and begins drying already dry glasses on the kitchen side of the pub. Tears well up, angry-sad-lost tears that she can't begin to process.

Behind her, someone strikes up a tune on a fiddle. Prob'ly Kevin.

"Not now, Kev," she says, afraid to turn around, afraid to see the pity in her customers' eyes. She can handle a pinch on the bum or a slap in the face, but pity tears her to pieces like wild dogs. The fiddle stops.

Will, she thinks for the thousandth time that day. *Goddamned William McConnelly.*

Her thumbnail starts worrying a small spot on the bottom of the glass, something that none of the patrons here would worry about in a million years. 'Cept maybe that cheapskate Coilin Walsh.

"Goddamn him, too," she whispers.

Sam scoffs at her own attitude. Nothing made sense today! She'd waited so long for her dream man to come, content with visions of laughter and dancing. Then he arrives, and what? He's a depressed widower with no will to live.

She laughs aloud at the phrase "will to live."

"Oxymoron," she says, talking to herself. "Or maybe jus' a regular ol' moron." She laughs again.

Behind her, the whispering gets louder. She knows everyone is talking about her, but she can't bring herself to care. Why should she? What did it matter, any of it? A tear spills onto her cheek, and she wipes it away with an angry backhand.

The grandfather clock in the corner begins to chime. Sam counts the bells as she often does, with a little rhyme her ma used to teach her numbers. She misses her parents terribly, though she doesn't wander about the country trying to find fairy kingdoms to hide in.

She counts, "One fer sorrow, two fer mirth, three fer a weddin', and four fer death. Five fer silver, six fer gold, seven fer a secret ne'er to be told. Eight fer a wish, nine fer a kiss, ten fer a bird you must not miss."

That's all of the original rhyme, but Sam continues on with her own words she added eight months ago. They came to her after the first few days of her visions of Will.

"Eleven fer parents lookin' down from above, and..."

Gong.

"Twelve, fer a future filled with—" Sam chokes on the words, then they sputter out with a sob—"dancin' and love."

She pushes the dishtowel into her mouth to keep from screaming. Behind her, the fiddle begins again. She pulls the dishtowel from her mouth.

"Stop it!" she cries. "I told yeh already! No music tonight!"

The bar is silent long enough for Samthann to curse herself for losing her mind in front of everyone. Then the fiddle picks up again, this time an even merrier tune. A drum joins in, and then an accordion.

Yer about to wollop a fiddle player, Samthann, she thinks.

Sam whirls around, red-faced and furious. "Are yeh deef?" she screams.

The music stops, but even with the scream, Sam is not the center of attention. The crowd stares at a man dressed in clothes from another century. He stands near the band and places a €10 note in the tip jar. It joins two others.

"How can we dance," asks Will, "if we don't have music?"

"W-Will?" she stammers. "William McConnelly? Am I ill? Am I dreamin'?"

"Journeys end in lovers meeting, Samthann. Every wise man's son doth know."

The next few moments, for Sam, unfold in slow motion.

Will holds out his hand, and Sam's towel falls from hers, unbidden. The fiddle, drum, and accordion begin to play again.

"Dance with me!" shouts Will over the music.

Sam looks down at her feet, which stubbornly refuse to take a step.

"Samthann!" says Will.

Sam's right foot manages to shift half a step, and then the left follows. It's like she's walking through syrup—not just her feet, her whole body.

"Come on, woman!" says Will. "I gave up a million years of peace and quiet for you!"

He laughs and, in the blink of an eye, the spell is broken.

Sam hurls across the room. "That's how yeh court a girl?" she roars. "'I gave up a million years a' peace and quiet fer yeh'?"

Will laughs, this time, louder.

Samthann's rage bubbles in her veins. She raises a hand to slap the bugger, to ring his bell like a church steeple on Sunday morning. Before she can land the blow, he throws his arms around her and pulls her in for a kiss.

She bites his lip.

"Ow!" he yells. He tries to back away, but Samthann pulls his head to hers and presses her lips against his. She breaks the kiss and pushes her head into his chest, crying and laughing.

"Yeh did give up years a' peace an' quiet, didn'tcha?" she says.

Will's hands grip her shoulders and she looks up into his smiling face. "I'm looking at you," he says, "and it's like the first time I've really seen you. I don't think I gave up anything."

Sam laughs again and starts dabbing at her eyes. "I look a right mess today," she says. "All yer fault, a' course. If yeh'd just stayed—"

"All my fault," Will agrees. "Can I apologize with a dance?" Will pulls Sam into the middle of the small, bare space of floor near the front door. He bows. Sam laughs and curtsies. Will's right hand finds her waist, and his left hand her right. He leads Sam into a modified two-step, which doesn't quite fit the music. Will steps on her foot, and she laughs and backs away.

"That's what they call dancin' in America?" she asked.

"I'm not sure I'd call it dancing anywhere," Will replies. "I'm out of practice."

"I'll lead a bit," Sam says.

It takes a moment, but she finally has him flying around the room, out of breath and panting like a dog. Most of the pub claps along or bangs their pint glasses along with the beat of the song.

The song ends, and Will collapses onto a bar stool.

All the regulars applaud, and a few call for more drinks.

"Wait yer turn, yeh dopes," Sam shouts. "I need a moment with this gentleman here."

Whistles and catcalls greet her announcement.

Sam waves them off as she rounds the bar to pour Will and herself a drink. "Is jus' one okay today?" she asks, "Or do yeh need three or four?"

"One is fine, thanks," Will says, trying to catch his breath. He looks around the bar. "Seamus and Conor aren't here, so—"

"Why do yeh keep on with that bollocks?" asks Sam. This time, she doesn't feel the normal aggravation. Just curiosity. "Three whiskeys fer me friends and all? Yeh've been layin' that on ever since yer first night here, or maybe the second. The first night yeh had a bit a' guaze up yer nose."

"Thanks to the door," laughs Will.

"Tá," Sam agrees. She passes a glass of Jameson across the bar to Will, keeping one for herself.

"And I only ordered extra drinks when Conor and Seamus were here."

"Who are Conor and Seamus?"

"Oh, lord," says Will. "Not this again."

"Will? Can yeh give a lass some details so's mebbe she can understand?" She covers Will's hand with hers.

"They've been with me every time I've come in," Will says. "Two old...what do you call them? Gaffers?"

"I've never seen nobody with yeh, Will."

"I swear it. Every time I ordered three drinks it was because they were with me, or joining me later."

"Why didn't they order their own?" Sam asks. *Ha! Gotcha there, William McConnelly!*

"They said you wouldn't serve them, 'cuz you didn't like them much."

Sam laughs. "This is silly. I gave yeh the drinks 'coz we Irish don't mind a double fister as long as yeh pay yer tab. I thought it a wee bit strange that yeh'd order three, since yeh only have two hands."

"Leipreachán," says Fergus.

They turn to see that the doctor has brought his empty pint glass to the bar.

"Hi, Fergus," says Will.

"Evenin', Will, or should I say, mornin', since it's past twelve."

Fergus turns to Sam. "Samthann, love. We're getting' mighty dry out there. I know yer havin' a moment here with the lad, an' it's good to see some real color in yer cheeks after such a spell. Still, good ale needs drinkin', the ol' fellers say." Fergus smiles. "An' I'm one a' the ol' fellers."

Sam grabs his pint glass and refills it. "What were yeh sayin' about leipreacháns, Fergus?" she asks.

"The two ol' byes Will's talkin' about."

"You saw them?" asked Will.

"Tá, I did. See 'em now and again, always with the tourists. Yeh see, leipreacháns can't drink alcohol. It's agin their nature, but they love the taste of it. So, they have a magic, yeh might say, when a lad or lass happens ta buy 'em a drink, that they get the taste of it, but the one who buys it gets the alcohol."

Will stands, excited. "That makes so much sense! I was always getting drunk on so few drinks! Except for the night with the pùca."

"I won't ask," says Fergus. He grabs the fresh pint from Sam.

"But if Samthann couldn't see them," says Will, "how did you?"

Fergus smiles and wiggles his bushy eyebrows like Groucho Marx. "Leipreacháns are seen when they want ta be, I reckon. Hell, bye. I live in Ireland; I don't question the magicks. I just let 'em be. Cavort with leipreacháns and yeh'll have more than a broken nose, I can tell yeh that fer certain."

"For sure and certain," says Will.

"Tá," says Fergus. He walks away with his pint.

"Well, that's good," says Sam.

"What?" asks Will.

Sam smiles. "I work in a bar, Will. I don't need another drunk in me life. If the leipreacháns were workin' their magicks on ya though, I understand."

Will's attention shifts to the floor. "I guess I should say that...ever since the fire, I've drunk more than my share. Prob'ly a leprechaun's share...or however Fergus says it. 'Leipreachán.'" He pushes his drink away. "I don't think I need it anymore, though." He smiles, and Sam thinks it's even more beautiful than the smile in her dreams.

"I outswam a selkie," Will continues, "outdrank a pùca, outwitted a kelpie, and came through fire unscathed...except fer this."

Will pulls his shirtsleeve up and shows Sam the scar.

She gasps a little. "It's the triple spiral from Newgrange," she says. Her eyebrows knit. "I believed yeh before, I guess, but it was a little without believin', if yeh understand what I'm sayin'. This, though." Sam touches the mark and Will shivers.

"Yer not a fairy, are yeh?" he asks.

Sam laughs and turns. "No wings," she says.

"Not all of them have wings."

"Huh?"

"Nothing."

Their hands touch, then enfold. Sam pulls Will into another kiss across the bar. This one is deeper, more passionate. The world fades, leaving Sam and her dream man alone in the universe.

"Are yeh shuttin' the doors now or can we get another pint?" shouts someone far away.

Sam and Will break apart, she laughing, and he looking somewhat bedazed.

Sam grabs a stack of pint glasses. "C'mon, luff. Let's get these byes some drinks, shall we?"

"Sure," says Will. "I look like a waiter at a theme restaurant, anyway."

"We don't have theme restaurants in Ireland, 'cept in Dublin." Sam rounds the bar with a tray of full pint glasses.

Will follows her, carrying six handled mugs. "I wonder why?" he asks.

"Theme restaurants are pretend," she says. She plants one more, quick kiss on his lips. "Everything here, even the magicks, is one hunnerd percent real. Even me."

"I, STATE YOUR NAMES," SAID FATHER SIMMONS.

"I, William McConnelly," said Will. At the same time, Cara said, "I, Cara Brady."

"Take you, state your intended's name."

Will and Cara said each other's names, Will resisting an urge to say, 'intended's name.'

"For my lawful wife or husband, to have and to hold from this day forward, for better, for worse, for richer, for poorer, in sickness and health...."

Will and Cara repeated the lines as the priest indicated.

"Til death do us part."

They finished the ritual words, sending them into the universe. The only real thought in Will's head was the kiss that was about to come, then party with cake and dancing, and much later, a bed that would welcome them officially as Mr. and Mrs. Cara and William McConnelly.

"This is it," Will says. Carefully, he removes the top of the urn.

Not a single cloud hides the sun from the hundreds of green hues that distinguish the trees and grass and bushes encircling the small field in the hills. From here, it's only a few minutes' walk up the path to Seamus and Conor's little hut, if it's still there, or down the hill to the fairy field that can never again appear to Will. He closes his eyes and feels the soft Irish breeze brush past his face like a feathered fan.

Samthann lays her hand on Will's shoulder. He feels the weight of all the things she wants to say, yet she remains silent. Will wants to reply. He has things he can say now, too. After all, this isn't the hard part, sprinkling the ashes of his two first loves in this beautiful place. The hard part is wanting to remember every second, every millisecond, so he can bring those memories out on hard days. Sam is beautiful, but neither she nor Will are perfect. There will be hard days, just like there were with Cara and Samuel.

Beauty lies not in perfection, he thinks, *but in the flaw that allows us to appreciate the perfection.* It's a quote from something, but he can't remember what.

In the distance, unseen by Will and Samthann, unseen by any mortal eyes, three figures sit on a large tree limb. They stare at the tableau on the grass with quiet impatience.

"C'mon, bye," whispers Seamus. "Yeh can do it now. Let 'er go."

"Let both of 'em go," Conor says, correcting Seamus. "That be Aidan's daughter *and* grandson, fer sure and certain."

"Tá," says Seamus. "Fer certain and sure."

"He will release them now," the third figure says, her elongated eyes taking in more than the others. She sees not only the visual realm, but that of the heart.

"It'll be fer the best," says Seamus.

The Fairy Queen stares, unblinking, at Will. "The first time I saw him, his aura was gray, tinged with black, torn."

"And now?" asks Seamus.

"Oh, there's still a touch of brown here and there, but the rest is a nice, healing yellow. I managed to pull enough of the pain from him that he's on the mend now. He'll be better in a few months, though one is never the same after a loss such as his."

"Tá," says Conor, "an' thank ye kindly from me whole family."

"Who is he," asks the Queen, "this Aidan? You said he was related, but...."

"Ah, he's me bye, actually. A little dalliance with a beautiful Irish lass during the war. A mistake, obviously."

"A beautiful Irish lass abed with an old leprechaun?" she says. "Perhaps the mistake was not yours?"

As the bell of her laugh touches the tree bough they sit on, several blooms swell into deep red apples.

"Ah!" says Seamus. He pulls one of the apples from its stem and almost takes a bite. Conor grabs his hand.

"You don't want to eat that," says Conor. "Fruit a' the fay ain't good fer a leprechaun, unless yeh want ta fergit who yeh are fer a spell."

Seamus stares at the apple.

"That'd be a laugh." He places the apple in his knapsack. "I'll save it fer later, though."

"There weren't no dalliance with an ol' leprechaun," Conor says. "I took on the likeness of that American singer fer a few days. What were his name, Seamus, the "'don't be cruel' bye?"

"Elvis Presley."

"Tá, that's it. The lass couldn't help herself. Up 'til then, I thought it were impossible fer humans and fay ta conceive, so I left."

"Imagine his surprise," says Seamus, "when he goes back ta visit and finds her with child."

"You kept in touch with the boy over the years?" asks the Fairy Queen.

"Tá. Just a letter now and agin, naught but friendly words, 'til he sent this." Conor removes a crinkled envelope from his knapsack. He hands it to the Queen, who opens it and reads, "You know the story. My grand-daughter and great grandson taken in the fire. Aidan were sad himself a' course, but more worried about his son-in-law. Thought the bye might be thinkin' a' suicide."

In the distance, Samthann slides her arms around Will and hugs him from behind as he continues to stare at the urn.

"So yeh called in every favor and kindness yeh had to help this human," says the Fairy Queen.

"Tá," says Conor. "It took a lotta hands to make this magick. I fixed everything except the Questing Beast. She was the one test young William had to pass on his own."

"And he did," the Queen says, "with kindness and love and courage." She crinkles her little nose. "I would not have turned him down had he stepped into my kingdom. You two know that."

Conor nods. "Either way, his pain would have been taken, but in my mind, this is better. These two seem ta fit, almost like soulmates, if that were a thing."

"She dreamed of him," says the Queen. "So perhaps they are."

"Tá," says Conor and Seamus, both at the same time.

"I risk little fer humans. Still, it was...fun? I don't experience that emotion very often."

"It's a laugh ta play outside the box now and again," says Seamus. "I seem to remember a fight yeh had with Oberon over a little changeling child once, an Indian boy. That ended up amongst the humans, did it not?"

The Fairy Queen blushes a little, her cheeks turning a deep purple. "Don't mention Oberon," she says. "I'm still angry with him over the spell he used on me. I fell in love with a jackass! Or should I say, a man transformed into a jackass. The love we made was grotesque!" She pauses. "Though quite passionate."

"I never knew that part of it," said Seamus.

Conor added, "That explains a lot."

"Blessings on yer family," says the Queen. "While neither child is of your blood, it seems your Aidan loves William McConnelly like his own. In time, he'll love the girl just as well. She'll be blessed with three children, two girls and a boy. They'll be happy, though the magicks may cause them trouble now and again."

Conor bows his head. "Thank yeh, Yer Majesty."

She bows hers, then melts into nothingness.

"That blush on her cheek, Conor," said Seamus. "You e'er seen anything as beautiful as that?"

"Only the rest a' her nekkid self, Seamus," Conor replied. "As beautiful as a sunset, she is."

Seamus looks back at the field and almost falls out of the tree. "Look there, bye!" he says. "Don't miss it!"

Samthann shies away, and Will steps forward with the urn. He holds it at arm's length to the trees and the sky. He prays, "May the love of God and the peace of the Lord Jesus Christ bless and console us and gently wipe every tear from our eyes, in the name of the Father, and of the Son, and of the Holy Spirit. Amen."

Will gently tips the urn, and the last essence of his family drops into the wind. A gust grabs the ashes and pulls them into the air above the field, playing with them.

"What the hell?" breathes Samthann.

"Shhh," says Will.

The wind swirls the ashes into strange shapes and forms, almost as if it's writing spells. They travel higher and higher, until suddenly, the wind disappears. The ashes float gently onto the field.

"Like snow," Sam murmurs.

"Like glitter," smiles Will. He feels many, many things. He feels Samthann's hand creep between his bicep and chest. She grabs hold of his arm and lays her head on his shoulder. He feels the wind that took the ashes rise once more. It touches his cheek like a kiss. He feels the last drop of sadness fade from his heart, leaving it open for the possibility of a future. He feels...content.

"Ashes to ashes," he says. "Dust...to dust."

A Note On Pronunciation

I don't believe readers need a pronunciation guide to enjoy this novel. However, I find it fascinating how different Gaelic reads on the page versus how it's actually spoken. My first experience with the spoken language came from my college professor, Thomas Porter, at the University of Texas in Arlington. He would often read Irish poetry in Gaelic. The words leapt from his mouth like notes from an aria. I'm including a very small pronunciation guide (non-IPA), to honor the memory of an amazing professor and a beautiful language.

Dictionary Of Irish Pronunciations

- Aidan \ 'ay-dun
- Aintín \ 'ahn-teen
- Ar stealladh na ngrást / err 'shtal-uh nung 'rawst
- Athair \ 'ah-hare
- Betha \ 'bay-thuh
- Brú na Bóinne \ 'brewna 'bawnyay
- cara baineann \ 'ker-uh 'boo-nion
- Claidheamh Soluis \ 'klive 'sole-us
- Crom Cruach \ 'krawm 'kroo-uck
- Dowth \ 'dote
- Garda Síochána \ 'gar-dah shee-uh-'ha-nah
- Go raibh maith agat \ goh rehv mah a-'gut
- Is breá liom tú \ iss brah loom too
- Knowth \ 'note
- Leanán sídhe \ 'la-nun shay
- Leipreachán \ lep-ruh-'hawn
- mo chuislema \ 'hoosh-la
- Orlaith \ 'or-lah
- Oscail an doras \ 'ah-skale an-'door-us
- pùca \ 'poo-kuh

- Sí in Bhrú \ 'she-un 'brew
- Samthann \ 'sav-un
- Seanmháthair \ shan-wah-'her
- Sláinte \ 'slawn-shuh
- Sláinte mhaith \ 'slawn-shuh 'vaw
- Suigh síossuh \ 'sheez
- Tà \ 'tah
- Ta bron orm \ tah brone 'orm
- Taispeáin dom an bonn \ tuh'spaw-un 'dawm-ann 'bawn
- Tuatha Dé Danann \ 'too-ah de 'don-un

Trademarks & Copyrights

- Toyota Prius
- Ford Expedition
- William Shakespeare: *A Midsummer Night's Dream* (Hippolyta, Puck, Titania, Oberon, Hermia), *Romeo and Juliet* (Mercutio, Gregory, Sampson), *Hamlet* (Claudius, Horatio), *Macbeth*, *The Tempest* (Caliban), *King Lear*, *Timon of Athens*, and *Julius Caesar*
- Chevrolet Suburban
- Tarrant County College
- Mr. Sowerberry in *Oliver Twist* by Charles Dickens
- *Playboy Magazine* founded by Hugh Hefner, owned by Playboy Enterprises, Inc.
- Pottery Barn
- Corona Beer
- Pabst Blue Ribbon Beer (PBR)
- Ryan Gosling
- *Teen Beat* magazine
- *The Princess Bride* by William Goldman
- *The Notebook* by Nicholas Sparks
- Pink by Victoria's Secret
- BMW (Beamer)

- *Monty Python and the Holy Grail* by the Monty Python Comedy Troupe
- Diddle Diddle Dumpling, My Son John – Nursery Rhyme
- Walmart
- Keystone Light - Coors Brewing Company (Molson-Coors)
- Macy's
- Neverland in *Peter Pan* by J.M. Barrie
- Coke - Coca Cola
- 7-11
- 7-11 Super Big Gulp
- Jack Daniels
- Vanilla Lace Body Spray by Victoria's Secret
- McShan Florist
- Trinity Hall Irish Pub – Dallas, Texas
- Jameson Irish Whiskey
- Hot Wheels by Mattel
- Styrofoam
- YouTube
- Notre Dame Cathedral
- Guinness beer
- Bushmills Irish Whiskey
- Connemara Irish Whiskey
- Shamrock Rovers Football
- Elmer Fudd, cartoon character produced by Warner Bros. *Looney Tunes/Merrie Melodies*
- Daffy Duck, cartoon character produced by Warner Bros.
- Courtyard by Marriot
- Café Brazil
- The Highland Dallas Hotel
- Sweet'N Low Artificial Sweetener
- Southern Methodist University (SMU)
- Aer Lingus Airlines
- O'Hare International Airport in Chicago
- Kingsford Match Light charcoal briquettes
- American Airlines

- Google
- Queens College
- Dallas Cowboys
- Michael Phelps
- *Wicked* by Stephen Schwartz, book by Winnie Holzman
- Bus Éireann Transport
- Volkswagen Golf
- *Shrek, the Musical* by Jeanine Tesori and David Lindsay-Abaire, Dreamworks Theatrical
- Fiat – since 2021, owned by a subsidiary of Stellantis
- Dasani
- Matchbox, Registered trademark of Mattel
- Enterprise Rent-A-Car
- Disney – The Walt Disney Company
- Bilbo Baggins, Sting, hobbit, and the mines of Moria in *The Lord of the Rings* and *The Hobbit* by J.R.R. Tolkien
- Andre Norton
- Dr. Seuss
- *Children of a Lesser God* by Mark Medoff
- John Wayne
- Clint Eastwood
- *Lord of the Dance* – Michael Flatley
- Clarkes Butchers
- Kroger
- Target
- Kenny's Grocers
- The Forde Ian
- *The Kardashians, Keeping Up with the Kardashians,* a reality T.V. show that airs on E! cable network
- Tylenol
- "The Cupid Shuffle" by Cupid
- *Bulfinch's Mythology* by Thomas Bulfinch
- Irish Festival of Dallas
- Fair Park, Dallas
- *Dallas*, the television series, originally aired on CBS

- The Rowan Tree Restaurant
- Callahan's Nursery
- The Stanley Cup
- "The Rainbow Connection" by Paul Williams
- Kermit the Frog and *The Muppets*, created by Jim Henson
- Microsoft Windows 10 by Microsoft Corporation
- MacBook (Mac) by Apple
- Microsoft Word by Microsoft Corporation
- Windows Visa operating system produced by Microsoft
- Friedrich Wilhelm Nietzsche
- Regions Bank – Regions Financial Corporation
- Amleth, Prince of Denmark
- King James I of England
- Saturn Automobile – The Saturn Corporation
- Ronnie Wood, guitarist of The Rolling Stones
- State Fair of Texas
- *A Christmas Carol* by Charles Dickens
- Cheshire Cat, from *Alice in Wonderland* by Lewis Carroll
- Donegal Bay
- Slieve Liag
- Bunglass Cliffs
- One Man's Pass
- Ford Pinto
- The Blarney Stone
- Winston Churchill
- *On the Road* by Jack Kerouac
- *The Boy in the Stryped Pajamas* by John Boyne
- Agatha Christie
- Suffolk Strangler
- James Joyce
- Bugs Bunny, created by Warner Bros. Cartoons, Inc.
- Acme Corporation, Warner Brothers Cartoons
- Popeye the Sailor Man – cartoon character created by Elzie Crisler Segar, owned by Turner Entertainment and distributed by Warner Bros.

- Hernán Cortés
- Juan Ponce de León
- Diffagher River
- Elwood P. Dowd, in *Harvey* by Mary Chase
- Jimmy Stewart
- Casper, the Friendly Ghost from Classic Media
- Lego – owned by the LEGO Group
- Brian Boru
- Oscar – popular name for an Academy Award
- Oscar Wilde
- Sandymount
- William Butler Yeats
- Muhammad Ali
- "The Raven" by Edgar Allan Poe
- *The Terminator* by James Cameron
- Arnold Schwarzenegger
- *Alien* directed by Ridley Scott, written by Dan O'Bannon. Based on a story by Dan O'Bannon and Ronald Shusett
- Saint Patrick
- Liam Neeson
- United Nations
- South Lebanon Army (SLA)
- "Dancing Queen" by ABBA, written by Benny Andersson, Björn Ulvaeus, and Stig Anderson
- Salvador Dali
- Rumple Minze Peppermint Schnapps
- The Claidheamh Soluis
- The Tuatha Dé Danann
- The Goddess Danu
- Lugh
- Leanán sídhe
- The Questing Beast, The Beast Glatisant
- Road Safety Authority
- The Fomorians
- Crom Cruach

- Brú na Bóinne Visitor Centre
- Cistercian Abbey
- Saint Malachy
- Knowth
- Dowth
- Newgrange Stone Age Passage Tomb, Sí an Bhrú
- Wookie, in *Star Wars* by George Lucas
- *Starry Night* by Vincent Van Gogh
- The overture to *Don Giovanni* by Mozart
- *Batman* by Bob Kane and Bill Finger, DC Comics
- SpaghettiOs by Campbell Soup Company
- *Don Quixote* by Miguel de Cervantes
- *Scooby Doo*, Hanna-Barbera
- University of Texas Longhorns
- Odor-Eaters
- *Moonlight Sonata* by Ludwig Von Beethoven
- Michelangelo
- *Doctor Faustus* by Christopher Marlowe
- Clue from Hasbro
- Jägermeister
- Clydesdale horse
- Garda Síochána (Police of Ireland)
- Ford Focus
- *Rip Van Winkle* by Washington Irving
- Timberland
- Pellinore of Listenoise
- Camelot
- Joseph of Arimathea
- *The Tragical History of the Life and Death of Doctor Faustus* by Christopher Marlowe
- Groucho Marx
- Elvis Presley

Sneak Peek

Some Monsters Never Die Sneak Peek

Sneak peek at the first book in the Monsters and Mayhem series Some Monsters Never Die by E.A. Comiskey

Richard always believed he'd enjoy a few golden years before Death's bony hand reached for him. But what does he get? He gets to live across the hall from friggin' Stanley Kapcheck with his shiny bald head and perfect teeth that are all his own; Stanley Kapcheck who struts around like a peacock in his leather coat.

Honestly! What kind of respectable senior citizen wears leather?

But Stanley isn't your average senior citizen. He's a Hunter—a slayer of all things unnatural. He reveals to Richard that the one monster that has eluded him is the same beast that killed Richard's wife, and it's due to kill again before the next new moon. The two men load up on ibuprofen and prune juice and embark on a cross-country demon-hunting adventure, but when The Devil Herself kidnaps Stanley, Richard realizes the line between Hunter and hunted is very thin, indeed, and the ornery octogenarian only has a few days left to trap The Devil, save Stanley, and slay the monster who murdered his bride.

Chapter One

Richard

OLD AGE WAS the most vicious of bullies. Life had already scorned him, knocked the books out of his hands and beat him to a pulp. Now, here came Old Age to kick sand in his face. It wasn't fair. All his life, he'd been promised a retirement from hardship—a handful of golden years before Death's bony hand reached for him. Now, when it was far too late to do anything about it, he realized the whole blasted world had conspired against him.

There were no golden years. Only a lonely descent toward oblivion.

Everest Senior Living Facility was not the nursing home of his nightmares. As a younger man, in his seventies, Richard had woken in a cold sweat with visions of dirty, closed-in rooms, abusive nurses, and seeping bedsores. The reality of his old age was nothing like that.

The old-folks home was bright, full of sunlight that streamed through enormous, plentiful, spotless windows. Perky young girls who smelled faintly of coffee bustled about with rhinestone-studded stethoscopes draped around their necks.

The food was bland and mushy, but at least as good as what he'd lived off in the years since his sweet Barbara had died, and they served ice-cold prune juice at every meal, so his guts kept moving like they were supposed to. Thanks be to the Holy Lord above, there were no olive loaf sandwiches. He'd eaten enough olive loaf to last a dozen lifetimes.

All in all, Everest was as good a place as any to be abandoned by your family while you waited for death.

Well, it would have been, if it weren't for Stanley Kapcheck. Stanley with his shiny bald head and perfect teeth that were all his own. Stanley had a flat stomach and a British accent. He wore a leather coat.

Honestly! What kind of respectable senior citizen wore leather?

Pretty nurses, young enough to be his grandchildren, giggled and blushed when Stanley spoke.

Richard loathed Stanley.

Was it so much to ask for a man to grow old and die the way nature intended? Something was weird about a man Stanley's age who still wore well-shined lace-up shoes that he tied himself.

Consequently, the sight of Stanley's pristine wingtip tapping on the white tiles of the dining hall floor was chipping away at the core of Richard's soul. And if that weren't enough, the pompous old peacock had an extra helping of chocolate pudding on the table in front of him. That new girl with the wild black curls had brought it to him, offering it like she was presenting her dowry.

Richard used the back of his chair and the edge of the table to push himself to his feet. He held on for a moment to make sure his balance was good and steady, and then moved his hands to his walker and shuffled in Richard's direction.

The insufferable old fart smiled at him. "Good evening, Dick! You're looking well. How's that hip of yours?"

How dare he act like they were friends? And, Lord, but how he hated being called Dick.

Richard lifted his chin and looked down his immense nose at Stanley. "I see you have two puddings."

"Yes, a little indulgence is good for the soul, don't you think?"

"No. I disagree completely. I think this world is a sick and broken place where people indulge all too often and abstain not nearly often enough."

"Oh, come on now." Stanley reached forward and patted the round paunch of Richard's stomach. "It seems perhaps you've enjoyed one or two indulgences over the years."

That was it. That was going to be the comment that sent his blood pressure so high something inside would finally burst. He pointed a shaking finger at the other man and tried to get a word out, but his lips were pressed into a thin, tight line of fury and he couldn't quite seem to remember how to get them to move.

"Mr. Bell," the wild-haired girl said. "Did you want to have dessert over here with Mr. Kapcheck? Here, let me move your pudding for you." In a flash, she scooped the little bowl away from his seat and plopped it down across from Stanley. "There you go. Now you can sit with your friend."

She trotted away to refill the teacup Mrs. Wiler was holding in the air and left Richard standing there, red-faced and trembling with rage.

"Your shoes are ugly!" Richard spat the words out of his mouth with all the force he could muster.

Stanley threw his head back and laughed.

Richard spun on his heel—or, well, he turned around with pathetic, tiny, careful little steps and did his very best to stomp out of the room. It was difficult since he lived in mortal fear of falling again and therefore never lifted either foot more than an inch or two off the ground.

Back in his room, he lowered himself into the soft brown arm chair and clicked the TV on, just to have some noise. He sat there, staring at some stupid nature documentary. After a minute or two, he realized that he never enjoyed a single bite of dessert, but he'd left Stan Kapcheck sitting in the dining room with three bowls of chocolate pudding laid out in front of him.

The unfairness of life was a burden nearly too great for someone as old as him to bear.

Chapter Two

Finn

FINN WAS one hundred percent certain that cigarettes were the only thing keeping him from ballooning up to three hundred pounds. If he was smoking, he wasn't shoveling potato chips into his mouth.

He lit a Marlboro and leaned back, making the soft leather of the enormous desk chair squeak. Outside the window, a hummingbird flitted around the red plastic feeder and buzzed away again. The smoke curled up in his lungs, sank into his blood, kissed his soul, and made its way back out of his body as he exhaled.

On the computer screen, the little black cursor flashed against the blank white page.

He'd done an internet search for tips on how to conquer writer's block.

Exercise. Take a walk. Get a change of scenery.

What a joke.

Another long inhale filled him up so completely he thought maybe he could float right out the window and fly away.

Letting it go, the weight on his shoulders returned twice as heavy.

The blank page mocked him.

He breathed in.

Upon exhale, he whispered to the empty room, "Dear God, send me a Muse. " Slick tendrils of smoke wrapped around the words and carried them toward heaven.

With the cigarette dangling from his lips, he stood, grabbed his keys from the hook next to the door, and headed out into the brilliant sun. Joe's was open, and the owner would serve him a cold beer any time of day, no questions asked.

A little pink Vespa was parked outside his front door. A girl, presumably the owner of the preposterous scooter, sat on the hood of his car, her smooth, tanned legs crossed like a school child's. For all that, she sported every attribute of a grown woman. At the sight of him, she flashed perfect white teeth. Tiny dimples formed on her round cheeks. "Hi there!"

He plucked the cigarette from his mouth. "You're sitting on my car."

"I didn't want you to leave without me," she said.

"Why's that?" It had been years since the first fan had approached him on the street. He'd been so flattered then it left him cocky for a full week. After a while, fame lost its appeal. They all asked the same questions. Half of them wanted him to make them famous writers, too. The other half expected him to be one of the characters in his books. None of them really cared who he was, outside of his life as a writer. This girl, though, had the distinction of being the first groupie to seek him out at his home. It seemed a level of stalkerly ambition worth a decent conversation, at least.

Plus, the t-shirt stretched tight across her pert, unbound breasts created an interesting diversion from the all-consuming thoughts of self-pity he'd battled the past few weeks.

"Can I have a cigarette?" she asked.

He fished the crumpled pack from his pocket and offered it to her. She let him light it for her and inhaled like the smoke was salvation. "I haven't smoked in forever."

"If you can go this long, you should probably keep up the clean streak."

She inhaled again and blew the smoke out in a long, thin stream through the purse of her full pink lips. "Where you goin'?"

"Have we met before?"

"Maybe you've seen me around. Everybody around here knows each other, right? So, where you goin'?"

He studied her face. She didn't look the least bit familiar. "I would remember you."

She hopped down and stepped over to him. The cigarette fell to the ground and she crushed it under the heel of her white sandal. "Where you goin'?"

"I'm going to Joe's to get drunk."

"It's cheaper to get drunk at home."

"Only alcoholics drink alone."

She grinned up at him. "So, you're looking for company?"

She was Venus on a half shell, offering herself up for his pleasure. How could he resist? Why should he resist? Damn! Remember that. It would be a perfect line in the new novel. Twenty words down, seventy-nine thousand, nine hundred and eighty to go. "Care to join me?"

She bounced on her toes. "I thought you'd never ask. I would love to join you for a drink."

"You are old enough to drink, right?"

"In all fifty states," she promised.

It seemed like there should be some voice in his head listing reasons why it was a bad idea to invite this tiny, adorable stalker to go to the bar with him. He listened hard. The voices were as silent as they had been when he'd stared at the computer, so he reached around her and opened the passenger door.

She slid in and ran a hand over the gearshift. "I adore this car. You have amazing taste."

He watched her fingers glide over the molded plastic. Still, there was no voice, but there was more than a little seismic activity south of the equator. "What's your name?" he asked.

"Tell you later," she said, looking up at him through lashes so long they surely had to be fake.

The door slammed a little harder than he meant for it to. His boots thumped against the pavement and the car sank under his weight when he dropped into the seat. He crushed the cigarette out in the car's ashtray. "Tell me now."

She pouted. She had a perfectly bite-able bottom lip.

"Please," he said.

"Sara."

He had to ask. "What do you want, Sara?"

"I want to drink a beer with you at Joe's."

He lit a fresh cigarette, put the Mustang in gear, and headed toward Joe's.

Chapter Three

Richard

THE LIGHT TAP on the door came like clockwork, just after the start of the eleven o'clock news.

"It's open!" Richard called out, as if it weren't always open. Doors at Everest didn't have locks. A pretense of privacy was maintained, but the charade wasn't lost on him. Strangers washed his underpants and strangers cleaned up under his bed. Strangers asked about his morning stool and peeked in on him while he slept. Privacy was a privilege afforded to those who could still contribute to society.

The door swung open and a child with a shiny blonde ponytail on the very top of her head bounced into the room. "Evenin', Mr. Bell. How you feelin' tonight?"

Over her shoulder, Richard caught a glimpse of Stanley leaning against the wall in the brightly lit corridor. He wore jeans and a lilac button-front shirt. His legs were crossed at the ankles. He caught Richard's eye and smiled. Jerk. Looked like a darn wrinkled up old gigolo on a street corner.

The little girl peeked into the bathroom. They always did that. What were they looking for, anyway?

"That hip bothering you at all?" she asked.

"Only when I sit or stand," Richard told her. When he'd fallen off the curb in front of his house and shattered his hip, the doctors had assured him that the newfangled titanium implant would be better than the original. They'd lied. They always lied. Medical school probably had a course—Effective Falsehoods 101. He hurt all the time. It wasn't just his hip, either. Since they'd officially declared him an old man, he hurt in every joint of his body.

The girl was undeterred by his gruff attitude. "Time to lay down then?" she asked.

"I'll be layin' down for eternity soon. I'd like to sit up and watch the eleven o'clock news now, if you don't mind."

She giggled as if he said something funny and took his wrist between her slim fingers. Glancing at the TV, she told him, "I really love her. She's so much more relatable than the woman who was on there before."

The woman who was on there before? Was she talking about Barbara Walters? Of course, Barbara Walters wasn't relatable. She was iconic. She was untouchable. She was exactly what a TV personality should be. These pretty young things in short skirts were more concerned about looking like the latest celebrity than in finding incorruptible sources. Not that he had anything against pretty girls in short skirts, but there was a time and place and the nightly news was not that place.

Nurse Ponytail let go of him and gave him a long look. "Can I ask you a personal question, Mr. Bell?"

That was new. Not once, since he'd moved into this place, had anyone asked permission before getting personal. Out of curiosity as much as anything, he said, "You can ask. Don't promise I'll answer."

She tugged on the ends of her lavender stethoscope. "I just... You seem pretty unhappy."

He stared at her, waiting for something more than a statement of the obvious.

"Do you still enjoy life?"

It took a moment to even process the question. Enjoy life? Images flashed in his mind. He was a boy on the farm, swinging from a rope in the hayloft and landing in a pile of fresh, sweet-smelling straw. He was racing in the State track and field championships, the crowd screaming his name. It was his wedding night and he learned about the astonishing secret power that women held over men. He held his newborn child in his arms and thought his heart would burst with pride and joy. His wife lay in a hospital bed. His company gave him a gold watch and a pat on the back for forty-two years of loyal service. He buried his best friend. His daughter told him she just didn't have time to give him the care he needed and she was having him moved to a rehabilitation facility.

To his astonishment, hot tears pricked his eyes for the first time in decades. "I..."

"Yes?" She leaned in toward him, listening with unusual intensity.

"I don't..."

A loud banging startled him so badly his heart gave a painful squeeze. The door swung open and there stood Stanley.

"Dick! Thought I'd stop in and see if you'd like to join me for a nightcap in the cafeteria. Of course, they don't serve alcohol, caffeine, or sugar, but we might be able to sweet talk the ladies into some sugar-free cocoa."

Richard's mouth fell open and he snapped it shut again. If Nurse Ponytail had proposed marriage, he'd have been less surprised than he was by the invitation from Stanley.

"Come on, my friend!" Stanley insisted. "If we're not there by eleven thirty, they'll have all the peanuts packed up and we'll miss out on that perfect combination of salty and sweet."

Nurse Ponytail giggled and patted Richard's arm. "Sounds like you boys are gonna have fun. See ya later, Mr. Bell."

Stanley stepped into the room and held the door for her, giving a courtly little bow of his head when she bounced past him. He let the door fall shut behind her and turned toward Richard. "Are you all right?"

"What in tarnation are you talking about?"

"Did she hurt you? Take anything?"

Richard glared at Stanley. "You havin' a stroke or something?"

Stanley seemed to relax. "Great. You're all right." He looked over his shoulder, like he was checking to make sure the door was still closed tight, then came to sit on the corner of the bed so he was practically knee-to-knee with Richard.

"That woman is not what she seems, and I'm quite certain she has her sights set on you as her next victim."

Richard felt the hot blood in his face. "I know you take me for some kind of fool, Stan Kapcheck, but I tell you I'm no man's stooge. Get out of my room. Play your stupid jokes on someone else."

Stanley had the audacity to look truly hurt. "Dick, I…."

"Just get out of my room!" Richard bellowed.

Stanley's lips pressed into a tight, thin line. "All right, then. That's fine, Dick. I'll get out of your room and you can deal with that creature by yourself when she comes back for you."

"I'm sure I can manage five feet of blonde ponytail."

"Very well, then," Stanley said, rising to his feet.

Just after the door clicked shut, Richard growled back, "Yes, it is very well."

It irked him to his core that Stanley moved so fluidly when he rose from the bed and left the room. He was as graceful as any athlete—as graceful as Richard himself had been in the years before life became all about soft food and nurses who called him cute. With a sigh, he clicked off the television and shuffled into the bathroom to wash up before bed.

He never would have known anyone had come in, except that the door made a tiny, high-pitched squeak that caused his hearing aid to give feedback. He dropped the washcloth on the edge of the sink and spun around. "Dagnabit, Stanley Kapcheck, I told you…"

The creature stood before him, five feet of pink scrubs with bat-like wings, red eyes, and long, dripping fangs.

Richard stumbled back, tripped over the toilet and fell against the wall. The jolt ran through his bones like an explosion. "Jesus, Mary, and Joseph!"

"I will have your memories, Richard Bell. I will devour the sweet, rich memories full of the glory days," it hissed at him.

The door swung open again and Stanley appeared behind her shoulder.

She launched herself toward Richard as he cowered against the cold tile wall, but Stanley's arm lashed out in a flash. The pointed end of a broken stick burst through the thing's chest and, with a wheezing exhale carried on a plume of black smoke, she dissolved into a pile of ash on the floor.

Stanley stood there, panting.

Richard's lips took on a will of their own and started forming a series of incoherent sounds. Maybe he was having a stroke. This was how a stroke had always felt in his imagination.

Stanley skirted the pile of filth, keeping his wingtips shiny, and extended a hand. "I told you she was coming for you," he said.

"I...she...teeth..." Richard managed.

"Yes," Stanley agreed. "The teeth are horrible. And those big, batty wings. Dreadful creatures. We should go before the others realize what we've done here."

Richard blinked up at him. He allowed himself to be helped up. "Others?"

"The strigoi never exist in solitude. They move in packs."

"Strigoi," Richard squeaked in a weirdly feminine voice.

"Strigoi," Stanley said. "No doubt about it. Get your coat. We have to move quickly."

"Coat?" Richard asked.

Stanley crossed the room and knelt in front of Richard's walker. He took the fanny pack from the top of the dresser, strapped it around the front handles, then filled it with a tiny water pistol, a crucifix, and a baggie full of garlic, all retrieved from his own pockets. Then he took the yardstick that lay on the table next to Richard's jigsaw puzzle and snapped it in half over his knee. He slipped both jagged pieces into the long, narrow pouch meant for an oxygen tank. Thankfully, Richard wasn't yet so far gone as to need to lug one of those around. Then he stood, retrieved Richard's Wellington Plastics jacket, and held it out. Richard let Stan tuck him into the garment just as if he were a girl on a date.

"Don't hesitate to use that squirt gun if you need to. Holy water won't kill them, but it will slow them down long enough so we can do what we need to do." He positioned the walker in front of Richard.

Richard stared down at the little bag's unzipped compartment. The toy gun's red plastic handle was just barely visible. "It's a joke," he muttered. It pleased him to hear that his voice had returned to a masculine tone, even if it remained somewhat tremulous.

Stanley gripped him by the shoulders. "Look at that pile of ash, Richard. Does that look like a joke to you?"

Tiny black tendrils of smoke still rose from the ash. It smelled like burnt eggs. His stomach turned.

"We need to get out of here," Stanley said.

Richard nodded and headed for the door, but the other man grabbed his arm. "Don't be foolish, man! We can't go that way. They're not going to let us just waltz out the front door."

"Well, what do you suggest then?" Richard asked.

Stanley gestured toward the window.

"You've gotta be kidding."

"Really, Dick, you must learn what a joke looks like. It's time to go, and that's the only way out if you intend to save your wrinkled old hide, because this place is crawling with more just like her and they're not going to be happy to find her remains in your room."

Richard glanced at the mess one more time, grasped the handles of his walker, and headed toward the window.

www.ingramcontent.com/pod-product-compliance
Lightning Source LLC
Chambersburg PA
CBHW061302190726
48288CB00002B/316